TIMES REMEMBERED

TIMES REMEMBERED

Susan Glen

WARNER BOOKS

A *Warner* Book

First published in Great Britain in 1995
by Warner Books

A CIP catalogue record for this book is
available from the British Library.

ISBN 0 7515 1017 3

Typeset by Solidus (Bristol) Limited
Printed and bound in Great Britain by
Clays Ltd, St. Ives plc

Warner Books
A Division of
Little, Brown and Company (UK)
Brettenham House
Lancaster Place
London WC2E 7EN

PART ONE

1959

CHAPTER ONE

The setting sun cast long shadows across paddocks where ponies grazed in scattered groups. A solitary mare looked up as Justin Lang climbed from his car and stretched his stiff limbs, but lost interest when he picked up a holdall and turned towards the house. The front door was unlocked and he stepped into the hall, pausing while his eyes adjusted to the dimness. He had stayed away for far too long and it felt good to be home. He wondered where everyone was, but before he could call out the two family labradors bounded towards him, almost bowling him over with their exuberant greetings.

'Is that you, George? You're late. I was getting worried.'

Sarah Lang came out of the kitchen, a tea towel in her hands. She was a small, untidy woman who was neither fat nor thin, but solidly built. Her short, mouse-coloured hair was streaked with grey and framed a kind but plain face, with gentle eyes of a nondescript blue. She had no time for feminine indulgences and, apart from a rare slash of lipstick, never used cosmetics. The smart women who brought their children here for riding lessons thought her drab, but she had a wonderful smile, a smile which lit her face as the older of her two sons disentangled himself from the dogs.

'Hello, Mum.'

'Justin! We didn't expect you back until next week. You

should have let us know you were coming.'

'It was a spur-of-the-moment decision. Paris was sweltering and I was low on funds.'

'I could have sent some money had you asked.'

'I know, but it didn't seem fair, not with Nick going up to Cambridge next month.'

He kissed her cheek. Sarah was proud of her sons. Justin, now twenty-one, was about to enter his fourth and final year at the Royal College of Art in London, while Nicholas, who was three years younger, had left school this summer with a string of A Levels and a guaranteed university place.

'You look tired,' she said. 'And you've lost weight. I do wish you would eat properly. How you have survived three years without contracting rickets or scurvy is a mystery.'

'I do eat. I had a sandwich on the ferry.'

Sarah sighed. She ought to be used to the vagaries of his eating habits by now. 'Supper has been ready for ages. I was waiting for your father, but I think we ought to start without him.' She squeezed his hand. It was wrong to favour one more than the others, but Justin had always been special. 'Take your bag upstairs while I round up the others and get the food on the table.'

'Where are they?'

'Helen is in the back yard playing with a new kitten. The farm down the road had another litter and were desperate to get rid of them. I'm not sure where Nicholas is. Probably in the shed fiddling with his motor bike.'

'No I'm not,' a voice said from the kitchen. 'If that's Dad, can we eat now? I'm starving, and I promised to meet Joe at the pub in half an hour.'

'It's not your father.' Sarah glanced over her shoulder.

'Who is it then?'

Nicholas came out of the kitchen. He grinned when he saw his brother.

4

'The wanderer returns. One of these days you might think to tell us you are coming home. It's good to see you again, Justin.'

They did not always see eye to eye, for their personalities were too diverse. There were times when Justin cared too much about too many things, while Nicholas possessed a hard and selfish streak. He invariably put himself first, and always would. But tonight their differences were laid aside as they threw their arms about each other. Physically, they were very alike. Both towered over their mother, Nicholas having shot up to over six foot, while Justin was an inch and a half shorter. They had inherited their father's rugged good looks; his straight nose, determined mouth and strong jawline. But it was Nicholas who bore the stronger resemblance to his father, for he had the same pale blue eyes and sandy hair which bleached blond under the summer sun. On the other hand, Justin's colouring was inherited from neither parent. His eyes were grey and his hair a rich chocolate brown which was styled in no particular fashion and, as now, was usually in need of a trim.

'Lucky beggar, living in France for two months,' said Nicholas. 'I expect to hear the sordid details later.'

'You'll be disappointed.' His brother bent down to pick up the discarded holdall. 'It was a working holiday and I had to rough it in hostels, some of which were pretty grim.'

Nicholas took the holdall from him. 'Come off it, Justin! Do you think I'm naive enough to believe you spent the entire eight weeks doing nothing but painting?'

Sarah watched them walk up the stairs, wrangling in a good-natured manner. She loved having her family together, and regretted those times were becoming more infrequent. Justin had established his independence three years ago when he moved into London, and once Nicholas left for university she knew he too would find his feet and make his own life. She went back to the kitchen, which was large and untidy and filled with the pleasant aromas of a casserole simmering in the oven. The back door was open and Helen was running across the lawn, dragging a paper bow attached to a length of string behind her. A tabby kitten was racing after it. Sarah watched them for a moment.

Helen was nine years old and small for her age. She had been a late baby who was adored by her father. She was purely her mother, except for her eyes, which were the same pale blue as Nicholas'. Unfortunately, there was nothing else which she and her brothers shared. Helen was a plain, timid child who was painfully shy and terrified of the ponies. Justin and Nicholas had grown up on horseback, but Helen had screamed like a banshee when she was lifted into a saddle for the first time. She had been three years old and, although nobody had forced her since then, she never lost that initial fear.

Sarah picked up the two pans of prepared vegetables and put them on the stove. If she told Helen that Justin was back the child would want to dash upstairs. She adored her older brother, whereas there was very little affection between her and Nicholas. But it was better for the two boys to have some time alone without Helen pestering them. Sarah smiled. They were young men now, but to her they would always be boys.

'Helen, come in and wash your hands,' she shouted.

She glanced at the wall clock. George always telephoned if he was working late. Where was he?

By nine o'clock Sarah was worried. George was not home, nor had he telephoned.

'I expect he is bogged down in figures and has forgotten the time,' Justin said.

Sarah doubted it. George was not like that. Justin was. As

6

a child he had thought nothing of wandering off with a sketch pad and not coming home until hours later, when daylight was fading. Even now he would disappear for days, sometimes weeks at a time, rarely bothering to tell anybody where he was going.

She walked to the window. The nights were beginning to draw in and it was already dark outside. 'I'd better go and see if Helen is ready for bed,' she said.

Justin sensed her anxiety and stood up. 'Would you like me to telephone the office?'

'I know it's probably a waste of time, but I shall feel happier if you do.'

Justin waited until his mother had gone upstairs before dialling the London number. He did not expect a reply, nor did he get one. He put down the receiver and leant against the wall, his eyes closing as a numbing weariness crept over him. Nicholas had gone to the Dog & Duck to tell his friends he could not join them tonight. But knowing Nicholas, he would stay for a drink and be away for most of the evening. He could hear Helen giggling and his mother softly scolding. This had been a long day and he had an uneasy feeling it was far from over.

The telephone rang, startling him. As he picked up the receiver he was aware of his mother standing at the top of the stairs.

Sarah barely dared breathe as she listened to her son. He was talking in monosyllables, but she knew he was speaking to either his father or somebody who knew where George was. She saw him scribble on the pad which was kept beside the telephone. The hallway was not brightly lit but she could see how pale he had turned, and it was with a sense of foreboding that she came down the stairs.

'What's happened? Has there been an accident?' she asked when he rang off.

7

He did not reply immediately, and she glanced down at the pad but, as always, his handwriting was illegible. It was beyond Sarah's comprehension how someone who drew so well, wrote so atrociously.

'He has been arrested for stealing company funds.'

'Oh, my God!'

Justin took her arm and led her into the living room. He made her sit down, then poured some brandy into a glass and put it in her hands. She drank it slowly.

'I'm all right now,' she said. 'How could such a thing happen? Your father is not a thief. He has worked there for more than thirteen years. How on earth could it happen . . .?'

Justin squeezed her shoulder. 'I don't know, but someone has obviously made a dreadful mistake.' He paused as he heard the distant drone of his brother's motor bike. Nicholas was going far too fast along the narrow country lanes. 'I said we would fetch him. He's still being questioned by the police, but they should be finished by the time we get there.'

Sarah put down the empty glass and stood up. 'There is no need for you to come. You look exhausted.'

'I'm not letting you drive into London on your own, not at this time of night.' He smiled. 'For a start, you'd get hopelessly lost.'

He was right. Sarah had only ventured into London twice during the years they had lived here, and she had hated it on both occasions. 'What about Helen?'

'Nick is eighteen years old and perfectly capable of looking after her. Neither of us are children any more.'

'Of course not.' She turned her head away so he would not see the tears which sprang to her eyes.

But Justin did not have to see. 'Don't worry. We'll get through this together. All of us.'

8

What none of them could predict was the sheer escalation of events.

George Lang worked in the London-based offices of Russell Industries, one of the largest suppliers of ball bearings in the country. He had been offered a job there after the war, but Sarah was a country girl who refused to raise her children in the city's grimy, bombed-out streets. At first, he had lodged in a boarding house, coming home for weekends. But with the improvement of the train services he began to commute on a daily basis from Brighton.

He cursed the day he stumbled upon a discrepancy in the books. It had obviously been overlooked by the auditors, but because it niggled him he started to work backwards, digging deeper and deeper until he unearthed an unbelievable bag of worms. Money had been disappearing for years. Not small sums, but amounts which ran into six figures.

He told two people. One was the personal assistant to Terence Russell, the owner of the company, and the other Terence Russell himself. George was asked to remain silent while private investigations were conducted and then, less than a week later, he was arrested when leaving the office. He had been set up, and knew that Terence Russell must have known about the missing money all along. But there was no way George was going to prove it, not when he was up against his employer's wealth and power.

A week had passed since his arrest and, for the time being, the press had stopped hounding them. They were sure to swarm back once the trial started. For there would be a trial. The police had held him for twenty-four hours, and it was only after a brief court appearance that he had been released on bail. As if that had not been humiliating enough, he had walked into the street with his wife and son, to be met by a volley of flashing cameras and insulting questions fired by an officious press who were out to crucify him. The only person who could have informed them about his arrest was Terence Russell.

He stood beside an open window, watching Sarah instruct a small class of beginners who were sitting on the ponies like sacks of potatoes. Although she had said nothing, he knew there had been a number of cancellations since his arrest. And it was not only Sarah who was suffering, but his children. He felt increasingly guilty about them, for they would have a tremendous burden to bear when the inevitable taunts began. Of them all he knew Justin would weather it best. He was not only the oldest, but beneath that sometimes vague exterior was an iron will.

It was Justin he had talked to three nights ago, long after the rest of the family had retired. He told him everything, and through it all his son sat grim faced and silent. Afterwards, George made him promise to say nothing to his mother. She had more than enough worries.

Today, Justin had driven into London on business of his own, saying he would be back in time for supper. Nobody bothered to ask where he was going. Long ago he had adopted an infuriating habit of ignoring any question he did not want to answer.

George was about to move away from the window when he saw Nicholas grab the reins of one of the smaller ponies, which was stubbornly refusing to obey its ineffectual rider. Even he was avoiding his friends. He had helped his mother every day this week, something he rarely did.

It was all becoming too much. It was bad enough that he had become a prisoner in his own house, but the catapulting effect on his family was beginning to hurt.

He could feel a tension headache coming on and decided to walk on the Downs. But as he strode into the hall he changed his mind. A good dose of sea air was what he needed. He picked up his car keys and a jacket from the line of hooks behind the door.

'Where are you going, Daddy?' Helen asked.

He swung round. The child was standing on the stairs, the sleepy kitten cradled in her arms.

He smiled. 'Out for a while.'

'Can I come with you?'

'Not today.'

'Why not?'

Because ... because what? He simply did not want her with him.

'I am going to the Dog & Duck later on,' he lied. 'You know you can't come in there.'

She looked so crestfallen that he went to the foot of the stairs and kissed her cheek.

'Goodbye, Helen,' he said as he left the house.

Justin sat patiently in his car. He would sit here all night if necessary, until the man he intended to confront came home.

It was five-thirty when a black Rolls-Royce pulled up and a smartly dressed chauffeur leapt out. He opened the rear door and as Terence Russell emerged Justin tightened his grip on the steering wheel. He had only seen photographs of Terence Russell in the business sections of the newspapers, and was surprised by how large a man he was. He strode across the pavement, then paused below the steps, glancing back at the car. He looked irritable as he said something which Justin was unable to hear.

He disappeared into the house, while a younger, red-faced man clambered awkwardly from the vehicle. Justin recognised the son, and was amused to see him so obviously out of favour with his father. Because he was heir to the Russell business empire, the society columnists listed him as one of the most sought-after bachelors in the country. They failed to mention that he was small and unattractive, with shifty eyes, a weak mouth and even weaker chin.

Justin knew there was also a daughter, but being a schoolgirl she was probably shielded from the excesses of the popular press. Mind you, he thought, if she was as unattractive as her brother it was not surprising. Then he remembered his father mentioning they had different mothers. There had been a scandal during the war, when Terence Russell's first wife left him to live with an Australian soldier who was temporarily based in London. Later, when the war ended, she went with him to Australia. Whether she deliberately abandoned her young son or had been prevented from taking him with her was a matter of speculation. But there could have been little love in the marriage, for less than a year later Terence Russell remarried, losing his second wife to a higher force when she died eight months after the birth of their daughter. It was a classic tale of tragedy, and ample proof that money could not buy happiness. But Justin could feel no pity for the man, not when Terence Russell was bringing about the ruination of his own father.

The Rolls-Royce moved away, leaving the street deserted. It was now or never. Justin was aware of his pounding heart as he crossed the road. He bounded up three well-scrubbed steps to the front door, and it was then, as he paused to gather his resolve, that he heard a taxi pull up behind him. He ignored it as he lifted his hand to the doorbell. Whatever happened now, he knew his courage would not fail him, not when it was fed upon festering resentment.

'Excuse me, but tradesmen are meant to use the basement entrance. There is a sign down here had you bothered to read it.'

Justin swung round, startled by the sharp, feminine voice.

The taxi was pulling away, and on the pavement below him stood a tall, young woman with upswept hair. She wore a pale yellow suit which was obviously Chanel, and was displaying the kind of inbred arrogance he despised.

'I read it.' His grey eyes were smouldering.

'Oh!' She suddenly sounded unsure of herself. 'I'm sorry, but you look . . .'

'. . . like a tradesman?'

'Yes . . . I mean no . . .'

A crimson flush spread upwards through her cheeks, disappearing into the roots of her hair, which was neither blonde nor brown, but the colour of ripened wheat fields at harvest time. It was only when he looked more closely that Justin realised she was little more than a child of perhaps fifteen or sixteen. It was her height, combined with the adult clothes and unsuitable hairstyle, which had initially deceived him. But with an eye trained for detail he now saw that the well-cut suit barely disguised a gangling adolescent with a slender, boyish figure, narrow hips and flat chest. There was a trace of developing character in her angular face, and an impish quality which appealed to the artist in him. Her nose was finely shaped, if slightly over-long, her cheekbones high and prominent, and she had a generous, upturned mouth. Her eyes were her most outstanding feature. They were large and almond-shaped with long lashes which shadowed their unusual turquoise colouring.

She was someone who would stand out in a crowd and not be easily forgotten. Could she be the daughter? She was about the right age, although only in height did she resemble Terence Russell.

The blush had burnt itself out, leaving her face colourless. He rightly guessed that her outburst had been an act of bravado which she was now regretting.

'I should not have spoken to you like that,' he said.

'I'm the one who should apologise. After all, I was rude to you first.' She paused, embarrassed by the directness of his gaze and her inability to make him out. He was casually dressed in a lightweight jacket and open-necked shirt, with shaggy hair, the ends of which touched his collar. He could not be a friend of Geoffrey's, for her brother did not cultivate tall, good-looking friends who might upstage him. She mounted the bottom step. 'I am Philippa Russell.'

'I suspected you were.'

He smiled, and Philippa felt her breath catch in her throat as a genuine warmth caressed her. Then it was gone, replaced by a grim determination. She glanced at the door. Bradshaw was certainly taking his time, but for once she didn't mind. There was something intriguing about this young man, and she found herself hoping the butler was in his rooms at the top of the house, for then he would be at least another two or three minutes.

'Are you here to see my father?'

'Yes,' he replied.

Whatever business he had, she sensed it was not pleasant.

'Do you have an appointment? If not, you will get no further than the entrance hall. Our butler is an old hand at getting rid of unwanted callers.'

The door opened and she saw his momentary hesitation. No, he does not have an appointment, she thought. But he was prepared to try and bluff his way in.

'Good afternoon,' said Bradshaw, obviously not seeing the girl standing at the bottom of the steps. 'May I help you?'

Philippa held little sway over the staff, except for the chauffeur, Mike Taylor. But there were occasions when she was able to exert her influence and, by using surprise as her weapon, she did so now.

'I presume my father is already home.' She swept past

both the young man and the startled butler. 'This gentleman has an appointment and is already late. Please take him through.'

Bradshaw frowned as he watched her cross the hallway.

'Mr Russell arrived a few minutes ago. He never mentioned an appointment.'

Philippa swung round. 'I expect it slipped his mind. He has been rather busy lately. Well, Bradshaw, don't dither. He's been standing on the doorstep for long enough as it is.'

The butler made a disapproving sound which was somewhere between a cough and a grunt. The chit of a girl would be going back to school in another week, and not a moment too soon.

'If you would come this way, sir,' he said to the young man. 'I shall announce you.'

'Thank you,' said Justin, his eyes seeking those of his unexpected ally.

Philippa met his gaze, blushed, then fled up the stairs. She stopped on the landing, wishing she had the courage to stay down there longer, for then she would have heard his name. She met many young men when staying at the homes of her friends. They were usually older brothers, or the sons of close family friends, but none of them had ever affected her in quite the same way as this shabby-looking stranger.

Terence Russell paced his study, a glass of whisky in one hand and a cigar in the other. The sheer audacity of the Lang boy had taken him by surprise. The cheeky, young whelp had pushed past Bradshaw, slammed the door, and delivered an impassioned speech which gave vent to his feelings but not once degenerated into a plea for his father. He left as abruptly as he had come and, furious though Terence was, he could not help but compare George Lang's son with his own. Geoffrey was weak, like his mother, and Terence knew

15

that however hard he pushed, his son would never have an inner fire. The best he could do was prepare Geoffrey for the day when he took over Russell Industries.

The door swung open. Terence stopped in mid-stride.

'You wanted to see me?' his daughter asked.

'Yes, young lady. And the next time you come marching in here, knock first. Shut the door and sit down.'

'I'd prefer to stand, thank you.'

His mouth tightened. 'Why did you tell Bradshaw to let that abusive young man into my house?'

'He wasn't abusive to me.' Philippa met his furious gaze. 'And I was under the impression this was my house too.'

'Don't think you are too old for the strap, my girl, because I can assure you that you're not. Why did you let him in?'

'Because he wanted to see you. He was perfectly respectable. I might have thought twice had he a gun or a knife tucked in his belt.'

Terence Russell stepped forward and slapped her cheek.

'Go to your bedroom, and stay there until I give you permission to come down.'

Had he cared anything for his daughter he would have recognised her defiant stare as a reflection of his own stubbornness. But he did not see it and after she had slammed out of the room his only thought was to ensure she was better disciplined when she returned to school.

Before he drove home, Justin went into a pub for a much-needed drink. He dallied for a while, sipping a half pint of bitter and eating crisps. He was still inwardly trembling from the enormity of what he had done, for it had taken every shred of courage to face Terence Russell under his own roof. He was under no illusion that his personal crusade would change anything, but he had had the satisfaction of rendering the man speechless before making a dignified retreat.

He left London later than anticipated, and by the time the South Downs came into view evening was drawing in fast, with the setting sun casting mellow hues of red and gold over the gently undulating hills. He put aside the events of the day and concentrated instead on memorising the colours, so he could translate them into a painting.

He did not know his father was a part of that painting. He was standing high up on the cliffs at Beachy Head, staring across the calm waters of the English Channel. There had been a lot of people here earlier, but the families had gone, leaving mainly childless couples who were making the most of the warm, late summer evening. It was already September, and very soon the first signs of autumn would make themselves known, with chill mornings and damp mists settling in the valleys.

But George Lang wouldn't be here to see another autumn. He had decided there was only one way out of this mess. One way to save his family from even greater humiliation. He was sorry he had been unable to say goodbye, but knew Sarah would understand the reasons. It would be hard on her for a while, but she was strong and would fight to hold the family together.

George Lang was aware of an unusual calm as he walked forward. The horrified people who witnessed what happened told the police the same thing. He had been smiling before he stepped off the edge of the cliff and plunged to his death.

Justin could usually vent his emotions with a frenzied attack on his sketch pad, but there were occasions when he needed the distraction of a more physical activity. Today was one of them. He came downstairs in breeches and boots, intending to take his mother's thoroughbred over the Downs. But Sarah waylaid him in the hall, saying they needed to talk.

The four of them sat in the kitchen, Sarah, her two sons and Helen. The funeral had been held the day before at the local church. The vicar was kind considering the circumstances of George's death, and the local community had put in an appearance. But there was an air of hypocrisy hanging over the proceedings, and Sarah was glad when it was over and done with. She wanted to put this nightmare behind her and remember George as he had been before the accusations began. Enough damage had already been done, and it would probably leave a lasting impression upon them all.

She gazed sadly at her three children, her eyes resting longest on her older son, without whom she could never have got through this horrific week. For Justin, the last remnants of youth had been shed when he opened the front door to the two grim-faced policemen. From that moment he took it upon himself to shoulder the responsibilities of the ensuing days – an endless stream of questions from the police and the coroner; the callous persistence of the press, who haunted them until a better story came along; and the morbid curiosity of the people in whose midst they had lived for thirteen years.

And the other two? Bit by bit Helen was withdrawing further into herself, despite their efforts to shield her from the worst of what was happening. Even Nicholas was quieter, and although he appeared to be the least affected, she knew he was holding the hurt deep down inside him. He needed to release his anger, like his brother was doing, but he refused to discuss his father's death with her, and she did not want to ask Justin for help. He had done more than enough.

'I reached a decision last night,' she now told the three of them. 'I don't want to stay here any longer. I intend to give a month's notice on this place and then go home. It will be better for Helen, and for us all in the long run.'

Her announcement was met by a stunned silence. The two boys glanced uneasily at each other.

'This is home.' Helen sounded confused and frightened.

'I know, darling,' Sarah said. 'But we only rent this house. With Daddy gone it's not going to be easy to meet the monthly payments. But I still own the house where I lived as a little girl, and where we used to live until we moved here.'

Tears sprang to the child's eyes. 'I don't want to leave! I don't want to live in some horrible town!'

'It's not in a town.'

Sarah reached out to comfort her daughter, but Helen slipped off her chair and ran to Justin. He lifted her on to his lap and held her close.

'Nick and I were born at Flint Iron Farm.' His voice was gentle. 'It's a lovely old farmhouse in the middle of Dartmoor. There is a village close by, but it's miles from the nearest town, not so very different from here.'

Helen shuddered. 'Dartmoor is a prison.'

'Of course it isn't,' he laughed. 'Dartmoor is mile upon mile of open moorland. There is a prison, but it's a long way from where we will be.'

'What will you do with the ponies?' Nicholas asked.

'Take them with us. If nobody else has opened a riding school in the district then I shall.' Sarah paused. 'Sooner or later I am going to need the additional income. Your father and I never did manage to save much.'

Justin's eyes were resting on her face and, like her, she knew he was thinking it ironic that his father had killed himself because he had been accused of stealing thousands of pounds. In reality, they were practically penniless. Thank heaven she had refused to sell Flint Iron Farm when they moved here. It had been in her family for five generations, and to her it would always be home. It was not strictly a farm any more, for there were fewer than twenty acres of land attached to it. But there was sufficient grazing for the ponies and a wooden barn in which they could be stabled.

'It must be in a terrible state by now,' Justin said. It had been rented to a family for a short while, but they couldn't take the harsh winters and moved out within a year. Since then it had been empty.

'The house is solidly built, and I'm sure there is nothing a good scrub and a layer of paint can't put right.'

Justin thought his mother over-optimistic, but did not have the heart to disillusion her. 'We could go and see it. But wouldn't it be better to stay here for winter and move back in the spring?'

'I don't want to spend another winter here, with people looking down their noses at us. And it would be easier on Helen if we started afresh. Nobody in Povey Ashton will treat us as outcasts.'

'Why do we have to leave?' Helen asked, her voice trembling. 'Why can't we stay here?'

Justin lifted her chin. 'People don't understand about Dad, sweetheart. And when you go back to school you're going to find a lot of the children are nasty to you because of what their parents have told them.'

'But he didn't steal anything!'

He kissed her forehead. 'We all know that, but nobody else is going to believe us.'

'Not even our friends?'

He hesitated. So few of their so-called friends had stood by them.

'Some of them do,' said Sarah. Her unspoken words hung on the air. Both Justin and Nicholas knew the number of true friends the family shared between them could be counted on the fingers of one hand.

'There is something else you have forgotten,' said Nicholas. 'What about me? Justin lives in London for most of the time, but what am I meant to do? I can't very well pop home for a weekend if you're living on the other side of the country. And I don't suppose I'll be getting a car now.'

Sarah saw the sudden anger in Justin's eyes, and spoke quickly, before a row erupted between them.

'You'll either have to remain in Cambridge, or else stay with Justin and Noel, if they'll have you. As for the car, it's out of the question. Certainly for the time being. Nothing is ever going to be quite the same again, Nicholas.'

Shame-faced, her younger son looked away.

'If money is going to be a problem I could get a teaching job,' Justin volunteered. 'After three years I have the qualifications.'

'You will do no such thing!' Sarah's voice was sharp. 'Your father would want you to finish your final year, and I insist upon it. We are not broke, darling, but because of the circumstances of his death there will be no money from the insurance company and, for a while, we shall have to count our pennies a little more carefully.'

She stood up and put the kettle on the stove. After she had made a pot of tea they discussed their future plans. It was eleven-thirty when they finished.

'I'd rather you rode in the paddock,' Sarah said before Justin could slip away. 'Copper could do with some schooling.'

He turned round slowly. 'I'm not about to do anything stupid.'

'I know, Justin. But *she* might. You know how strung up she gets when she hasn't been exercised. Do it for me. Please.'

She thought he was going to refuse, but then he nodded his head. She knew she was being over-cautious. Justin was more than capable of handling the mare, however silly she

21

might be. If it had not been for art dominating his life he could have become a top horseman in any equestrian sport. Both she and Nicholas were competent riders, but neither of them possessed the natural flair which placed Justin in a class above them.

He was barely out of the door when Nicholas stood up. 'I think I'll go and watch,' he said. 'Come on, Helen, some fresh air will do you good. You spend too much time cooped up inside the house.'

His sister hesitated, then followed him.

Sarah watched them through the window, conscious that their father's death had brought them closer together than they had ever been. She started to gather up the dirty cups, but one slipped through her fingers and smashed on the linoleum floor. She stared at it in dismay and then, as the explosion welled up inside her, she sat down and cried.

CHAPTER TWO

Philippa Russell glanced at her watch. Her father had allowed her to have the car providing it was back by three. But they had got lost in the narrow, country lanes and if they did not find the place soon, would be forced to turn back. Officially, she was meant to be visiting a friend who lived in Surrey. Unofficially, Mike Taylor had chatted up a junior in the personnel department, persuading her to give him George Lang's home address.

Terence Russell had employed Mike as his chauffeur five years ago, when Philippa was a lonely ten-year-old whom he drove to and from boarding school. He had been twenty-five then, a slightly built man of medium height with thinning brown hair and a doleful expression which was at odds with his cheerful disposition. He was nothing like his dour predecessor. He chatted to her and made her laugh. Philippa rarely talked with her father, for he simply was not interested in anything she had to say, while Geoffrey had no time for her at all. But she could always turn to Mike, even though their friendship had to remain secret. In public she was Miss Philippa and he Mr Taylor. In private it was different.

She looked at him now. 'You must have taken another wrong turn. All we are doing is driving deeper into these wretched hills.'

'These wretched hills happen to be the South Downs.

Don't they teach you anything at that fancy school? And this has to be the right road. Look, there's the T-junction. If we turn left, it should be a quarter of a mile further on.'

Philippa was sceptical. The woman at the farmhouse where they had stopped to ask directions had been helpful but not overly bright. She gazed at the thick hedgerows which lined the banks on either side of them. There was no verge and she had the claustrophobic feeling of being boxed in. It was little wonder Mike was driving at a snail's pace.

'It's so desolate out here,' she said. 'I always thought people like them lived in semi-detached houses in the suburbs.'

'People like who? I never realised there were any hard and fast rules about who lived where. They have as much right to live in the country as anyone. You remember that the next time you pass judgement on people you know nothing about.'

The girl's cheeks were scarlet. 'I thought he would live closer to the office, that's all. It has taken forever to get here, and he must have been making the journey twice a day.'

'Brighton is not too far away and it has a reasonable train service.'

They reached the junction, but Mike did not pull out, even though there were no other vehicles in sight. He stopped the car and shifted the gear into neutral.

'What's the matter?' Philippa asked.

'Before we get there, you and I should have a little talk. I know how hard it must be sometimes, having no mother to guide you and a father who is always busy. But don't you think I should be told the real reason why you wanted to come here today?'

A wave of panic washed over her. 'I want to say I'm sorry for what happened. My father won't. What other reason could there be?'

'What about a nice-looking, well-spoken lad, who would have benefited from a decent haircut?'

Philippa stared through the windscreen, concentrating on the skudding clouds. 'I don't know what you're talking about.'

'Don't you? Mr Bradshaw enjoys gossiping over a cup of tea in the mornings. He told me about the Lang boy coming to the house and the trouble you were in because of it. Since then you've been wandering around in a dream, not hearing what's said to you half the time.'

'You're imagining things, Mike. I barely spoke to him. I don't even know his first name.'

'Does that make any difference? You want to see him again, don't you?'

He sighed when she did not reply. She was not being awkward. She was a vulnerable young girl who was crying out for guidance and affection.

'There is nothing to be ashamed of, Philippa.' He spoke softly. 'You try and act as though you are twenty and sophisticated, but inside you are a very normal fifteen-year-old who is neither a child nor a woman. I'm not so old that I cannot remember the uncertainties of my own adolescence. Am I right about the boy?'

'Yes.' Philippa hated herself for admitting it.

Mike put his hand beneath her chin and turned her head, forcing her to look at him. He was smiling. 'Try to remember that however pleasant a young man he might have seemed, his father has been lying in his grave for less than twenty-four hours. What if neither he nor his mother want to see you? By going there now you could be badly hurt.'

'I'm not backing out, not after coming this far. I want them to know at least one member of my family cares. And what does it matter if I am being foolish? I'll never see him again after today.'

'All right, let's get this over with. There are times when you remind me of your father. He can be equally stubborn when he sets his mind to it.'

'Am I really like him?' she asked.

Affectionately, he patted her cheek. 'Would I be saying so if you weren't?'

As the car moved forward Philippa wondered if Mike was right. Was she being pig-headed for her own selfish reasons, or did she genuinely want to convey sorrow for what had happened?

'There it is,' said Mike.

She looked up and saw a driveway fifty yards ahead. There was a weathered board pressed into the hedge.

'But that's a riding school!' she exclaimed.

'It also happens to be where they live. Look at the name on the board. Are you still determined to go in?'

'Yes. But it would probably be better if I walked. The Rolls might look ostentatious. Can you park out here?'

'I don't see why not. Will you be all right, or shall I come with you?'

'No,' she said. This was something she had to do on her own.

At least she was not over-dressed, having opted for a loose shirt, slacks and flat shoes. She had nearly put up her hair as it made her look older, but changed her mind and left it bouncing on her shoulders instead.

As Philippa got out of the car she heard a thud of hooves on dry ground, followed by a short burst of clapping and a child's voice calling for more. Her nerves were starting to run riot, but because Mike was watching she did not dare to hesitate. This was a riding school, after all. There was probably a lesson in progress. She took a deep breath. It was now or never.

She strode confidently into the driveway, only to come to

an abrupt halt. In a paddock to her right a chestnut horse was cantering towards a high, three-bar jump. The rider was not wearing a hat and, with a sense of shock, Philippa realised who it was. He did not see her, as his entire concentration was focused on the horse and the jump. She watched in fascinated horror, subconsciously aware that he rode with the skill and confidence of a professional.

The horse tried to rush the final approach, and with little visible effort he steadied it. And then the animal left the ground, virtually flying over the jump as though it were nothing more intimidating than a fallen log. There followed another round of delighted clapping. Philippa forced her eyes away from the horse and rider, seeing a young girl with plaits sitting on a wooden gate. Beside her was a fair-headed young man who had a steadying arm around her waist.

It was the child who saw Philippa first. Her eyes widened and she whispered something to her companion. The young man turned his head. They had the same eyes and were obviously brother and sister, but what shook Philippa was his strong physical resemblance to the rider. She had automatically presumed there was only one son, and was ill prepared to face a brood of George Lang's offspring. She wondered if there were more of them in the tree-shaded house.

'Justin!' shouted the fair-headed young man.

The rider circled the horse and brought it to a halt. This time he did not smile. His facial muscles hardened and Philippa saw anger flare in his dark eyes. As the horse sprang forward she took a backward step. She could feel her heart pounding as she wondered whether it was going to jump the wooden fence which separated them. But at the last moment Justin Lang pulled the animal around, so that it stood side on to her, tossing its head and champing impatiently at the bit.

'What the hell are you doing here? Hasn't your family

done enough damage without you coming to gloat?'

The colour drained from Philippa's face. 'I only want to . . .'

'I don't give a damn what you want! This is our property and you are trespassing. Now get out!'

Tears sprang to her eyes but she was not going to let him see her cry. She turned away.

'Who was that?' she heard the younger brother ask.

'Nobody important.'

Mike was right. She should never have come.

PART TWO

1963 to 1968

CHAPTER THREE

After two years abroad it was strange to be in England. When her father sent her to a Swiss finishing school Philippa did not bother to come back, preferring to spend her holidays with friends. She had left the school six months ago but had remained in Europe, wandering without purpose from country to country, usually with friends but sometimes alone. Not once had her father suggested she come home. Instead, he encouraged his daughter to stay away by giving her unrestricted access to whatever funds she required. There had been no reason for her to return, until now.

She had sent a telegram giving details of her arrival, but nobody was at the airport to meet her, so she found a porter, and went in search of a taxi. But four international flights had arrived almost simultaneously and there was a long queue of people waiting at the empty rank.

'A bus to Victoria would be quicker,' the porter said. 'They leave every twenty minutes.'

It was more sensible than standing here. Philippa had forgotten how cold November could be, and her light-weight suit offered no protection against the icy wind.

'Can you take me to the terminal?' she asked.

They seemed to walk forever and her teeth were beginning to chatter when she heard someone call her name. She looked round and saw Mike hurrying to catch her up. He was not much different than when she had last seen him. His hair was receding, and she was taller than him now.

'There was an accident and I was held up in traffic,' he said. 'I thought I had missed you.'

'Oh, Mike, it is marvellous to see you again.'

Philippa forgot she was no longer a child and threw her arms around his neck. He hugged her tight before stepping back and holding her at arm's length. She had been a schoolgirl when he last saw her. Now she was an attractive young woman with poise and sophistication.

'You have grown up beautifully, Philippa. Your father would have been proud of you.'

'No he wouldn't,' she said. 'You know as well as I do that he never liked me. What happened? Geoffrey's message said nothing, other than he was dead.'

'He was driving the Bentley. It crashed into a tree and he was killed instantly. There was nobody else involved and the police still don't know what happened. I think he must have lost control. He's had a lot on his mind recently, what with everything going from bad to worse.'

'What do you mean?'

'Your brother will explain it to you.'

'Explain what?'

'You must ask Geoffrey. It's not my place to say. And ... good heavens, child, you're shivering! Couldn't you find anything more appropriate to wear?'

'I was in Italy and had nothing else with me.'

Mike took off his jacket and draped it around her shoulders. 'I have an overcoat in the car,' he said as she started to protest. 'Come along, before you catch pneumonia.'

It was warm inside the Rolls-Royce. While he supervised the luggage Mike left the engine idling and the heater on full. Gradually, Philippa brought her chattering teeth under control.

'Did you tip the porter?' she asked when he climbed in beside her.

'Of course. You owe me a couple of pounds.'

He spoke lightly, for she knew he could claim back the money on a legitimate expense account, but there was no smile on his lips and he was avoiding her gaze. Philippa shivered, but not because she was cold.

'There is something which you are not telling me,' she said.

Mike had not wanted to do this, but it was only fair that she know. He took a deep breath. 'The funeral was yesterday. Your brother insisted.'

Philippa closed her eyes. How could Geoffrey do such a thing? He must have known she would come. After all, Terence had been her father as well.

'Could I see the grave before you take me home?'

'Of course. I am sorry it had to be like this.'

The flowers which covered the newly turned earth were sodden and windblown. Philippa stood ankle-deep in autumn leaves, staring at the largest of the wreaths. The card was still attached to it and read 'In Memory of Our Loving Father. We Shall Remember You Always. Geoffrey and Philippa'.

What love? For all her life they had been strangers. He had given her things material, but never his love. Philippa had not cried when she heard he was dead, nor did she shed a tear now. She felt nothing as she turned away from the grave to where Mike was waiting.

'I need to know what other surprises are about to be sprung upon me,' she said.

'I can't tell you, Philippa. I don't know the full details. Even if I did, it wouldn't be right.' He glanced up as a drop of rain splattered against his cheek. 'Have you finished here?'

'Yes.'

He watched her walk towards the car. The child had become a woman and he hoped she had the strength to face what was coming.

It was six o'clock when they reached the house, and the rain was falling steadily. Her father's house ... or was it her brother's? Philippa declined the umbrella Mike offered. She walked up the steps and pressed the bell.

Geoffrey opened the door. He was wearing old flannels and a V-necked sweater. 'Oh, it's you,' he said, his impersonal eyes looking her up and down. 'You'd better come in. What is that thing you are wearing? The latest in Paris fashion?'

Philippa frowned. She had forgotten how sarcastic he could be. 'Mike ... Taylor ... lent it to me,' she said. 'Have you been drinking, Geoffrey?'

'I've had one or two, but not enough to make me drunk.'

He stood aside and she walked past him into the hall. It was a beautiful hall, with an arched ceiling and a chandelier which sparkled like a hundred stars. But because this had always been a male-dominated house it lacked the warmth of a proper home. Now, the brightness from the chandelier merely showed up the dust on the furniture and the dirty floor.

'I'll take your luggage to your room,' Mike said.

'That's all right. Bradshaw can do it.'

'Didn't he tell you that Bradshaw has gone, and Mrs Litton as well?' Geoffrey asked. 'I'm surprised Taylor is still here. He knows there is no money to pay him.'

It took a moment for his words to sink in. 'Is that true?' she asked Mike.

'Yes. I have already told Mr Geoffrey I would prefer to remain in the flat until the end of the month, when my employment will terminate.' He looked uncomfortable. 'I'll take these upstairs.'

As he moved away Philippa turned on her brother. 'What is going on?'

'I'd rather not discuss it out here,' he said. 'Taylor, I have an appointment with the solicitors tomorrow. Please be here by ten. My sister will accompany me.'

Philippa went into the drawing room. He followed her, closing the door behind them. She did not wait for him to explain further, but launched into an attack.

'What right did you have to bury Father without my being present?'

'So Taylor did tell you something.' Geoffrey flopped on to the sofa and picked up a glass half filled with neat whisky.

'He took me to see the grave. Why, Geoffrey?'

'Because nobody knew where you were. I tried to contact you, but all I received was a cryptic message saying you were somewhere in the Adriatic with Sebastian Mortimer. I could not hold up the funeral for the sake of your love life.'

'I came back as quickly as I could. And before you hurl accusations at me, get your facts right. Sebastian happened to be one of a large group of people which also included his parents.'

'Then seeing you are so well in with the family I suggest you get back there and persuade this Sebastian Mortimer to marry you. I wasn't kidding, Philippa. We are broke, and in three weeks' time this house won't belong to us any more.'

She resisted an urge to sit down. 'How can we be broke? It's impossible.'

'The Inland Revenue nailed Father for tax evasion. They say he owes them millions. The company has gone into receivership and everything has to be sold to help meet the debt. Had he lived, there was a possibility he would have been jailed for fraud.'

Philippa heard the front door close and walked to the window, pulling aside the heavy velvet curtain. She watched as Mike got into the Rolls-Royce and drove away. She let the curtain drop. No wonder he had been reluctant to tell her anything.

'How could it happen?' she asked.

'I don't know. He fiddled the books and pocketed the money.'

'You worked with him, Geoffrey. You must have known what was going on.'

'No, I didn't. There were certain aspects of the business which he never confided in me.' He stood up. 'Do you want a drink?'

'No, thank you. Haven't you had enough?'

'Not nearly enough. I have my own theory. I think he deliberately took the Bentley out with the intention of killing himself. Why else would he wrap the car around a tree trunk? It was a dry day with clear visibility and virtually no traffic. He conveniently killed himself and left us to face the consequences.' He tipped more whisky into his glass. 'Because of what he's done we are no longer socially acceptable. I have been dropped like a hot brick and so will you.'

Philippa curbed an impulse to knock the glass out of his hand. 'Why don't you fight back?'

'What with? Face facts, Philippa. We are not wealthy any more. All Father's assets have been frozen and neither of us will be able to lay a finger on any of his money. I don't know how much cash you've got on you, but I am practically skint.'

'Are you trying to tell me you have been working all these years for nothing?'

His smile was cold. 'Like you, I have not been hiding my light under a bushel. I didn't see any need to save for a rainy day.'

Philippa closed her eyes. This was too much to absorb at once.

'What are we going to do?'

'I don't know about you, but I'm going to have another drink.' He drained his glass. 'Don't worry, you won't be left destitute. Father's solicitor is arranging for a small lump sum which should tide you over for a while. There are some papers which need your signature before the money can be released. And there is your inheritance, of course. It's tied up in a trust which nobody can touch. Unfortunately, you can't either, not until you are twenty-five.'

Philippa's disdain showed as she looked at him. 'Is there any food in the house?'

'I expect you'll find something if you rummage about. Did they teach you to cook in Switzerland? From what I remember you couldn't even boil an egg without burning it.'

'Go to hell, Geoffrey!'

He grinned as he raised his glass. 'I may do just that.'

Philippa found some stale bread and a slab of cheese with lumps of green mould clinging to it. Geoffrey was right, she couldn't cook. There had never been any need for her to learn. She toasted two slices of bread, covered them in cheese, then placed them under the grill. There was half a jar of instant coffee in the pantry, and some old newspapers which had been thrown into a corner. They caught her eye because of the photograph of her father on the top copy. She picked it up. There was also a brief piece in the newspaper beneath it. She took them to the Formica-topped table.

The Profumo scandal was dominating the news at the time, yet her father had made the front pages. As she ate, Philippa read through the sequence of events leading to his death. There was no sympathy for him. In fact, he was called a hard and ambitious man. She pushed the newspapers aside. Who was she to disagree? If he had a gentler side she had never seen it. She remembered that time four years before when another man had killed himself. Had he been an innocent scapegoat who had got in her father's way? Nobody would ever know now.

Leonard Perkins of the firm Perkins, Crisp & Perkins was a drab-looking man who wore a pin-striped suit and sat with his hands clasped over his stomach. His face had the unhealthy pallor of a person who rarely went out of doors, and he had probing eyes which sent shivers coursing down Philippa's back. But he also had the look of a man who could be trusted.

Geoffrey had a hangover. His eyes were slits and he kept drumming his fingers against his thigh. He let Leonard Perkins do most of the talking, although he interrupted every so often in a manner which Philippa found irritating. He was right about the inheritance. Terence Russell had put aside a small sum of money soon after she was born. With interest, it had accumulated to six thousand pounds, but was so tied up in legalities that his daughter was unable to draw a penny of it until she was twenty-five.

'My brother was given his inheritance at twenty-one,' Philippa pointed out. Geoffrey had also blown the lot in less than a year, but she did not mention that.

'Your father stipulated twenty-five,' said Leonard Perkins. 'It is a condition which I am unable to circumvent.'

'Surely you can do something? I need the money now – or at least some of it. What good will it be to me in another six years?'

'You will get some money, Philippa.' Geoffrey sounded impatient. 'But you will not get that money. Father was not going to have every down and out chasing you for what they could get. Please give her the document, Mr Perkins.'

'What document?' Philippa looked from one man to the other.

'This one.' Leonard Perkins opened a file, removed a typewritten sheet of paper and placed it in front of her. 'If you will sign here I should be able to release some money by the end of the week.'

She stared at the dotted line on which his thumb was resting. 'What is this?'

Geoffrey exploded. 'For heaven's sake, Philippa, my head is splitting! Sign the damn document and let's get out of here. It is perfectly above board. In fact, you will come out of this a lot better off than me.'

'I suggest you take your brother's advice,' said Leonard Perkins. 'Because you are under twenty-one he is legally your guardian. We have discussed the matter in some depth and have reached the conclusion this is in your best interests.'

'Just sign it,' Geoffrey said. 'Had I been able, I would have done so on your behalf.'

'I want to read it first.'

The breath hissed between her brother's teeth, but Leonard Perkins nodded his approval. Philippa picked up the document and read it slowly. Then she turned to Geoffrey.

'Why didn't you tell me about Moor View?'

'Because I knew you would become sentimental.'

'But I didn't even know my grandfather had left it to me. I presumed it was sold when he died.'

'The house was sold and the money used to pay off his debts. Father couldn't touch the pottery. Don't be a fool, Philippa. The place is barely managing to keep going. By liquidating what few assets there are and selling the land, you'll receive a respectable sum which will give you enough leeway to decide what you want to do with your life.'

Some of the happiest days of her childhood were tied to that pottery. When she was a little girl Philippa had been allowed to spend the summers with her grandfather, but when she was nine he had died and she never went there again.

She pushed the document across the desk. 'I am sorry, but I am not signing away my grandfather's pottery.'

Leonard Perkins admired her stance, foolhardy though it was. 'I can understand how you must feel. However, Moor View Pottery is on the verge of bankruptcy and if you do not take it into voluntary liquidation now, it will eventually be forced upon you. When that happens you will have to wait a year, maybe longer, for whatever money is left. You are in a no-win situation, Miss Russell. You have no business experience and, even if you did, the company desperately needs an injection of hard cash. No amount of good intentions can save it now.'

'I want to see it for myself.'

Geoffrey stood up. 'I've had enough of this. I'll wait outside. I have no idea what you hope to achieve, but I am beginning to understand Father's caution as far as you were concerned.'

He stormed out, slamming the door behind him.

'Your brother is not out to rob you,' Leonard Perkins said. 'On the contrary, he has gone to considerable trouble on your behalf.'

'Then why didn't he want me to know I was about to sign Moor View away?'

'Because he was afraid you would react in precisely the manner you have. In all honesty, you do not have a hope of getting the pottery back on to its feet. Be sensible, sign the document and have done with it.'

Two centuries of family history were tied up in the pottery. They were the only family who had ever cared for her. Philippa was obdurate. 'I shall decide what I want to do when I have seen it. Thank you very much, Mr Perkins. I apologise if I have wasted your time.'

'You haven't.' He smiled. 'Take a look at your pottery. Once you have seen the problems I am sure you will come round to our way of thinking.'

CHAPTER FOUR

Overnight, Philippa had to learn to count her pennies, and there were precious few of those. The bank accounts had been closed and the only money she had was what she had brought back with her. In less than three weeks she wouldn't even have a roof over her head. The house was being auctioned with all its contents, as were the Rolls-Royce and the mews flat above the garage where Mike lived. She knew the chauffeur was looking for another job. What she did not know were Geoffrey's plans. Since their visit to Leonard Perkins he had barely spoken to her. When she told him she was going to Devon to see the pottery he poured himself another drink and acted as though he had not heard.

Philippa had decided to travel by train, as it would be cheaper than taking the petrol-guzzling Rolls-Royce, but when she mentioned it to Mike he was horrified.

'While you still have the trappings of wealth, flaunt them,' he told her.

Which was why he drove her there two days later.

Philippa was nervous. 'Do you think I should have warned them I was coming?' she asked. 'I thought it better to see the place as it really is, not done up for my benefit.'

Mike knew she was finding it difficult to adjust to her present circumstances and up to now had refrained from passing an opinion. But she had no family, other than a spineless brother, to guide her, and no close friends in whom she could confide.

'You should have taken the money,' he said. 'You have a habit of leaping into situations where you end up getting hurt. It happened with that boy you were determined to track down, and will happen again with this run-down pottery.'

Philippa was surprised he remembered that incident. It was such a long time ago. On the other hand, his remarks stung her into retaliation. 'I don't see any comparison! I was younger and more impressionable then. My grandfather left me Moor View for a purpose and I shall do everything I can to live up to his expectations.'

'Stubborn, that's what you are. Just like your father.'

She might have been flattered once, but not any more.

'I shall never be like him. I shall never cheat people, nor ruin their lives like he did.'

'I never insinuated you would. But if Geoffrey had half your guts, it might never have come to this. He is not as innocent as he makes out. He must have had some inkling of what was going on.'

It was something Philippa was unable to understand. But she did not want to think about Geoffrey or her father. As she gazed at the bleak countryside her thoughts wandered to that short-lived, adolescent crush of four years ago. The pain was long past and the memory brought a smile to her lips.

'Why don't you stretch out in the back?' Mike asked. 'We still have a long way to go.'

'I'm too strung up. What about you? Do you want to stop for a rest?'

'I'm fine. I enjoy driving. I wouldn't do it otherwise.'

'You don't have another job yet, do you?'

'No, but I'll find one.'

'You should have left us earlier, like the others did.

Geoffrey warned me our name would become mud, but I didn't want to believe him. It's true, nobody wants to know us any more. I rang some of my old schoolfriends yesterday – the ones I used to spend weekends with. They were polite, but remarkably busy. They said they would get in touch, but I know they won't.'

'Then you're better off without them,' Mike said. 'And don't worry about me. There are plenty of jobs about. Look, we're approaching the eastern edge of Dartmoor. Did your grandfather ever take you there?'

'Only to the outer fringes to see the ponies.'

'It's a bleak place at the best of times. I went through it one summer, but wouldn't like to risk it in winter, not with the sudden mists which come down.' He switched on the wipers as large drops of rain splattered against the wind-screen. 'Are you nervous?'

'A little. Mostly because I don't know what to expect.'

Moor View was smaller than she remembered, or was that because she had last seen it with the eyes of a child? The three-storey brick building was situated on the northern side of Tavistock, and when Mike drove into the yard she thought how dreary it looked in the rain – rather like the murky workhouses described by Dickens. The only out-standing feature was a bottle-shaped oven which was no longer used and stood forgotten and decaying at the bottom end of the yard. It was a depressing place. Philippa wondered if everyone else was right and she was wrong. Perhaps it would have been wiser not to come.

Inside was equally dismal. There was no proper reception area, only a poky office where a middle-aged woman thumped at a typewriter. She stopped, her eyes narrowing when the young woman with an older, uniformed man walked in. Philippa had swept her hair into a low but fashionable beehive, applied a bare minimum of make-up, and wore a camel coat which she had bought in Paris three years before. The coat might have been old, but the classic cut was one which had not dated. It looked expensive, as did the leather handbag, gloves and shoes.

'Yes?' the woman said, her voice filled with hostility.

The girl smiled. In reality, she wanted to spit. 'I should like to see Mr Slater.'

'He is busy. You'll have to make an appointment.'

Philippa sensed Mike's annoyance, but he refrained from rushing to her defence. She had insisted he come with her, partly for moral support, but mainly because it was unfair to leave him sitting in the car for any length of time.

She removed a glove and then started on the other. 'I am delighted to hear business is so good. Now would you kindly inform Mr Slater that Philippa Russell wishes to see him.'

The name meant nothing to the woman and for one awful moment Philippa thought she was going to refuse. But she picked up the telephone, dialled an extension, and spoke briefly into the receiver.

'He's coming,' she said, and returned to her typing.

There was a spare chair in the office, but she did not invite Philippa to sit down, nor did the girl presume to do so. Instead, she walked to the rain-streaked window and stared at the slag heap where inferior china was traditionally dumped. It was pretty obvious, even to her untrained eyes, that Moor View Pottery was in the decline. How could she have the presumption to think she could save it single-handed? She had never done a stroke of work in her life. She was a social butterfly who knew nothing of the machinations of business.

The door opened behind her and the typing stopped.

'She insisted on seeing you,' the woman said.

Philippa turned slowly, unsure of the reception she would

45

get. The Gideon Slater she remembered was a tall, slightly built man with a cheerful smile and kindly eyes. Now, she saw him as a man of medium height who had thickened with age. He was in his mid-sixties, and although his face had lost its finer contours the smile and the eyes were still the same.

'Little Philippa! Whoever would have thought you'd grow so tall! I wish your grandfather could see you now. He would be bursting with pride.'

The tension melted away. 'I was not sure whether you would recognise me.'

'I would recognise you anywhere. You have a look of your mother about you. I have been waiting a long time for this day. Is a hug in order, or would it be too unseemly?'

'I would love a hug.' She knew then that everything was going to be all right. Gideon knew what he was doing. He would guide her through this thorny, new world. 'I never knew about Moor View until now. I thought it had been sold when my grandfather died.'

'It is your inheritance. He went to great pains to ensure it could never be taken from you.' He paused, his eyes searching her face. 'Your father's death must have come as a shock.'

'We were never very close.' She could tell by his expression that he understood.

'You'd better come to my office.' He hesitated, his eyes resting on Mike.

'This is Mike Taylor. He's . . .'

'Miss Philippa's chauffeur,' supplied Mike, displaying the kind of formality which she never demanded from him.

Gideon greeted him politely, then turned to the tall young woman. 'You will want to see around the pottery, of course, and I insist you join me for lunch. Perhaps your man would like to go into town for a while. I am afraid we have no canteen facilities here.'

Philippa glanced at Mike.

'What time do you want me to fetch you?' he asked.

'What time do you suggest?'

'About three. It's a long drive back, mostly in the dark.'

He smiled warmly, then left.

'This is Christopher Blake's grand-daughter,' Gideon told the glowering woman. 'She is the owner of Moor View.'

She had obviously worked that out for herself and did not look very pleased.

'I don't know how we would manage without Betty,' Gideon said. 'She is a treasure.'

'I am sure she is,' Philippa purred. She was not there to make waves.

Gideon's office had belonged to her grandfather and memories of him still lingered in the clutter on the mantelpiece. A coal fire had once burned in the fireplace. It had been replaced by an electric one, the burning coals lit by a red bulb and a revolving fan. They chattered idly while waiting for Betty to bring some tea. Philippa liked Gideon. He was a forthright man who knew what he was doing and did not beat about the bush.

'Your father should have been protecting your interests until you came of age,' he told her. 'He did nothing. I advised him of the mounting problems, and have a bulging file to prove it. He ignored my letters and refused to accept any telephone calls. Your grandfather made no provision for him to receive anything from the company, and I sometimes wondered if he deliberately wanted us to go under. It has been a long and hard struggle, but we have kept going, even if we are hanging on by our fingernails.'

Philippa could believe anything of her father now.

Whatever he had done was for himself. She had never mattered and, when it came to the final crunch, neither had Geoffrey. Because Gideon was frank with her, she felt it was only fair she was the same with him.

'I have been advised by my brother and my father's lawyer to liquidate the company. Despite your efforts, the pottery is on its knees, and there is nothing I can do to help it. I am broke. All my father's assets have been frozen, and although I came here in style, that was Mike's doing, not mine. I suspect he paid for the petrol. He insisted the tank was full when we left London, and I expect it will be full when we leave here. Everything my father owned is to be auctioned, including the car and the house.'

'So that's why you came, to prepare us for the worst.' Gideon picked up a paper knife and turned it slowly in his hands. 'It's been expected for a long time. We're already down to a skeletal staff and only keep going by manufacturing cheap souvenirs for the holiday resorts. Moor View is nothing like it was in your grandfather's time. In those days it was renowned for fine bone china, with our dinner services being sold to some of the best homes in the country.'

'What went wrong? How could it deteriorate so rapidly?'

'It wasn't rapid at all,' he said. 'The war brought an end to the boom we were enjoying, and after the war there was no money around. Your grandfather invested every penny he had in the business, but it kept backsliding. There was never enough money to replace worn-out machinery and everything deteriorated even more quickly after your grandfather died. Your father sold the house to pay his outstanding debts, and would have sold Moor View too, if he could. I knew he would do nothing to help us. Most of the machinery runs on a prayer, and now the oven is starting to play up. It broke down in the middle of a firing last month.

It was only half full, but there was nothing we could salvage.'

Philippa sipped her tea. It tasted as foul as it looked. 'How much longer can you keep it running?' she asked.

'A year. Perhaps a little longer if we are lucky.'

She stared beyond him, through the window at the murky sky. Her grandfather had wanted her to take his place, but how could he know his beloved pottery would be running on a shoestring while she was a virtual pauper. She thought of her inheritance lying in some musty bank vault gathering interest.

'Could you show me around?' she asked. 'But only if it is not inconvenient.'

He smiled. 'Moor View belongs to you, Philippa. You have the right to do whatever you want.'

She had not earned the right to do anything, but appreciated his kindness.

They lunched in a charming restaurant which had oak beams and a log fire burning in the fireplace. Away from the pottery they spoke more freely of its problems. Moor View was crying out for investment, but it also needed to revert to the fine bone china with which it had once been associated. To achieve that would take a substantial amount of money, more than Philippa could possibly lay her hands upon.

When they returned to Moor View a biting wind had blown up, but the rain had stopped. Gideon walked with her to the car.

'Everyone will be wanting to know how long they can expect to keep their jobs,' he said. 'Will it be a matter of weeks or days? I should like to give them as much warning as possible.'

Philippa looked at the ugly building. Shafts of light shone

49

through the windows and reflected in the puddles. Generations of the Blake family must have stood in this very same place and she was the last of them. Would they thank her for giving up so easily? Would her grandfather forgive her? Would she forgive herself?

'I shall telephone you on Monday,' she said. 'I need to speak with my father's lawyer.'

Gideon kissed her cheek. 'I'll be here.'

'You've already decided to keep that white elephant of a place, haven't you?' Mike asked.

Tavistock was behind them and he had driven into a patchy mist which cut visibility to a few hundred yards.

'I have to. It's difficult to explain, but I feel I belong there.'

'You should never have come. Use your common-sense. You have no money, and very soon will not have a roof over your head. Take what you can get, Philippa. You'll end up with nothing if you don't.'

'And will regret it even more if I do.'

It had been a long day and Philippa had no desire to cross swords with her brother. She crept into the house, but was only halfway across the hall when the drawing room door opened.

'Where have you been all day?' Geoffrey demanded.

'In Tavistock. I told you last night. Mike drove me there.'

He frowned. 'The sooner that man leaves the better. You seem to forget he is a servant and should be treated as such. You can tell me about the state of your precious pottery later. I have a friend who wishes to meet you.'

'I am tired, Geoffrey. It has been a long day and I'm not in the mood for a drunken evening with you and your friends.'

'I happen to be sober as a judge. And Maggie is the one person who has been decent enough not to turn her back on us. The least you can do is display some manners.'

'You're a fine one to talk of manners!' Philippa flung her coat over the banister, then strode past him into the room.

The woman who stood with her back to the fireplace was in her early twenties and quite unremarkable to look at. Her hair was brown and short, the bouffant style framing a moon-shaped face with blue eyes, a straight nose, and narrow lips which had a firm set to them. She was small and dumpy, and expensively dressed in all the wrong clothes. The red suit made her look sallow and the cream-coloured satin blouse was too frilly for someone of her stature. But she had the assertiveness of a person who was used to giving orders and having them carried out. She was certainly not a stereotype of the big-busted blondes who were more to Geoffrey's taste.

Philippa held out her hand. 'Good evening. I am Geoffrey's sister. Half-sister,' she corrected, ignoring his furious gaze.

'Margaret Huntington-Smythe,' the woman said. She had not expected the girl to be quite so young, and admired her self-possession. 'All my friends call me Maggie. I am so pleased to meet you at last.'

There was something vaguely familiar about her. 'Have I seen you before?' Philippa asked.

'Probably in the society pages of those magazines you used to buy,' Geoffrey said. 'On a more formal basis, she is Lady Margaret Huntington-Smythe and owns the Huntington Art Gallery in Bond Street.'

'Doesn't your father own a hotel chain?'

Maggie smiled. 'Yes. He is opening another one next year. That will make ten. Come and sit down, my dear. I am sure Geoffrey will not mind making us some fresh coffee.'

Her rather pointed look left him with no option. 'Girl talk, Maggie?' he asked as he walked to the door.

'Something like that. You should have told me what a lovely young woman your sister is.'

Philippa had the grace to blush as Maggie took her hand and led her to the sofa.

'From what Geoffrey told me I expected a shy little thing who wouldn't say boo to a goose. Men have no idea, especially when it comes to their sisters. I wanted to come over before this, but have been tied up with an exhibition and was unable to get away from the gallery until now.'

'It's kind of you to bother,' Philippa said. 'You are the first person to come near us since I came back. Geoffrey warned me we would be ostracised. At first, I thought he was exaggerating.'

'It is called social snobbery. Once the scandal has died down you will be acceptable again. I thought Geoffrey was over-reacting when he told me about Australia, but the more I think about it, the more sense it makes. A year or so away will give people time to forget. And they do say Australia is the land of opportunity, although I have never felt any urge to visit it.'

Philippa listened with a growing sense of horror. Geoffrey's mother lived in Australia with her sheep-farming husband. He had not so much as hinted he intended to go there. She clasped her hands together to stop them from shaking, then stared into the fire so that she would not have to meet Maggie's probing gaze.

'I know nothing whatsoever about my brother's plans.' Her voice was trembling, but she was unable to control it.

'Surely he said something? He's leaving in a fortnight.'

Everything fell into place. Philippa understood now why Geoffrey was so insistent she get rid of the pottery. He was running out on her and wanted to go with a clear conscience.

'No, he has said nothing at all.' She stood up. 'Would you excuse me?'

'Philippa . . .'

She did not reply. She fled from the room, unable to face any more revelations. She ran straight into Geoffrey's arms.

'Where do you think you're going?' His fingers tightened about her wrists.

'Obviously not to Australia!'

He let go of her and took a step back. 'I was going to tell you when the time was right.'

'Like the day you were leaving? Or were you going to send me a letter? Goodbye, Philippa. Go to hell, Philippa!'

'You don't understand. I'm finished here. I've been tarred with the same brush as Father and nobody will even consider employing me. I need a new beginning and Australia is a logical place to start. You're old enough to look after yourself, and I certainly don't want you hanging like a stone around my neck. Anyhow, my mother is not too happy about me turning up on her doorstep, so you can be sure she would not tolerate your presence.'

She was not going to cry. Her eyes sought his, but he refused to meet them. It was then Philippa realised she was the stronger and her hurt turned to contempt.

'If you cannot stand up to prejudice here how do you expect to succeed in another country? You have no backbone, Geoffrey. You don't even have the guts to stand up to me.'

'I apologise for my sister's lack of manners,' Geoffrey said. 'It comes from being given too much freedom and not enough discipline.'

'I found her perfectly charming.' Maggie's voice was

cold. She had heard what was said, not deliberately, but because Philippa had left the door open when she fled. 'Was she right? Did you intend to walk out and leave her destitute?'

'Of course not. I am doing everything I can to ensure she has enough money to get by, for a while at least. But she is stubborn and ungracious. I don't think she fully comprehends the position we are in. Whether rightly or wrongly, Father always cushioned her against life's blows. He let her spend money like water. Now there is no money she blames me and thinks I am out to rob her.'

There was a bitterness in his voice which did not escape Maggie. 'You don't like her very much, do you?'

'I barely know her. She is six years younger than me. We saw little of each other when we were children and even less as she grew older. She wouldn't come to Australia if I went down on my knees and begged.'

'But that's not the point, is it? You have treated her shabbily. Where is the coffee you were meant to be bringing?'

Geoffrey looked startled. 'In the kitchen. I'll get it.'

'Don't bother. I'll take it to your sister. Where is her room?'

She knocked lightly and when there was no reply she walked in. The girl was sitting on the bed, tears streaming down her cheeks. She turned away when she saw Maggie.

'I'd rather be alone,' she said.

'I think you have been alone for too long.' She placed the tray on the dressing table and filled two cups. 'Here, drink this.'

Philippa dabbed at the tears with a sodden handkerchief. Maggie was a total stranger, but she felt at ease with her, as though they had known each other for years. Maggie handed the girl one of the cups, then sat beside her. Philippa found her closeness comforting.

'How did you and Geoffrey get together?' she asked.

'We met at Oxford and have seen each other on and off since then. We were never seriously involved. I am not his type, nor he mine. I suppose you could call us friends, but not particularly close ones.' She paused. 'I would like to be your friend, Philippa. You are extremely young and need someone to whom you can turn.'

'I am nineteen, and capable of looking after myself.'

'Are you? No doubt it was easy enough when you had access to unlimited funds, but your circumstances have changed. I don't think Geoffrey is completely broke, but I doubt whether he has much money left. He has been spending too much time at the gambling tables. I heard he lost thousands last year. He may be a bastard, but I promise you will not be left penniless.'

Philippa put down her cup. 'I have money, but it is in trust and I cannot touch it until I am twenty-five. I can't even use it to raise a loan. Two days ago I learnt that I have inherited a run-down pottery from my mother's side of the family. Because it is not making any profit everyone wants me to sell.'

'I take it you don't want to?'

'No. My grandfather entrusted it to me. The pottery, a string of pearls and that photograph is all I have left of my mother.'

Maggie picked up the wooden frame which held a fading black and white photograph.

'She was extremely lovely. You look a lot like her. If you want your pottery so much, then nobody can take it away from you. But you also have to consider whether you will be capable of running it and, more importantly, making a living from it. I know what I'm talking about, because I was determined to change the image of the gallery when I took it over from my father. Until then it had been one of those discreet places where old masters changed hands behind locked doors. I wanted to open the doors and exhibit today's up and coming artists. Like you, everyone told me I was making a mistake, but I persevered and now it has taken off. What about you, Philippa? What plans do you have for this pottery of yours?'

'None. Without money there is nothing I can do for it.'

Maggie put down the photograph and stood up. 'You look exhausted. Sleep on it for now and if you decide to keep your pottery, then do so, and to hell with what everyone thinks. Look, I'll telephone you tomorrow. We can arrange lunch and discuss your situation in more detail.'

'I'd like that.' Philippa smiled. 'Thank you. I feel better already.'

'Good. Now what have you done about finding alternative accommodation? You can only stay here for another fortnight.'

'Nothing as yet. At the moment I have no idea where the rent money will come from.'

'I'll sort that out with Geoffrey. You are not alone any more, Philippa, and everything will fall into place. Now try and get a good night's sleep. Worrying never helped anyone.'

She kissed the girl on the cheek, then went downstairs to tackle Geoffrey.

'I think you are making a mistake,' Leonard Perkins said. 'However, if it is what you want, who am I to stop you? There are some documents which you will need to sign. Perhaps you would care to make another appointment later in the week.'

'How much is all this going to cost?' Philippa was blunt because she had to be.

Leonard Perkins rarely smiled, but he came close to it now. He liked the girl. She knew her own mind and was not one to go back on decisions.

'Legal fees have already been covered by an earlier retainer. Despite what you may have heard, not all lawyers are out to rob. I have managed your father's legal matters for many years, and would sort out your affairs, whether or not any payment was forthcoming.'

Philippa believed in first impressions, and she had trusted him from the outset.

'Will you continue to act for me?' she asked. 'Should Moor View ever get back on its feet I shall need a good legal adviser.'

He did not reply immediately and she thought he was going to refuse.

'I will do so gladly, Miss Russell. If it is possible to make a go of that pottery, then I believe you will do it.'

Geoffrey was less polite. Amongst other things, he called her a fool and suggested she start looking for a job unless she intended to live off Moor View, in which case it would be broke in less than a month. But it was easier said than done, for Philippa had neither experience nor training. She scoured the evening newspapers and went to an employment agency. The latter politely suggested she contact the personnel department of one of the high class stores, such as Harrods, who made a policy of recruiting well-spoken counter staff. Not only was she insulted by the slur on her intelligence, but Philippa had too much pride to work at a store where she was once a customer.

Another week slipped by and she still had no idea where she would go. Geoffrey was no help and Maggie had not contacted her since they had lunched together the week before. Sharing a flat seemed a good idea, but the people she telephoned lost interest once they heard she was not working. They wanted a guaranteed rent and some insisted on references. She looked at a couple of bedsits, but they were cramped and dismal and the rents extortionate. She was becoming frantic. Time was running out and it was no longer a case of moving into an hotel suite until something better turned up. Nothing better was going to turn up.

To make matters worse she was surrounded by the valuable antiques and silverware which had belonged to her father and had now been inventoried by Sotheby's. Neither she nor Geoffrey could take so much as a teaspoon. They were here under sufferance, temporary caretakers in their own home.

And then, six days before she was due for eviction, Maggie telephoned. There was a small basement flat which might suit her. It was in Notting Hill Gate and was presently rented by a young couple who were going to Africa to do missionary work. They were vacating it in two days' time. Maggie took Philippa to view it that afternoon. It was a stone's throw from the tube station and the shops, in a quiet street of white-painted houses. It did not possess Belgravia's opulence, but nor was it a slum.

The flat had its own entrance next to the dustbins. There was no central heating and the narrow entrance hall had a damp feel to it. There were two rooms, the one in front being the living room and the other a bedroom. They were both small and sparsely furnished with old, mismatched furniture, threadbare carpets and unlined curtains. But they were clean, as were the box-like kitchen and functional bathroom.

'You were very quiet in there,' Maggie said as she eased her Jaguar into the flow of traffic which was heading towards the Bayswater Road. 'I know it's not a palace, but it would be better than a bedsit and the rent is controlled, so it can't suddenly be put up by an unscrupulous landlord. In fact, I don't see why Geoffrey cannot pay the first three months in advance. That should give you time to get on your feet.'

It was certainly better than anything Philippa had seen so far, and it had the advantage of being self-contained.

'How did you find out about it?' she asked.

'My father owns a lot of property in London. Don't worry, it doesn't belong to him. He only invests in up-market buildings. Accommodation which falls under the Rent Control Board is not easy to find, and even though it is a far cry from what you are used to, you could make it cosy with your own furnishings.'

'I don't have my own furnishings. We are not allowed to take anything from the house other than our personal belongings.'

Maggie glanced at her. Geoffrey was right in one respect. Philippa knew very little of the ordinary world. 'It is the silver and paintings and antique furniture which you cannot walk off with. Nobody is going to quibble if you raid the servants' rooms. The butler had a small living room, didn't he? And I don't see why you can't keep your own bedroom furniture. Your father's lawyer should be able to advise you. After all, space limits the amount you can take.'

'I'll go and see him,' Philippa said. 'But what if somebody else wants the flat? Lots of people must have seen it.'

'You have first refusal. It hasn't been advertised yet. The present tenants were not meant to leave until after Christmas, but their plans have been altered. It's a case of finding someone immediately or paying a month's rent in lieu of notice. By taking it, you would be doing them a favour.'

Leonard Perkins asked for a list of the items which she wished to take, and within twenty-four hours it had been approved. Maggie borrowed a van from an art dealer she knew and Mike drove it, bringing along a friend to help shift the furniture. Geoffrey shut himself in the drawing room and refused to have anything to do with any of them. Philippa was glad of that for she knew he would look down his nose at her new home.

Five days after finding the flat she left her father's house for good. She had said goodbye to Mike the previous afternoon. Maggie had not only come to her rescue but had procured him a job at her father's Caernarvon hotel. He had left by the night train. It had not been an easy parting and, as a final gesture, Philippa kissed his cheek. She did not care if he was only a chauffeur. She was no better than him now.

Her farewell to her brother was a reflection of their relationship. There were no hugs or kisses. No damp eyes. He wished her luck and said he would not have time to visit as he had a ship to catch in another week. Where he intended to stay once the house was gone he did not say, nor did she ask. He promised to write, but she knew this was goodbye and she would never see nor hear from him again. Before she left he handed her a cheque.

'It's the best I can do,' he said. 'Try not to squander it. Your rent is paid for the next three months. By then you should have found yourself a job. But if you have a grain of sense you'll pack up and go back to Europe.'

'There is nothing left for me there,' Philippa told him. 'Goodbye, Geoffrey. I hope Australia is everything you hope for.'

'Goodbye, Philippa.'

He held out his hand, as though she were nothing more than a passing acquaintance. She grasped it briefly, then turned away and walked through the front door for the last time.

She glanced at the cheque before thrusting it into her handbag. It was for a hundred and fifty pounds and, except for the dwindling amount left in her purse, represented all the money she possessed. She was alone now. There was nobody to fall back on. It was a case of sink or swim, and Philippa had always been a strong swimmer.

CHAPTER FIVE

Harlequin House was situated three miles south west of Povey Ashton. It was an isolated mansion which stood in fifteen acres of overgrown garden and pasture. When the last direct descendant of the Walsh family died three years before the start of the Second World War the property was sold, then resold twice. It had then lain empty for a decade. When part of the roof fell in and pigeons nested in the rafters the villagers declared it to be the death knell for the old house.

But in June 1963 a firm of builders descended upon Harlequin House. The village began to buzz with rumours and in less than twenty-four hours it was established that the property had been bought by Lord Rudolph Huntington-Smythe, who intended to turn it into an exclusive hotel. The news was treated with caution. An hotel on their doorstep would mean jobs, especially for the younger generation, who tended to drift into the towns once they left school. But it would also attract an influx of tourists.

Povey Ashton was snuggled in a narrow valley, five miles from the popular village of Widecombe-in-the-Moor, and only the most persistent hikers or lost motorists stumbled inadvertently into it. The roads were narrow and badly sign-posted, and the village had little to offer other than a tranquil, old world charm. There was also Flint Iron Tor, which was a squat, uninteresting hill when compared with

Dartmoor's better-known tors. Tourism would bring noise and people and cars to block the single, narrow street. The majority of villagers were against it on principle.

But there were exceptions. The local pub, the Pack Horse, would benefit, as would the village shop-cum-post office. The stables at Flint Iron Farm might profit as well. Horse riding was a good way of viewing the moors and Sarah Lang could do with the extra business. The riding school was managing to pay its way, even though many of the local children had their own ponies. Sarah was a good teacher who had virtually bomb-proof ponies and never took unnecessary risks with her pupils. Her reputation had been established by word of mouth, some of her children coming from the towns situated on the outer fringes of the moors. But she never seemed to make enough money during the summer to see her through the long winters, when her only pupils were the really horse-mad children. And sometimes, when it snowed and the roads were blocked, not even they could get through.

At these times her two sons helped out, despite her protests that she could manage, which she could not. But Sarah never regretted her decision to come back here, despite the hardships. They had arrived at Flint Iron Farm like a pack of vagrant gypsies with their livestock in tow, but nobody had turned up their noses nor snubbed them. The villagers were pleased to see one of their own return and wholeheartedly offered whatever assistance they could. They remarked on how the boys had grown into good-looking young men, and how like her mother Helen was. One and all condemned the heartlessness of the city and the man who had driven George Lang to his death.

Of course it had been difficult at first. There were massive adjustments to be made, and it had not been long before the boys were away again, one to Cambridge and the other to

London. Helen made friends with the postmaster's daughter, who was the same age, so that when she started school she did not have to face her first day alone. Nor was she ostracised by the other children. What had happened in Sussex might have been a continent away from here.

Helen was thirteen now, still terrified of the ponies and painfully shy. But she was doing well at school and had picked up the soft, West Country burr. Nicholas teased her about it whenever he came home, but not Justin. Helen adored her older brother and lived for the days when he was here. They were, thank goodness, a well-balanced family who had come through their earlier traumas without any visible scars.

Justin had chosen to remain in London after he left the Royal College of Art. His friends were there and he had made a life for himself. But Sarah knew he struggled to survive. Artists were two a penny and even the good ones, like Justin, did not find recognition easily. The few paintings he did sell were usually underpriced and he was forced to earn money by teaching and commercial art, both of which he hated. In the latter field it was Nicholas who pushed work his way, who repeatedly tried, without success, to persuade him to take it up as a career.

Nicholas had done well for himself. During his final year at Cambridge he had been head-hunted by one of the top advertising agencies. Originally, he wanted to go into banking or stockbroking, but decided to give advertising a try. He was young enough to change careers if it did not suit him. But he was hooked from the minute he walked into the offices. He went in as a junior executive on a high salary and a car allowance, both of which he was expected to work for, sometimes all night and often through the weekends. But the work was invigorating and he threw himself whole-heartedly into it. His ideas were good and he was steadily building up accounts. Much of his success was attributable to his brother, for Justin could transfer his ideas on to paper better than anyone in the large art department. Nicholas used him frequently on a freelance basis, and Justin helped out because the cheques that followed were always welcome.

Harlequin House Hotel was to be opened in April 1964. The mansion had been painstakingly restored to its original condition at a cost that was more than anyone dared to contemplate. It was no ordinary hotel. The stables were converted into an indoor swimming pool and the grounds carefully landscaped to hide a cleverly designed nine-hole, mini golf course.

On a freezing morning in February, with snow lying ankle deep on the ground, Sarah received a letter from a London-based solicitor. Her heart missed a beat as she wondered whether it was something from the past about to catch up with her. She tore open the envelope with trembling fingers. The letter was short and to the point. Lord Rudolph Huntington-Smythe wished to offer the guests at his hotel riding facilities on the moors. As her stables were within easy reach of Harlequin House and had an excellent reputation in the area, would she be prepared to accept a trial contract from April until the end of summer?

Sarah read the letter again and again, and that evening she telephoned Justin for advice.

'Look, I'll come home at the weekend and we can go over it properly,' he said after she had read out the letter.

'Will Alice be coming with you?'

'No. She has two shows on Saturday. I'll be there about midday. Give Helen a kiss for me. Goodbye, Mum.'

Sarah put down the receiver. She was pleased at the prospect of having him to herself for a couple of days. He had brought Alice with him at Christmas, so the time they were able to spend alone was virtually non-existent. It had been the first time she had met the girl and her initial impression had been of a delicate china doll. Alice was exceptionally pretty, with an English rose complexion and long, golden blonde hair which fell to her waist in a silken sheaf. She was slender and petite, the top of her head barely reaching Justin's shoulder, and because she had been ballet trained she moved with a natural grace. She was, in fact, near to perfection, and although Nicholas would occasionally gaze enviously in her direction, he knew better than to step into his brother's territory. Not that Alice would have looked at him, for she was obviously much more in love with Justin than he appeared to be with her.

Sarah did not know where or how they had met. Alice was a dancer by profession, but she had given up the ballet and, at present, was in the chorus of one of the West End's hit musicals. To Sarah, she and Justin were an ill-matched couple – or was she simply being an over-protective mother? At least she had the consolation of knowing they had been wise enough not to rush into what she feared might be a disastrous marriage.

Even though there was a coal fire burning in the living room they sat in the kitchen, where the old Aga cooker provided heat throughout winter. All major decisions were made in the kitchen. They always had been.

Justin was holding a mug of tea, his grey eyes thoughtful. Helen was as close to him as she could get. Lucky, the ineptly named cat which she had got on the day her father had been accused of embezzlement, was curled on her lap, his contented purr filling the room. The two dogs were stretched in front of the stove, one twitching in its sleep and the other snoring.

Sarah had her arms folded on the table. She frowned when Helen started to pick at a spot. Neither of the boys had suffered from the scourge of adolescent pimples, but Helen had broken out last year, and no amount of washing or dabbing on of antiseptic creams would budge the wretched things.

'Don't do that, Helen. You'll end up with a pitted skin and that, I can assure you, will be a thousand times worse than a few spots.' Her gaze fell upon her son. 'Well? What do you think?'

He took a sip of tea and then put the mug on the table. He hooked his hands around one knee. 'That you would be a fool not to give it a go. Trekking is becoming a popular way of viewing the countryside, and with a scheme like this you would be guaranteed a steady flow of riders for at least half the year. The stables are barely holding their own at the moment, are they?'

'So many of the local children have their own ponies and we're situated too deep into the moors to attract many children from the towns, not unless their parents are willing to drive them over. I need this new business, but I'm not sure whether I can cope on my own. I don't want to lose my regular pupils. It would be unfair on them. And then there's the problem of adult riders. Most of the ponies could take an average weight, but even the larger ones couldn't be expected to carry heavy riders over rough ground for any length of time.'

Justin laughed. 'Now you're putting obstacles in the way. This trial contract works both ways, you know. It's up to you to stipulate how many people you can cope with at one time – taking into account that the majority of them will never have seen a live horse, let alone ridden one. Initially, you will need to keep the rides small and stay out for no longer than two or three hours. You'd obviously need to invest in a couple of weight-carrying horses and, if it works out, you'll need an assistant next year. I can help you this summer. I've been stuck in the city for too long and need to get some country air into my lungs.'

'You mean you'll be here for the entire summer?' Helen asked.

He leant forward and tweaked her cheek. 'It looks like it, sweetheart.'

'By yourself?'

'Helen!' her mother admonished.

Justin glanced up. There is something he is not telling me, Sarah thought.

'Yes, I'll be by myself. Alice has signed a new contract and won't be able to take any time off until autumn.'

He did not elaborate and Sarah did not ask. She could only surmise they were not getting along too well.

Alice had known from the beginning that Justin did not have the same intensity of feeling for her which she had always felt for him. They had met at a party. She was with the lead dancer from a show she was in. This was the second time he had dated her, and the other girls were jealous because they had their eyes on him. But at the party he deserted her when he saw the producer of a forthcoming show. He was more interested in furthering his career than he was in Alice, and the only reason he had brought her here was because she looked good hanging on his arm.

She knew nobody and so stood disconsolate in a corner, until a tall young man with a dazzling smile and steel-grey eyes asked her to dance. He held her firmly, but did not run his hands up her body like most men did. He was charming and he made her laugh, and before the end of the evening she had fallen head over heels in love with him. They had known each other for three months before she let him make love to her, and six months when they decided it would be easier and cheaper if she moved in with him. That had been in April 1963 and now, almost a year to the date, he was telling her how he intended to spend a few months in Dartmoor helping his mother, while she remained here alone.

She walked to the window and gazed out. Three floors below people were hurrying about their business.

'Is it me?' She did not dare look at him. 'Have I done something to upset you?'

He stood beside the gas fire, frowning at her rigid back. She always blamed herself for everything, whether or not it was her fault. She rarely answered him back or raised her voice, and she was incapable of holding her own in an argument. Invariably, she would burst into tears. Then he would be filled with remorse, take her in his arms and say he was sorry. She was too full of insecurities. Her parents had died when she was young and she had been brought up by elderly grandparents. When they died she had been fostered by a family who let her continue with her ballet, but by then the hang-ups which were to haunt her for the rest of her life were deeply embedded.

'You've done nothing, Alice,' he said. 'My mother needs help and I need to paint something more than people and buildings. If you can get away you're welcome to come down. You know that. If not, there is the telephone, and I'll ask Noel to keep an eye on you.'

She shuddered. She disliked Noel Buchanan, but because he was Justin's friend she put up with him and said nothing.

'Are you fed up with me? Is that what you're trying to tell me?'

'No, of course not,' he sighed. He walked across the room and put his arms around her. She was tiny, so deceptively frail, that sometimes he was frightened of crushing her. He kissed the back of her neck. 'Look, we'll take a holiday together in the autumn. My mother should be on her feet by then and your contract will have run out. We'll go to Europe.'

She leant against him, her closed eyes holding back the tears. If she ever lost him she did not know what she would do. He was her life.

'I love you,' she whispered.

'I know. Come on, it's time you were leaving for the theatre. I'll take you in the car.'

'There's no need for you to come out. I can catch a bus.'

'No you can't.' He placed his hands upon her shoulders, gently turned her round, then kissed her forehead. 'Go and get your things. You don't want to be late.'

She nodded and smiled at him like a trusting child. He watched her walk into the hall and then turned away, staring sightlessly through the misted glass. How could he tell her this helplessness was wearing him down? That it would be good for them to be apart for a while. And that when he came back perhaps he could recapture the earlier passion she had aroused in him . . . perhaps.

Lady Margaret Huntington-Smythe was hopelessly lost. She should have kept to the main roads, rather than attempt to cut across this godforsaken stretch of moorland. She glanced at the map which was spread across the passenger seat. According to that, the village into which she had just driven did not exist.

It was one of those picture postcard villages with a single street that had neat lines of thatched cottages on either side of it. They looked charming but, in reality, were probably cramped and draughty. There was a deserted green at the far end of the village, with a pub opposite. She decided to go in and ask for directions. The sun was already low in the sky and she did not want to drive through these winding lanes in the dark. She parked her car at the edge of the green and, seeing a solitary man sitting at one of the outside tables, she walked towards him. From inside the pub she could hear a buzz of voices intermingled with loud laughter, but out here was an aura of peace, the kind which could only be found in the countryside.

She paused for a moment, listening to the frantic call of a blackbird. There must be a cat close by. Her wandering attention returned to the man. He was bent over the table, writing in a pad, and did not appear to notice her, even when her heels clicked on the stone path.

'Excuse me,' she said.

His hand continued to move across the paper. She wondered if he was deliberately ignoring her, or whether he was a dim-witted, country yokel.

'Excuse me,' she repeated in a slightly raised voice.

Justin Lang had seen the Jaguar creep down the road, but was too engrossed in a pencil sketch to pay it much attention. He lifted his eyes, unconsciously smiling when he saw the well-dressed young woman who looked as though she had been transplanted from a garden party. Everything about her spoke of wealth and good breeding, and she looked apologetic for interrupting him.

He glanced down at the pad, then regretfully closed it. 'Can I help you?' he asked, rising to his feet.

This is no yokel, thought Maggie, despite his grubby jeans and open-necked shirt with rolled-up sleeves. His direct gaze and self-assured manner impressed her, although she did not know why. Handsome men usually turned her off, for they were invariably too full of their own self-importance.

'I'm looking for Harlequin House,' she said. 'Do you know where it is? I am totally lost. Don't they believe in using signposts out here?'

'It's how we retaliate against tourists. Unfortunately, we are fighting a losing battle. Harlequin House is less than three miles away. I can give you directions, or draw a map if you prefer.'

'Definitely a map. I have one in the car but it's hopeless. I don't even know where I am.'

'Povey Ashton,' he said. 'Would you like to sit down? It won't take a moment, but there are a lot of left and right turns which I'll have to explain.'

She sat beside him on the narrow bench, and as he flicked open the pad she caught a glimpse of some pencil sketches. Her curiosity was aroused.

'May I see your drawings?'

He looked startled and she thought he was going to refuse. Then he placed the pad in front of her. As she turned the first page she was aware of him watching her, waiting for a reaction. He was going to be disappointed, for one of her earliest lessons when she took over the gallery was how to school her features into a blank mask. The pad was half filled with sketches of the moors, the wild ponies, and the wandering flocks of sheep. The last two were of this village. Maggie slowly turned back the pages. The sketches veered between rough and finely detailed, but it was obvious this man was no amateur.

'Do you paint?' She knew it was a ridiculous question, even before she asked it.

'Yes.'

'Water colour or oil?'

'Both.' Briefly, his gaze met hers. 'I'd better give you those directions if you want to reach Harlequin House before nightfall.'

He took the pad from her and opened it on a clean page. But as he explained the intricacies of the map he was drawing she did not really listen. His work intrigued her.

She wanted to see more of it and to know who he was.

He finished. 'Is that clear?'

'Yes,' she replied, even though it was not. 'By the way, I am Margaret Huntington-Smythe.'

'A relation of Lord Rudolph?' He sounded unimpressed.

'His daughter. He wants me to see the new hotel, so I agreed to come down for the weekend. May I have the map, Mr . . . er . . . I'm sorry, but I don't know your name.'

'Justin Lang.' He tore out the page and handed it to her. 'I hope you enjoy your weekend.'

She had grown used to people fawning over her once they knew who she was. It was a refreshing change to meet somebody who could not care less. She decided to take the bull by the horns.

'I would very much like to see some more of your work. Do you have a studio nearby?'

In his dark eyes she saw a shadow of distrust. 'My studio is in London. Why? Are you thinking of buying a painting?'

'Perhaps. Does it have an address?'

'You'll find it in the telephone book.'

Maggie wondered at his reticence. The majority of artists she met were eccentric and outgoing, never missing an opportunity to flaunt their work.

She stood up. It was no use badgering him. She had his name and could easily find out more about him. 'Thank you for your help. Goodbye, Mr Lang.'

She glanced in the rear-view mirror as she drove out of the village. He was bent over his pad and had probably forgotten her already. But he was one person she would not forget in a hurry.

CHAPTER SIX

———◆———

Mermaid Hosiery was a difficult but challenging account. The company was owned by Alvin Harwood, a pig-headed Yorkshireman who had decided the time was right to move out of the local market into the national one. He had modernised his factory and increased production to a point where he needed new outlets. He had money to throw away, but had set ideas about how it should be spent.

He had already walked out of three top advertising agencies after being told his company needed to change its name because the word 'Mermaid' was not synonymous with women's stockings. Nor were the directors of McCullogh, Staines & Ray keen on having him as a client, but when Nicholas Lang asked if he could try and do something with it they had second thoughts. Why not, if he was willing to put his head on the block? But they insisted he work with Ernest Wakefield on this one. Ernest was one of their top executives. He had taken Nicholas under his wing when he first came here and the two of them had often collaborated since then. Nicholas was enthusiastic and Ernest reluctant, but they had an initial meeting with Harwood, then put their heads together to work out a solution.

After a sleepless night of chewed pencils and frayed tempers they had come up with a simple answer. They would use the mermaid as a logo, not base the entire advertising campaign around it as Harwood wanted. The Yorkshireman was not going to be easy to convince, but if they redesigned the Forties style mermaid, they would have the ammunition they needed. Nicholas did not bother with the art department. He went to his brother, and was rewarded with a delicately drawn creature with a lively, impish face, framed by a luxuriant fall of dark hair. Justin had woven strands of colour into the hair, giving a suggestion of seaweed and other aquatic plants. It flowed around her shoulders, artfully covering her breasts and blending into a magnificent tail of silver and gold and shimmering, rainbow flashes of colour.

Thereafter, the campaign had been easy to map out, their only stumbling block being Alvin Harwood. He was awkward from habit, but listened to everything Nicholas had to say and then, subject to a few changes, agreed to his proposals.

'I don't believe it!' Nicholas was jubilant.

Ernest poured them both a whisky, then sat on one of the comfortable chairs, his crossed feet on a table.

'We should try and get Steve Noble for the stills,' he said.

The photographer was renowned for his excellent use of movement combined with light and shadow, giving a surreal effect which never failed to catch the eye.

'What about the model? Do we go for an unknown, or try for one of the top girls?'

'If Harwood insists we use the same girl for a series of adverts, then you can write off the top names,' said Ernest. He sipped his whisky. 'Let's get hold of Steve first. See what he suggests.'

'The problem is that Harwood will accept nothing short of a virgin, and I doubt if Steve knows the meaning of the word.'

The two men laughed. It had been a tense fortnight and they needed to relax.

Most people thought Nicholas older than his twenty-three years. He was self assured and determined to get his own way in most things. Ernest, on the other hand, was twenty-eight, of average height, and nothing to write home about. His black hair was already flecked with grey, and his brown eyes alive with nervous activity. He smoked like a chimney and, since his divorce the previous year, had a tendency to hit the bottle a little too hard when he was not working. He had a sharp and creative mind which Nicholas sometimes envied, but was less successful when it came to handling people. That was why they made such a good team. They complemented each other.

'I'll get on to the agencies and ask them to submit some portfolios,' Nicholas said. 'An unknown model might suit us better. We could tie her to a contract and call her the Mermaid girl.'

Ernest stretched his arms above his head. 'It will only work if we can find just the right one.'

'I don't think that should prove to be a problem.'

Models are two a penny. It was every girl's dream to have her face on the front cover of *Vogue*, but few made it that far. Those who did were very special, or else had somebody pushing them up the ladder. The successful ones usually had both.

Steve Noble had fallen in love with photography at the tender age of seven when he found an old Brownie box camera at the back of a cupboard. Unlike other boys of his age, he did not spend his pocket money on sweets and comics, but saved his pennies to buy rolls of film. Developing them was costly, but he did a morning paper round and, later on, an evening one as well. At ten he was processing his own film, and at sixteen had set himself up as a street photographer. It had been a long, hard struggle to the top, and it was not until the beginning of the Sixties, with the emergence of youth as a strong buying power, that he began to make headway. His innovative photography suited the fast-moving times, and by the age of twenty-one he was recognised as one of the best fashion photographers in the country.

Two years on, at twenty-three, he had developed a professional arrogance and a reputation as a womaniser. It did not matter if his father had been a shopkeeper. The social barriers had come tumbling down and he was now a member of the new élite, the pop stars and models, photographers and actors, designers and writers, who were worshipped by the masses. Unfortunately, fashion brought him prestige but not money, and to finance his flamboyant lifestyle he was willing to dabble in portraiture and advertising, providing the subjects interested him. He particularly enjoyed working with Nicholas Lang. They were the same age, and were both driven by a desire to be the best at what they did. But Nicholas differed from other ad men in his willingness to give Steve a free hand when it came to the interpretation of his ideas.

Steve only had to glance at Mermaid's story-board to know he would do it. Nicholas wanted more than a pair of shapely legs. He wanted to portray youth and movement against a backdrop of London streets. It was a field in which Steve excelled.

The photographer flopped into a chair and swept back his shaggy fringe. He was slightly built with a boyish face and dark, intense eyes which missed nothing. His clothes were bright and casual, and had cost a fortune in Carnaby Street, the mecca of men's fashion.

'Who is the model?' he asked. 'She needs to be good if you want these to come off.'

Nicholas offered him a cigarette. He took one, even

though he was trying to give up smoking. It was a disgusting habit which he was finding difficult to kick.

'We haven't decided yet,' Nicholas told him. 'But we are thinking in terms of a new face rather than one which everybody recognises.'

'Cheapskate client?'

'On the contrary,' Ernest said. 'If he was, he wouldn't be paying your extortionate fees. We want to use the same girl for at least six months, and none of the well-known models will agree to tie themselves down for so long.'

Steve smiled. 'All right, show me who you have. You wouldn't call me in unless you had somebody in mind.'

'We've whittled it down to three,' said Nicholas. 'What do you think?'

He picked up three slim portfolios and handed them to Steve. He, in turn, gave them little more than a cursory glance before throwing them on to the floor.

'Are those the best you can find?'

Nicholas and Ernest exchanged glances. They had spent an entire morning sorting through portfolios and had finally picked out those three, agreeing to let Steve make the final decision if he accepted the assignment.

'What's wrong with them?' Nicholas asked.

'They're pretty, but so are a thousand other girls. You need someone who will jump out of the page at you. Those three do nothing at all for me.'

Ernest groaned. 'I need a drink. We are doing an advert for pantiehose, not looking for the next model of the year.'

Steve ignored him. He was looking at Nicholas. 'What about the others?'

'What others?'

'That pile of portfolios on your desk.'

'We have been through them with a fine toothcomb. Those are by far and away the best of the bunch. Let's call them in. If you still don't like them we can start again. This could turn into a big account, Steve, but only if I get it right from the start.'

Steve knew he could make something of the models Nicholas had chosen. He enjoyed working with women and was able to coax the best out of them. But he also liked a challenge, and none of these presented that.

'Can I look through your rejects?' he asked.

'Help yourself,' Nicholas shrugged. 'But you're wasting your time.'

Ernest took some glasses from a cupboard. 'This is going to be a long afternoon. Whisky or brandy?'

'Whisky and water,' Steve said.

Nicholas sighed. 'I'll have the same.'

He sat down, watching Steve flip through the portfolios. He ignored the information sheets. It was only the photographs which interested him. He recognised a couple of the girls. He had worked with them before, but neither had impressed him. Another had posed for a so-called art calendar. Steve wouldn't touch her with a bargepole. He liked his models to be pencil-thin with flat breasts and narrow hips. They were the ones who looked good in the higher hemlines, skinny rib sweaters, and hip-hugging trousers.

He put aside two of the portfolios, but Nicholas was unable to see which ones they were. When he had gone through them all, he went back to those two. One he discarded, the other he threw across the desk.

'I want to see this one,' he said.

Nicholas picked up the portfolio. It had been one of his first rejects. 'I don't know, Steve.' He showed it to Ernest. 'She is . . . well, she is . . .'

'. . . different. She is not classically beautiful, but bloody attractive, and she has presence. I could do something with that face.'

79

'We are focusing on the legs, not the face.' Ernest was getting impatient.

'She is five foot ten and, if the full-length portrait is anything to go by, has the legs of a colt. You asked for my opinion and I'm giving it. I may change my mind when I see her in the flesh. If I do, I'll consider one of your choices.'

'We'll call in the four of them,' said Nicholas.

There was no harm in pandering to Steve's whims. They were under no obligation to hire the girl, even if the photographer did like her. Nicholas looked at the name. Pippa Rowe. It meant nothing whatsoever to him, but there was something disturbingly familiar about her. According to the fact sheet she had done a little catalogue work and some ramp modelling in a couple of the larger chain stores. So why did he have the feeling he had seen her somewhere before?

Lady Jayne in Camden Hill was a popular restaurant. The food was well prepared, the service excellent, and the tasteful decor and subdued lighting contributed to its intimate atmosphere. The restaurant was not one which was frequented by celebrities. Husbands brought their wives here for an evening out and local businessmen filled it at lunchtimes.

After moving into her basement flat Philippa had seen a card in a shop window advertising for a part-time waitress in a local restaurant. She applied for the job because she was desperate, and went for an interview dressed as ordinarily as possible, in a plain skirt and jumper, with her hair pulled back into a bow. She wore flat shoes so as not to accentuate her height and very little make-up. But it was impossible to hide the expensive cut of her camel coat, or the self possession which was a legacy from her past life. She arrived

80

at the restaurant to find there were six girls ahead of her. They eyed her up and down, their expressions visibly hardening. She glared back. She needed this job as much, if not more than any of them.

Lady Jayne was jointly owned by Clive Boyd, the chef, and Malcolm Smith, the brains behind the business. At the restaurant their relationship was brisk and professional. Away from it was another matter, but they successfully contrived to keep their personal and business lives apart. Malcolm normally interviewed new staff, but on this occasion Clive decided to sit in.

He took no part in the interviews, something which the other girls found intimidating, but after politely acknowledging his presence, Philippa equally politely forgot him. She had never waited at a table, but had eaten in enough restaurants to know what was expected. Her confidence showed, although she was unaware of it.

'Why are you so keen to get this job?' Clive suddenly asked.

'Because I need the money.'

He stood up and walked to the door. 'Give her a week's trial,' he told his partner. 'None of the uniforms will fit her, but she will give the place class.'

Six months later she was still there, working six nights a week and lunchtimes. The hours were long and hard, the pay a basic minimum, but the tips were good. There were three waitresses with six tables each and a rapid turnover of clients. A table was no sooner vacated than it was filled again, especially at weekends when demand was high. All tips were put in a glass jar and every Sunday evening Malcolm would divide the money between them. It was tax-free cash which helped pay the bills and keep Philippa's head above water.

Her first winter was the hardest. Piece by piece she sold the silver and gold baubles she had so carelessly bought with her father's money. When spring came there was nothing left but her mother's pearls. She would never sell those, even though there were days when the only proper meal she had was at Lady Jayne's, late at night, after the restaurant had closed. She refused to give in to depression or despair and because she fought back she learnt how to survive.

She never did become friendly with the two other waitresses, but got along with Vincent Grant, an out-of-work actor who washed the dishes and insisted on seeing her home every night. She felt safe with him. He had the build of a rugby player and was never familiar. He told her funny stories as they walked through the deserted streets and always left her at the top of the basement steps, refusing to come in for a night-cap.

It was Vincent who suggested she try modelling.

'You look as good as any of the models in the magazines,' he said. 'A girl I know tried it for a while. The money is not bad and the work is a lot easier than waiting at tables. I'll ask her for the name of the agency she used.'

Philippa was less enthusiastic. 'I really don't think . . .'

'Nonsense! Nothing ventured, nothing gained. What harm is there in trying? Surely you don't want to work here for the rest of your life?'

She didn't. She was almost twenty and life was passing her by. She went to the modelling agency without any hope of getting anywhere, but they put her on their books and paid for the photographs she needed to make up a portfolio. Because she was tall and moved well they found her some work modelling spring fashions in a couple of West End department stores, and summer clothing for a mail order catalogue. Then the well ran dry and she was offered nothing else. She was told she must go round the photographers' studios. If one of them liked her, he would use her. Only the top models could sit back and wait for work to come to them. The others had to find it for themselves. But Philippa had no overwhelming desire to become a model, and was not about to jeopardise her job at the restaurant when it was her only steady source of income. No, she thought, modelling was not the answer. She needed to find something else.

She could not take any money from Moor View. Four people had been laid off during the winter, and she had also learnt that Gideon drew no salary for himself. He had not done so for over a year. The pottery was sliding downhill, and there was nothing she could do to stop it. The oven had broken down twice in February, and the bank was growing unhappy about their rising overdraft. Gideon had arranged a meeting with the bank manager the next week, but it was debatable whether he would agree to extend their credit facilities. She needed a miracle, and miracles were in short supply these days.

'Philippa, there is a telephone call for you. Cut it short, will you?'

It was lunchtime and the restaurant was filled to capacity. They were run off their feet and Malcolm looked impatient. She did not have a telephone at home. She could not afford to have one installed. There was a phone box on the corner of her street, and Malcolm did not object to her receiving the odd incoming call. She worked hard and never complained if he asked her to do overtime. He felt sorry for the girl. She obviously needed the money and, from the little he had been able to establish, she had no private life worth speaking of.

At the moment she had three tables waiting for service and a pile of dirty plates in her hands. 'I'm sorry, Malcolm,' she said. 'I've told everyone not to ring between twelve and two. Could you possibly ask them to ring back later, or else leave a number?'

'It's the modelling agency. They say it's urgent.' He gave her one of his rare smiles. 'Go on. I'll take those dishes into the kitchen.'

Philippa had a chance of an advertisement, and the modelling agency had made her an appointment for ten o'clock the following morning. Because there was a twenty-first birthday celebration that night it was nearly twelve-thirty before she was able to leave the restaurant. By then she was too tired to sleep, and knew she was going to look like a washed-out rag in the morning. Vincent, forever the optimist, told her not to be so negative and wished her all the luck in the world.

She was going to need it. Make-up helped, but did not completely disguise the shadows beneath her eyes. She dithered over her hair. She looked more sophisticated with it up, but left down it would detract from the flaws. During her year in Switzerland she had been told that a good wardrobe never dates. It was just as well, for she could not afford another. She chose her clothes carefully, finally settling on a navy suit with a short jacket and flared skirt. Beneath it she wore a cream-coloured satin blouse and her mother's string of pearls.

That year Courrèges had taken the fashion world by storm with his black and white space age look. Hemlines were rising and boots were worn with everything. There was a time when Philippa would have bought the originals, now she could not afford the cheap copies which filled the shops. She gazed at herself in a full-length mirror. She might not be wearing the latest clothes, but she looked good. She picked up a pair of gloves, unconcerned that they were no longer an essential fashion item.

She wished she could afford a taxi, but such a luxury was out of the question. So she took the tube to Oxford Street, then walked the rest of the way to the modern building in which the advertising agency was located.

It took up two floors and had a tastefully decorated reception area. The girl behind the desk was attractive, but her eyes were hard and her smile automatic. She asked Philippa to join three other girls, who looked her up and down with open disdain. There was something about them which told her they were professional models. Their make-up was immaculate and their clothes modern, but they lacked individuality, resembling three peas in a pod.

She was the last to be called in and, having studied the ingratiating expressions of the other three, had decided she was not about to beg for a job which it was doubtful she would be offered. She still had her pride, and either they liked her or they didn't.

Consequently, she swept into the office with the inbred confidence of a grand duchess. Ernest Wakefield was standing closest to the door and she walked up to him, her hand held forward. Startled, he took it.

'Good morning,' she said. 'I am Pippa Rowe.'

Ernest stared at her, not finding his voice until she released his limp hand.

'Good morning, Miss ... er ... Rowe. I'm Ernest Wakefield.' He indicated vaguely towards the desk. 'My colleague, Nicholas Lang. And this is Steve Noble. No doubt you have heard of him.'

Philippa's eyes flitted to the man standing beside the window. His hair was long and cut in pudding bowl fashion, and he wore a striped shirt with blue corduroy trousers. He was nobody she had ever seen, nor did the name ring a bell.

'I am afraid I have no idea who Mr Noble is.'

There followed an awkward silence. Steve saw she was telling the truth and not being brazen. In fact, she puzzled him. He knew a Paris original when he saw it, and the girl had the breeding of a prize racehorse. Whoever she was, he doubted if it was Pippa Rowe.

'Anyone who has aspirations of becoming a photographic model idolises Steve Noble. He works almost exclusively for the top fashion magazines and the three girls we saw prior to you were awed by his presence.'

Philippa swung round. Only Steve noticed how pale she was. For a moment she seemed unsure of herself, and then her confidence returned, together with a trace of defiance.

Philippa felt a reverberation of shock as she stared at the well-remembered face. She had only seen him once before. He had been sitting on a gate with his arm around a child, but his resemblance to his brother was unmistakable. She had never connected the name, either yesterday when the agency told her who to ask for, or today when Ernest Wakefield introduced them. There must be thousands of people whose surname was Lang, so why had fate cruelly chosen to bring her face to face with this particular one? Then common-sense returned, and pure bloody-mindedness. Why on earth should he remember a fleeting incident which took place five years ago? Anyhow, she had adopted a different name when she signed up at the modelling agency.

'I am not easily awed, Mr Lang,' she coolly informed him. 'I am fully conversant with the top designers and latest fashions. I did not know it was compulsory to follow the careers of those who promote them.' She looked at Steve Noble. 'I apologise if I have offended you. It was unintentional.'

He grinned. 'Do you always come on this strong?'

This time Philippa had the grace to blush. She had blown it. So much for employer and employee relations. She had forgotten all the basic rules. To bow and scrape was not in her character, but one did not hurl insults left, right and centre, and then expect to be given a job. In the circumstances, she chose to ignore Steve Noble's question. She turned to Nicholas Lang. He met her gaze and held it. His eyes were the palest blue she had ever seen. She shuddered, remembering the time his brother had told her to get off their property. His eyes had been darker, but he had looked at her in the same cold way.

She salvaged what she could from the situation. 'Is there anything you wish to ask me?'

'No,' said Nicholas.

'Walk to the window, will you?' said Ernest. 'Then turn round and come back to me.'

She did as he asked. Ernest leant back against the wall, his arms crossed and his eyes critical as he watched her. Nicholas also watched. The girl moved with an unconscious grace, seeming to glide over the carpet.

'What training have you received?' Ernest asked.

'None.'

'What about ballet?'

'I tried it when I was five years old, but couldn't take the discipline.'

'Where did you learn to walk like that?'

This time it was Nicholas Lang who spoke, and a strict finishing school was hardly the answer he sought. Oh well, Philippa thought, in for a penny, in for a pound. She knew she didn't stand a chance.

'Like what?'

The silence was deafening. You could have heard a pin drop on the floor above.

Nicholas glanced at the portfolio spread out in front of him. 'We shall need a telephone number where you can be contacted. I presume you are not doing any modelling work at the moment?'

'No,' she replied, and gave him Lady Jayne's number. She

didn't know why he bothered to ask. His secretary would probably telephone the agency and tell them she had been rejected. They, in turn, might or might not inform her.

'Thank you for your time, Miss Rowe,' said Nicholas. 'We'll let you know in due course.'

She pulled on her gloves with a defiant gesture and walked out as boldly as she had walked in.

By the next day Philippa had put the disastrous interview down to experience.

'Something better is sure to crop up,' said Malcolm as they set the tables. There were only the two of them to cope with the lunchtime crowd. One girl was sick and the other had a day off and could not be reached. Vincent would help clear the tables, leaving her and Malcolm free to concentrate on the orders.

It was one-thirty and she was run off her feet. Malcolm tapped her on the shoulder. 'There's somebody at the desk who insists on seeing you. I told him to come back later, but he refuses to leave. Get rid of him, Philippa. Quickly.'

Her heart plummeted to her feet when she saw Nicholas Lang watching her. What on earth was he doing here, when a telephone call would have sufficed? Or had he found out who she really was and come on some malicious errand of his own? Unconsciously, her face hardened.

'I'm busy, Mr Lang, and can't afford to lose this job. What are you doing here?'

'Pandering to a temperamental photographer.' He sounded angry. 'I do not like you, Miss Rowe. Unfortunately, Steve Noble does, and has threatened to walk out if we don't give you a chance. Here is his address. Be there tomorrow morning at nine prompt, and wear something that shows your figure and legs. I should add that the final decision will come from my client and I shall do everything in my power to dissuade him from using you. Is that clear?'

'Perfectly clear. You could have told me this over the telephone. If you dislike me so much, why did you bother to come here?'

'I did telephone, but was told you would not be in until later. I was curious, thinking you must have a share in the place. It's not a common occurrence to stumble upon a waitress who is dressed by Chanel.'

'The tips are good!' she fired back. 'My God, you're just like . . .' She was about to say his brother, but bit down the words.

'Just like who?' Nicholas asked.

'Like somebody I once knew. Look, I have to get back to work.' She was about to turn away, but hesitated as a thought occurred to her. 'The agency told me your adverts were for hosiery. Am I expected to wear frilly knickers and suspenders? If so, I would not want to do them.'

It was the first time she had seen him smile, and once again she was reminded of his brother. 'We are targeting your own age group. They will not be won over by frilly knickers or suspenders. Nor would Steve Noble condescend to photograph them.' He paused. 'A final word of advice. Get an early night. The camera emphasises every flaw, and your bags are showing. Goodbye, Miss Rowe. You will be informed of the results in due course.'

She watched him leave, then stared down at the scrap of paper which he had given her.

'Philippa, I need a hand over here,' Malcolm called.

'I'm coming.'

She smiled as she thrust the address into her apron pocket. Miracles did happen after all.

CHAPTER SEVEN

———◆———

Nicholas was working through a cost sheet when Steve Noble walked into his office. The photographer dropped a sheaf of photographs on to the desk.

'You have to use her now.'

Nicholas stared at him, his thoughts adrift. 'Who are you talking about? And what are these photographs?'

'The Rowe girl. Who else? She is special, Nicholas. Take my word for it. She could be even greater than Rosalind.'

It was the first time Nicholas had seen Steve so excited since he had parted from Rosalind Harper eight months before. They had worked their way up together. She had lived with him, and modelled for him and, on reaching the pinnacle of success, had left him.

Nicholas picked up one of the photographs. It was of Pippa Rowe. The camera had caught her suspended in mid-air, her limbs outstretched and her hair flying. It gave him the impression of a ceaseless flow of movement, which was the image of freedom which Nicholas had envisaged for the preliminary series of Mermaid advertisements. Steve knew that, of course, and this was the kind of work at which he was unsurpassed. Nicholas picked up another photograph. It was a black and white portrait, with light and shadow playing cleverly across the girl's face.

Steve grinned as he leant across the desk. 'She's different, isn't she? She does not have Rosalind's beauty, but makes up for it with that incongruous mixture of innocence and sophistication.'

Steve was right. There was something special about the girl. She had stood out in that mediocre restaurant, although Nicholas was not about to admit it. 'She comes over as gauche,' he said.

'Only because she has no idea how to play up to the camera. She needs taking in hand, which is what I intend to do. Give me a year and I'll have her face on the cover of every major fashion magazine, both here and in the States. You could be in at the beginning, Nicholas. You and Mermaid.'

Nicholas looked at the rest of the photographs. She still reminded him of somebody, but for the life of him he could not think who.

'Am I right in presuming you will not do the Mermaid shoot unless I choose her?'

Steve sat down. 'I won't do it if you use one of those other girls. I might consider it with an established model of my own choice.'

Steve had him over a barrel. He knew he was the main pivot in this campaign.

'You realise, of course, that Alvin Harwood has the final say.'

'I am sure he will listen to your advice.'

'There is something about her which I can't quite put my finger on. Is she difficult to work with?'

Steve smiled. 'She has more spines than a porcupine and, by the time I'd finished those shots, every single one of them was aimed at me. The odd thing is I know no more about her now than the first time we met. Most girls drive me mad with their inane chatter, but she barely spoke. And I don't think Pippa is her real name. She responds too slowly when you use it.'

'She works as a waitress,' said Nicholas. 'But I have the impression she is used to being served, not doing the serving.'

Steve raised his brows. 'I don't particularly care who or what she is. I'm more interested in what you are going to tell Harwood.'

Nicholas picked up one of the photographs. 'Personally, I find her arrogant. But you could be right about her being our Mermaid girl. I'll contact Harwood, and assuming Miss Rowe does not turn us down, I would like you to shoot next week.'

'It might have to be the week after. I'll let you know. You're not going to regret this. I'll give you the best shots you've ever seen.'

Nicholas believed him. There were people who would pay the earth to be photographed by Steve Noble, and if he was keen to mould this girl into a world-class model, then nothing was going to stop him.

This time Nicholas telephoned the restaurant shortly after two. It was Thursday and Philippa's mind was on the meeting she and Gideon had with the bank manager the following afternoon. The call took her by surprise. She had not expected to hear from Nicholas Lang again, not after their abrasive meeting three days ago.

His voice was clipped and she responded with cold formality. At first, she did not believe what he was saying. She had not only been chosen, but was expected to sign a contract which would restrict her from modelling any hosiery, other than Mermaid, for the next six months. There was also a chance it could be extended.

Six months. She might not work for more than six days during that period, but the contract was something concrete she could throw at the bank manager.

'I'm going away tonight and won't be back until after the weekend,' Nicholas told her. 'But if you come in tomorrow Ernest Wakefield can make the necessary arrangements.'

'I shall also be away tomorrow.'

She was aware of a pause at the other end of the line. He probably thought she was being deliberately awkward.

'Monday then,' said Nicholas irritably. 'Ten-thirty. Or can't you make that either?'

'I shall be there,' she replied. 'Goodbye, Mr Lang. And thank you.'

She put down the receiver.

'Good news?' Malcolm asked.

'Fabulous news. I've got that modelling job.'

He kissed her cheek. 'Congratulations,' he said. She deserved all the luck she could get.

Nicholas had promised to spend some time at home during the summer, but this long weekend was all he could manage. He left the office at five, early for him, collected a small suitcase from his Chelsea flat, then drove to the West Country in his red MG.

The sun was setting in a fiery sky when he turned into the drive. On either side of him ponies grazed in the paddocks. He passed the two-storey wooden barn which doubled as stables and a feed store. Some chickens were scratching in the straw by the open double doors, and a couple of pigeons flew out of the path of the approaching car.

He parked the MG behind his brother's rusting Morris and Noel Buchanan's equally dilapidated Triumph. Justin and Noel had met during their first week at art college. They were like chalk and cheese, both physically and in temperament. Noel was a year older than Justin. He was short and stockily built, with a bush of bright red hair and a square-jawed face which was interesting rather than good looking. His green eyes were sharp, and he had a sensuous mouth which would have looked better on a woman. His moods ranged from the depths of despair to raucous eccentricity, which was totally at odds with Justin's natural sobriety. But their friendship had survived over the years, strengthening after George Lang's death, when Noel had been amongst the few who had stood by them.

Nicholas took his overnight case from the boot, and by the time he reached the door his mother was standing there. He had last been home at Christmas, and now he felt like the prodigal son returned. Only Helen was distant, allowing him to kiss her cheek before darting away. But he and Helen had never been close and his years at university, followed by his decision to live and work in London, had driven a wedge between them. Justin's prolonged absence had the opposite effect, perhaps because he had become her substitute father. To make matters worse she had reached that awkward, adolescent stage, where she was cursed by persistent spots and a podgy, non-existent figure.

'Thank God we got through our teens relatively unscathed,' Nicholas remarked after she had gone to bed. 'You really should put her on a diet, Mum. It would also help with the spots.'

Sarah frowned at her younger son. 'Leave the child alone, Nicholas. She is already developing a complex, and I won't put up with you upsetting her.'

Soon afterwards she also retired, leaving the three young men to their own devices. They sat in the living room, drinking brandy and talking. It was a warm evening and the windows were open. In the distance Nicholas could hear bleating sheep.

'Mum is touchy,' he said.

'She is trying to make a success of this trekking business,' Justin told him. 'Remember she's not getting any younger, and the work is demanding. If she decides to carry on next year she'll have to get an assistant. I cannot always promise to be here.'

Nicholas glanced at Noel. The Scotsman's eyes held a warning, but Nicholas chose to ignore it.

'I suppose Alice is creating about you being away for so long,' he said. 'I keep meaning to pop in and see her, but I've been tied up with the Mermaid account.'

'There is nothing to stop her from catching a train on a Sunday morning and going back on Monday.' Justin's voice was sharp. He did not want to discuss Alice with anyone. Every time they spoke on the telephone they ended up arguing. She was being difficult on purpose, using her helplessness as a weapon to bring him back. But as he repeatedly told her, he would not be returning to London until the end of summer. 'How is the Mermaid account coming along?' Deliberately, he changed the subject.

'It's ready to go. We sign up the model on Monday. I brought some of the test photographs with me. Since you were in on this from the beginning, I thought you would like to see them.'

Justin nodded, but without any real interest. He had only drawn the logo because he needed the money.

Nicholas fetched the photographs from his room. The first one he handed to his brother was the black and white portrait.

Noel looked over Justin's shoulder. 'Now that's what I call an interesting face. Marvellous cheekbones and expressive eyes. Who is she? I can't recall having seen her before.'

'She is an unknown. Her name is Pippa Rowe. What do you think, Justin?'

His brother stared at the photograph. The last time he had seen that face it belonged to a child who was trying to look like a woman. Now, it belonged to a woman who had the startling appearance of an underfed waif.

'Her name is not Pippa Rowe. This is Terence Russell's daughter. You saw her once, Nick. Very briefly. She came to the house the day after Dad's funeral.'

Nicholas remembered then. She was the girl his brother had chased away. Or was she? After all this time Justin could be mistaken.

'It can't possibly be the same girl. Terence Russell was wealthy. This girl is a waitress in a tacky restaurant.' His mouth felt dry – a waitress dressed by Chanel.

'There was a rumour going round that Terence Russell killed himself to escape the humiliation,' said Noel. 'Unsubstantiated, of course. He had been robbing the tax man for years and everything he possessed was sold to pay off his debts.'

Justin stood up and went to the window. 'He got everything he deserved. When our father stumbled on to what was happening he was framed in an attempted cover up.'

Nicholas sighed. 'All that happened five years ago, and the girl, if it is her, could have had nothing to do with it. Terence Russell is dead and his empire gone. It's water under the bridge, Justin.'

'He is right,' Noel said. 'You can't carry your resentment forever.'

'I intend to use her, whoever she is,' said Nicholas.

'Her name is Philippa. You should tell her to use it rather than that cheap sounding pseudonym.' He walked to the door. 'If you'll excuse me, I'd better check the ponies.'

'Check the ponies . . .' Nicholas began.

Noel grabbed his arm. 'Let him go. He needs to exorcise his own ghosts in his own way. He is having a hard time right now. This project of your mother's is turning out to be more involved than they both realised. He can't paint as much as he wanted, and Alice is constantly nagging him. He ought to leave her, but he won't. There are times when he has too much principle for his own good.'

Nicholas put down the photographs and picked up the brandy.

'How about you and me getting drunk?' he suggested.

Justin and Alice were not getting along. He came back in the middle of September to tears and accusations that he no longer loved her. They argued incessantly and deep down inside he knew they could not go on like this for much longer.

His mother had insisted he have a share of the year's profits. It did not amount to a lot of money, but would help them through the winter months. In the first week of October he was called out on short notice to a school in Battersea, where the art teacher had come down with flu. The job was unlikely to last for longer than a few days, but it got him out of the flat for a while. He purposefully came home late, so that Alice was usually leaving for the theatre when he walked through the front door. For the moment they had called an uneasy truce, but it didn't last. When he walked in on Thursday evening Alice came flouncing into the hall.

'There's someone waiting to see you. A woman. She says you met her during the summer.'

His mind went blank. A few young women had flirted with him when he took out the rides, but he had not encouraged them, and they had soon given up. He had certainly told nobody where he lived, nor discussed anything touching the personal.

'Who is she?'

'How would I know? It's you she came to see, not me.'

He very nearly lost his temper. He felt like taking her by

the shoulders and shaking her hard.

'What's her name, Alice?'

'Why? Were you expecting more than one to turn up on the doorstep? It's Maggie something or other. I can't remember. Personally, I would not have thought her your type.' She glanced at her watch. 'I'm late, and your running me to the bus stop is obviously out of the question. Not when you have a lady friend to entertain.'

She snatched her coat from behind the door, picked up her tote bag, and slammed out of the flat. Justin did not move. This time Alice had gone too far with her accusations. He did not hear the door open behind him.

'I came because I didn't think you would remember who I was if I telephoned.'

He knew, even before he turned and saw her. 'You were looking for Harlequin House.'

'And found it, thanks to you. I am sorry for upsetting your girlfriend.'

'She'll get over it.'

He was being polite, but the hostility in his eyes made it clear he did not welcome her intrusion.

'Why are you here? I doubt whether it is to buy a painting.'

'I have something else in mind and would rather not discuss it in this draughty hallway.'

Maggie returned to the living room, which also doubled as his studio. He followed her, closing the door behind him. He immediately noticed that the canvasses he kept stacked against a wall had been moved.

'Did Alice give you permission to look at my paintings, or did you help yourself?'

'I asked first.' Maggie glared at him. 'Are you always so abrasive, Mr Lang? It is little wonder you have got nowhere as an artist. As for your work, you have talent, but are

98

spreading yourself over too wide a field. Your paintings remind me of a patchwork quilt. If you jumbled them all together you would find a little bit of everything.'

His facial muscles tightened. By criticising his work she had touched a raw nerve.

'You wheedled your way into my home and snooped without invitation through my work. I should like you to leave.'

Maggie had learnt to circumvent temperament. She ignored him and sat down. 'I have not finished, and I doubt if you will go to the lengths of physically throwing me out.'

He crossed his arms. 'I wouldn't bet on it, Lady Margaret.'

Maggie smiled. 'I take it you do not know that I own the Huntington Gallery in Bond Street. I am thinking of setting up an exhibition of your work. Would you still like me to leave?'

'Obviously not,' he replied. The abrasiveness was still there, but he was more relaxed than a moment before.

'I wouldn't mind a cup of coffee,' said Maggie. 'I would also like to look at your paintings again. It was difficult when your girlfriend was hovering over me. She seemed to think I was going to steal you away from her.'

She saw something that could have been exasperation pass through his eyes. 'Alice has always been insecure. You'll have to excuse her.'

He watched as Maggie walked across the room, propping up a couple of his canvasses so that she could see them better. It was unbelievable he should have met this woman outside a village pub. He remembered now that she was a known intimate of every London art critic and yet, until she told him, he had not made the connection between her and the Huntington Gallery.

★

'I'm going away for a while,' he told Alice a week later.

She stared at him, her eyes wide with fright. 'But you've not been back for long.'

'I need some new paintings for the exhibition, and I can't do them here.' He paused. He could not put this off indefinitely. 'There is something else. I think we should split up. We are not working any more. All we succeed in doing is making each other miserable.'

Her face, always pale, was ashen. Her voice trembled. 'You want me to move out?'

'Yes. I won't rush you, but I think it would be best if you left by, say, the end of January. That will give you almost three months. I'll stay out of your way as much as possible, and sleep on a camp bed in the living room.'

Alice began to shiver. She couldn't stop herself. Justin saw it but stood impassively on the opposite side of their bedroom. She sat on the bed, afraid she would fall if she didn't.

'I love you,' she murmured.

He did not go to her. He moved towards the door.

'I am sorry, Alice. I really am. Let's part friends, shall we? I am leaving early in the morning, so I'll spend tonight with Noel.'

'Where will you be going?' She was too shocked to ask more than the simplest of questions.

'I think it would be easier all round if you didn't know.'

'Is it with that woman?'

'If you mean Maggie, the answer is no. Our relationship is strictly professional. There is no other woman, Alice. If there was I would have the decency to tell you.'

He walked out, leaving her with tears streaming down her cheeks.

100

CHAPTER EIGHT

Philippa had entered a brash new world which fed on illusion and the adoration of the public. It was a world where the people at the top were treated, and acted, like gods, while those on the lower echelons, such as herself, were trodden underfoot. She put up with it because she needed every penny she could get, but time after time she had to hold down her temper. Her previous modelling stints had done nothing to prepare her for the professionalism to which she was now subjected – and nobody was more professional than Steve Noble. He continually pushed her to the limits of her endurance.

She very nearly pulled out at the beginning, when Nicholas Lang handed her the Mermaid Hosiery contract. She read the first couple of lines, then looked up to see him watching her.

'How long have you known?'

'My brother recognised you from the photographs I showed him. Do you object to our using your real name? I agree with him, Pippa Rowe sounds insipid and your own suits you much better. You might even find it advantageous from the publicity angle.'

'That depends upon the publicity. Why didn't you ask my permission first?'

He smiled. 'Because I wanted to see your reaction. Do

101

you mind if I call you Philippa?'

'You already are. I take it you have no objection to me?'

'I do not hold you responsible for what your father did. Anyhow, it is too late to change our plans. You are scheduled to start shooting next week, and before then Steve Noble wants you to spend some time with him.'

'Why?'

'Because you lack experience and it shows. You chose to be a model. As such, you are expected to obey instructions and keep your mouth shut.' He glanced at his watch. 'I have another appointment in fifteen minutes. Are you going to sign the contract?'

'Not until I have read it. I never sign anything which I have not read thoroughly.'

Steve Noble was unbelievably arrogant, but the man knew what he was doing. She spent two mornings with him, at the end of which she felt physically and emotionally drained. She wondered why he was giving up so much of his time to teach her a trade about which she knew nothing. She found out at the end of their second session. His assistant, Angie, had gone to lunch with friends, and they were alone in the studio. Steve declared he was satisfied with what they had done, switched off the arc lights, then put an arm around her waist and kissed her cheek.

'That was superb, darling. You're a quick learner.'

Philippa was stunned. Up to now he had done nothing but bark out orders and swear like a trooper.

'Let's have a glass of champagne.'

She disliked the way his hand moved down to her hip, and when his fingers caressed her buttock she had to stop herself from slapping his face. She spun away from him. It was a move she had perfected at the restaurant when dealing with rowdy customers.

'No thank you. I must be going. I have another appointment.'

'With a boyfriend?'

'Yes,' she lied.

He looked amused. 'You'll have to tell him he can no longer expect you to be at his beck and call.'

Nor yours either, she thought. 'He is not the possessive type.'

Steve had been unable to penetrate the wall Philippa had erected around herself. She kept her private life private and even now he was unable to tell whether she was bluffing. This time, he gave her the benefit of the doubt.

He went to a trellis table which was littered with photographs and scraps of paper. He picked up a calling card and held it towards her.

'Come in tomorrow morning and Angie will give you a selection of the best photographs. I want you to take them to this agency. Belinda will sign you up immediately.'

'I already have a modelling agency.'

'What you have is some tinpot concern which has no connections, or one high-class model on their books. Stay with them and you will get nowhere.'

'You seem to forget they got me this far!'

'Wrong, darling. I got you this far.' He placed his hands on her shoulders, trapping her against the wall. 'Your portfolio was in the reject list. I was the one who fished it out and insisted you be interviewed. And I was also the one who convinced Nicholas you were the right girl for the job. I can get you to the top, Philippa. Isn't that what you want?'

'Not particularly.' She tried to wriggle free, but he was too strong. 'The reason I want to get on is not what you think.'

'You want to make good the family name?' he asked.

'No! Now will you please let go of me?'

She thought he was about to refuse, but he suddenly released her and stepped back. 'If we are to work together, it is essential we are close.'

Philippa moved away from him. 'There must be any number of girls who would willingly give themselves to you. Why choose me? I'm no beauty.'

He leant against the table, watching her. 'You know the old saying, beauty is in the eye of the beholder. You have an interesting face, Philippa, and I like your spirit. It shows in the photographs. Go and see Belinda tomorrow. She is a hard bitch, but a good agent, and you need proper representation. She is expecting you. I telephoned her last night after developing the proofs.'

From thereon, Steve took it upon himself to manage Philippa's career. He taught her how to flirt with the camera and was dogmatic about what make-up she wore, stressing the emphasis must be on her eyes. He gradually achieved the effect he wanted, a little-girl-lost look, which made Philippa wonder whether she was growing younger or older. But his photographs were sensational, and even Nicholas was pleased when he saw the Mermaid proofs.

She did not tell Steve she was still waiting tables at Lady Jayne two or three nights a week, and at weekends. He often asked her for dinner, or to partner him at one of the clubs or discotheques which he frequented, but she always made the excuse of her non-existent boyfriend. She even gave him the name of Vincent, knowing he would never meet the real Vincent. For those first few months she successfully managed to keep her two lives separate. She would not be able to do so indefinitely but, in the meantime, she was saving a little money.

The breakthrough Steve had promised came unexpectedly. It was a wet and windy day in October when he walked into the dressing room where she was putting the finishing touches to her make-up.

'*Vogue* have agreed you can be the second model in the fashion shoot I am doing in Scotland next month. They had booked Janine Baxter, but she's sprained her ankle and won't be able to handle the Highland locations. You were not a popular choice as a replacement, but I persuaded them to let you have a go.'

Philippa put down her lipstick . 'I am actually going to be in *Vogue*?' she asked.

He grinned. 'Don't get carried away. Remember you'll be working with Rosalind Harper. I also taught her everything she knows, and she's been doing it for much longer than you.'

'I won't let you down,' Philippa said with more confidence than she felt. 'But won't it be awkward for you working with her again?'

'Of course not. We parted as friends. Nor is there any need for you to be nervous. She isn't bitchy.'

'I'm not nervous.'

'Good girl.'

He took her hand and pulled her to her feet. Then he kissed her. It was not a light-hearted, friendly kiss, for the pressure of it forced Philippa's lips apart. As his tongue explored her mouth she tried to pull away, but he was holding her in a bear-like grip from which she was unable to escape. She knew what he wanted and almost panicked. Then she used her common-sense and stopped struggling. Steve mistook that for compliance. His grip loosened and his fingers clawed at her breast. Philippa twisted away from him and backed across the small dressing room until her shoulder hit the wall and she was unable to go any further.

'Why do you keep resisting me?' He was breathing hard

and she did not trust the glimmer in his eyes. 'I am not prepared to wait forever, Philippa. If we are to continue working together, we must come to an arrangement.'

She felt trapped in here. He was blocking the only exit, but she did not let him see how afraid she was. 'I am fond of you, Steve, but I do not love you.'

'I'm not asking you to love me. I told you I like a close relationship with my models. I've kept my side of the bargain, and now I expect you to keep yours.'

'I made no bargain with you, and I certainly do not intend to sleep with you.'

'You can say goodbye to *Vogue* and the big time if I drop you.'

'Then it will have to be goodbye. I am not about to sacrifice my principles for the sake of ambition.' She pushed past him, her fear forgotten, and threw her make-up and accessories into a canvas bag. Steve watched her with the petulant look of a child who has been forbidden something he badly wants. 'I never came into this for fame. I simply wanted the money.'

He did not try to stop her when she walked out and she wondered if she was making a mistake. But the thought of sharing his bed was repulsive. She was not a prude. Some of her schoolfriends had lost their virginity at fifteen, but she had held out because she wanted her first time to be something special which she could share with someone she loved. Philippa had not met that someone yet. She might never meet him, in which case she would have to settle for second best.

At least they would be pleased to see more of her at the restaurant.

She worked late that night, and next morning was awoken by a persistent knocking at the front door. The bedroom was still dark, and when she switched on the lamp she saw it was five-thirty.

She dragged on her dressing gown, shivering as she stumbled into the hall.

'Who is it?'

'Who do you think it is at this time in the morning?'

She opened the door. Steve looked a wreck, as though he had not slept all night.

'What do you want?' In the road above them Philippa could hear the throb of an engine. Steve could not drive. He went everywhere in taxis.

'If you had a telephone put in this dump then I wouldn't be here. I want you in the studio at eight-thirty prompt. I've already had to juggle my bookings to fit you in.'

'I am not going to sleep with you.'

'I am not asking you to. Be there, Philippa. We've wasted enough time.'

She watched him run up the narrow steps, then closed the door and stood with her back against it. She did not know if rebuffing Steve Noble was much of an achievement, but she felt confident she could conquer the world if she set her mind to it.

Rosalind Harper had black hair, browny-black eyes, a pale complexion and perfect features. She was stunningly beautiful, yet friendly and unaffected by fame. Philippa felt plain and uninteresting and, having a supporting role to play, she quickly faded into the background. People walked up to Rosalind in the street and asked for her autograph, while Steve was like a dog after a bitch on heat.

He had not pestered Philippa since their quarrel a fortnight before but sometimes, when she saw him watching her, she had the impression that a future relationship was not entirely out of his mind.

They were scheduled to spend one day in Edinburgh, another in Stirling, and the other two by Loch Lomond. As they were on a tight budget there were only the three of them, and a woman who had charge of the wardrobe.

The sun shone while they were in Edinburgh, but when they left for Stirling it was cold and drizzling, which was how it remained all day. The final shots were to be taken in a pretty but deserted square. By then Rosalind was complaining bitterly, and Philippa was finding it hard to stop her teeth from chattering.

'One more shot,' Steve callously insisted. 'Philippa, I don't need you in this one. Ros, darling, walk towards me, then make a sharp left turn at the street lamp. I want to see that cape swirl. And stop pouting.'

'I'm cold and wet, and if I want to pout I damn well will! Where do you want me to start from? Here or over there?'

'Where you are will be fine. Get out of the way, Philippa!'

She leapt back, colliding with something solid which proved to be the only other person in the square besides them. She staggered sideways, and strong hands caught hold of her shoulders.

'I'm sorry,' she gasped.

'It was my fault. I should have been looking where I was going. Are you all right?'

Nicholas? Surely not? As the man released her Philippa swung round, the breath catching in her throat when she saw who it was. Memory can play funny tricks, and the similarity between Nicholas and Justin Lang was less pronounced than she had imagined. Physically, there was little to choose between them, but the grey eyes which gazed curiously into hers were not so hard as his brother's.

He appeared as shocked as she was that they should meet like this, accidentally, in a wet and windblown square. In five years he had changed very little, whereas Philippa was a different person. He took a step back, his eyes travelling with deliberate slowness from her face to her feet, then back to her face.

'My, how the mighty have fallen! Are you still as sharp of tongue, or have you mellowed since we last met?'

Philippa crossed her arms in a vain attempt to stop herself from shivering. A wind had blown up and dead leaves were showering upon them. Rosalind and Steve could have belonged to another world.

'I never fell, Mr Lang. I found my wings and flew. You, I see, are no less sarcastic.'

He laughed. 'No, you haven't changed. Are you as cold as you look?'

'I am not the slightest bit cold.'

'Like hell you're not!' He gazed beyond her. 'Nicholas said Steve had taken you in hand. He never mentioned Rosalind being back in the picture.'

'She isn't.'

'It may not be permanent, but the old chemistry is certainly working right now.'

Philippa turned to watch Rosalind sweep across the square. She and Steve were engrossed in what they were doing and, as Justin Lang had said, with each other.

'Do you know them?' she asked. He spoke as though he did.

'We met a few times when they were together.'

To Philippa's horror he stepped around her and walked towards them. Steve hated to be interrupted when a shoot was going well. She was about to shout a warning, but was too late.

'The light has gone from this side of the square,' Justin said. 'You're wasting film.'

Steve did not explode as Philippa had expected. 'What on

earth are you doing here?' he asked.

'The same as you. Trying to earn a living. Hello, Rosalind. You look magnificent.'

'So do you, darling.' She kissed his cheek. 'Thank you for stopping him. My feet are killing me. These shoes pinch.'

'You'll have to put up with them for a little longer,' said Steve. He was gazing at the other end of the square, where autumn leaves were falling in flurries of red and gold. 'I want to get some shots of you standing under those leaves.'

The wind was icy and Philippa's teeth were chattering again. She hoped Steve was not going to keep them here for much longer.

'How about joining us for dinner?' he asked Justin. 'We're on an expense account.'

'No thanks. I'm staying near Loch Lomond and don't want to drive back too late. It's a terrible road.'

'Come on, Ros, before the light goes altogether. We're moving into that vicinity tomorrow. We'll be there for a couple of days. Pop round. I can't remember the name of the hotel, but it's in a place called Drymen. There can't be many to choose from.'

As they moved away, Justin glanced at Philippa, smiling when she glowered at him. The child had matured into a remarkably attractive young woman who had lost none of her spirit.

'Have you finished with the other one? I think she could do with a hot drink. She's turning blue.'

'I am not,' she protested, a blush spreading into her cheeks.

'You can go if you want, Philippa. I won't need you again today. Can you see she gets safely back to the hotel, Justin?'

'I am perfectly capable of finding my own way to the hotel,' she protested.

Steve paused in mid-step, frowning as he looked from the

man to the girl. Something was sparking between them but he was unable to detect what it was. Intuition told him they had met before. He felt a stab of jealousy, then Rosalind pulled impatiently at his arm and the moment passed.

'It's up to you,' he said.

Philippa stared after him, unaware of Justin until he touched her arm. 'I very much doubt you will see either of them again this evening. There is a quiet café half a block from here. Let me treat you to a cup of tea.'

'I do not appear to have been left with any choice.' She knew she sounded ungracious, but she had not asked for this.

'You don't have to talk if you prefer not to.'

She looked at him, but there was no mockery in his eyes.

'Perhaps a cup of tea would not be such a bad idea,' she said.

The café turned out to be a rather lovely tea room which had emptied of the lunchtime crowd and was preparing for the late afternoon rush of shoppers. The only people in there besides them were a couple of middle-aged women. They sat at a table by the window, hidden from the outside world by thick lace curtains.

'Would you like something to eat?' Justin asked.

'No thanks.'

'You look half starved.'

'I need to be thin. The camera adds pounds.'

He was looking directly at her, something which Philippa found oddly disconcerting. She turned her head away, peering through the curtains into the street.

'This would be far more pleasant if you put your claws away and relaxed. As Nicholas so rightly said, what happened five years ago is water under the bridge. The main protagonists are dead and there is no reason why we

111

cannot be civil to one another.'

'You were hardly civil the last time we met.'

'That is not surprising when my father had been buried the day before. Whatever your intentions, your timing was lousy.'

Philippa avoided his gaze. He was going out of his way to be pleasant, but she still felt uneasy.

'I wanted to tell you how sorry I was. What your father did was so horribly final. It was like an act of desperation.'

'It was. He never stole anything in his life.'

'In the light of what happened later on you are probably right. You must have read the newspapers. Geoffrey and I were left penniless. We were even put out of the house. I think it was my father who embezzled the money and, when a scandal broke, killed himself rather than face a trial and perhaps jail. There is no concrete proof, for he took the truth with him to the grave. Geoffrey denied knowing anything, but I never really believed him. He went to Australia. I have not heard from him since, and I don't suppose I ever shall. As you have probably guessed, we were never a close family.'

In the silence which followed Philippa finished her tea. She was cold, but it was not the type of coldness which hot liquid would cure.

'I never realised how difficult it was for you.' As she put down the cup he reached for her hand. She looked alarmed, but did not pull away from him. 'It was not easy for us either. But we had each other. You're still cold. I wish you would eat something.'

'I'm not hungry. Truly. But I would like some more tea.'

'I'll order a fresh pot.'

He beckoned the waitress. He had an easy-going charm to which Philippa found herself responding.

'Are you also in advertising?' she asked for lack of something better to say.

'God forbid! In a roundabout sort of way Steve and I are in the same business, only he uses a camera while I prefer a paint-brush. For my sins, I am an artist.'

'Oh!'

'Only oh?'

'You don't look like an artist, or how I expect an artist to look. I cannot remember having met one before. Are you successful?'

He laughed. 'So successful I have to accept assignments from Nicholas in order to keep my head above water. I drew your mermaid.'

She was about to ask what he was talking about when it came to her. That delightful logo which featured in the Mermaid advertisements, and was woven into the tops of their stockings and pantiehose.

'Is that why you are here? To paint?'

'I have been promised an exhibition in February. I am trying to get together a selection of new work.'

More tea came. Behind him the door opened and a man and woman walked in, both laden with shopping baskets.

'Where is it being held? In Sussex?'

He looked startled. 'Didn't Nicholas tell you we left there in 1959? My mother wanted to move back to her old home in Devon. I was studying in London at the time and still live there.'

A suspicion crossed Philippa's mind. But surely it was too much of a coincidence?

'I expect this sounds absurd, but is your exhibition connected in any way with the Huntington Gallery?'

'Yes it is. How did you know?'

'Margaret Huntington-Smythe is a dear friend who helped me through some of the roughest times. She told me about an artist she stumbled across in Devon last summer. I never knew it was you.' She stopped. One way or another, it seemed their lives were fated to cross. First Nicholas, and now him.

Justin instinctively knew what was going through her mind. His own thoughts were running in the same direction.

'Shall I pour the tea?' he asked.

'I'll do it.'

Her hand shook as she picked up the teapot.

'Here, you had better let me.' He smiled and it was with a growing sense of alarm that Philippa realised she had never felt quite like this before. 'Will you have dinner with me tomorrow night? Drymen is close to where I am staying.'

'What about Steve and Rosalind?'

'They won't miss you. Please say yes.'

'Yes.' There was no going back. She was committed.

CHAPTER NINE

Philippa had not brought many clothes with her, but they included a long-sleeved, black dress, which needed no adornment other than her mother's pearls. It did not look out of place with Justin's casual slacks and a tweed jacket, nor in the intimate pub restaurant to which he took her. It was a perfectly respectable dress, although the length did raise a few eyebrows. Four inches above the knee was acceptable in London, but perhaps not quite so in a remote Scottish pub. Justin did not remark upon it, and Philippa did not care if she shocked a few dowdy matrons. She felt good, and knew she looked good from the way his eyes appraised her when they met in the hotel lobby.

'I took into account your obsession with looking stick-thin,' he said as they sat on opposite sides of a narrow table. 'This place may not look much, but people come from as far afield as Edinburgh for the fresh salmon. It has the advantage of being non-fattening.'

'I am not stick-thin! Nor do I diet.'

'Don't you ever drop your defences? You have more bristles than a broomhead.'

'It might help if you brushed them up the right way.'

He smiled, that wonderful smile which had melted her bones when she was fifteen years old, and did the same now.

'How about calling a truce?' he asked. 'I promise not to

bait you if you will desist from sticking barbs in me.'

'I am sorry. I've had a hellish day. Steven can be a real bastard sometimes.'

'It's his artistic temperament. Do you want a drink, or would you prefer wine?'

'Wine. But only one glass.'

Philippa began to relax. He was a most attractive man, and what harm could there be in a little, light-hearted flirtation? She had not been on a proper date since her father's death.

Philippa had borrowed one of the capes from the collection she and Rosalind were modelling. It was classier than her camel coat, which was looking jaded from continuous wear. She pulled it tightly around her when they left the pub. The sky had cleared and a full moon was reflecting silver against the frost-covered ground.

'Would you like to walk?'

At first she had found it unsettling, this knack Justin had of reading her thoughts.

'Where?'

This village was almost non-existent and had no pavements.

'By the lake is pleasant.'

'There are no lights down there!'

He laughed, and she felt his fingers tighten around her arm. 'There is nothing to be afraid of. It is perfectly safe.'

'I'm not afraid.'

'You're getting bristly again,' he teased.

She looked into his face. 'All right, I'll come down to the lake, but you can shoulder the blame if my shoes fall apart.'

'I am not about to embark on a ten-mile hike. We can drive to the jetty where there is a proper path.'

She could tell he was laughing at her, but in a nice sort of way which brought a smile to her lips.

★

The loch was beautiful in the moonlight. Philippa didn't notice the cold wind as it rippled across the water. A fish leapt skywards, its scales gleaming like quicksilver. In the hills behind them she heard the sigh of pine trees, and the eerie call of a hunting owl.

'I wish I could catch hold of this moment and keep it forever,' she said.

'You can, in your mind.'

Justin had his arm around her waist, and she leant against him. It seemed natural for them to be standing here like this. A thin wisp of cloud passed in front of the moon, quickly followed by a thicker band which shadowed it. The wind strengthened as it whipped itself into a frenzy over the open surface of the lake.

'A storm is coming. We'd better go.'

'Not yet,' she pleaded.

'We'll get soaked if we don't. They blow up quickly here.'

His face was suddenly very close. He lifted his hand to her cheek, then brushed his lips against hers. To be kissed in the moonlight by a good-looking man whose sex appeal hadn't entirely escaped her was a heady experience. Philippa hesitated for no more than a heartbeat before she kissed him back. He reacted by putting his arms around her, holding her so close that she could feel the heat of his body pass through her like an electric current.

Her awareness extended no further than him and the dormant sensuality he had aroused in her. She had never been kissed like this before and did not want him to stop. It was the unexpected deluge of rain which drove them apart. They ran, hand in hand, to his car, but by then they were both wet through.

Justin grabbed a tartan rug from the back seat. 'Take off that cape and wrap yourself in this.'

Philippa ran her hands down the front of the soaking garment. 'I borrowed it from the collection we're modelling. What if it's ruined?'

'To hell with the cape! Here, lean forward and let me help you.'

The rug made little difference, for her thin dress clung soddenly to her, while her hair dripped down her back. She shivered. Outside the squalling wind buffeted the car and pea-sized pellets of hail bounced off the roof.

Justin started the engine. 'I'm taking you to Lochdunnan. It's closer.'

'Lochdunnan? What's that?'

He cupped his hand against her cheek. There was no warmth in his palm and she realised he must be as cold as she was.

'The place where I'm staying. It belongs to a friend and is not far from here.'

He switched on the headlights, and with the confidence of somebody who knew the area well, sped out of the gravel car park on to the dark and empty road.

Philippa huddled into the rug. Her emotions were in a turmoil and she had no idea how to bring them under control.

'Justin.'

'Yes.'

'Nothing.'

His hand touched her thigh. There was no need to tell him how she felt. He already knew.

The car laboured up a winding road, with the headlights glancing off high banks and solid lines of pine trees.

'Where is this place? On top of a mountain?'

'More or less. We're almost there.'

They were suddenly confronted by a wall and studded

wooden gates which had been left open. Justin drove through them into a cobbled courtyard, then turned left along a narrow passage, also cobbled, to a smaller yard with an open-fronted garage. Behind it, Philippa glimpsed another wall.

'Where are we? It looks like a castle.'

'It is a castle. Surely you have been in one before?'

'Only as a tourist. I had a schoolfriend once whose parents owned a château in France. It was one of those fairy tale places with spiralling towers and cornices. From the outside it was breathtaking, but in reality it was damp and draughty, with rats in the roof.'

'I think you'll find Lochdunnan a little different. It's in the hands of the National Trust and they have done an exceptional job with its upkeep. This is the entrance to the private apartment. Wait here while I open the front door.'

He got out of the car, but Philippa did not wait. She grabbed the cape, then followed him through the pouring rain. As she squelched over the cobbles she had the oddest sensation of being perched on top of the world.

Justin swung round, almost collided with her, then grabbed her arm and led her into a large hall which had a staircase running up one wall. There was central heating. She could feel its welcoming warmth.

'I'll show you around afterwards. First of all, you need to get out of those wet clothes. Unfortunately, nothing of Morag's will fit you. She is about half your height and dumpy.'

'Who is Morag?' Philippa asked as he took the cape from her and threw it on to a chair.

'Alistair's wife.'

'Who is Alistair?'

'Noel's older brother.'

'Who is . . .'

119

'. . . for heaven's sake, Philippa, I'll explain it to you later.'

She had a hot bath and then padded downstairs, her hair damp and a towelling robe tied securely around her waist. Justin was in the kitchen, making coffee. He was wearing a navy fisherman's jersey and grey slacks. He turned round and Philippa blushed.

'I must look awful.' It was a thin attempt to disguise the increasing confusion she felt when she was near him.

'You could never look awful, however hard you tried. Here, drink this while it's hot.'

Their hands brushed as she took the mug from him. They went into the living room, which was furnished with old but comfortable furniture. She sat on the sofa, close to a two-bar electric fire.

'No family treasures?' she asked, looking around.

'Most of them were sold off years ago. There is a little porcelain and some paintings on show in the main part of the castle.'

'Why don't you sit down?' she asked, aware that his eyes had never left her face.

'I prefer to stand.'

She was facing a situation which was beyond her experience and, seeing her hesitation, he was keeping his distance. She put down the mug and cautiously began to feel her way through this unknown jungle of human relationships.

'I am not sorry about what happened by the lake.'

'Neither am I.' He sounded tense. 'I had better find you something more appropriate to wear, then take you back to the hotel. It's getting late and Steve will be sending out a search party.'

'What I do is none of Steve's business. Anyhow, I expect he and Rosalind will be otherwise occupied by now.'

'I still have to get you back.'

She did not want to leave, but how could she tell him without sounding cheap? She looked up and as their eyes met the air between them became explosive.

'I'll only go if you want me to.'

'Do you know what you are saying?'

'Yes.'

The master bedroom was dominated by an imposing four-poster. There was also a fireplace, and Philippa watched as Justin dropped to his knees and put a match to the rolled-up balls of paper which had been placed under a pile of logs.

'Who lays the fires and does the cleaning? Or do you have a friendly ghost?'

'Nothing so dramatic. The caretaker's wife looks after the place.'

He stood up and reached for her hand. She came to him eagerly, but when they kissed, he sensed her nervousness. It was with genuine surprise that he realised she had never done this before, and so he was more gentle than he might otherwise have been. He did not rush her. He waited until the fire had taken, then switched off the light and began their love-making in earnest. It was he who removed his clothes first, so that when he slipped the robe from her shoulders she would not feel awkward or embarrassed. But by then she was swept up in their passion, and as his hands drifted exquisitely over her body, she willingly gave herself to him.

To love was to trust. It never crossed her mind this might not be for always.

Justin took her back to the hotel at dawn and she was in her room when Steve burst in. He slammed the door and glared at her.

'Did you sleep with him?'

'I don't believe that is any of your business. Did you sleep with Rosalind?'

He ignored the question. 'Are you seeing him again?'

'Yes. Tonight.'

'Then take my advice and ask him about the dancer.'

After he had gone, Philippa gazed at her reflection in the mirror. She looked like the same person she had been yesterday, but knew she was not. What had Steve been trying to insinuate? She did not believe Justin would knowingly deceive her. What they had shared last night had gone far beyond the raw desires of lust and sexual fulfilment.

Steve was probably furious because she kept turning him down. But she was not going to let him get under her skin, whatever he said.

The day could not pass fast enough, and when it was finished Philippa checked out of the hotel. She had asked Justin to wait in his car, and was about to leave when Steve waylaid her.

'I've got you booked tomorrow afternoon,' he said. 'If you don't show up, that's it. I wash my hands of you.'

'I'll be coming back with you and will be at the station in the morning.' She kissed his cheek. 'Please don't be angry, Steve. I never meant this to happen. Now it has, can't you be a little bit happy for me?'

'I might if I knew it would last.'

'It will.'

'I wouldn't be so sure about that. When it goes wrong don't expect me to pick up the pieces.'

'There won't be any pieces to pick up. Goodnight.'

They did not go out. Justin cooked cheese omlettes which they ate with chilled wine. They caressed occasionally, but mostly they talked, and when he suggested a tour of the castle Philippa thought she had misheard him.

'At night?'

'Strange though it may seem, it has been electrified. There is a main switch, and we can get in through that locked door at the back of the hall. You don't have to worry about the ghost. It never appears before midnight.'

'There is a ghost?' she asked, her eyes widening.

'Of course. Every self-respecting castle should have a ghost.'

'Are you having me on?'

He hugged her. 'Sort of. But according to Noel there really is one. It gets sighted every hundred years or so, usually by an inebriated member of the family.'

She laughed, but baulked when Justin took her arm.

'Ghost or no ghost, I don't fancy exploring at this time of night. What happens if the lights go out?'

'They won't.'

'What if they do?'

'I'll find you a torch if it will make you feel more secure.'

The castle was much smaller inside than Philippa had expected it to be. The great hall was cavernous, with faded tapestries hanging from the walls, but the other rooms were claustrophobic. They avoided the dungeons and ended up in the portrait gallery, which was a wide passage with a door at each end. She understood then why he had been so insistent they come here. It was a place where he could talk unemotionally, without fear of their mutual desire getting in the way.

They sat on a hard bench in the middle of the gallery and Justin held Philippa close to him. And while she stared at the paintings of fierce-looking Scotsmen and their equally fierce looking women, he told her about Alice.

'It was over a long time ago,' he said. 'We should have parted then, but somehow I never got round to telling her.

123

I finally did so before coming here.'

Philippa looked at their clasped hands. 'What about her? Does she still love you?'

He did not reply immediately. When he did, he spoke slowly, as though he were considering something which had not struck him before. 'I am not sure if it is love or dependence. Alice is nothing like you. She is insecure and in constant need of reassurance. She wore me down in the end. I reached a point where I was unable to sustain her any longer.'

Philippa was not jealous, but Justin must have read something in her expression. He kissed her tenderly.

'It won't happen to us,' he promised. 'I love you too much.'

Because he had been honest with her, Philippa told him about the pottery.

'Did you hear a word I said?' she asked when he passed no comment. They were in the four-poster bed and he was gazing at the dying flames of the fire.

'Every one of them.' He smiled. 'May I express an opinion, or would you prefer me to keep my nose out of your affairs?'

She straightened up so that she could see him better. 'Are you going to tell me I should cut my losses and sell it?'

'No. But you might as well. Pouring in money without knowing what it is being used for is a recipe for disaster. If you want to run a successful business then you must know everything about it. Consider the consequences of my mother owning a riding school and not knowing one end of a horse from the other. Do you follow what I am trying to say?'

'Yes. But I don't actually have any money worth speaking of. Not yet. Moor View is scraping by on a massive overdraft which I have committed myself to pay off. That is why I have to succeed at modelling. My father must have spent a fortune on my education, but what good has it done me? Waiting at tables or standing in front of a camera seems to be all I am capable of doing.'

He put his arm around her. 'You are more than capable of being whatever you wish, sweetheart. If you really want to make something of your pottery, then you must spend more time in it. Your manager is there to deal with the day to day problems, but the important decisions must come from you, not him.'

'Without Gideon the pottery would have ceased to exist a long time ago. Even if I knew what I was doing, I wouldn't have the gall to walk in and take over.'

'What happens when he retires? If he worked for your grandfather he cannot be a young man. You need to sit down and think through your problems. What you have inherited is not a plaything, but the livelihood of a lot of people.'

'I know. Why do you think I was so determined to keep it in the first place? You are right, of course. I never had any plans. I sort of assumed it would keep going, which it has. But that's not enough, is it?'

'Not nearly enough. Your heart is in the right place. Now you need to get it in line with your head.' His lips brushed against hers. 'That is enough serious talk for tonight. Are you cold?'

'A little. I am also frightened. I never stopped to think what I was doing until now.'

His laughter was gentle. 'You frightened? You don't know the meaning of the word. Even as a schoolgirl you were a force to be reckoned with.' Abruptly, he moved away from her.

'Where are you going?'

'To put more wood on the fire.'

Philippa watched as he crossed the room, then crouched down to throw fresh logs on to the flickering embers. She hugged her arms around her updrawn knees. She could not recall a time when she had felt this happy, but she had never been in love before. The unexpected pang of anxiety was like a shadow looming on the horizon. They had spoken of everything, except what would happen when she left here.

'When will I see you again?' she asked.

He looked up. 'I shall be finished in another week.'

'You mean it, don't you, Justin? I would much rather you told me now than leave me to hope and wait.'

He tossed a final log on to the fire, unfurled his supple body, and walked towards her. He sat on the edge of the massive bed.

'Of course I mean it.'

The warmth of his kiss dispersed the shadows of doubt. As he bent over her Philippa was aware of a lingering aroma of pine smoke which clung to his body. It was something she would always associate with him.

CHAPTER TEN

'What's wrong, Justin? Why have you come back in such a foul mood? It can't be the paintings. They are excellent.'

He had been home for less than an hour and was prowling the room like a caged animal, his eyes dangerously bright. Alice gripped the back of a chair, her fingers digging into the frayed fabric.

'You know what is wrong, but act as though nothing has happened. I meant what I said, Alice. It's over between us and I don't think you should stay here any longer. I should like you to move out as soon as possible.'

She was unaware of her fingernails ripping into the chair. 'Is there someone else?'

'What difference does it make now?'

Tears flooded her eyes. She was at a loss to understand what she had done to make him turn against her. She loved him deeply and, until recently, was certain he had loved her too.

'How long have you known her?'

'Known who?'

'I am not a fool, Justin! Please don't treat me like one. If you are throwing me over for another woman, surely I have a right to know?'

His eyes were hard and inflexible as he gazed at her. 'Whether or not there is somebody else is beside the point.

Let go, Alice, because you are only succeeding in hurting yourself.' He turned away. 'To hell with this. I'm going out for a while.'

'But you only just got back.'

'You don't own me.' He strode towards the door.

'I'm pregnant.'

That stopped him.

'How?' His face was ashen and his voice sounded dreadful.

She lowered her eyes. 'I went off the pill when you were away during the summer and forgot to go back on until you had been back for a couple of weeks. I knew you would be angry if I told you. As the odds were against me getting pregnant, I never gave it another thought.'

'Obviously, you should have. Are you certain about this?'

'I saw the doctor last week. I missed a month and you know how regular I am . . .' Her voice trailed away and uncontrollable tears rolled down her cheeks. She sank into the chair and covered her face with her hands. 'I don't know what to do.'

'Are you sure it's mine?'

Alice lifted her head, her expression reflecting disgust. 'How could you? You know there has been nobody else. This baby is yours, and I don't want it any more than you do, but I'm the one who is stuck with it.'

There was no compassion in him as he looked at her. 'Have you considered an abortion?'

She recoiled. 'Is that what you want?' She was trembling violently and could not stop herself.

The anger left him. 'Of course not. I had no right to suggest it.'

He went to the sideboard and took out a bottle of cheap brandy and two glasses. He poured a little into each glass and took one to her.

'Drink this. It will calm you.'

'I don't need calming!'

'Yes you do. We both do.'

He walked to the window. It was raining. Why was it always raining in London, or was the greyness more noticeable here? What choices were left open to him? Alice had nobody else. She wouldn't even have a job when her waistline thickened. Nobody was going to employ a pregnant dancer, and how could she support herself, let alone a child? His child. If he were Nicholas he would put himself first. But he was not Nicholas, and would never be able to live with himself if he cast aside this pathetic girl at a time when she needed him most.

'We'll get married immediately.'

Alice gazed at his harsh profile. 'You don't have to marry me. I'll manage somehow.'

'I said I would. Please don't make this any harder than it already is. At least the child will be born legitimate.'

He leant against the window and, for one last time, allowed his thoughts to linger on something which had been cruelly snatched from him, and was now beyond his grasp. It would be kinder to them both if he did not contact Philippa again. Let her think he had deliberately deceived her. She would be hurt, but she was young and resilient and would soon forget him.

'Justin,' said Alice, her hand touching his.

He moved away from her.

'Leave me alone. Haven't you done enough damage?'

It was three months since Nicholas had last seen Philippa Russell. Both he and Ernest had used her during that time, but their negotiations had always been with Steve Noble.

At the moment, Nicholas was working on a perfume promotion and wanted to use Steve who, in turn, wanted to use Philippa. But Nicholas was unsure whether the girl was capable of the high level of elegance he sought, which was why she and Steve were sitting opposite him now. He wanted to make his own unbiased judgement.

She had changed, but he could not lay his finger on what was different about her. She had not gone out of her way to impress him. She was dressed in a suit with knee length, black leather boots, wore very little make-up, and had left her mane of tawny hair loose. Yet she looked marvellous, and he had been unable to take his eyes off her from the moment she came into his office. He should have remembered that elegance was an unconscious part of her, as it had been the first time they met. He wondered why he had doubted she might not be right for the perfume ad and its follow-up promotion.

Philippa knew why she was here. Steve did not believe in beating about the bush, and had told her she was about to be scrutinised. So she made no concessions. Either Nicholas used her, or he did not. It was as simple as that. Less simple was this meeting. Her nerves were already on edge as she waited for Justin to come back from Scotland. He had told her one week, and it was a fortnight since she had left there. Surely, he must return soon? And now she had to sit in this office, an arm's length from his brother.

Nicholas and Steve were discussing the boring technicalities which did not involve her and she wondered how much longer the meeting would go on. Nothing definite had been said, but she presumed she would be doing the promotion. She shifted into a more comfortable position.

'Has Justin told you we met in Scotland?' Steve asked.

Philippa tensed. What was he up to? She had refused to discuss Justin with him, even when he wore her down with his questions.

'Not that I recall,' Nicholas replied.

And then Steve displayed the kind of perception she did not expect from him.

'Is he back? He promised to get in touch. I took some photos of Loch Lomond which he particularly wanted to see.'

'He's been back for a week,' Nicholas said. 'I expect he has been too busy. He and Alice were married yesterday. It caught us all on the hop, as he never bothered to inform anyone beforehand.'

He was looking at Steve, but when the photographer suddenly turned to Philippa, so did Nicholas. All the colour had drained from her face, and the inner radiance she had emanated moments before was gone.

'Do you feel all right?' Nicholas half rose from his chair.

Her blank eyes met his. 'It's rather hot in here. As you don't seem to need me any longer, can I go?'

'Would you like some water?'

Philippa shook her head. Her legs were like jelly when she stood up. She swayed, then steadied herself – he and Alice were married yesterday – the words pounded through her brain. If Justin had lied about Alice, then he must have lied about everything else.

'I'll come with you,' Steve said.

'Please don't.' Her voice was curt. 'All I need is some fresh air.'

Steve looked worried as she left the office.

'Look, I'll phone,' he said. 'I ought to see her home.'

He was at the door before Nicholas stopped him.

'What's going on, Steve?'

'What do you mean?'

'Between you and her?'

The photographer frowned. 'I don't think that is any of your business.'

Steve caught up with her in the main entrance, but only because she was standing in the foyer, heedless of the people rushing to and fro. She was crying.

'I would never have asked about him had I known.' He stood in front of her, trying to shield her from the curious glances of passers-by. 'I really am sorry that you had to hear it so brutally, and from his brother.'

Philippa said nothing. She wiped the back of her hand across her wet cheeks and tried to get away from him. But Steve was blocking her path and she was incapable of thinking beyond a pain which was worse than anything physical.

'I'll take you home,' he said.

'No! Leave me alone. You were against us all along. I don't want you gloating now.'

'I tried to warn you not to get mixed up with him because I knew he . . . because they have been together for a long time. It was inevitable he would go back to her.' He reached for her hand. 'Let's get out of here.'

She followed him because she did not have the will to resist. She stood huddled in her coat while he searched for a taxi. When he finally hailed one down, he bundled her into it and gave the driver his own address.

'You said you were taking me home.'

Steve smiled. 'I don't think you should be alone at a time like this. I won't touch you. If I cannot be your lover, then I'll be your friend. And if I have to pick up the pieces, I will. Starting from tomorrow, I intend to work you to a standstill. You may not thank me, but work is the best cure for a broken heart.'

She stared at him, then sobbed violently and threw herself into his arms. Steve stroked her hair and said nothing. He meant what he said. He felt no sexual desire. They had come this far without the intimacy he craved, and perhaps their relationship was closer because of it.

Justin took his collection to the Huntington Gallery on a Monday morning in January. Noel Buchanan went with him, and when he introduced the Scotsman to Maggie she felt a faint stirring of recognition. She knew him from somewhere, but could not place the face or the name. She liked him. He was amusing and outspoken, and outrageously dressed in emerald green trousers and a scarlet turtle neck sweater, which clashed horribly with his carroty hair. In contrast, Justin looked tired and pale and barely spoke.

'I hope he's not going to break down on me,' she said when he was fetching the last of his paintings from the car. 'It happens sometimes. I was handling a promising young artist a couple of years ago who couldn't take the strain. He never reached the same standard again. It was a great pity.'

Noel was propping canvasses against the office walls. He straightened up. 'He's been working too hard. Not only on this collection, but he's also been teaching during the day, and spends too many evenings doing whatever commercial art his brother throws his way. Her doctor has forbidden Alice to work during her pregnancy and, to put it bluntly, they are skint.'

Maggie sat on the edge of her desk. 'How do you know all this?'

'Because I am his friend. Please don't repeat anything I have said. Justin is cursed with pride and refuses to let anyone, not even his family, know how badly off they really are.'

He stopped when he heard a murmur of voices in the gallery. Justin was coming back.

Maggie had tea brought in, then turned her attention to the array of paintings which filled her office. She did not hurry, but studied each one in concentrated silence, assimilating both their good and their bad points. He could turn his hand to practically anything, and did, but the canvasses which depicted a touch of genius followed a similar theme. It was those she would use in the exhibition.

'You don't think they are good enough?' he asked when she was finished.

His expression was not that of a man who would buckle under pressure. He had learnt a long time ago how to take the blows, then rise above them and fight back.

'What you have presented me is a mish mash of conflicting styles. You seem unable to decide which direction to take, so I shall make the decision for you, certainly as far as this exhibition is concerned.' She picked up a canvas of ponies grazing in the stark setting of mist-covered moorland. 'This is what you do best. You are a country artist, Justin. You were brought up in rural surroundings and have a sharp eye for the fine detail a town person would miss. The other stuff is good, but not outstanding. It would certainly not impress the critics, and they are the people with the power to make or break you.'

'When you refer to the country do you mean the scenery, or the animals, or something more obscure?'

'I mean everything. Your country scenes blend into a perfect whole, whatever the subject. Will you object if I only use them and throw the others out?'

'No,' he replied.

'Good. Let's get them sorted.'

They were almost done when Maggie remembered who Noel was.

'You are one of the Lochdunnan Buchanans. You used to pull my hair and tease me because I had a crush on your brother. I called you carrot tops once, and you refused to speak to me for a week.'

Noel looked up. 'You must be that evacuee who was sent to live with the MacMullen's until the end of the war.

Alistair and I used to call you Mags, which you hated.'

'I was hardly an evacuee. They are my aunt and uncle, and I still visit them occasionally.' She turned to Justin. 'We spent a lot of our early childhood together. The Buchanans were our nearest neighbours.'

He had no desire to be drawn into a conversation concerning Scotland. He had his own painful memories of his last visit there. He picked up a couple of the larger paintings which she wanted to use. 'I'll put these in the store-room.'

Maggie opened the door. 'There are times when that man can be downright obnoxious,' she said when he had gone.

Noel grinned. 'I know. But he'll always come through when you need him.'

'Have you been friends for long?'

'Almost ten years.'

She picked up a glass paper-weight and ran her fingers over its smooth surface. 'Do your family still own Lochdunnan?'

'No. My parents were forced to hand it over to the National Trust after the war. They didn't have the money to maintain it. We moved into Edinburgh, but were allowed to keep a small apartment at the back.' The grin faded. 'They were both killed in a car crash in 1954. Alistair inherited the title and brought me up. He's married now, with two sons, but he makes a point of going to Lochdunnan every year so the boys will not lose sight of their heritage.'

They were from similar backgrounds and Maggie could understand what he was saying. It was a sad fact that the hereditary owners of homes such as Lochdunnan were no longer able to afford their upkeep. Her father had been lucky, for by investing in property he had made enough money to hold on to his own estates.

'I take it you are also an artist,' she said.

'I sculpt. I don't have the temperament for dabbling with paint.'

'Are you any good?'

'I get by.'

'Don't listen to him.' Justin had caught the tail end of the conversation. 'He has been getting so many commissions he will soon have to turn them away.'

'I already have,' said Noel. 'I don't mind a bit of hard work now and again, but I object to slavery. And talking of slavery, I think I have done my fair share today. How about a drink and some lunch?' He winked at Maggie. 'We can reminisce over old times.'

A flush came to her cheeks. 'I'd like that.'

Something indefinable passed between them. Justin had seen Noel flirt often enough to know what was happening now. He could not understand why, for Maggie was the complete opposite to everything Noel sought in a woman. Her money might have been an enticement, but he doubted it. Perhaps he wanted nothing more than to talk with somebody who remembered, however vaguely, the times before the death of his parents.

'I promised Alice I would be back,' he said. 'I don't like leaving her alone too long. You two go ahead.'

Neither of them protested.

'I shall need you tomorrow to help with the cataloguing,' Maggie told him.

'I'll be here at nine o'clock. I can take away the other paintings then.'

As he left he heard Maggie laugh at something Noel said. He did not think them well matched, whatever their backgrounds. But who was he to criticise when he had made such a mess of his own life.

Maggie was keeping an anxious eye on Alice Lang. She was

a pretty little thing, but far too pale, and so delicate that a gust of wind could have blown her away. She wore a plain shift which hid her waistline. There was really no need, for nobody would have guessed she was six months pregnant.

The exhibition was going well. All but one of the invited critics had looked favourably upon Justin's work. But the ones who mattered most were impressed, and it was they who held his future in the palms of their hands. They had gone now, leaving a small core of friends and the inevitable hangers-on.

Nicholas had come alone, out of sheer pique because Philippa had refused to accompany him. He had asked her out on several occasions, but each time she turned him down. Nobody had ever refused him before and he found her disinterest infuriating. This was the first time Maggie had met him, and her initial impression was of a cold fish who lacked his brother's charm.

'If I yell fire do you think they will bolt into the street?' Noel came up behind her, placing his hands on her shoulders. 'Then we could lock the doors and slip away. I'm starving.'

Maggie laughed. She liked Noel, and her father approved of him. The Buchanans may not have been wealthy, but their line could be traced to the earliest Scottish kings.

'I'll give them another five minutes and then dim the lights.' She looked around the gallery, stopping at Alice. 'Do you think she feels okay? She looks awful.'

Noel followed her gaze. Alice was standing alone, a glass of orange juice in her hand. She had been aloof all evening, and Justin had been too much in demand to stay at her side for long.

'She's stronger than she looks,' he said. 'She had to be. She was a dancer. Maybe I should have a word with Justin.

Tonight may have been too much for her.'

Alice had not wanted to come. She knew she would be out of place, but Justin insisted she be there. She felt queasy before they left the flat, but did not tell him. He would think she was making excuses. She felt worse now, and longed to lie down. But this was his night and she was too frightened to ask if she could go home. There was Nicholas, who was lounging about on his own, but he had been drinking steadily all evening and drove too fast, even when sober. She did not get along with Noel, and found Margaret Hunting-ton-Smythe intimidating. She knew nobody else in the crowded gallery.

'Would you like to sit down in the office? It will be much cooler.'

Alice swayed dizzily, and would have lost her balance if Maggie had not grabbed her arm.

'You definitely need to sit down,' she said.

'I'll be all right,' Alice protested.

'My dear girl, you look ready to pass out at any moment. You shouldn't be standing around in your condition. Come along. Lean on me if you like.'

'I feel sick, that's all. I don't want Justin . . .'

'Noel is getting him. And stop worrying. I was about to chuck everyone out anyway.'

Alice did not have the strength to resist. There was a throbbing pain in her back and she really did feel awful.

Nicholas knocked back another glass of champagne. He knew he was drinking too much, but didn't care. He saw Maggie take Alice into the office, and Noel forcing a path towards Justin. He sighed. His brother was a fool. He should have insisted Alice have an abortion rather than go through with this sham of a marriage. He put down his glass. By the time he reached the office Alice was sitting down and Maggie was handing her some water.

'You should never have come,' he said. 'Would you like me to take you home?'

'It's all right, Nick. I'll look after her.'

The girl looked up. She was afraid, not because of anything Justin would say or do, but because of everything that would remain unsaid. He had married her, but in doing so had given nothing of himself, other than his name and a tolerant kindness. Brutality would have been preferable, for then he would have displayed some visible emotion.

'Thank you, Maggie.' Justin's eyes were resting on Alice. 'Why didn't you tell me you felt ill?'

'I'm not ill, only a little nauseous.' There was the merest trace of defiance in her voice, but suddenly it was gone. 'I didn't want to ruin your evening.'

Maggie saw his jaw clench. 'It's not ruined. It's finished now. I'll take you home.'

He put his hand beneath her elbow, but when she stood up an excruciating pain shot through her.

'What is it?' he asked as she doubled over.

She did not answer. Her legs buckled and he swept her into his arms. There was no weight to her, and he could count her ribs with his fingers. It was a miracle she had managed to carry a baby this long. If she got through her full term, the child, if it lived, was sure to be small and sickly.

Maggie rushed forward, alarmed by the girl's pallor and the way she was clenching her lips, as though to stop herself from crying out.

'You have to get her to a hospital,' she said.

'No . . . no hospital. Take me home, Justin. Please.'

His smile was reassuring. 'Of course I'll take you home. Nick, could you bring my car to the entrance? It's about fifty yards up the road.'

He struggled to fish the keys out of his pocket. Nicholas took them from him.

'I'd better drive,' he said.

'I'm so sorry ... so very, very sorry,' Alice murmured before slipping into semi-consciousness.

'Justin, she needs a hospital,' Maggie insisted. 'She could be losing the baby.'

He shook his head. 'I don't want to alarm her any more than necessary. She's always been terrified of hospitals. I wish I knew why, but I don't think she remembers herself. Could you telephone her doctor and ask him to come to the flat? Noel knows who he is.' He paused. They were meant to be having dinner together. 'And then you two go on to the restaurant. I don't want this to spoil everyone's evening.'

'I couldn't,' Maggie said.

'Yes you could,' Noel told her. He picked up a telephone directory and flicked through its pages. He knew there was nothing he or Maggie could do, and Nicholas would stay with his brother.

'She's asleep.' Justin closed the door behind him.

Nicholas stood up and handed his brother a tumbler containing straight whisky. Justin sank into a chair, the glass cradled in his hands.

'Thank you for staying.'

'Did you think I wouldn't? What are you going to do now?'

'What do you mean?'

'You heard what the doctor said. She was advised not to go ahead with the pregnancy. She could have had a legal abortion, but refused. She didn't even consult you.'

'Don't rub it in, Nick. What's done is done. If anything like this happens again she could not only lose the baby but her life. What choice do I have but to stand by her?'

'She's certainly wrapped you up in a neat little parcel.'

'That's enough, Nicholas! You are drunk.'

'A little, but not nearly enough.' He walked to the window, pulled back the curtain and gazed at the street below. 'It was a pity the exhibition had to end like this. Perhaps it's as well Mum couldn't come. She would have been worried sick.' He dropped the curtain, wandered across the room and picked up one of his brother's sketch-pads. He turned the pages slowly. 'Maggie thinks your star is in the ascendancy. But if you are short of money, don't be too proud to ask for help. It's not going to be easy for you, especially with Alice being bed bound until the baby is born.'

An uneasy smile creased Justin's lips. 'I don't want to borrow money, not unless I get desperate. Would you like something to eat, or do you have alternative plans?'

'Nothing whatsoever.'

'No girlfriends waiting with bated breath? I was surprised when you turned up alone. After all, you have a reputation as an eligible bachelor about town.'

'I did ask somebody, but she turned me down, and I was too furious to ask anyone else.'

Justin laughed. 'That must have been a crushing blow to your ego. Who was the brazen young woman?'

'Philippa Russell. She preferred to go night clubbing with Steve Noble.'

Had Nicholas been looking at his brother he might have guessed something from his expression. But he did not look up immediately, and when he did there was nothing for him to read in Justin's face.

'She has changed since you last saw her. But, of course, you did see her. Steve mentioned meeting you in Scotland last year.'

'Briefly, in Stirling. Rosalind was there as well.' Justin finished the whisky. He had not realised until now how indebted he and Philippa were to Steve for his continuing silence.

Nicholas was frowning. 'You don't approve, do you, big brother?'

'It's not a case of my approving. But there has already been enough bad feeling between our families.'

'Then it is high time the past was put behind us. If I have to be the one to hold out the olive branch, then so be it.'

Their eyes met. It was Justin who looked away first.

CHAPTER ELEVEN

Alvin Harwood decided the next series of Mermaid advertisements should be shot closer to home, and declared the Yorkshire Moors an ideal backdrop. Nicholas disagreed. The Mermaid Hosiery campaign was drawn up on more sophisticated lines. Not too sophisticated, of course, as it was targeted at a young and affluent market who needed to identify with the product. He told Harwood that the starkness of the moors would do nothing whatsoever for Mermaid's image. They argued and Harwood threatened to move his account elsewhere. But when Nicholas kept his head and coolly told him to do so, it was Harwood who lost his nerve. Nicholas Lang might be a brash young man, but since he had taken over Mermaid's advertising, sales had soared and were still climbing.

In the end they compromised. They would use London for the television advertisement which Nicholas was planning to shoot during summer. For the stills they would go to some northern cities. Liverpool was still predominant in the music scene, and Blackpool was an ever popular holiday town. Their brashness could be offset by the quieter splendours of York, and perhaps Durham with its ancient cathedral. Nicholas and Steve were working on the schedule when Ernest suggested they try a few shots in one of the Midland towns. Nicholas was unimpressed.

'Most people dream of getting out of those industrial wastelands. They don't want the dreariness brought home.'

'The Midlands do not begin and end in Birmingham,' Ernest retorted. 'There are some charming towns if you bother to look.'

'No,' Nicholas said. 'Harwood stipulated the north, and the north he shall have.'

Steve let them argue. He was thinking of Philippa. Since her unfortunate foray in Scotland five months ago she had driven herself to the point of exhaustion, accepting every assignment which came her way. There were a lot of them now. *Vogue* was starting to commission her on a regular basis and a variety of other magazines were jumping on the band-wagon. She continued to work almost exclusively with him, but would occasionally sit for other photographers if he okayed them. As a result of the exposure she was becoming identifiable, and as her popularity grew people were begin-ning to recognise her.

She had finally given up the job at Lady Jayne's, but it vexed Steve that she continued to pour every penny she earned into some run-down pottery in the West Country. For a start, she ought to be moving out of that awful flat into more up-market accommodation, but she refused to discuss the matter.

They had returned from Paris two days ago. The schedule had been punishing and the weather foul. In front of the camera Philippa had been effervescent, away from it she was jaded and edgy. He knew she was not looking forward to the Mermaid shoot. She needed something to bring back the sparkle, and Steve suddenly realised what that something could be.

'I wouldn't mind kicking off from one of the pottery towns,' he said. 'I hear those old bottle ovens are a sight worth seeing. And a few shots inside a pottery would be interesting.'

Nicholas stared at him. Ernest was dumbstruck.

Steve got his way because nobody could think of a legitimate reason to turn him down. The effect on Philippa was dramatic. She was over the moon at the prospect of seeing a working pottery.

She had no idea Steve was doing this for her. Industry bored him and he was unable to whip up any enthusiasm. He had brought Angie because he said she was good with the spotlights, but the fact that he was sleeping with her had something to do with his decision. Nicholas had offered a make-up artist and hairdresser, but Steve didn't want to travel in an entourage. Philippa had learnt her trade well and could cope with the free flowing Mermaid image.

The pottery could not accommodate them in the morning, so they did the outside locations first. It was a windy day and Philippa's hair was all over the place. In desperation, Steve made her stand face on into the gale while he shot her against a background of disused bottle ovens. He thought them the ugliest structures he had ever seen, but instinct told him these photographs would be outstanding. Philippa looked marvellous as she leant into the wind, her clothes and hair billowing out behind her.

They moved to three locations, each time drawing a crowd of curious onlookers. The old men shook their heads and the women tutted. The essence of the Sixties had not yet penetrated this corner of the world. Above-the-knee hemlines, heavily made-up eyes and backcombed hairstyles were in evidence, but Angie's skin-tight hipster pants, worn with an equally tight skinny rib sweater and no bra, left mouths gaping. Steve and Philippa could have come from another planet. His hair was shoulder length and he was wearing a psychedelic shirt with blue corduroy slacks, while Philippa was all eyes and legs, in what was loudly proclaimed as a disgustingly short skirt which no decent mother would allow her daughter to wear. The comments did not deter them. On the contrary, they became more outrageous as the morning progressed.

By eleven they had finished. The crowds dispersed, sadly wondering what the younger generation was coming to. Philippa threw a jacket over her shoulders and sat on a nearby bench, hugging her arms about her in an effort to keep warm. She watched Steve and Angie pack up their gear, then noticed a newspaper which had been jammed into the slats at the other end of the bench. She pulled it out and flicked idly through the pages. It was a local rag and of little to interest to her, but on the second page from the end, amongst the advertisements, she saw something which caught her attention. She searched her accessory bag for a pen and scrap of paper, then wrote down an address.

'Will you need me before this afternoon?' she asked Steve in the taxi.

'No. Why?'

'There's an auction I'd like to see. Can you drop me there?'

'What sort of auction?'

'A pottery. Everything is up for sale. Scrounging around for second-hand parts is something I have never considered.'

'Heaven help us! You *are* becoming obsessed. All right, I'll drop you off. But I want you back by two. Nicholas went to a lot of trouble to set up this afternoon's shoot.'

'Have I ever let you down? Here's the address. Can you give it to the driver?'

'If you walk in looking like that you're going to be ogled,' Angie said. She was squashed in a corner, cushioning the spotlights.

'I've grown used to it.' Philippa's voice was dry. She would have liked to go back to the hotel and change, but there was not enough time.

Steve grinned maliciously. 'I almost feel like coming with you, just to see the sensation you cause. I doubt there will be another woman in sight.'

Philippa smoothed down the folds of her skirt and stretched her long legs.

'It will give these staid menfolk something to tell their wives when they go home tonight.'

'Do you think they will tell their wives? . . . Will *dare* tell their wives?' Steve howled with laughter.

What Moor View could do with all this, Philippa thought as she gazed at moulds and potter's wheels and machinery which did not look as though it was about to disintegrate. There had been an initial stunned silence when she walked into the crowd of predominantly male buyers. They eyed her up and down, then decided it would be more prudent to ignore her altogether. It was not entirely successful, for whenever she approached a jostling group they opened up before her like the Red Sea parting for Moses, doffing their hats and grinning like a claque of village idiots.

This looked as though it had once been a thriving pottery, yet it had gone bust. So how did she have the gall to imagine she could keep Moor View going? She glanced at her wrist, but her watch was in the bag which Steve had taken back to the hotel. She decided it would be safe to stay a while longer, and stood in a quiet but draughty corner, listening to the bids and making a mental note of the prices being paid.

'You look cold,' somebody said. 'I thought you would appreciate some tea.'

A man held a paper cup towards her. She took it from him.

'Thank you.'

'You're welcome.' He smiled. 'I suppose you realise that you look as at home here as a leper on a health farm.'

Philippa laughed. 'I was interested in the auction and didn't have time to change beforehand.'

She did not elaborate, nor did he ask. He was shorter than she was, but solidly built, probably in his early thirties, with dark hair which was conventionally cut, and serious eyes. There was nothing striking about his square-cut features, but he looked like a man who knew where he was going.

Philippa sipped the tea. 'Are you here to buy?'

'No. Sentimentality. This was where I spent the first year of my apprenticeship. It could have been a profitable business if the family which owned it had relinquished some of their power and taken the advice of their managers.' He paused. 'By the way, I should tell you that I am probably the only person here who knows who you are. Nobody else can make head or tail of you.'

'Have we met before?' She featured predominantly in women's magazines, but it seemed unlikely he would recognise her from those.

'A long time ago,' he replied. 'You were a little girl, and I used to see you with your grandfather at Moor View. He would be pleased to know you are trying to hang on to it, even though my father thinks you are fighting a losing battle.'

Her eyes widened. 'Your father?'

'Everyone says we are nothing alike. I'm Rodney Slater.'

Nicholas found Steve glancing through magazines in the deserted public lounge.

'What are you doing here?'

Steve had not expected him and made a show of putting away the magazines, giving himself time to gather his wits.

'It's good to see you too, Nicholas. Is there a reason for

this visit, or were you passing through?'

'I wanted to see how the shoot was going. Obviously it isn't. Why?'

'A minor hiccup. They happen sometimes. I had to cancel this afternoon. We'll do it first thing in the morning.'

'You're meant to be leaving here first thing in the morning.'

Steve shrugged. 'So we'll leave later than planned. What difference does it make?'

'What difference does it make?' Nicholas scathingly repeated. 'This trip may be an insignificant breeze for you, but every minute you waste comes out of my client's pocket. We agreed the schedule and now, in less than twenty-four hours, you've thrown it out of the window. Half a day lost tomorrow and a full one the day after.'

'Sit down, Nicholas. You're getting yourself worked up over nothing.'

Nicholas ignored the advice. 'And where is our prima donna? She is conspicuous by her absence.'

'Philippa has a headache and is lying down.'

It was a feeble excuse, but all Steve could think of. He saw disbelief in the pale blue eyes.

'You work your models until they drop, and Philippa is no exception. If she had a headache you would tell her to take a couple of aspirin and get on with the job. If she is that ill, I insist on seeing her.'

'Don't bother. She's not here.'

'Where is she?'

'I don't know. There was something she wanted to do. She promised to be back, but she wasn't, so I cancelled the shoot.'

Nicholas felt a cold fury erupt inside him. 'Back from where?'

Steve sprang to his feet. 'How should I know? I'm not her

149

keeper!' He got a grip of himself. It was no good letting Nicholas get to him. 'Look, we can make up the time. I have never let you down before, and far worse things have happened. But I warn you, Nicholas, if you intend staying here, get off my back and leave Philippa alone. We work best as a close-knit team and if you are going to interfere we might as well pack up and go home.'

He walked to the door.

'Where are you going?' Nicholas demanded.

'For a walk. What else is there to do in this dump?'

Rodney Slater's impression of Philippa Russell was of a beautiful, self-assured young woman, who was also intelligent. He asked her to lunch, hoping they could continue their conversation in comfort, and was surprised by the enthusiasm of her acceptance. He took her to an inexpensive restaurant where the food was basic but good. Once there, Rodney found himself studying her carefully, partly because his wife, Daphne, would pester him with questions about what she was really like, but mostly from curiosity. She was no ordinary person. She was not yet twenty-one and, like a phoenix, had risen from the ashes of a well-publicised family scandal to become a top model. It was also something of an achievement that she still owned Moor View. True, it could not go on for much longer, but his father had expected it to close down long before this.

At first, they talked of the past, but inevitably the conversation drifted towards the present. Philippa was cautious, feeling her way through a subject on which she felt less than adequate. She had tried to learn more about the pottery and its internal workings, but Gideon treated her like a child who was incapable of understanding the intricacies of business, while Betty was a brick wall which it was impossible to circumvent.

'Gideon never told me you were in the same business,' she said over coffee.

'It's traditional. The Slaters have been a part of Moor View for as long as your family have owned it.'

'Then why are you here, not there?'

Her eyes were resting on his face. Daphne was sure to ask what colour they were. He decided they were neither blue nor green, but somewhere in between.

'Because I have a family to support, and Moor View is in its death throes. My father has nothing to lose. He should have retired years ago, but stayed on because he loves the place. I need stability. I have a four-year-old son and a baby on the way.'

'Whatever Gideon may have told you, I am not about to let the pottery go without a fight. I'm trying to learn more about it but, quite honestly, I find your father indulgent rather than helpful. He doesn't seem to realise that I am no longer a child.'

'What do you want to do with it?' Rodney was as blunt as she was.

'I want to build it into a viable business. Modelling is a short-term career which I am hoping will earn me enough money to set Moor View on its feet. But it needs a lot more than money. The last time I went there I realised what was wrong. It lacks youth. I am not running down the skills of the work-force or your father's devotion, but it needs someone with new ideas who is not afraid to try them out. Gideon won't take chances. He says they would be disastrous. So the pottery is going nowhere, except downhill.'

'Are you suggesting I could be that person?'

'It's more than a suggestion.'

She was impressed by Rodney Slater, judging him to be a steady man who would not take unnecessary risks. But there again, he was not staid. If he had to gamble, he would.

151

'You would like me to run Moor View, yet be wholly answerable to you for my actions?'

'I could hardly expect that of anyone. I would like you to work with me, in a wholly independent capacity. What Moor View needs is somebody who knows what the public wants and is capable of giving it to them.'

Rodney leant forward. This was a subject he knew inside out.

'What do *you* think the public wants?'

'Brightly coloured, chunky chinaware. It's what the shops are selling.'

'The shops sell what is popular at the time. The specialist shops sell what is popular all the time. Think about it. There is a marked difference between the two. Moor View has virtually no modern equipment. What it does have are craftsmen whose skills are wasted. I believe it should specialise, concentrating on small batches of high quality chinaware. You will find my father disagrees with me. He thinks it ought to compete in an already over-crowded market.'

Philippa picked up the coffee pot. Rodney did not want more, but she refilled her own cup.

'If the conditions were right would you consider taking over Moor View?'

'Ten years ago I would have been brash enough to give it a go, but I can no longer afford to take the chance. My father tells me the oven is unreliable. You have one kiln. If it keeps breaking down you face financial ruin.'

She thought of the money her father had left her, tied up in legal loopholes for another four years.

'There must be repairs which can be done until I can afford a new oven. I am not talking through the top of my head. Given time, I shall be able to afford one. Or do you think it unscrupulous to force Gideon into retirement?'

Rodney ran his thumb around the rim of his empty wine glass. 'My father would like nothing better than for me to step into his shoes. It's me who refuses to jeopardise my family.'

Philippa had never gambled, but she did so now. 'Not even if I guaranteed you a salary equivalent to whatever you are presently earning? I could also have my lawyer draw up a contract which will give you a free hand to make whatever changes you consider necessary. There is no capital, and I have a massive bank loan to pay off, but I could scrape together enough to get you going.'

'Your offer is tempting, but I cannot accept it.'

There had to be something which would make him change his mind. Moor View would have a fighting chance with him at the helm.

'You would be Managing Director, and I will give you fifteen ... no, twenty per cent of the company shares. You will not only have a positive say in the running of Moor View, but will also be on the board.'

He grinned. 'Do you have one?'

'I would if you joined me. It's the opportunity of a lifetime, Rodney, and once we begin to make a profit you'll be the first to benefit.'

'There won't be any profit unless Moor View succeeds.'

'It will if we work together. I won't be a burden. I want to learn. Talk it over with your wife, and Gideon too. Personally, I think we can do it, but I have always been an optimist.'

'You make it very hard for me.' The muscles around his mouth were tight. 'I shall think it over very carefully, but I'm making no promises.'

'I have not asked for any. I shall not be back in London until next Wednesday, which will give you plenty of time to make your decision. I'll give you my home telephone number.' She reached for her handbag. 'What time is it? I have a photo session at two-thirty.'

He glanced at his watch. 'You had a photo session. It's almost four.'

'It can't be!'

He held up his wrist so she could see for herself. 'You know the old saying, time flies when you are having a good time. Will you be in trouble?'

She threw caution to the winds. 'To hell with it! This is far more important.'

Steve was probably sulking. She asked for him at the reception desk, and was told he had gone out. She left a message saying she was back, then took her own key. He must have cancelled this afternoon's session, which meant she could clean off her make-up, wash her hair and languish in a hot bath. By then, she would be in the right frame of mind to withstand one of his tantrums.

'Where have you been?'

The breath caught in her throat. Surely, it could not be? Fate would never be so cruel.

'Do you realise that your disappearing trick has made a complete mockery of a minutely planned schedule?'

No, it was not. Nicholas had a more clipped voice, but you had to listen carefully to hear the difference. He was standing in the doorway of the public lounge, his hands on his hips and his pale eyes glowering. He was furious. But Philippa was in no mood to be browbeaten by anyone, least of all him. She glared back, her mouth a determined line.

'What are you doing here, Nicholas? Checking up on us?'

'It appears I should do so more often. You have not answered my question. Where were you?'

'I do not believe it is any of your business.'

He stepped forward. 'I disagree. Whatever you were doing was done in my client's time and you were being paid for it.'

'Then deduct this afternoon from my fees. I have no intention of quibbling over a few pounds. As for your precious schedule, Steve would have deviated from it somewhere along the line. He always does. Now, if you would excuse me, I should like to go to my room.'

Nicholas was not used to being answered back, especially by a feather-brained model whose only function was to look good.

'I have not finished with you! Come in here.'

'For a lecture? Forget it. I am answerable to Steve, not you. Where is he, by the way?'

'Here. I went for a walk.' Steve looked from one to the other, feeling the waves of tension which bounced back and forth between them. 'I told you to leave her alone, Nicholas.'

'I am perfectly capable of looking after myself,' Philippa said.

'And I have every right to know where she has been and why you are so eager to cover up for her.'

Nicholas was used to getting his own way, so was Steve.

'The only right you have is to demand high quality work from us, and that you shall have. Come along, Philippa, I'll take you to your room.'

He held out his hand. She took it.

'You had better keep your promise, Steve. Because I intend to penalise you for every day you overrun your schedule. In case you are unaware of it, there is a clause in your contract which I can invoke.'

'Do what you want. But if you withhold so much as a penny of our agreed fee I shall never work for you again, nor will Philippa if I can help it. You need us far more than we need you.'

155

As they stepped into the lift Nicholas wondered, not for the first time, if they were lovers.

Philippa said she wanted an early night, so Steve took Angie to a nightclub. She ordered coffee and a toasted sandwich from room service and had barely put down the phone when there was a knock at the door. She opened it, her expression contemptuous when she saw Nicholas standing there.

'What do you want?'

'To apologise. I saw Steve go out and wondered if you would join me for dinner.'

'No thank you. I am having something sent up. We have an early start tomorrow and I am sure you will be the first to criticise if I do not look my best.'

Nicholas did not rise to the bait. He wanted to mend bridges, not pull them down. 'I was wrong to lose my temper, but try and understand my predicament. How would it have looked if Alvin Harwood had been with me, wanting to see how the shoot was going?'

'But he was not with you. Had he been, I think he would have understood. If you will excuse me, Nicholas, I want to wash my hair.'

'Do you dislike me?' he asked before she could close the door. 'Or do you still resent what happened between our families? You and I were the victims, not the perpetrators. Don't you think it time to forgive and forget?'

Her expression hardened. 'If I had not forgiven and forgotten I could never have brought myself to work for you. Thank you for asking me, but I don't think dinner would be a good idea.'

Nicholas smiled. 'Even my company would be better than sitting alone in a dreary room.'

'That happens to be a matter of opinion.' He was

156

unsettling her. Nicholas lacked his brother's warmth and humour, yet there was an uncanny similarity between them.

'Look, let's start again. Please have dinner with me. We can stay in the hotel if you prefer, and you won't even need to change. You look perfect as you are.' He paused. 'I promise not to talk shop, nor will I ask where you were this afternoon.'

Philippa wavered. Dinner with him would be better than an evening spent alone, as long as she remembered he was not Justin, nor ever could be.

'I'll meet you in the bar in fifteen minutes. I have a reputation to maintain and I expect half the town is down there, hoping to catch a glimpse of the model from London. Why do you think Steve slid off? He hates being gawped at.'

The dining room had probably never been so full on a midweek evening. Philippa did not let down the curious. She looked magnificent in a short, pastel-coloured dress, and wore her hair built up with cleverly inter-woven false pieces which the inexperienced eye could not detect.

Nicholas was used to beautiful young women fawning over him, and automatically presumed Philippa would be the same once she had thawed out. He was wrong, for she remained indifferent to him the entire evening. She drank no more than half a glass of wine, barely touched the steak and salad she ordered, and left him to do most of the talking.

'Am I boring you?' he asked after a while.

'Of course not. It's been a long day, that's all.' In truth, there was no part of her life which she wished to share with him. 'When will you be leaving?'

'Tomorrow morning. I happened to be in this neck of the woods, and dropped by to see how things were going. I am not here to spy on you and Steve. I know better than that.

He is a brilliant photographer, but has always been temperamental.'

'He respects you.' Philippa sipped her wine. 'You give him a relatively free hand, whereas other advertising agencies expect to get exactly what they ask for. That's why he rarely accepts commissions from them.'

'What about you and him? I notice you have separate rooms.'

Her smile was conspiratorial. 'Only because we don't want to shock the natives. He sneaks into my room late at night and I throw him out at dawn.'

Nicholas was not sure how to take that, but then she laughed and he knew she was joking.

'I should like to see you again,' he said. 'Or will you turn me down?'

This evening had been pleasanter than Philippa had expected, but she did not want to take it any further. To become entangled with another member of the Lang family could only bring pain.

'I don't know.'

'Perhaps we could have dinner, or go to a discotheque. Get to know each other better.'

'I mean it, Nicholas. I really don't know.' She pushed back her chair. 'Thank you for the meal. No, don't bother to get up. Stay here and finish your drink. Goodnight.'

When she had gone Nicholas lit a cigarette and ordered a large brandy. He wanted to see her again, but was confused as to why. Was it because he found her an irresistible challenge? Or was he attracted by the beguiling young woman she had become? Whichever it was, he would need to tread carefully, for she was not going to be won over easily. He did not doubt he would succeed, for Nicholas never failed in anything he set out to do.

CHAPTER TWELVE

At the end of May, Alice gave birth to a baby girl. She was a tiny, red scrap with a shock of dark brown hair which could have been transplanted from her father's head.

The first time Justin saw his daughter she was in an incubator, screaming her lungs out. He looked at her for a long time, waiting for the surge of paternal love which never came. He felt nothing, not even the basic stirrings of protectiveness. She was simply another burden for him to bear.

When he was allowed to see her, Alice looked small and shrunken and extremely ill.

'I am only allowed to stay for a few minutes.' He kissed her cheek.

'Did you see the baby?' She had been given pain-killing drugs and her thoughts were disorientated.

'Yes,' he replied. 'How do you feel?'

'Tired, but happy. She's perfect, Justin. Don't you think so?'

He recalled the pinched-looking face which resembled nothing in particular.

'Of course she is.'

Maybe Alice sensed his lack of enthusiasm, or perhaps she felt she had let him down. They had never discussed this child. On the few occasions Alice did mention it he paid her scant attention.

'I am sorry it wasn't a boy.'

He laid his hand over hers. 'I never hankered for a son. I grew up with a younger brother and sister, and girls are far easier to handle. What are you going to call her?'

'I don't know. I thought she would be a boy. I wanted to call him Michael. It's a strong name for a boy. You name her, Justin. I want you to.'

'We can wait a few days until we find something which matches her personality.'

'New-born babies don't have much of a personality. No, you choose. I'll be happy with whatever it is.'

He did not want such an onerous task, but if he refused she would be upset.

'I'll think about it. You're half asleep. Would you like me to leave?'

'Not yet.'

He sat on the bed and talked about the past, not the future. He could see no future worth speaking of. When a nurse came to shoo him away Alice was asleep.

Justin stood in the brightly lit passage. He had no idea what time it was. He had brought Alice here last night and, for all he knew, it could be night-time again.

'You could have had the decency to let somebody know where you were.' The belligerent voice startled him. 'I was about to leave for my weekly squash game when Mum telephoned in hysterics because she had been unable to raise either you or Alice all afternoon. I went to the flat, and one of your neighbours told me she saw you leave at two o'clock this morning and presumed the baby was coming.'

There was still the look of an executive about Nicholas, even though he was wearing jeans and an old jacket over an open-necked shirt.

160

'I didn't think you would appreciate being woken so early, only to be told that Alice was going into labour.'

'Probably not. But I would have liked to know what was happening. So would Mum. This is her first grandchild and she's over the moon about it.' He grinned. 'So, what is it, a boy or a girl?'

'A girl.'

'And Alice?'

'Very weak and tired. She is sleeping now.'

Nicholas studied his brother's face. 'You look worn out, big brother. What you need is a strong drink followed by a slap-up meal. But first I want to see my niece. I'm an uncle! Do you know how old that makes me feel?'

The student nurse was very obliging. She held the baby close to the glass.

'She's a bit squashed-looking,' he said. 'I can't see any resemblance to you or Alice, although the hair colouring could be yours. I always thought babies were born bald. Do you think the nurse has the right one?'

'She's tagged. And I expect you were a bit squashed-looking after you popped out of Mum's womb.'

Nicholas shot his brother a filthy look, but Justin ignored him. He was gazing at his daughter. He did not look like a proud father, and seemed relieved when the nurse took the baby back to the incubator. As he turned away, Nicholas fell into step with him.

'You ought to telephone Mum. I promised one of us would. Have you decided on a name? She is sure to ask.'

'Alice wants me to choose one.'

'Then I'd hurry up if I were you. Otherwise she is going to suggest you name her after a long-departed relative, probably great aunt Ermintrude. Helen narrowly missed being called that!'

Justin smiled. 'I can't think straight at the moment. But

no child of mine is going to be lumbered with a name like Ermintrude!'

Nicholas was in a lavish mood and splashed out on a bottle of champagne. After all, they did have something to celebrate, although nobody would have guessed it from his brother's morose expression. Nicholas knew Justin must be tired, but he had known him work forty-eight hours at a stretch without showing any ill effects. No, this was more than tiredness. It was an accumulation of disappointments which had built up from the day he married Alice.

He was also dogged by cash flow problems, made worse now he had a family to support. His exhibition may have been a critical success, but it was going to be a long time before he became well enough established to live off his work, if he ever did. Nicholas wondered if he should say something to their mother when she came up the next day. He was fetching her from the station and would have the opportunity. But if Justin learnt he had interfered he was liable to get on his high horse and they would end up by arguing.

After dinner, Justin suggested a nightcap and Nicholas accepted, hoping they would find it easier to talk in the flat.

'Have you given any thought to the future?' He sipped the cheap brandy which was all his brother had been able to offer. 'This flat may be cosy for two, but it will be hell when Alice brings the baby home.'

'We can cope for a while longer,' came the negative reply. 'We still have to decide whether or not we want to remain in this area.'

'I take it you would prefer to move back into the country and she wouldn't?'

Sometimes, it was easy to forget how well Nicholas knew him.

'Alice has always lived in the city. The countryside frightens her. And she wants to go back to work.'

'What about the baby?'

'That's her responsibility, not mine.' Justin peered into his empty glass. He had drunk a lot tonight, but the alcohol was having no effect on him. 'I have been offered a full-time teaching post and I'm in half a mind to take it.'

'I could get you a job tomorrow at triple the salary, and not necessarily at McCullogh, Staines & Ray, although I would be the one to suffer if you went elsewhere.'

'I hate commercial art. You know that. I find it too restricting and I could never put up with the demands of an advertising agency. Anyhow, I haven't decided whether I should take it. Maggie has a prospective buyer lined up for a couple of my paintings. I'm waiting to see if she sells them. If she does, we'll be solvent for a while.'

Nicholas emptied his glass, then balanced it on the chair arm. 'If I ask you a question, will you give me an honest answer?'

'Don't I always?'

'You used to. Nowadays, you are more evasive. We both know Alice is stifling you. Why do you insist on being so loyal to her? You should have got out a long time ago. You still could. You know she tricked you into this marriage.'

Justin's eyes were sharp as they rested upon his face. 'Get your facts right, Nick. She was pregnant, but it was me, not her, who suggested marriage. I don't have your mercenary attitude, and Alice would fall to pieces if I left her now. Despite what you may think, I am still fond of her. I also have a responsibility towards the child.' He stood up and walked to the far side of the room, where he stopped to look at a half-finished canvas. 'What about your life, Nick? Shall I pick it to pieces like you are doing with mine?'

'Pick away,' his brother replied. 'I work hard during the

163

day and play hard at night. I like to go night-clubbing with a pretty girl who will not be averse to rounding off the evening in my bed.'

'There are times when you display the mentality of a spoilt child. Don't you ever tire of meeting the same people night after night and week after week?'

'Contacts, not people,' Nicholas corrected. 'In my line of work it pays to be seen with the right people. My clients like it, and I'm not complaining.'

'At your age it's about time you got yourself a steady girlfriend. Too much bed-hopping and your reputation is going to take a few knocks. The majority of your clients are middle-aged men with families. They may indulge in the odd affair, but you can be sure they want their business associates to be squeaky clean.'

'Oddly enough, I am working on it. Ernest and I are thinking of starting our own agency. If we do, I shall need the trappings of respectability. I have taken a shine to Philippa Russell. I don't know why. Maybe it is because she keeps turning me down. Nobody has done that since my university days.' Nicholas smiled. 'Her popularity has taken an upward surge recently and her career keeps getting in the way. She's in the States at the moment, doing a layout for American *Vogue*, and when she gets back she and Steve will be off again flitting around the world until the end of summer. But she has to slow down eventually, or collapse from exhaustion.'

He did not notice the abrupt lack of colour in his brother's face, for Justin was standing in shadow.

'Have you considered what you would term the impossible? That she dislikes you?'

Nicholas let the sarcasm wash over him. He had seen little of Justin these past few weeks and was beginning to realise how much strain his brother was under. He wondered if he should ask his mother to stay over for a few days.

'I think Philippa is playing hard to get,' he said. 'We had dinner when she was doing the last Mermaid shoot and a couple of times, when she thought I wasn't looking, I caught her watching me. She had an odd expression on her face, but it was not one of dislike.'

Justin went to the window and flung it open, breathing in the chill night air. It was feasible that he and Nicholas could be attracted by the same woman, as could Philippa see the same qualities in them both. His heart dropped like a stone. For him the past was over and there could be no future with her. It would be ironic if she found happiness with his brother.

'I shall call her Jennie. You can tell Mum when you fetch her.'

Nicholas was feeling exceptionally slow tonight. 'Jenny? What are you talking about?'

'My daughter, of course.'

Justin left the window and picked up the brandy. Nicholas was staring at him.

'Jenny? Don't you mean Jennifer?'

'No.' Justin refilled his brother's glass. 'I mean Jennie, spelt with an "ie".'

'I'm not sure if Mum will approve.'

'She will have to put up with it. I can name my child whatever I want.'

CHAPTER THIRTEEN

Rodney Slater moved to a rented house in Tavistock at the beginning of August, accompanied by his wife, son Peter and newly born twin daughters. His father guided him through his first week at Moor View, then he was on his own. Philippa was still abroad, which gave him time to settle down and assess what preliminary changes needed to be made. When she appeared three weeks later, those changes were already in hand. Most noticeable was that the obnoxious Betty was gone. She had not wanted to work for a younger man and chose to retire with Gideon. In her place was Louise Albright, a cheerful young woman in her mid-twenties who had recently married.

Philippa and Rodney spent a whole day closeted together. He wanted Moor View to become more studio-orientated, producing an exclusive range of individual pottery. He also wanted to manufacture high quality chinaware. But all that was still a long way off. For the moment, they had to continue with the cheap range of tourist items which was their bread and butter.

Philippa was earning good money now and was able to hand him a cheque for £1000, to use as he saw fit. She knew it was a drop in the ocean, but it would enable him to buy the raw materials he needed to make an initial firing of a bone china tea service. It would be a strictly limited edition which might not work. Even if it did, Rodney did not expect to go into any sort of production before the end of the year. There was too much to be done beforehand.

'We have to take one step at a time,' he told her.

With Rodney there were no 'ifs'. He breathed new life into Moor View and by November some individual items were filtering into the local shops. The pottery barely covered its costs, but the effect on the employees was dynamic, and Philippa could feel renewed optimism when she went there.

It was in January 1966 that Rodney made a breakthrough with his tea set. He had cast a variety of moulds, some of them successful and others disasters which ended up on the slag heap. But now the final design was ready and Philippa was impressed. The china was finely textured and had a pleasing fragility, its colour being off-white with a bluish tinge. The pattern was taken from one of the old pattern books. It was hand painted, the predominant colours being moss green and grey, with ochre tendrils which offered an eye-catching splash of colour. To give added quality there was a narrow border of gold, not paint, but expensive gold leaf.

'This is fabulous, Rodney.' She held the cup to the light. 'It's almost translucent. I don't know how you managed it with our rag-bag equipment.'

'It took a lot of sweat and dedication. It was not cheap to produce, and we will have to sell at a high price through specialist outlets to recoup our money. If we decide to go ahead, you will have to arrange another bank loan.'

She put aside the cup and picked up the teapot, holding it in both hands. 'I don't think that should present any problems now the existing loan is down to a manageable figure.' She lifted the lid off the teapot and peered inside. 'Will it turn a funny colour when filled with tea?'

'All teapots turn a funny colour. The tea leaves stain them.'

'I mean when you pour in the water. Does the level show from the outside?'

'Of course not,' he laughed. 'Only if you hold it up to the light like you are doing now. Well, do we go ahead?'

The question was irrelevant. 'When will the first batch be ready?'

'By Easter, barring any disasters. Before then we must decide if we will continue with this line should the demand be sufficient. We also have to plan our next project and discuss the contract for the souvenirs. It's due for renewal in September. I know that's still a long way off but, in terms of the agreement, both sides have to give three months notice as to whether or not they intend to renew. They bring in a steady, if unspectacular flow of bread and butter money, but do nothing for Moor View's image. Personally, I think we should cut our losses and ditch them. They are killing our reputation.'

'You are the expert. Do what you think best.' Philippa put down the teapot. 'How will you get these tea sets into the specialist outlets? Do you have any contacts?'

'None whatsoever.' He smiled, and in his expression she detected a shadow of ruthlessness. 'We need publicity, and the best way is by having your name linked with Moor View. I know you would prefer not to, but we both have to make sacrifices if we are going to get this company up and running.'

He was right, although Philippa was loath to make public the one part of her life which she had successfully managed to keep private.

'If I announce I own a pottery it will be a five-minute wonder which is quickly forgotten.'

'You are already involved in the world of advertising. There must be people whose brains you can pick. Better still, couldn't you persuade somebody to draw up a cheap,

168

but effective advertising campaign?' Nicholas came to mind, but what would he want in return? 'We also need to produce a catalogue. Initially, it will consist of two or three pages. A good photographer would make an enormous difference. You must be on excellent terms with any number of those. Daphne tells me your name has been linked with Steve Noble. I understand he is one of the best.'

Nobody could accuse Rodney of not being blunt. Philippa shuddered at the thought of Steve and inanimate objects.

'I shall do my best, but I cannot promise him.' She caught his eyes. 'Contrary to popular rumour, he is not, nor ever has been my lover.'

It was the first time she had seen a grown man blush.

When Philippa returned to London her elation was short lived. Steve was like a bear with a sore head and Nicholas was away until the end of the week. She left a message with his secretary for him to contact her. She had been out with him twice since he had turned up at the Mermaid shoot in the spring. He had pestered her so much that she had agreed to dinner in December.

He had taken her to a popular show, followed by a late supper, and she had been surprised by how much she enjoyed his company. He had then asked her to partner him to a New Year Ball, an invitation she willingly accepted. It was there she discovered she was socially acceptable again, on coming face to face with many of the so-called friends from her childhood. Nicholas was amused by the way she greeted them politely before proceeding to cut them dead. She had not seen him since then. She had been too busy, and so had he.

Steve was impossible all week. Not a day passed when they did not quarrel about something, and when Friday came Philippa breathed a sigh of relief. Nicholas was due back later that day and she was meeting Maggie for lunch. Halfway through the morning, in the middle of a three-hour session with Steve, four dozen red roses arrived by special delivery.

On the card was written 'Dinner tonight at 8.00'. It was signed Nicholas, and written in his distinctive hand. He must have come back earlier than planned and arranged for the flowers to be sent immediately.

'I was beginning to think you had forgotten me!' Maggie put down her second glass of sherry and sprang to her feet.

'No chance of that,' said Philippa, kissing her cheek. 'The session overran and I couldn't get away any earlier.'

She sat down and ordered a glass of wine. It was two months since she had last seen Maggie, and she looked different. She had lost weight and her hair was cut in a fashionable geometric style which made her look younger.

'You look marvellous,' Philippa said.

'You look strained. Is Steve working you too hard?'

'No, I am working me too hard. Steve is being pig-headed. He likes to be out and about, not stuck in a studio. You really do look great. What prompted the change of image?'

Maggie shrugged. 'I was putting on too much weight. Do you have to rush back?'

'No. I'm free for the rest of the day.'

'Good. We can enjoy a leisurely lunch, and then you can come back to the flat for tea. I have invited someone over who is eager to meet you.'

'Who?'

'Noel. I wanted you to meet him a long time ago, but you were never around when he was.' She paused. 'He proposed to me last week and I accepted.'

Philippa was stunned. It took her a moment to find her voice. 'Congratulations. I am so happy for you. Do you have a ring yet?'

Maggie's eyes were glowing as she laid her hand on the table. The ring was a cluster of diamonds surrounding a sapphire. It was pretty, but no different from the rows of rings which could be seen in any high street jeweller's shop window. Philippa tried to remember what, if anything, she knew about this Noel.

'Is he the sculptor?' she asked.

'Yes. We have decided on a September wedding, which Daddy insists takes place in our local parish church.' She too looked at the ring. 'He's not wealthy, but neither is he a fortune hunter.'

'Will you be giving up the gallery?'

'Good heavens, no! I am a career woman, not some starry-eyed housewife.'

'What about children?'

'I'd like one, perhaps two. But I shall arrange my life around them.' She paused when the waiter brought Philippa's wine. 'I want you to be my maid of honour.'

There was a hint of sadness in Philippa's smile. 'Thank you, but you know I cannot accept. It is your day, Maggie. What if I inadvertently hogged the limelight? Your father is sure to arrange for some society photographers to be there, and other members of the press could turn up.'

'I don't care about the press.'

'But I do, and would prefer to come as an ordinary guest.' She raised her glass. 'Here's to your happiness.'

'Are you sure you won't change your mind?'

'Positive.'

Philippa did not need to be introduced to Noel Buchanan. She recognised him. 'You are the spitting image of your ancestors. I saw their portraits at Lochdunnan Castle.'

'You never told me you went there,' Maggie said.

'Only briefly. It was my first assignment for *Vogue*. You must remember, I went with Steve and Rosalind Harper in November sixty-four.'

Noel stared at her. 'I can't recall my brother giving permission for anyone to film there. You must have joined a tour.'

Too late, Philippa realised her mistake. Lochdunnan had been closed to the public, and he knew it.

'I must have,' she said. 'It was a long time ago.'

It was not an auspicious start, and although he said nothing more about Lochdunnan, she was uneasy in his presence. She left as soon as she politely could.

By the time Nicholas arrived her nerves were on edge. She would have preferred to go somewhere quiet, but he had booked a table at the most popular restaurant in London. It was exorbitantly priced, and celebrities went there for the specific purpose of being seen. Conversation was impossible, as they were constantly interrupted by people who knew them.

'I thought you would be impressed,' Nicholas said when Philippa pushed aside her plate. She had not enjoyed the meal and had eaten very little of it. 'You are the only woman I have brought here who hasn't been.'

'How many have you brought?' She grinned. 'You forget I grew up with all of this. There was never any novelty or glamour that I remember. It was an accepted way of life.'

He leant his elbows against the table, his pale eyes studying her face. 'What does interest you, Philippa? You shun nightclubs and turn down invitations to parties which people would kill to get into. I know, because I often meet Steve and your other contemporaries at them.'

172

A waiter removed her plate and offered her a menu. Philippa declined it and ordered coffee. 'I dislike large crowds and noisy music. And those so-called parties are farcical. Steve took me to one last year. Half the guests were having it off in the bedrooms, and any other vacant room they could find, while the other half were queuing up for reefers. I was bored to tears.'

Nicholas laughed. 'We obviously receive invitations to different kinds of parties. Why did you want to see me?'

'Because I need some advice. But we can't talk here with all these interruptions.'

'Here was I thinking you had finally succumbed to my charms. Shall we forget the coffee and go back to my flat?' He saw anger in her eyes. 'I am not about to seduce you, Philippa. I doubt I should get very far if I tried. We can go to your place if you prefer. Or do you have a better idea?'

He lived in a tastefully furnished flat close to the Chelsea Barracks. It had luxurious, thick-pile carpets and central heating. Philippa knew she could afford to live like this if it were not for Moor View. After he had made fresh coffee he told him about her pottery.

'Are you intimidated by the prospect of me owning a business?' she asked when he passed no comment.

'Surprised would be a better word,' he said. 'Does Steve know? But of course he must. You keep no secrets from him. Somehow, I cannot picture you working in a pottery, not with those nails. What do you want from me?'

'Some ideas for an advertising campaign – a small one. We cannot afford to pay you.'

'If I freelance I shall be breaking the rules of my contract of employment.'

Philippa's expression did not change. 'I thought you, of all people, would not be afraid to take a risk.'

Nicholas stood up and poured brandy into two goblets. He offered her one and she took it gratefully. She needed something to steady her nerves.

'I never said I wouldn't help you.' He was smiling. 'But I shall need to look over this pottery of yours. Tavistock is not too far from my home. We could go down for a long weekend. You need not worry about your reputation, as my mother and sister can act as chaperones.'

Philippa found herself looking at Nicholas in a different light. Up to now she had been wary of him, even though, since their initial antagonism, he had never treated her with anything but respect. He was a businessman and could be ruthless, but he was also very like his brother.

'Steve and I are leaving for the Caribbean a week on Sunday. We'll be away for ten days, so it will have to be after that.' She drank a little of the brandy. 'I would rather not stay with your family. It could be awkward. I understand from Maggie that Harlequin House is not far from the village where you live. She has been nagging me to visit it, so I could kill two birds with one stone.'

'My mother does not hold grudges. You will like her. But if you will feel more comfortable, by all means stay at Harlequin House. I have not seen the place since it was done up. I expect it is quite different now. When we were children, Justin and I occasionally rode over there. The house was empty and we used to climb in through a broken window.'

Philippa panicked. Would Justin be there? No, of course not, for he lived here, in London, with his wife and child.

'I am impressed,' said Nicholas. 'This stuff is good, although your production line leaves a lot to be desired. Am I right in presuming you are operating on a hit and miss basis?'

'We want to specialise, which means more craftsmanship

174

and less mass production,' Rodney told him. 'All our lines will be limited, including this tea service. What we want to know is whether you will be able to create an interest in what is essentially an old-fashioned concept. Philippa assures me you are the best in your field.'

She could have throttled him for saying that. Nicholas turned to her, his pale eyes glowing.

'Does she now?' he asked.

'I said you were among the best. If you can help create a market for this, then I might concede you are the best.'

He smiled. 'Specialised goods require a specialised market. With your budget it will be difficult, but not entirely impossible. Firstly, I shall need a lot more technical information. I like to know what I am dealing with before I consider marketing strategy.'

This was Rodney's field, not hers, and Philippa told him so. As the two men talked she let her thoughts wander. They had done the full tour, showing Nicholas both the best and the worst. He had been surprised by the size of Moor View and she wondered if he had expected a dingy studio with a single potter's wheel.

Rodney launched into a technical description of the firing technique used on the tea service. She went to the window, gazing into the yard where the weeds had been cleared from the banks and turf laid. By the old bottle oven a lone daffodil struggled for survival. She made a mental note to have daffodil bulbs planted in all the beds, then next year Moor View would be how she remembered it as a child.

She could feel a warm glow inside her, and not only because she was conscious of Nicholas watching her. For the first time Philippa was thinking ahead positively. Progress was slow, but her pottery was going to be a success. There would be another spring, and many more after that.

★

It was dark outside and raining. Everyone else had gone home and an eerie silence had settled over the pottery. Philippa's back was aching from sitting for too long on a hard chair, and she was hungry. All she had eaten was one of the rubbery sandwiches which Louise had brought in at lunchtime.

Nicholas looked up from a stack of notes. There were lines of weariness beneath his eyes. It had been an even longer day for him. He had driven here.

'You would definitely benefit from a pre-launch campaign,' he was saying. 'Create enough interest and the buyers will approach the pottery, which automatically places you in a stronger position. As you are ready to launch now, you need something which will hit the public in the face. Rodney is right, Philippa. Moor View has to be linked with you. Philippa Russell has become a household name and, as such, is instantly recognisable.'

'I know,' she said. 'I will do whatever is necessary. But remember our prices will be too high for the general public.'

'While any advertising will need to be restricted to the trade magazines which the public never sees,' Rodney added, 'the nationals are beyond our reach.'

'I realise that.' Nicholas was sounding very confident. 'Give me a few days to put something together and then we'll discuss where we are going to place it.' His eyes sought Philippa's. 'What about Steve? I presume you have roped him into this.'

She grinned. 'I did mention it during our last trip, when he was in one of his better moods. He told me he does not take snaps of cups and saucers, but he might consider doing it for me. I think we can safely call that a yes.'

This was his neck of the woods and Nicholas took Philippa

for dinner at an excellent fish restaurant in Plymouth. Afterwards, they walked along the Hoe, but it was bitterly cold and they returned to the car.

'What would you like to do tomorrow?' he asked. 'Mum is expecting you for Sunday lunch, but other than that we are free to do what we want. Let's forget business and enjoy ourselves.'

Philippa was not looking forward to meeting Sarah Lang. She imagined her as a tall, thin woman with swept-back hair and a booming voice. Unfortunately, there was no way she could avoid Sunday but, as Nicholas suggested, they could enjoy themselves tomorrow.

'I'd like to see Cornwall. It is one of the few places where I have never been.'

'You'll find it rather different from the Caribbean,' Nicholas laughed.

He took her back to Harlequin House and walked with her into the lobby.

'I'll fetch you at nine,' he said.

He kissed her cheek and left.

CHAPTER FOURTEEN

———◆———

Philippa was enchanted by the Cornwall Nicholas showed her. It drizzled for most of the day, with mists drifting in from the sea and giving the rugged coastline a sense of timelessness. The weather also had the effect of keeping away all but the hardiest tourists. He dropped her at Harlequin House shortly before midnight, promising to fetch her at ten the following morning.

She went up to the suite where Maggie had insisted she stay as a non-paying guest. It was twice the size of her flat, with magnificent views over the moors. She made herself a cup of tea in the little kitchenette, then sat beside a window and stared into the darkness. The cloud was beginning to lift and she could see a couple of stars. Nicholas had not attempted to kiss her when he left, not even on the cheek. He puzzled her. She knew his reputation as a womaniser and yet, with her, he was the perfect gentleman. Too perfect in some ways. After spending two days in his company she was beginning to like him much more than she had thought possible, and she was sure he liked her too. So why was he going to such lengths to keep his distance? She was no nearer a solution when exhaustion drove her to bed.

She dreaded Sunday. She woke early and panicked over what to wear. Nicholas had said casual, but casual in London had an entirely different meaning to casual in the country.

She knew there were horses, and it stood to reason there would be dogs and cats and perhaps some other animals as well. She decided to dress down, and wore jeans with a pullover, very little make-up, and her hair pulled back from her face. Even so, she bore little resemblance to the average girl next door.

Sarah Lang turned out to be nothing like Philippa had expected. She was plain and dumpy, with short hair which was more grey than brown, and a kindly face. Neither of her sons resembled her.

'So you are Philippa,' she said when they met. 'No wonder my son is enamoured. You are every bit as lovely as your photographs.'

Nicholas enamoured? She glanced in his direction, but he had his back to her as he hung their jackets on a crowded row of pegs.

'He was determined I meet you,' she said. 'I hope my coming here is not too awkward.'

'Awkward? Of course not. I hold no grudge against you, my dear. You must have been a child when all the unpleasantness happened.'

The easy-going charm was something her older son had inherited. With Nicholas it was more of an effort. Justin had inherited something else as well, for when Sarah smiled a chill passed through Philippa. The smile was his.

'Where is Helen?' Nicholas asked his mother. 'I told her to be here.'

'She's gone to visit some friends in the village and promised to be back in time for lunch. Don't scowl, dear. It is not a tragedy. Anyway, I thought you had made your own plans for this morning.' She took hold of Philippa's arm. 'I have half an hour before my next lesson. Come into the kitchen and I'll make us some tea.'

The kitchen was large and untidy, with two dogs sprawled

179

on a rug in front of an old-fashioned stove. Two cats were curled up on chairs, and another on a scrubbed wooden table. It was a homely, lived-in room. The kettle had already boiled and Sarah quickly made the tea. She also placed a large cake and a tin of biscuits on the table.

'You are thin as a rake,' she said when Philippa declined any food. 'A little cake won't hurt you. Lunch won't be ready before two. I have to give a riding lesson first, and Nicholas wants to take you for a hack on the moors. He says you can ride. But don't let him force you if you don't want to.'

The more she got to know Sarah Lang, the better Philippa liked her. She was straightforward and genuine. For this family the death of a husband and father must have been a tragedy. For Philippa, the death of her father had been an inconvenience.

Later on, while Sarah organised a group of schoolgirls, Nicholas saddled up two bay cobs. While he did so, Philippa stroked the nose of an inquisitive chestnut mare.

'That's Copper,' he said. 'She belongs to Mum. She's nearly fifteen and getting a bit long in the tooth, but used to be a marvellous jumper. She might have got somewhere had Justin persevered with her. He's the only other person who was allowed to ride her. The trouble was he had the skill and not the inclination. With him, art always came first.'

'I saw him ride her once.'

'Of course you did. I'd forgotten. Here, you take Ben. He's steady as a rock, and wouldn't blink an eye if a bomb exploded under his nose. Do you want a leg up?'

'I can manage.' She had learnt to ride in Hyde Park's Rotten Row in her early teens. It had been a short-lived craze, but she had been fairly proficient, and being able to ride was an advantage when she visited the homes of friends who owned their own horses.

180

Her skills, such as they were, soon came back, and within fifteen minutes she was trotting like an old hand and confidently attempting a canter. Nicholas was as excellent guide, surprising her with his knowledge of the countryside. He took her to the base of Flint Iron Tor, which was smaller than it looked from a distance. Close up, it was oddly shaped, resembling a toad with a sloping back, and a crown of upright slabs of rock where its head should have been.

'If you feel up to it, there is a reasonable path leading to the top,' Nicholas said. 'The view from there is well worth seeing.'

'I should love to go up, even if I am stiff as a board tomorrow.'

The path was rocky in places, but not too steep, and she could see the imprints of other shod hooves. They dismounted at the summit and Nicholas hitched up the reins, letting the horses graze.

'They won't stray,' he said, taking her hand and leading her to a narrow, stone ledge which jutted from the side of the tor.

He was right about the view. It was breathtaking. He put an arm around her waist, and she leant against him as he pointed out the more distinctive landmarks, the drifting herds of wild ponies, and a kestrel hovering high above their heads. Every so often Philippa glanced at him, needing to reassure herself that this was Nicholas, not Justin. In the atmosphere of this place she was finding it increasingly difficult to distinguish between the two.

'Let's sit down,' he said after a while.

'Shouldn't we get back?'

'There is no hurry. My mother is a haphazard housekeeper at the best of times, and always puts the animals first. I'll be surprised if lunch is ready by three.'

'I like your mother. She is nothing like I imagined.'

181

He sat on a fallen slab of stone and drew her down beside him. 'I said you were working yourself into a state over nothing. She would have told me if she didn't want to meet you.'

There was a hint of spring up here. Primroses were flowering between the rocks and a carpet of yellow flowers was interwoven with the spiky grass. Philippa heard a shod hoof strike stone, and somewhere close by a bird called. Nicholas said her name. As she turned her head his hands gripped her shoulders, and then his mouth came down on hers. It was a lingering kiss, but strangely chaste, which left her yearning for something more. What that was she dared not contemplate. One man had swept her off her feet. Did she expect all men to do the same? Had she experienced true love, or an erotic sexual desire which would have burnt itself out?

'What are you thinking?' Nicholas asked.

His face was close to hers and his hands still resting upon her shoulders.

'How lovely it is here, and how much I would like you to kiss me again.'

He did, and although she put her arms around his neck and he held her close, it was not the same. She knew it was never going to be the same.

Helen had been a child when Philippa last saw her. Now she was sixteen and nothing like her brothers, except for the pale eyes which she and Nicholas shared. She was a shy, overweight teenager who said barely a word as they ploughed through an enormous meal.

'You peck at your food like a bird,' Sarah remarked as she watched Philippa eat.

Nicholas sprang to her defence. 'She is a model and has to be thin.'

Philippa's smile was for him, her words for his mother. 'The food is excellent, but I never have been a big eater. My figure has nothing to do with it. I don't put on weight easily, and have never dieted.'

'Lucky you. I only have to look at food to get fat.' It was the most Helen had said. She poured a liberal helping of custard over her apple pie, then gazed shyly at the young woman who sat opposite her. 'How do you make your eyes look like that? I practise for hours but mine always look messy.'

Her brother looked irritated. 'Don't be a pest, Helen.'

Sarah frowned, and Helen turned crimson. Philippa was sorry for the girl. Her own teenage years had been miserable, but for totally different reasons.

'Don't mind him,' she said. 'I'll let you into some of the trade secrets later on.'

Helen had a large bedroom, with a view of the moors which was partly obliterated by a row of trees.

'You're lucky to have all this at your back door,' Philippa said after she had shown the girl how to make up her eyes. 'I live in a basement flat with no view at all, other than brick walls and dustbins.'

Helen had been admiring herself in the mirror, but she suddenly leapt to her feet. 'I'll show you an even better one.'

She took Philippa to a larger room than hers. It had natural beams, a sloping ceiling and inglenook windows with box seats beneath them. There were rugs on the floor, and the walls were covered in pictures. It felt empty, as though it had not been used for a long time.

'This is the best view in the house.' Helen knelt on the cushioned box seat and threw open the window.

Philippa stood beside her. The moors stretched as far as she could see, and dominating them was Flint Iron Tor.

'Whose room is this?'

'Justin's.'

'Are those pictures his?'

'Of course. Every painting in the house was done by him, except for the hunting prints in the hall.'

Philippa went to the nearest wall and studied a muddled selection of water colours, oils, pencil sketches and ink drawings. Most of them were of the moors; the ponies and sheep; the birds and wild animals which lived here. None of the pictures gave the impression of an amateur, although there were distinct changes of style, as though he was trying to find himself. He had drawn Harwood's mermaid, and Maggie always enthused about him, but she had never realised how good he was.

'Is that oil painting in the living room his? The one of the ponies in the storm. It seems so . . . so professional.'

'My brother is professional. He is also a very fine artist, who deserves more recognition than he gets.' Nicholas was standing in the doorway, frowning as he looked from the woman to the girl. 'What are you doing in here?' he asked his sister.

'Showing Philippa the view.' There was a sharpness to Helen's voice, which was quite unlike the tones she had used when speaking of Justin.

'I wanted to see it,' Philippa said, defending her. 'Well, aren't you going to tell Helen how pretty she looks?'

She could tell by his expression that Nicholas disapproved of the eye make-up. It was fine on her, but not on his baby sister.

'You look all right, Helen,' he said begrudgingly. 'But don't go into the village looking like that. Mum is doing the washing up. Why don't you help her?'

She scuttled past him into the passage, then thudded down the stairs.

'My sister, the baby elephant,' he joked.

'You and she don't get along, do you?'

'We never did. Justin has always been her favourite. There was no need for you to spend so much time with her.'

'I enjoyed it. She is so gloriously naive that I feel about a hundred years old.'

'You don't look it.' He came into the room and reached for her hand. 'I thought you might like to walk off some of that food. Later on, we can go to the Pack Horse for a drink.'

'I should offer to help your mother.'

'She wouldn't let you.'

She walked with him to the door. 'When did he find time to do them all?' she asked, referring to the paintings.

'These are only a few of what he has done over the years. He did the water colour above the bed when he was fourteen. It won first prize in an inter-school competition.'

The painting did not look like the work of a schoolboy. It was of two horses pulling a plough and the background was one Philippa recognised – the South Downs.

She suddenly wished Helen had not brought her in here.

There had been many occasions when Philippa missed having a mother to whom she could turn for advice. Now was one of them. For a time there had been Mike, and more recently Steve, but she needed to talk with another woman, not a man. She sensed Sarah Lang would understand, had her own sons not been involved. Which left Maggie. She went to her flat early one evening on the off-chance she would be in. She was, but Noel was taking her out later on.

Maggie poured them both a glass of wine. 'Is this about Justin and Nicholas Lang?'

'How did you know?'

'Noel told me Lochdunnan is closed from October to

March. The only way you could have seen it was if someone showed you privately, and Justin happened to be staying there at the time.'

The colour drained from Philippa's face and her fingers tightened around the glass. 'Who else knows?'

'Nobody, and I promise nobody ever shall. What happened there?'

'I made a fool of myself. I thought I was in love, and that he loved me back. I was wrong. It was not love at all, but an uncontrollable physical attraction.' She drank a little of the wine. 'I don't suppose it would have taken long to discover we had nothing in common. Steve warned me, but I wouldn't listen. Justin told me he was leaving Alice and, like a besotted fool, I believed him. His lies were a deliberate and cruel way of getting back at me for what my father did.'

Maggie was gazing into her own glass. 'He told nobody, not even his brother. He must have had some respect for you.'

'Rubbish! He didn't want her to know.'

'You should not make hasty judgements, not without knowing the full facts.'

Philippa stared at her. 'Do you know something I don't?'

'What would I know? I happen to like him, that's all. Nicholas can be charming when he chooses to be, but there is something cold and calculating about him which makes me uneasy. He is obviously different with you. And that is what this is about. Not you and Justin, but you and Nicholas. Are you in love with him?'

Philippa hesitated. She was finding it difficult to plumb the depths of her feelings. 'I think I am falling in love with him, and I'm frightened.'

'Of him learning about you and his brother? It won't happen, not unless you tell him yourself.' She leant forward and squeezed her friend's hand. 'It is not a crime to be involved with two brothers, separately, of course. It happens all the time. If you like Nicholas, go out with him and have some fun. He is a good-looking young man who has the money to show you a good time, and heaven knows you deserve it. Ever since I've known you, your life has been devoted to work. You are still very young, but don't let the years slip by until you suddenly find you have grown old and bitter. It could happen. It was happening to me until Noel came along.'

'I could not bear to be hurt again.'

'The chances of that happening a second time are exceedingly remote. Even if the worst should happen, you have the strength to survive. Story book romances do not exist. We invent them. I am marrying Noel because I love him, but I'm not really sure how much he loves me.'

Philippa found that shocking, for she had thought theirs a fairy tale romance.

'Why does love have to be so complicated?' she asked.

'Because that is how it has always been,' Maggie replied.

CHAPTER FIFTEEN

Nicholas and Philippa were the darlings of the gossip columnists that summer. They were referred to as the perfect couple, the very essence of the beautiful people upon whom the sun never set.

Nicholas thrived on the publicity, while Philippa was amused by it. Despite what the newspapers intimated, she and Nicholas were not lovers, nor had he put any pressure on her in that direction. She had taken Maggie's advice and was enjoying herself. She was in a position where she could choose her modelling assignments and, at long last, Moor View was beginning to find its feet.

The advertising campaign which Nicholas drew up was simple and to the point, while the photographs Steve reluctantly took gave a touch of class to the double-paged leaflet which was the nucleus of a future catalogue. Some free publicity was gained from press releases which Nicholas sent out to the trade magazines, but the half-page advertisements which appeared in a handful of glossy magazines infuriated Philippa.

'You had no right, Nicholas! This is something which Rodney and I must decide. How much did they cost?'

'Nothing at all.' He shrugged. 'I was owed some favours and it was a case of pulling the right strings. Be grateful, darling. They are a one-off gamble which might not work.'

They did. A small stream of orders were received from various parts of the country, while the pottery's own mail shot produced a steady response. Rodney and Philippa started to plan for the future. Until their cash flow improved expansion was restricted, but Rodney's idea of a selective studio pottery within the main frame was starting to show results, and the tea service had sold so well that they decided to continue with similar lines and ditch the souvenirs. They were also toying with the idea of a series of collector plates, but for those they needed to commission an artist. Rodney did not know Nicholas had a brother who was talented in that field, nor did Philippa tell him. Justin and she had gone their separate ways. They could not change course now.

The only cloud on the horizon was Maggie's impending wedding. Justin was to be best man and it was inevitable he and Philippa would meet.

The wedding took place on a mild Saturday afternoon in late September and turned out to be the society event of the year. Nicholas and Philippa were driving to Gloucestershire in the morning and coming back the same evening. They were unencumberd, as Sarah and Helen were going by train and staying overnight at a hotel.

They left early enough to stop off for a drink and for Philippa to smarten up, and pin into place the broad-brimmed hat she had chosen for the occasion. It was cream-coloured and unadorned, except for a strip of pale lilac ribbon which matched her equally simple outfit. She knew how good she and Nicholas looked together, and as they walked, hand in hand, along the roughly paved path to the three-hundred-year-old church, the photographers must have thought so too, for flash bulbs exploded all around them.

She glanced at Nicholas, who was enjoying being the

centre of attention. He is the exact opposite of his brother, she thought, and suddenly went cold. She would have given anything not to be here at this moment. And then they were inside the church with its uneven, stone floor and a heady scent of flowers which could not quite overpower the older smells of age and decay.

She looked straight ahead, her fingers digging into the palm of Nicholas's hand.

'Is something wrong?' he asked.

'I wasn't expecting so many photographers,' she lied, slipping her hand from his.

A movement of colour at the front of the church caught her eye. It was Noel Buchanan, dressed in full Highland regalia. With his flaming hair he could have been a resurrection of the first fierce Buchanan. He was talking to an older man with horn-rimmed spectacles, who bore a vague resemblance to him. She rightly guessed him to be Noel's brother, Alistair.

'I would rather not sit at the front,' she said.

Nicholas turned to her, his eyes puzzled. 'You're jumpy as a cat. Anybody would think it was your wedding, not theirs. We can sit anywhere you like, but out of common courtesy we ought to greet my family first.'

As he tucked her arm beneath his Philippa saw Sarah and Helen standing beside a stone pillar to the right of the altar. With them was one of the most beautiful young women she had ever seen. She was small, slender and graceful, with golden hair which flowed down her back. If there was any criticism Philippa could level, it was that she was too pale. In fact, she looked decidedly delicate beside the robust Lang women.

'Who is that?' she whispered.

'Alice. Justin's wife. Thank heaven they found a baby-sitter. I had visions of Jennie screaming through the

190

ceremony. I can't imagine either of them have had a good night's sleep since she was born.'

He decided to cut through an empty pew and, as Philippa followed him, she had an uncomfortable sensation of being watched. She stared beyond the three women, into the shadows, and there she saw Justin. He was exactly how she remembered him. Defiantly, she met his gaze. He smiled, and she steeled herself for the encounter which she had dreaded for so long. How could she greet him without her resentment showing? Then Sarah said something and Nicholas answered her. The spell broke and Philippa turned her head away from the man who had once been her lover.

She was aware of him holding back as his mother and sister spoke with her. She was introduced to his wife, who offered a limp hand and a gracious smile. There was a genuine sweetness about Alice Lang which made it impossible for Philippa to dislike her.

'You and Philippa have already met,' she heard Nicholas say, and realised he was talking to his brother.

'Briefly, many years ago. The last time was when you were subordinate to Rosalind Harper. I remember Steve was giving you a hard time. I don't suppose he would dare bully you now.'

His voice bridged the awkwardness of the moment. Philippa was both grateful and alarmed that he should instinctively know how to put her at ease. She took a backward step and came face to face with him. His smile was tense, but his grey eyes were shuttered, reflecting no emotion whatsoever.

'Steve bullies everyone, especially me if I don't get something right the first time.' She did not offer him her hand, nor did he hold forward his.

'Shouldn't you be supporting the groom?' Nicholas asked.

'More than likely I'll be propping up the groom. His nerves got the better of him and he lunched on a half bottle of whisky. Alistair is feeding him peppermints in the hope his breath will not knock the vicar flat. The bride will have to take her chances!'

Except for that fleeting moment in 1959, when Nicholas had been sitting on a gate and Justin on a horse, Philippa had never seen the two brothers together. They were very alike, yet different. Nicholas was a little taller, which she found surprising, and with his chiselled good looks and sun-bleached hair he was also the more eye-catching. But he lacked the warmth and humour of his brother – that unconscious charm which had swept her off her feet two years ago and was now playing havoc on her nerves.

She reached for Nicholas's hand. 'I think we ought to find a seat.' She spoke more sharply than she intended. 'Maggie will be arriving soon.'

The reception was a sumptuous affair held in a marquee on the lawn of Lord Rudolph Huntington-Smythe's palatial country home. After the meal and obligatory speeches, there was dancing to a live band. Philippa rarely danced any more. After a day in front of a demanding camera she did not have the energy for today's fast-paced gyrations. But she got up for a slow number, and when the music continued in the same tempo she and Nicholas remained on the floor. He moved well and she felt comfortable in his arms.

'May I cut in?' a familiar voice said. 'It would please Mum no end if you asked her for a dance.'

'You have lousy timing, big brother.' And then, to her horror, Nicholas handed Philippa over as though she were a loaf of bread. 'Be careful, he has two left feet.' He kissed her cheek, and she watched dumbstruck as he strode away.

'We shall cause an obstruction if we stand here. And

192

Nicholas tends to exaggerate. I promise not to trample on you.'

He was not holding her close, but she found his nearness disturbing. 'I do not want to dance with you. I would rather sit this one out.'

'I have no intention of letting you go, and if you make a fuss my brother will want to know why. Please, Philippa. I owe you an apology.'

A couple jostled into them and she automatically began to move in time with him. 'You owe me nothing. I knew what I was doing, and what happened was as much my fault as yours.'

'I know you will find it hard to believe, but I meant every word I said at Lochdunnan.'

Philippa ground to a halt. 'Of course you did. That's why you went back and married your dancer.' The savageness of her reply clearly startled him. 'You have your wife now, and I have Nicholas. Unfortunately, I cannot avoid you altogether, but want as little to do with you as possible.'

His hands dropped to his sides. 'I am sorry I hurt you so badly. I'll take you back to your table.'

She turned away, conscious of him behind her. They did not speak again. He held out her chair when she sat down, and then led his blushing sister on to the dance floor. Shortly afterwards, she asked Nicholas if they could leave because she had a splitting headache.

They did not talk on the way back to London. Philippa closed her eyes and pretended to be asleep.

'Are you feeling any better?' Nicholas asked when she finally stirred.

'A lot better, thank you.' She straightened up. They were travelling through the suburbs and there were rows of identical houses on either side of them. 'What time is it?'

193

He glanced at his watch. 'A little after eleven. Do you want to stop off somewhere for a drink?'

'Round here? Everywhere will be closing.'

'No, not here. The clubs will be coming to life about now. Or we could go to my flat if you would prefer peace and quiet.'

She gazed at his profile, at the determined chin and firm mouth. He sensed her watching him and turned his head a little. In the yellow glow of the street lights the muscles in his face appeared unusually taut. Philippa raised her hand and stroked her fingers across his cheek. They could not go on like this, either of them.

'Let's go to your flat,' she said.

This time she stayed. This time she let him take her to his bed, where they made love. For Nicholas, physical contact was enough, and although her body responded eagerly to his, a part of her longed for the beauty and serenity which she had shared with his brother. But it was to exorcise the ghost of Justin Lang that she had come here tonight, and if she did not quite succeed then the fault was hers entirely.

'We made the newspapers. Look.'

Philippa put down the coffee she was drinking and took the newspaper from him, laying it flat on the sofa beside her. On the second page was a close-up of Noel and Maggie, with a photograph of Nicholas and her below it.

He handed her another three papers. Each one had similar photographs.

'How many Sunday newspapers do you buy?' she laughed. 'You can't possibly read them all.'

'I compare their viewpoints and see who is advertising what. Here, I kept the best for last.'

It was one of the cheaper rags and, this time, there was

only one photograph. It was of them, hands clasped, walking into the church. The caption above it read 'Wedding Bells?'.

'Well?' Nicholas asked.

'Well what?'

He took hold of her hands.

'Well, are there going to be any wedding bells?'

She stared at him, unsure if he was serious. His lips brushed over hers.

'Will you marry me, Philippa?'

It was the last thing she expected him to say.

'Yes,' she whispered. 'Yes, I will.'

Marriage had not always been in his mind, but the more Nicholas thought about it, the more appealing the prospect became. It would give him stability and a gorgeous wife other men would envy. He had originally intended to seduce her during the weekend they spent in Devon, but changed his mind once they got there. He was realistic enough to admit, if only to himself, that the pottery played a part in his decision. But he also desired something more permanent than the meaningless relationships he had indulged in up to now.

That night, they had dined in a local restaurant before returning to his flat. They were drinking champagne and he had his arm around her. He put down his glass and laid his hand over hers.

'We'll choose a ring tomorrow,' he said.

'What ring?'

'Your engagement ring, darling. Surely you want one?'

'Do I? It never entered my head.'

Nicholas laughed. 'You are having nothing but the best – a diamond ring and a lavish white wedding. Heaven knows where we shall go for our honeymoon. Is there any country which you have not visited?'

'One or two. But seriously, Nicholas, I would prefer a Register Office, with no fuss and a few close friends.'

'My mother has never forgiven Justin and Alice for doing that. She knew nothing about the marriage until afterwards, and I had to walk out of a meeting when he telephoned me one hour before the ceremony took place. We are going to do this properly, in Povey Ashton, in the spring. You will make a ravishing bride, Philippa.' He lifted her hand to his lips. 'And don't worry about the cost. I'll take care of everything.'

'I always thought it was the bride, not the groom, who insisted on a white wedding.' She was smiling. 'All right, Nicholas. But please don't make it too lavish. I don't want a bevy of bridesmaids, and I shall buy my own dress.'

'One bridesmaid would not be flamboyant, and it would be a nice gesture to ask Helen. She would be thrilled.'

Philippa suspected this was no spur of the moment decision and wondered how he would have reacted had she said no. Knowing Nicholas, he would not have reacted at all. He would have set about persuading her in some other way.

'Penny for your thoughts,' he said.

'They aren't worth a penny.'

Philippa was half asleep when Nicholas slid his arm from beneath her and sat up.

'Are you awake?'

'I am now. What's the matter?'

He switched on the bedside lamp. 'I love you,' he said, putting his arms around her. 'I love you and I want you to move in with me.'

She kissed him tenderly. 'I love you too. But it wouldn't work. I'm in and out at impossible hours, and until Christmas will be abroad more often than I am here.'

'I am stuck in the office most nights, but those are problems we can surmount. I want you with me now.'

Philippa wriggled free from his tight embrace. 'Don't rush me, Nicholas. I'm not ready to live with you yet. I need some breathing space.'

'Then move in at Christmas.'

'Can't we carry on as we are until after we're married?'

She saw a spark in his eyes which could have been anger, but when he spoke his voice was gentle. 'Did anyone ever tell you that you're a prude? If you refuse to live with me, will you do me another favour?'

The clock read three-thirty and there was not a sound in the street below. She might be awake, but she was not in full command of her wits. Unfortunately, Nicholas was bright as a button.

'Can't it wait until morning?'

'It could. But I would prefer your answer tonight.'

His bed was a wide divan with no headboard, and she had to lean against the wall.

'What is this favour?'

'It's not for me, but for my brother. I know you and Rodney would like to go ahead with the series of plates, but cannot do so until you find a good artist who will not demand an exorbitant fee for his work. I'd like you to commission Justin.'

Philippa's face hardened. 'Doesn't that smack a little too much of nepotism?'

'He's a damn good artist. Ask Maggie if you don't believe me. Why do you dislike him so much?'

She gazed into the depths of his pale eyes, knowing she could never tell him the truth. 'I never forgave him for being so rude to me after your father's death. I know it sounds silly now, but fifteen can be a tender and impressionable age.'

'If you give him a chance, you'll find he's not at all like that. He is practically broke, Philippa, and in desperate need of money. I push whatever work I can his way, but he is too proud to admit how bad things really are. Even Mum doesn't know. He'd never forgive me if I told her.'

'I thought Maggie was selling his paintings.'

'She is trying to, but despite the success of the exhibition it is a slow process. One day I believe he will receive the recognition he deserves, but until then he is struggling to support a family and keep his head above water.'

Philippa laid her cheek against his shoulder. 'He must be highly irresponsible to start a family when he is so badly off. Why should it fall upon your shoulders to pull him out of the mire?'

Nicholas did not answer immediately. For a moment, she thought he wouldn't. When he did speak there was a fierce pride in his voice which took her by surprise. 'I suppose it would be hard for you to understand, especially as your brother dumped you when times were hard. Justin was always there when we needed him. During the nightmare which followed our father's death it was he who held the family together. He has a knack of sorting out other people's lives, but making a mess of his own. He didn't want to marry Alice. A couple of years ago they were on the verge of parting. He left her alone in London while he spent the summer helping my mother set up the trekking centre. Alice retaliated by getting pregnant and, being the noble person he is, Justin married her.'

As the pieces fell into place, it was with a sense of shock that Philippa realised Justin had not been lying to her. The knowledge came too late to change anything, except perhaps her tolerance.

'Give him a chance,' Nicholas said. 'For my sake. You won't regret it.'

'If I asked him now he would suspect you were behind it.'

'Not if you used Maggie as an intermediary.'

She owed Justin nothing, and yet she was touched by his brother's concern. 'I'll see what I can do,' she promised.

CHAPTER SIXTEEN

Noel and Maggie came back from their honeymoon and moved into the large house off Sloane Square which her father had given them as a wedding present. Within a week she was back at the gallery, enthusiastically planning the exhibitions she intended to put on the next year.

She was in the office when Justin came in. Usually, he went straight through, but her assistant said she was on the telephone and would he mind waiting. When Maggie came out he was at the far end of the gallery, studying her latest acquisitions. She had seen him a few days earlier, but they hugged fondly, and he kissed her cheek.

'Thank you for coming at such short notice.'

'I'm glad to get out for a while.'

She knew what he meant. He was finding it increasingly difficult to work in the cramped flat, with Alice moaning at him and Jennie screaming.

'This is good news. I have been approached by somebody who wants to commission some work from you. It's an offer you should seriously consider. Look, why don't you go into the office. I'll be with you in a moment. There are a couple of things I need to do first.'

Maggie was a rotten liar and had been certain he would see through her. But he went unsuspectingly into the office, closing the door behind him.

'Good morning. I apologise for the deception, but I wanted to be sure you came.'

Philippa was standing to one side of the window, with the glare of artificial lights full on her face. They drained the colour from her cheeks, giving her an ethereal quality which was at odds with the determination of her expression. She was wearing a short, brown leather skirt which clung to her hips, and matching knee-high boots which accentuated the length of her legs. Her long-sleeved shirt was brightly coloured and adorned by rows of junk jewellery which she had picked up down the Portobello Road. Like anything she wore, they looked good on her.

His smile was unconscious. From head to toe she was the top fashion model she had become.

'You could have picked up the telephone,' he said. 'When you marry my brother it will be impossible for us to avoid each other.'

'This has nothing to do with Nicholas.' She moved away from the light. 'I don't know what Maggie has told you, but I shall be grateful if you will hear me out.'

'It must be important for you to go to this trouble. Did my brother buy that chunk of stone you are wearing? Ernest cannot be pleased. They need every penny they can get to start up the new agency.'

She barely glanced at the diamond on her left hand. She had asked for something simple, so Nicholas had given her something simple. That it was the kind of ostentation she deplored was another matter altogether. She was terrified to wear it most of the time, in case the wretched thing got lost.

'He sold some stocks.' Her voice was dismissive. She sat down, her back rigid and her exquisite legs stretched in front of her. 'I did not ask you here to discuss my wedding.'

'You did not ask me here at all. You got Maggie to do your dirty work. What do you want, Philippa?'

A flush of colour stained her cheeks. 'It would help if you sat down.'

'First of all, I should like to know what I am doing here. Are you afraid I'll tell Nicholas about our little fling? You don't have to worry, I could never do that to him.'

Words had the ability to wound, and his did. What had been a little fling for him had meant a lot to her at the time. But she would never admit it, nor was she about to let him see the chinks in her armour.

'This has nothing to do with that sordid little affair. You would have told Nicholas before now if you had any intention of doing so. He knows about this meeting, by the way. We have no secrets from each other—' she hesitated – 'except for one. I would tell him everything if I thought he would understand.'

'He won't.' Justin was equally sharp. 'Do you love him?'

She was startled. 'I would never have agreed to marry him if I didn't.'

Again he smiled, and deep down inside Philippa felt the stirrings of some dormant emotion. It was gone as quickly as it had come.

In turn, Justin saw a light flare, then die in her eyes. He was perceptive enough to guess what it meant, and felt a wave of indefinable sadness. Theirs had been a hopeless love from the beginning. He wondered whether his brother realised how lucky he was.

An uneasy silence stretched between them. It was Philippa who broke it.

'Can't we forget the past and be friends? After all, we shall soon be related, if only by marriage.'

'Do you honestly see me as some kind of enemy?' His voice had softened, as had his expression.

'I resented you for a long time, but not any more. I wish you had let me know Alice was pregnant. If you could not face me, a one-lined note would have been kinder than nothing.'

'Who told you? Nicholas?'

'We were talking and he volunteered the information.' Her eyes levelled with his. 'I wanted to see you because I need an artist to do some freelance work for the pottery. We want to issue a series of collector plates over a six-month period. If the project is successful, there will be a second and possibly a third series.'

'Did Nicholas put you up to this?'

His voice was like a whiplash. Angrily, Philippa leapt to her feet.

'No, he did not! Moor View is mine. I may be marrying your brother, but that does not entitle him to meddle in the affairs of my pottery. I have seen enough of your work to know how good you are, and Maggie is forever singing your praises.'

Justin walked towards her, but stopped an arm's length away, his grey eyes smouldering.

'We are on the verge of making a success of it.' Philippa subsided into the chair. 'Nicholas helped with the initial publicity, but only because I asked him. Rodney Slater is running Moor View now, and we are experimenting with new ideas, the plates being one of them. To make them sell we have to use a known artist who has a universally acceptable style. The subject matter is open to discussion, but Maggie has suggested horses. She thinks you have the potential of becoming another Stubbs.'

Not a muscle twitched in his face. 'I am flattered. However, you are overrating my abilities. Nor am I a known artist.'

'You are becoming known, and if the plates are successful they could boost your career. Each one will be sold with a full history of the artist.'

203

He leant back against the desk, his arms crossed. Seeing she had his full attention, Philippa began to relax. 'You have probably guessed I am not in the position to pay the sort of fee a well-established artist would demand. Practically every penny I earn is being re-invested in Moor View, which is still running in the red and will be for a long time yet.' Her eyes met his. 'Will you accept my offer?'

'You always were impulsive. You have not offered me anything other than the doubtful privilege of supplying your pottery with a series of paintings.' He spoke candidly, without any trace of malice. 'Before I consider such a proposition I need a lot more information, not only about these plates, but the degree of artistic licence I would be allowed. And you cannot expect me to work for next to nothing simply because you are marrying my brother.'

'Your advice would be sought in all major decisions relating to the plates. I don't think I can be fairer than that. As for payment, I have no idea what your paintings are worth. They are probably more than we can afford, but I have other inducements. A permanent studio at Moor View is one of them. You could use it whenever you wanted, and for whatever you wanted.'

'Permanent?'

Did she detect a spark of interest, or amusement? She could not tell.

'I am sure you will find it advantageous to have a studio in that part of the country. I am looking to the future, Justin. If everything works out as I hope, then I would like to call upon your services every so often. I realise you are an independent artist and will not want to be tied down to the pottery, but if you had an interest in it you might look upon us more favourably. If our first collaboration is a success, I am willing to give you a ten per cent share in the business. You will also be paid for your work. You may not get much at first, but I promise the situation will improve.'

She had matured, the cocksure young girl he had first met on a doorstep. She might not have grasped all the intricacies of running a successful business, but her instincts were good.

'Before I decide one way or the other I would like to look over this pottery of yours,' he said.

'Nicholas and I will be driving down in a fortnight. We have to see your mother and make a start on the preliminary arrangements for the wedding. Can you come then?'

'Yes,' he replied.

Philippa stood up. 'Maggie promised to send in some tea. She must have forgotten.'

She walked past him, then paused.

'I am glad we have finally put the past behind us. If nothing else, we have achieved that much today.'

Alice had reluctantly agreed to come.

'Your mother hates me,' she said.

'Of course she doesn't,' Justin told her. 'She wants to see Jennie, and it will give you a well-deserved rest. You look far too pale and are always complaining how tired you are. I wish you would see the doctor. He could give you a tonic.'

She hated doctors and illness. She had never known why. It was a fear which stemmed from early childhood; from some long buried incident she could not remember, but which persistently haunted her. Perhaps it was tied in with the death of her parents. Perhaps it was better not to know.

'There is nothing wrong with me which a good night's sleep will not cure! It's always me who has to get up when Jennie screams.'

She saw Justin's mouth tighten. It was an old argument and one which they had never resolved.

'If you left her to scream she would soon get fed up and

go back to sleep.' He had told her the same thing umpteen times.

'And the one night I did not go to her could be the night when something goes seriously wrong. Let's face it, Justin, you don't want her any more now than you did before she was born. Jennie means nothing to you. She never has.'

Alice dropped into a chair. She did not complain for nothing. She was always tired these days. There were times when she literally dragged herself around the small flat, dutifully doing the chores she detested. And day by day she felt Justin distance himself from her. She was certain there was no other woman, but neither did he make love to her very often. Their marriage had been falling to pieces since Jennie was born, and their financial situation did not help. She wanted him to accept his brother's offer of a permanent job, but he refused. He was determined to be an artist, unfettered and independent. They had managed before, when she was working and there were only the two of them, but circumstances had changed, and he would not change with them.

In the bedroom, Jennie started to cry.

'For God's sake leave her!' Justin swore. 'I want to know whether you are coming with me.'

Alice gripped the arms of the chair. 'All right, I'll come. But when we get back I'm taking a part-time job. We need the money, and I feel like a prisoner shut in here all the time.'

'That is entirely your fault.' There was no concern in his voice, only more anger. 'What are you going to do with Jennie? I refuse to be lumbered with her.'

Alice shrank into the chair, unnerved by the sharpness of his voice. 'I'll take her with me. Someone I knew years ago has opened a dancing school. She has offered me a teaching job. I said I would think about it. Jennie would be no problem.'

206

'She will be if you desert your class every time she so much as whimpers.'

Tears started to her eyes as Jennie's cries turned into that high-pitched, partly hysterical wail which was so distressing. Alice did not go to her immediately. She lasted for one, almost two minutes, before leaping to her feet. Justin's expression was scornful, but she ignored him as she ran from the room.

Nicholas and Philippa were unable to leave London until the Friday evening and had to be back on Sunday. He and Ernest had been kicked out of McCullogh, Staines & Ray at the beginning of the week, when it became known they were about to start their own agency. Consequently, they had brought their plans forward, deciding to open during December rather than January. They had looked over some premises and decided upon a second-floor suite in the fashionable part of Kensington. Parking would be easier for their clients, and they would be far enough away from their old firm to avoid embarrassment.

The lease was to be signed on Monday morning. Then there was furniture to buy and staff to hire. They had more money than expected, for McCullogh, Staines & Ray had paid them generously. They did not want ex-employees shooting their mouths off to the press about unfair dismissal. They had been too late to prevent a handful of clients from switching agencies, Mermaid Hosiery being prominent amongst them.

Justin and Alice, with Jennie thankfully sleeping most of the way, left on Thursday afternoon. They were not tied down by busy schedules and Justin wanted to look over Moor View without Philippa breathing down his neck. He intended to make his own judgements. Alice sulked when he went off without her on Friday morning. He had told her nothing about the pottery until then. But she was in good hands, for the trekking season was over and Sarah had the time to fuss over her and Jennie.

Unlike his brother, Justin was not surprised by the size of Moor View, which was actually smaller than he had expected. It was one of those raw November mornings, with mist sitting in pockets on the moors and a drizzling rain making sodden heaps of the autumn leaves. The pottery looked drab when he drove into the yard, but inside he found an air of optimism. A young woman with a strong Devonshire accent took him straight to Rodney Slater. She was wearing a trouser suit, apparel still frowned upon in many London offices. Justin smiled – that had to be Philippa's doing. Rodney was tackling a pile of paperwork. He knew Philippa was coming the next day and wanted to get this done. He expected Justin Lang to be with her, and was surprised when Louise popped her head round the door and announced he was there.

It took no longer than a handshake for the two men to weigh each other up, each liking what he saw.

Philippa insisted she go to Harlequin House, despite Nicholas arguing there were plenty of rooms at Flint Iron Farm. He accepted her decision with ill grace, but was visibly annoyed when she refused to let him stay overnight.

Nor did she want him at Moor View on Saturday, as the business she had to conduct there did not concern him. But he turned up at Harlequin House early in the morning.

'Everything is arranged,' he told her. 'Justin will drive Alice into Tavistock, then I'll take her on a sightseeing tour of Plymouth and the two of you will join us for lunch. Believe me, you are getting the better deal. At least she has agreed to leave Jennie at home. That kid has lungs you would not believe. She woke me up twice last night.'

Philippa was irritated by his meddling. 'I do wish you had not made so many arrangements without consulting me first. There are a number of things I need to discuss with Rodney, and Justin is dithering about the plates. He may need a lot of persuasion. What if we run late?'

'You won't. He came down early and spent yesterday with Rodney. He has not said anything, but I am pretty sure he has already made up his mind. Oh, and another thing, we have to see the vicar tomorrow morning about the wedding.'

Philippa did not like being manipulated, and was furious with him. She was also angry with Justin for having the gall to visit Moor View without informing her beforehand.

She felt less intolerant by the time they reached the pottery. Her mood improved further when Rodney took her aside, leaving the two brothers to finalise their plans for later on.

'I take your word about him being a good artist,' he enthused. 'Did you know he has a basic knowledge of firing and glazing, and is also aware of the problems encountered when transferring a conventional painting on to china? He not only has the expertise we need, but the ideas as well. Have you made him an offer?'

'A permanent studio – we have more than enough room on the top floor – and a ten per cent share-holding if the first series of plates are successful. I hope you don't mind about the shares, but they were the only real inducement I could think of. We haven't got round to haggling over money, but he knows about our cash flow problems.'

She saw approval in Rodney's eyes. 'You can dispose of your shares in any way you like. But my intuition tells me you are doing the right thing. He has suggested we launch the plates on a series of native pony breeds, and is bringing some sketches for us to see.'

Philippa stared across the yard, at the profile of the dark-headed brother. He was going to do the plates. The money was immaterial, for he had already made up his mind.

The two men drew apart, Nicholas blowing her a kiss before climbing into the MG where Alice was patiently waiting.

'Rodney, is your father at home? I'd like to pop round and see him later this morning.'

'He should be.' He looked puzzled. 'I can telephone to make sure.'

'I'd be grateful if you could. I have nobody to give me away and wondered if he would do it.'

'I am sure he will be delighted,' Rodney said.

It was something which had been haunting her, and last night she had suddenly thought of Gideon. Everything was falling into place – the pottery, the wedding, her life. Her next priority was to get a driving licence. A car was a liability in London, but down here it was a necessity, and she intended to spend a lot more time at Moor View when she was married.

Justin joined them as Nicholas sped out of the yard. 'I have the sketches. They should give you a rough idea of what I was talking about.' He spoke to Rodney.

'You are going to do the plates?' Philippa said.

Their eyes met. 'Yes, I am going to do your plates.'

Then he smiled – that wonderful smile which banished all care from his face. He had not smiled at Alice like that. He had not even kissed her goodbye. Nicholas and I shall not have a loveless marriage, Philippa thought. We care too much for each other.

CHAPTER SEVENTEEN

The first day of April dawned cold and wet, but by ten-thirty the grey clouds blew away, leaving a pale but clear sky.

April Fool's Day, Philippa thought as the car pulled up outside the church and the waiting press surged forward. She had done her best to ensure they would not learn when or where the wedding was being held, but with a guest list like theirs it was virtually impossible. Half an hour ago Justin had telephoned from the village, telling his mother to warn Philippa of the intrusion.

Gideon remained wonderfully calm as he helped her from the car. She saw Helen standing inside the porch with the official photographer. The girl had been told to keep away from the press and Philippa needed no assistance with the plain, high-necked dress which fell naturally into place. It was not pure white, but a cream-coloured, synthetic satin which did not crush, overlaid by delicate, pearl-studded lace. She had rejected the traditional veil, preferring to weave a band of fresh spring flowers into her hair. At the time it did not occur to her that the flowers were a symbol of the Flower Power cult which was filtering over from America. But it was an angle which the reporters were quick to take up.

She posed prettily for the photographers and answered some questions before Gideon led her away. It was only then, as she walked along the uneven path, that Philippa felt butterflies in her stomach. This is it, she thought, the point of no return. She suddenly wished Geoffrey were there, for he was the only real family she had.

'Nervous?' Gideon asked.

'Terrified!'

She could hear the organ inside the church and tightened her grip on his arm. The photographer darted forward to take some pictures and she called for Helen to join them. The girl was also dressed in cream satin, but without the overlay of lace. She looked almost pretty, with her hair piled on her head and make-up covering the spots and emphasising her pale eyes.

'You look beautiful,' she told Philippa. 'It's a shame about those awful people being here, but they promised to stay on the road. Justin was furious and had a terrible row with Nicholas. I thought he was going to hit him. Luckily, Mum arrived in time to calm them down.'

Philippa stared at her bridesmaid. 'Why were they arguing?'

'Why do you think?' Helen spoke in a deadpan voice. 'Those reporters are here because Nicholas tipped them off.'

Philippa was shocked. How could he? Were it not for his brother she would have arrived unprepared.

'It doesn't matter,' said Gideon as the organ broke into a spirited version of the Wedding March. 'Come along, they're waiting.'

'You'd better hurry up,' Helen hissed. 'One of those reporters is trying to sneak up behind us.'

Gideon glanced over his shoulder. 'No, wait.'

Then somebody else spoke. Somebody whose voice she recognised.

'Good luck, Philippa. Mr Slater told me you were getting

married today, and I wanted to be sure you were happy.'

She let go of Gideon's arm. 'Mike!'

He was older than she remembered. His face was thinner, with deep lines around the eyes and mouth, and he was going bald. She was aware of the watching reporters, but knew they were too far away to hear what was being said.

'I've missed you, Mike. Why did you stop writing?'

'Because you are not a child any longer, but a successful young woman. Here, I brought you some fresh heather from the Highlands.'

He came to her, pressing it into her hand. 'I can't stay. I have a train to catch.'

'Oh, Mike, surely you're not going to disappear again?'

'Very shortly you will have a husband to care for you. What do you need me for?' His smile was both gentle and sad. 'It's strange you should marry into that family.'

'Is it? Won't you come into the church?'

'I am back in private service and have to be in Scotland this afternoon.'

'Will I ever see you again?'

'Who knows? Goodbye, Philippa. Have a wonderful life.'

He cupped his hand against her cheek, then turned away, striding through the randomly growing daffodils and disappearing around the side of the church.

'We must go in,' Gideon said from behind her.

She turned to him. 'Why didn't you tell me you were in contact with Mike?'

'Because he asked me not to. He telephoned last week. He wasn't sure whether to come, but I thought you would like to see him.'

Philippa pushed the heather into her hair, above her right ear.

'They've started on the Wedding March for the second time,' Helen said.

'Do you think Nicholas is getting nervous?' Philippa asked Gideon.

'I am getting nervous,' he replied. 'Nicholas must be thinking he is about to be stood up.'

She laughed. It no longer mattered if Geoffrey was not here. Mike had come.

They walked into the church. It was warm and brightly lit. Philippa ignored the sea of faces as her eyes sought Nicholas. He was standing shoulder to shoulder with his brother, looking unusually pale. Yes, she thought, we shall have a happy life together, and because she loved him she was able to forgive him for deceiving her, and inviting the press to what should have been their private day.

Philippa forgave Nicholas a good many things over the next few months. They were both working hard. He and Ernest often stayed late at the office, while she gradually found herself doing more advertisements for Lang & Wakefield, and less of the fashion modelling which she preferred. And because Nicholas did not want her jetting around the world, the work became increasingly soul-destroying. She would have given up modelling then had it not been for Moor View. The pottery was making a slow recovery, but still needed additional finance.

The first series of plates had been more successful than they anticipated, the demand noticeably growing after the entire set had been issued. Rodney and Philippa consulted with Justin, who agreed the new series be put on hold and the first given a limited re-issue. This time they experimented with direct mail order rather than rely on the larger retail outlets. Initially, the cost of advertising and employing extra staff drained their resources, but the resultant flood of orders proved a profit could be made without the middle man taking his cut. It dictated the direction they would take in the future.

Philippa still dealt on a personal basis with Leonard Perkins of Perkins, Crisp & Perkins, and it was he who suggested she persuade Justin Lang to become more involved with the pottery. Rodney agreed.

'We should make him artistic director with a token salary and a say in how the business is run. He has an excellent eye for design and colour, and his contributions can only be to our advantage. It makes sense to offer him a position he cannot turn down.'

'Can't he?'

Philippa's scepticism was justified. They spent the better part of a day trying to convince Justin to join them. By the end of it, Rodney was showing signs of exasperation.

'Amongst other things, it will give you the opportunity to influence the future development of the company,' he said.

Justin stared at him. 'What on earth makes you think I want to influence its development?'

Philippa had been listening to them, but now she lifted her head, her gaze resting on Justin's face.

'You are not being offered charity. I cannot afford to give money away. And as I told you once before, I do not have any intention of fettering you to Moor View. The position will give you stature on the work floor, and you will be free to hand in your resignation whenever you wish.'

Something passed between them which Rodney was unable to interpret. It was obvious Justin took exception to Philippa's well-meant, but tactless remark about charity. His reply was cutting.

'If it is so important to you, I shall reluctantly accept.' His angry eyes rested on her face. 'You should spend more time here, Philippa. You must find the business world more

215

stimulating than the stream of mindless advertisements in which you appear these days.'

It was a cruel dig which hit home and brought about a premature end to the meeting. What he had said was true, for Philippa was becoming increasingly unhappy at the way Nicholas was using her to attract clients. He kept saying this was the last time, but it never was.

When she told Nicholas about Justin, he was furious, retorting that his brother had no business acumen and no right to become a director of Moor View. In contrast, he was not only her husband, but had put himself on a limb in order to do the preliminary publicity. Philippa exploded, and they had their first serious quarrel when she said the affairs of the pottery were none of his business.

Never again did she ask for his help. She no longer needed it. The break-through came in September, when a local chain of four Devonshire hotels placed an order for breakfast, dinner and tea services. A pattern was chosen from the old pattern books, and Justin incorporated the hotel crest into it. For the very first time the pottery came out of the red, managing to sustain the majority of its own expenses.

Also for the first time, Philippa found her money beginning to accumulate. She and Rodney were able to sit down and decide which areas would best benefit from additional investment. Their ultimate goal was a new kiln, but she had ear-marked her inheritance for that.

Moor View's success meant she could consider retiring from modelling. Nicholas did not agree.

'You are still at your peak, and in greater demand than ever,' he argued.

'Which is the reason I should give up now. I've had enough. I'm sick of living my life in a goldfish bowl. I want to be your wife, not Philippa Russell.' She had talked about this before, but never so seriously.

'Wait until Christmas, and see how you feel then. We're trying to attract a new account, a large one. We have every chance of swinging it if you agree to do the initial advertisement.'

She stared at him in disgust. 'I am doing too many adverts, Nicholas. Not only am I getting over-exposed, but I'm starting to hate them.'

Nicholas frowned. The agency was struggling to succeed in a highly competitive market. The big, international accounts preferred the larger agencies, which they thought more stable and better able to portray a corporate image. This account had American connections. He and Ernest needed it, but they were not going to get it without Philippa.

'One more, darling. It will be the last. I promise. Look, you're always complaining about not doing enough fashion. Why don't you arrange some sessions with Steve, then decide whether you still want to give up.' He kissed her gently, but she did not respond. 'I realise this has not been the easiest six months for either of us. Let's go away for Christmas. Anywhere you want.'

'Your mother is expecting us.'

'Mum never expects me.' This time he kissed her hard, his mouth grinding against hers.

She pushed him away. 'Don't, Nicholas, I'm not in the mood! I have to go and see Maggie.'

'To hell with Maggie! You say you want to be my wife. It's about time you started to act like one. I give you a free rein, Philippa. I have no idea what is happening at Moor View, but do not interfere because you have made it patently clear it is none of my business. However, as your husband I do have some rights.'

Philippa's expression was icy. 'I promised to love and

honour, not obey. Remember that, Nicholas. Because you want me to, I shall stick it out until Christmas. I shall also do your advertisement, providing your precious client is willing to pay my going rate.'

Nicholas breathed deeply to calm himself. They were heading towards another argument unless someone held forth the olive branch. Philippa usually took the initiative, but this time he defused the situation.

'Let's not argue about something so trivial,' he said. 'Forget about Maggie this evening. We can eat out and then do a couple of the clubs. It would do us both good.'

A repentant smile pulled at the corners of her mouth. 'I have to go. The baby is due any day now, and Noel is in Scotland until tomorrow. But I don't have to stay long, and it's no good going anywhere before ten. I'll be back by then.' She hated the clubs with their pounding music and cliques of celebrities who did the rounds in the hope of being seen. But Nicholas liked to be counted amongst those celebrities, and she too wanted to calm the rippled waters.

'Shall I run you over?' Nicholas asked.

'I can drive myself. It's not far.'

'I don't know why you insist on keeping that toy car. It's not as though I haven't offered to buy you a decent one.'

It was an old grievance. She had bought the red Mini last December, after passing her driving test. The car was her pride and joy, and ideal for London traffic. But she only used it in the city because Nicholas would not let her drive to the West Country alone.

'I like my Mini,' she said. 'And have no intention of exchanging it for something larger.'

Alec Duncan Buchanan arrived six days late, on a wet October morning, with a gale rattling the windows of the exclusive Knightsbridge clinic. He was the image of his father, even at the tender age of six hours, which was when Philippa first saw him. Maggie and Noel wanted her to be his godmother, Justin having been cajoled into being her opposite number. When she told Nicholas he grunted. He had more important matters on his mind. His prospective new account was turning sour. The man had the money but was looking for bargain basement rates.

'Let him go,' said Philippa. 'He's a cheapskate and there must be plenty of bigger fish in the ocean.'

'He has an American subsidiary. If we can swing this account, it will give us the opportunity to break into that market.'

She was snuggled against him, half asleep. They had eaten at their favourite restaurant, then come back early because Nicholas had brought home a pile of work. Three brandies later he was almost finished, and rather than go to bed without him, Philippa waited.

'You have been established for under twelve months. Don't you think the American market is over ambitious?'

'It won't be this time next year.' He looked at her. 'You look tired, darling. Why not go to bed? I won't be much longer. I think I may have found a way around the problem.'

'Good. You can tell me tomorrow.' She kissed his cheek. 'I love you, Nicholas.'

But love could not overcome every obstacle and when Nicholas did the unforgivable, it was Steve to whom Philippa turned. They had been friends for a long time and she knew he would understand how hurt she was.

'What happened?' he asked.

'Nicholas had me work flat out for three days on a television commercial, then paid me less than a quarter of the agreed fee. He said he had come to an arrangement whereby he would get the account if I did the commercial for peanuts.' She drank the champagne which Steve placed in front of her. He refilled her glass. 'If he had explained the situation I would have worked for nothing. All it took was a little trust.'

'It's only money, love. Is it worth jeopardising your happiness, even your marriage, for something so unimportant? True, he has played you a dirty hand, but it's not as though you are desperate for money any more.'

'It's not the money. It's the principle.' She ran a forefinger around the rim of the glass. They were sitting in his living room and the light from a nearby lamp reflected off her diamond engagement ring and the wide band of gold above it.

'What are you going to do?'

'Refuse to make any adverts, even if he goes down on his knees and begs.' She looked up. 'I want to retire from modelling, Steve, but I want to be remembered for something more than a string of commercials. I'd like to come back into full-time fashion for a while.'

'The door has always been open. You only have to walk through it. When do you want to start?'

'Immediately.'

'What about Nicholas?'

'He will have to put up with it. Before we married we agreed to follow our separate careers. I was foolish enough to allow him to interfere with mine, and now I intend to redress the situation.' She picked up her glass. The champagne was the best vintage and there were bottles of it in Steve's fridge. 'What about next month's trip? Has it been settled, or are you still having problems?'

Steve had not expected that. She had emphatically stated she would not do another foreign assignment. And now she was asking about a two-week stint in South America.

'We're still arguing about it. They left it too late and all the top models are tied up. Now they want to use two girls who are barely out of their teens. I disagree. I was thinking of bowing out altogether and letting them get another photographer.'

'I'll come,' Philippa volunteered. 'As it's for *Vogue*, I am sure they will not object to me.'

'You'll be welcomed with open arms. But are you sure this is what you want? Nicholas is not going to take kindly to you being away for so long.'

'Nicholas will have to put up with it.' Her reply was curt. 'What about the second model? I would prefer to work with somebody I know.'

Steve hesitated. 'Would you object to Rosalind? There will be a lot of resistance, but we could overcome it if we stick together. She needs the money and is finding it difficult to get back into the business.'

Philippa had heard unsubstantiated rumours about Rosalind Harper leaving the middle-aged Italian count she had married eighteen months ago. She had gone to Italy with him, breaking contracts and making enemies of some important people in the fashion industry. Steve had said very little at the time, but he had always cared for her.

'She was good to me when I first started. Of course I won't mind working with her.'

She recalled those autumn days in Scotland – the magical Rosalind stalking through a swirl of autumn leaves, and her own hopeless, first love. It all seemed to have happened a long time ago.

She held up her glass. 'Let's drink to new beginnings.'

Steve grinned. 'And happy endings.'

Moor View had not only boosted Justin's finances when he was most in need of money, but had also sped up the process started by Maggie when she had exhibited his works at the Huntington Gallery two years earlier. The plates had generated more interest in his work, and recognition could now be measured by the number of paintings being sold.

The money meant he and Alice were finally able to move out of the cramped, one-bedroomed flat into something more spacious, where Jennie had her own room and he a separate studio. They were still in Chelsea, at the unfashionable lower end, close to the Fulham Road. Alice had wanted him to get a mortgage and buy a small house with a garden in the suburbs, where they would have the respectability of a young, married couple with a child. Justin refused, and signed a one-year lease on a rented flat. If he did tie himself down, it would be out of London altogether, in the countryside, not suburbia. But that was unlikely to happen, for Alice made no bones about how much she hated the country.

Soon after they moved, Alice went to work three afternoons a week at her friend's dancing school off the Bayswater Road. She was not well paid, and most of the money went to the nursery school where she left Jennie after Justin made it clear he would not be responsible for the child over long periods of time. There was no question of her returning to the chorus line. The hours were too incompatible and it was doubtful whether she could stand the strain any more. She had never regained her stamina after Jennie's birth. The doctors said she was anaemic and, for a while, she took foul-tasting tonics and brightly coloured pills. But she had given them up because they made no difference. She felt as tired with them as she did without.

Nursery school had been a blessing as far as Jennie was concerned, for it got her away from her mother's pampering and amongst toddlers of her own age. She had grown from a screeching baby into a chubby two year old with her father's colouring, and features which were a happy mixture of both parents. She was a bright, talkative child, who was incapable of sitting still for any length of time, except in Justin's presence. Then, under his watchful eye, she would play quietly with her toys, or else scrawl in a colouring book, careful not to make greasy marks on the carpets or furniture.

She was playing a fantasy game now, with a tattered teddy bear and a stuffed rabbit which had floppy ears. Every so often she would pause and gaze at her father, wanting his approval, but not getting it. Nicholas had often noticed how she never did. He found it strange his brother had so little time for his own daughter, when he had shown such tolerance with Helen as a child.

It was Sunday, and if Justin had not asked him for lunch he would have gone to the office and worked, like he had done yesterday. He refused to admit it, but he missed Philippa. They had a blazing row when she told him she was going to South America, and were still not talking when she left. He had come home on the Tuesday evening, certain she would have cancelled the trip and be waiting for him. Instead, he found a neatly written itinerary of where she could be reached. He had rolled the sheet of paper into a ball and thrown it into the kitchen bin, only to fish it out a couple of hours later. He smoothed down the rumpled paper and left it beside the telephone, but he did not ring her. She was in the wrong, not him.

Alice came into the room. They had eaten a late lunch or early supper, depending upon how you looked at it, and she had been washing the dishes, having refused an offer of help from Nicholas, who would never dream of washing a cup in his own home, let alone dirty plates. Her blonde hair was tied back from her face. She looked tired, and was painfully thin.

'Come along, Jennie,' she said. 'It's time for your bath and then bed. Kiss Daddy and Uncle Nicholas goodnight.'

Jennie was about to protest, then glanced at her father and thought better of it. She stood up and, dragging the teddy bear behind her, toddled on stubby legs to Nicholas first and then Justin. He let her kiss his cheek, but displayed no outward signs of affection. Nicholas knew his brother's deference could not be attributed to any doubt over her parentage. You only had to look at Jennie to know she was his daughter. The resentment could only stem from his feelings towards Alice. They had nothing in common, except for their child.

Alice picked up the discarded rabbit, then scooped the child into her arms.

Justin frowned. 'She's not a baby any more. She has legs and is far too heavy for you to carry around.'

Twin flushes of colour stained Alice's cheeks. 'It's only across the hall. Why don't the two of you go for a drink? The pubs should be open now. Don't worry about me. Bath-time always takes ages, and she likes me to read her to sleep.'

It was drizzling, and the reflection of the street lights on the pavements made them glisten. Christmas was still three weeks away, but many houses had gaily lit trees in their windows. Few cars were about and even fewer people. The two brothers had been cooped up all afternoon and, in mutual consent, walked rather than drove. They headed towards the Kings Road.

'Is Alice all right?' Nicholas asked. 'She looks – well, not ill exactly, but she's a terrible colour, and I swear she has lost weight since I last saw her.'

'The flesh has been falling off her since she went back to dancing, but she won't see a doctor.' Justin was staring straight ahead, his hands thrust into his pockets. 'I was thinking of going home next week rather than waiting until Christmas. We'll probably stay there until after New Year, which will give Alice the break she needs. Will you and Philippa be coming down?'

'We were planning to go abroad, but I don't know what we'll do now. I have not given it any thought.'

Justin glanced at his brother. His face had hardened and his mouth was set in an uncompromising line. He had barely mentioned Philippa this afternoon. She had been gone for five days and was not due back until the week after next.

'It's no good burying your head in the sand and pretending the problem doesn't exist,' he said.

'What problem?'

They turned into the Kings Road. There was more traffic here, and people. A couple of girls, huddled under a colourful umbrella and wearing short PVC raincoats and knee-high boots, walked towards them. They giggled and fluttered their false eyelashes at the two good-looking men, but the brothers swept past without noticing them.

'Did you think Philippa would not see through your ruse of using her to build up the agency and attract new clients? You have not married a dumb blonde, Nick, but an intelligent young woman who is more than capable of thinking for herself.'

'Brother or not, what happens between my wife and me is none of your business! Considering the mistakes you have made in your own life, I do not think you are qualified to lecture me on mine.' Justin took hold of his arm and, glowering, Nicholas swung round to face him. 'I told you I did not want to discuss it.'

'Don't be a fool, Nicholas. If you can't talk to me, who can you talk to? She went into modelling for the money. She

225

no longer needs it, yet is expected to continue working for your benefit.'

His brother's eyes narrowed. 'You too have profited from my wife. It was because of me she asked you to do those plates. At the time, I did not realise she would go mad and make you a director. She doesn't even tell me what is happening at the pottery. Moor View is a big secret.'

'A successful marriage needs a lot of give and take, and up to now you seem to be doing all the taking and Philippa the giving. As for my so-called directorship, it is nothing more than a courtesy title which was forced upon me. I am not profiting by it.'

'You could have refused.'

'I did, repeatedly. But was landed with it all the same.' Nicholas started to walk. 'Why did you marry her? Because you love her, or because you can profit by her?'

He stopped. 'Of course I love her. I am not mercenary.'

'I know you, Nicholas. You probably do love her in your own way. But I suspect you love what she can do for you even more.'

'I am a realist, Justin, not a dreamer. I need a wife who is an asset, and Philippa is certainly that.'

'Then heed my warning and never let her find out. Remember she started life as a spoilt rich kid who was suddenly thrown on to the street. She had the will to survive, and will continue to do so, with or without you.'

'If you are so certain she wants to give up modelling, tell me why she ran off with Steve?'

'I should have thought that was obvious. It's her way of saying you do not own her. Whatever you may think, she is not having an affair with him.'

It was lightly said, but his brother stiffened. 'Why not? She slept with him before me. She was no virgin when she came to my bed.'

226

'Oh, for heaven's sake, grow up! We are living in the Sixties, not the Middle Ages. Anyhow, the divine but ageing Rosalind is with them. Surely you knew that?'

'How would I know anything? We were not talking when she left!'

Justin sighed. There were times when Nicholas could be infuriating.

'You must decide what you want, a professional model or a wife. If it is the former, then you would have been kinder not to marry her. She loves you, which is a lot more than you deserve. You even turned your wedding day into a public exhibition.'

'Have you finished? Or am I expected to listen to this drivel for the rest of the evening?'

'I've finished, except for one last piece of advice. Patch up this ridiculous quarrel, then sit down together and talk out your problems. Try and tell the truth, Nick. In the long run, lies will get you nowhere.'

'I never lie. I simply hedge around the truth.' He grinned. 'Cheer up, big brother. Philippa and I are having some teething problems, but once we have sorted ourselves out we are sure to live happily ever after.'

Perhaps he was being over-optimistic, but Justin knew he would try, for a while at least.

CHAPTER EIGHTEEN

Because it had developed a minor fault before take-off the plane was three hours late into Heathrow. Philippa had been sick during the flight and all she wanted was to get home and lie down. She was leaning on Steve's arm when they left the customs area, with Rosalind following behind carrying the hand luggage. She did not see Nicholas waiting, but Steve did and whispered in her ear. She looked up, her pallid skin disguised by a rich tan. She started to say something – anything – but he was quicker.

'I missed you.'

She melted into his arms. 'I missed you too.'

Rosalind and Steve exchanged relieved glances, and when Nicholas offered to drive them into London they declined.

'Didn't you bring the MG?' Philippa asked. He had his arm around her and she felt good leaning against him.

'I thought you would have too much luggage.'

In reality she had very little. He must have borrowed Ernest's Rover. She was glad he had, for the MG was too close to the ground and the motion would probably make her want to throw up.

'Why were you thanking Rosalind?' Nicholas asked as they walked through the car park.

'For being kind to me. Rosalind is one of the kindest people I have ever known. I wish she and Steve would get together. But I doubt if they will now. They have grown apart.'

He pulled her closer to him. 'Are you warm enough?'

His concern sent a warm glow of happiness through her. She was glad to be back.

'I bought you a present,' he said.

'That's sweet of you. What is it?'

'This.' He stopped beside a new Jaguar. 'A classy lady should drive a classy car. Cute though your Mini may be, it would cave in like a sardine can if you were involved in an accident.'

He opened the boot for the porter, gave him a generous tip, then handed the keys to Philippa.

'It's your car. You drive.'

It was a generous gesture for Nicholas. He hated being driven.

'We've had a long flight and I'm tired. I would prefer to be the passenger.'

The wooden finish on the dashboard and the smell of new leather reminded her of the past. Of Mike Taylor and her father's Rolls-Royce.

'Can you afford this?' she asked.

'Would I have bought it if I couldn't?' He turned the ignition key.

'Nicholas, I have something important to tell you.'

He twisted round. She would not meet his gaze, and under the tan he was aware of an unexpected sallowness. He felt a tight knot in the pit of his stomach as he switched off the engine.

'What is it?' His voice sounded hoarse.

She was staring at a discoloured cement wall. 'I'm pregnant,' she blurted out. 'The day after we arrived on location I started to throw up. Steve rearranged the schedule for a couple of days, but Rosalind guessed what was wrong and insisted I see a doctor.' Her breath caught in her throat. This had been as much a shock to her as it must be to him. Motherhood was something which had never occurred to her. 'I suppose I should have been more careful, but sometimes, when I was working, I had to skip the pill for a few days. I thought I had sufficient protection.'

Nicholas folded his hand over hers, then kissed her with loving tenderness.

'Let's go home,' he said.

The morning sickness stopped as abruptly as it had started, and by the end of February Philippa was not only feeling good, but looked it as well. Her swan song had been an elaborate close-up for a *Vogue* cover. Modelling was another part of her life which she had left behind. Steve knew she would never return to it. Nicholas had other ideas, but for now he was the solicitous husband pampering his pregnant wife. At first, Philippa found it strange to have time on her hands. She organised the transformation of the spare bedroom into a nursery and wished Moor View was closer. But the pottery was too far away and she did not want to provoke a row by going there.

Then, one evening in March, Nicholas told her he had to visit Manchester for a couple of days, to woo a new client.

'I am sorry, darling,' he said. 'But the man is being awkward and Ernest will never be able to handle him. I think I can secure the account, but if I do it will mean putting in extra hours. I don't like leaving you here alone. Would you object to staying with my mother for a while? She will be thrilled to have you, and I could drive you down this weekend.'

It was what she had wanted all along.

Nicholas promised to come down regularly, but his trips

were spasmodic, and more strain showed in his face each time Philippa saw him. He refused to tell her what was wrong, but she guessed he had problems with the agency. Up to now he had found it too easy, unlike Moor View, which had been an uphill struggle and still was. They needed the new oven badly, but until she got her inheritance next year they had to pray the old one would last.

She returned to London at the end of June, a month before the baby was due. She was weighed down by the great lump in her belly, and felt lethargic and irritable. During the day she did not move around much, letting her friends come to her, but Nicholas often took her out in the evenings, when it was cooler. They stayed away from their old haunts, taking gentle walks beside the Thames, or sometimes driving further afield, to less populated places.

It was on one of those occasions that she tackled him about the agency. They had driven to Henley and were sitting on the sloping lawn of a favourite pub, with the river lapping an arm's length from them. He was drinking lager, she orange juice. Nicholas had said very little, and in the evening sunshine his face was grey.

'Please tell me what is wrong.' Philippa laid her hand over his. 'Something is, however much you deny it.'

'We have lost a couple of clients. I know it doesn't sound much, but they were both large enough accounts to justify taking on extra staff. One of them was the bastard with the American connections.'

The one Nicholas had under-paid her for. It was ironic he should be the one to walk out.

'You still have Mermaid. You always told me you could survive if you kept that.'

'No advertising agency can survive indefinitely on one account. We need to expand, not stagnate. And Harwood is being difficult about the new model. He wants you back.'

231

Philippa turned her head away, gazing at some ducks bobbing on the water. 'I am not coming back, ever. I got out while I was still at the top. I am not going to be like Rosalind, begging for crumbs. My life has taken another direction now. I am perfectly content to be a wife and mother.'

'Once the novelty of having a child has worn off your obsession with that damn pottery will start all over again. Well, you had better pray it continues to flourish, because if the agency carries on at its present rate, we might not be around at the end of the year.'

A runnel of shock passed through her. 'You never said you had financial problems.'

'One leads to the other. We are over-extended, with an unsympathetic bank manager breathing down our necks. This is a bad time of year to pick up new accounts. Everything is on hold until the end of summer.' His eyes sought hers. 'There is no need for you to worry. Should the worst happen, we will get by until I can find a job.'

She thought of the battering his pride would take if he had to go round the agencies, cap in hand. She thought too of the money squandered on a luxury car which she did not want.

'How much do you need to see you through? I still have the last of my modelling money.'

'I doubt whether it would be enough.'

'There's nearly eight thousand pounds. I was going to put it towards the improvements we're making at Moor View next year. It's yours if you want it.'

She saw the glimmer in his eyes and in that instant knew he would take it all if she let him, not only the eight thousand pounds, but the inheritance for which she had waited so long.

He leant across the table and kissed her cheek.

'Thank you, darling. I shall pay back every penny.'

It was an empty promise, and she knew it.

The next morning she took a taxi to the offices of Perkins, Crisp & Perkins. She did not have an appointment, but Leonard Perkins kept her waiting for no longer than five minutes.

'I have to leave for Court in fifteen minutes, Mrs Lang.' He folded his hands in the customary manner over his stomach. They had known each other for five years and he still maintained a formal relationship.

'Then I shall come straight to the point. I want to protect Moor View, keep it safe for my child, like my grandfather kept it for me.' She saw his sudden alarm and smiled. 'I am not expecting anything to go wrong. I am perfectly healthy. It is merely a precaution, Mr Perkins.'

He nodded. 'A simple document would suffice. I take it there are certain conditions you wish to include?'

'Yes.' She hesitated. She had not told Nicholas, nor did she have an intention of doing so. Moor View meant no more to him than it had to her father. And like her father, Nicholas would take everything he could from it, then leave it to rot. 'Should it ever become necessary, for whatever reason, I want Rodney Slater and Justin Lang to become joint trustees. They are to run the business unimpeded until my son or daughter comes of age.'

His eyes widened. 'Your husband's brother, but not your husband?'

'Yes, Mr Perkins. Not my husband. I want the pottery to be in the hands of people who care for it. Unfortunately, I do not consider Nicholas to be amongst them.'

A fortnight later Philippa went into premature labour. Dawn was breaking over the horizon when Nicholas rushed her to the private clinic which Maggie had recommended. But it was not until late in the afternoon that their son was born.

'I'd like to call him Christopher,' she said when Nicholas saw him for the first time. 'Christopher after my grandfather, and George in memory of your father.'

'Mum will be pleased.' He placed a tentative finger in the palm of his son's hand. The tiny fingers closed around it, their grip surprisingly strong. 'I'll telephone her later with the good news. I've been trying to get Justin all afternoon. He must be out.'

Philippa was not really listening. She was gazing at the baby which lay in her arms. He had enormous blue eyes and not a hair upon his head. The love she felt for him was quite different to anything she had experienced before, and she was determined he was never going to know the pain of being unloved, as she had.

While Philippa and Nicholas admired their infant son, a young, over-worked doctor in the casualty department of a public hospital walked towards the man who had been waiting for over three hours. On the bench beside him a child was curled up asleep. The father had placed his jacket beneath her head and she had one arm around a tattered teddy bear and her thumb in her mouth.

Alice had been brought here by ambulance after collapsing during a dancing class. Whatever was wrong, Justin guessed it must be serious from the doctor's expression. He glanced at Jennie, then stood up.

'I am sorry for keeping you waiting, Mr Lang, but this afternoon has been chaotic. Your wife appears to be fine now, but I would like to admit her for further tests.'

'Tests for what?'

'She is suffering from acute anaemia. I suspect it might be leukaemia, but we cannot be certain until the tests are complete.' He paused. He had never become hardened to being the bearer of bad news. 'If it is, we do have effective treatment and, in some cases, a total cure.'

Justin scooped the sleeping child into his arms. She moaned, but did not wake. Her head lolled against his shoulder and her teddy bear fell on to the floor. The doctor picked it up.

'May I see her now?' he asked.

'Of course.'

Justin forced a smile to his lips as he walked towards the curtained cubicle.

PART THREE

1973 to 1976

CHAPTER NINETEEN

'Why can't I have a pony of my own?' Kit asked.

'Because we live in London and have nowhere to keep it.'

'Why can't we live here?'

'Because Daddy works in London. Now stop asking silly questions.'

The child pulled a face. 'Can I canter to the gate?'

'Yes. But wait for me when you get there.'

Philippa smiled as the pony sped away. She would also like to live here, if only for part of the year, but Nicholas refused to discuss the matter. Moor View was doing well and she could go out tomorrow and buy a cottage. Nicholas knew it and resented the independence she was careful not to flaunt. He was unable to understand she had outgrown the London scene. The fun-loving innocence of the Sixties had been overtaken by a more sombre decade. The flower children were gone and hard drugs had replaced marijuana. There was social unrest, runaway inflation and the increasing horrors of debilitating strikes. Moor View was a small, independent pottery whose workers belonged to no union, but the prolonged power strikes of 1972 had hit them hard at a time when the business was finally coming into its own and making a respectable profit.

They had weathered the storm up to now, as had Lang &

Wakefield, but according to Nicholas things were going to get worse before they got better. Like our marriage, Philippa thought. The rot set in soon after Christopher was born, when she refused to go back to modelling. Since then it had deteriorated into an empty shell, but at least she had the satisfaction of knowing there had been no infidelity on Nicholas's part. Maggie was not so lucky.

The year before a reporter had found out about an affair Noel was having with one of his models and had blown it out of all proportion. Maggie stood by him and, for a while, guilt kept him from wandering. But Nicholas had heard he was carrying on again. If Maggie knew she was telling nobody, and Philippa was not about to hurt her friend by saying anything.

Kit was waiting by the gate and rode on ahead while she closed it.

'Daddy's come!' he yelled, startling her.

Philippa looked up to see him trot Sam around the side of the barn and on to the driveway.

'Kit!'

If he heard, he ignored her. She started to run, afraid he would fall on the gravel, but when she reached the drive Kit was tumbling off the pony and into his father's arms. She held back, giving them more time together. She often criticised Nicholas for putting work before family, but he was not a bad father. He cared, which was more than her own father had done.

Nicholas saw her and smiled. In the sunlight he looked tired and tense. She walked towards him, but stopped when Jennie came out of the house, a strange expression on her face as she watched the display of affection between father and son. She was a pretty child with her father's colouring, and tall for an eight-year-old.

'Hello, Jennie.' Philippa greeted her first because she

could see the hurt on the girl's face. Justin had no time for his daughter, and her mother was too ill to pay the child any attention. Philippa held out her arms. Jennie hesitated for a moment, then ran to her. She hugged the child and kissed her forehead. 'Where did you spring from?'

'Uncle Nicholas brought me. Daddy says I have to spend the rest of the holidays here. He and Mummy will be coming down soon.'

Philippa glanced at Nicholas. He shook his head, mouthing a firm 'no'.

'You'd better unsaddle Sam,' he told Kit. 'Remember to brush him before putting him out. Jennie can help you.'

They had always got along, despite the age difference. They ran to the pony and snatched up the reins, laughing as they led him to the barn.

'Why did you bring her here?' Philippa asked.

'You had better come inside.'

He took her into the kitchen, where there was a pot of tea and some empty cups on the table.

'Do you want some?' he asked.

'No, thank you.'

She watched while he filled a cup, adding milk from a glass jug. He looked up, his eyes meeting hers. She was pleased their son had not inherited those pale eyes.

'Alice is dying. She was rushed to hospital this morning, and Justin does not want Jennie there.'

Philippa reached across the table and laid her hand upon his. Over the years she had come to know how close Nicholas was to his brother. 'Are you sure? Alice has been in and out of hospital for the past twelve months.'

'I am sure,' he said. 'It has only been a matter of time. You've seen how rapidly she has gone downhill.'

In reality, Philippa had seen little of Alice. The last time had been two months ago, when she had looked alarmingly

241

frail and gaunt. She knew Nicholas often dropped by after he had finished at the office, but he rarely spoke of his visits, even when she asked him.

'Mum and Helen are getting ready,' he was saying. 'I'm taking them back with me.'

'Today?'

'Yes. I'll have to take your car and leave you the Porsche. Drive it carefully, Philippa, it is a powerful vehicle and not a plaything.'

She stared at him. 'Surely you don't expect me to stay here?'

'Somebody has to look after the children, and at a time like this Justin needs the support of his family.'

'And what am I meant to be?'

'My wife,' he coldly replied, his tone making it clear she was an outsider, and always would be as far as his family was concerned.

Alice died an hour before dawn.

Sarah and Helen came home by train, while Nicholas stayed with his brother. He and Justin drove back the next day, staying for one night before returning to London. Justin looked awful. He spoke little and ate less. In the afternoon he took Jennie riding on the moors, and somewhere in that wilderness he must have told the child about her mother.

Kit sulked because he was not allowed to go with them, so Helen took him out for the day. Pauline had been there for three years and was capable of taking out the afternoon ride, but Sarah went with her, which left Nicholas and Philippa alone in the house. He looked exhausted, having driven between there and London three times in as many days, with the prospect of having to drive back shortly.

'Can I do anything to help?' Philippa asked as she massaged his knotted shoulder muscles.

'You could arrange for the Slaters to look after Christopher and Jennie on the day of the funeral.'

'They are coming to it. They didn't know Alice well, but want to be there out of respect for Justin. Rodney's parents are going to have Peter and the twins, so I don't suppose another two will make any difference.' She hesitated. 'Won't Jennie be coming with us?'

'Justin says she is too young. He has arranged for her to stay here for a while. That feels good, darling. Can you move a little to the right.'

She did as he asked. Alice was to be cremated and her ashes buried in a West London cemetery. Justin had been dogmatic. Alice hated the countryside and he refused to give way when Sarah insisted she be laid to rest in Povey Ashton.

'Shouldn't I come back with you tomorrow? Somebody has to make the arrangements for afterwards.'

'Noel and Maggie are attending to it. We'll be using their house.'

Once again Philippa felt like an intruder. She turned away from him.

'I'll come down on Sunday so that I can drive you to London on Monday morning,' Nicholas said. 'The service is not until the afternoon.'

Philippa glanced at him. 'I am not helpless. Neither are Sarah and Helen. Between the three of us we should be capable of driving ourselves.'

His smile was unexpected. 'Of course you are. I'll take the Porsche and leave you the Jag.'

'Do you want me to stay on after the funeral?'

'And leave Moor View? Isn't the pottery the reason you insist on coming here every summer?'

She bridled at his sarcasm, but kept her temper in check, not wanting to argue with him. 'If you spent more time with Kit and me you might understand why I bring him here.

You should try and get some sleep. You're exhausted.'

'I am too tired to sleep.' He stood up and went to her. 'Come upstairs with me.'

'In the middle of the afternoon?'

'Nobody will be back for ages.'

'What about Justin?'

'I expect he has taken Jennie to Flint Iron Tor.'

Philippa was startled. 'Why there?'

'Why not? It's isolated and a good place for talking. I took you there once. It was the first time we kissed.'

'I remember,' she said, touched that he also did.

She had no desire to make love in a hot bedroom in the middle of the afternoon, but pretended enthusiasm where there was none. Afterwards, while watching him sleep, she wondered where their lives were going.

Summer was over. Philippa was taking Kit home the next day and Jennie asked if she could go with them. She had heard nothing from her father and was a confused and frightened little girl. When Philippa telephoned Nicholas he said his brother was busy sorting out the flat and was coming down soon. His brusque manner suggested more, but whatever it was, he did not tell her. It was also the first time he would not be driving her back.

Sarah wanted to give the children a treat on Kit's last day, so she took them into Torquay, leaving Philippa free to tie up some loose ends at the pottery. She was in her office, looking through the previous month's sales figures, when the door opened.

'May I come in?' Justin asked.

'You know you are always welcome.' She pushed back her chair and stood up. 'Did you go home first? Sarah has taken the children out, but they should be back soon. Jennie will be thrilled to see you.'

He closed the door and stood with his back against it. He had lost weight. His cheeks were hollow and his clothes hung off him.

'I'm not going back to the house. My mother already knows. I telephoned her this morning. You must have gone, otherwise she would have told you.'

'What about Jennie?'

'She has her grandmother and Helen. She does not need me as well.'

'Of course she needs you. You are her father.'

Their eyes clashed, but his reflected none of the anger she felt. What she saw was pain.

'I'm sorry. I should not have snapped at you like that.'

'You and I always did have a knack of rubbing each other up the wrong way.'

'Not always,' she said quietly. 'Not at Lochdunnan.'

'No,' he agreed. 'Not at Lochdunnan. That was a mistake which has been dearly paid for.'

'I never realised until now how much you loved Alice.'

'I admired her courage. She kept on fighting, even when there was no hope. I suppose that could be construed as love. I wanted to send Jennie here a long time ago, but she stopped me. Then, at the end, when she knew she was dying, she told me to send her away.'

'What about your daughter? Don't you owe her something?'

'I cannot cope with a child at the moment. I'm going away for a while. My mother understands.'

'Does Jennie? You have seen her once since her mother died, and now you are going to walk out of her life without a word. For heaven's sake, Justin, you didn't even allow her to attend the funeral.'

He crossed the room and leant across the desk, his dark eyes smouldering.

'Do you think she should remember her mother as a lifeless body lying in a coffin? I don't and, as you keep telling me, her well-being is my responsibility. How do you remember your father? The last time I saw mine was when I had to identify him. I couldn't let my mother do it, and Nicholas was only eighteen. Believe me, there is very little left which is identifiable when somebody jumps off a cliff.' As he turned away the anger seemed to drain from him. 'So don't lecture me on how to bring up my daughter.'

'I didn't know.'

'Nobody does.'

Philippa longed to go to him, but she didn't.

'I am not deserting her,' he said after a while. 'What Jennie needs now is love and stability, neither of which I am capable of giving her.'

'How long will you be gone?'

'A month. Perhaps longer. Which is why I needed to see you.'

He tossed an envelope on to the desk.

'What is this?'

'My resignation. You said I was free to hand it in whenever I wanted. I should have done so a long time ago. I have contributed nothing to Moor View this year.'

'It was not part of our bargain that you should. We have other artists on our books now, although your work is superior to anything they can do. We are already receiving enquiries about the Christmas plate.'

The first of the Christmas plates had been issued in 1970. They were numbered and limited to three firings, and had sold out within days. In subsequent years they had kept to the same formula and were invariably over-subscribed before the first firing took place.

'I shall not be doing it this year,' he said.

Philippa was gripped by an icy chill as she realised what

he was doing. 'You are running away. You don't even know if you are coming back.'

'Think what you will. I am running away from nothing.'

'I am not going to accept this.' She picked up the envelope and tore it in half. 'I have a valid reason, but never said anything before because I didn't want Nicholas to find out.'

He was frowning. 'When have I told Nicholas anything he has no business knowing?'

Philippa flushed. 'This is different. You *have* to remain part of the structure of Moor View. Should anything happen to me, my lawyer holds a Power of Attorney which will enable you and Rodney to run the business until Kit comes of age.'

'What about Nicholas?'

'He is not included.'

'Does he know?'

'Would I be telling you if he did? Nicholas has no more feeling for Moor View than my father had, and I never want it to fall into his hands.'

'My dear girl, what on earth do you think will happen to you?'

'Probably nothing. But surely you have noticed how our lives have a curious way of crossing. I am not talking about my marriage, but other things. What happened to our fathers, for instance.'

'You silly little fool.' He took her hands in his. 'Go back home to Nicholas and put those ridiculous thoughts out of your head. I know he may not always show it, but he misses you when you're not there.' Gently, he kissed her cheek. 'If it will put your mind at ease, then we'll leave things as they stand. Goodbye, Philippa.'

It might have been coincidence, but no sooner had Justin left than Moor View ran into trouble. Philippa had not realised until then how much of the pottery's success was attributable to him. The quality of his own work spoke for itself, but he had also taken on additional responsibilities, leaving Rodney free to run the practical side of the business. He may have spent little time at the pottery since Alice's health started to fail, but not a moment of that time had been wasted. His presence was going to be sorely missed.

Philippa had barely settled Kit into his new school when she had to return to Tavistock for a couple of days. Nicholas was annoyed.

'You're over-reacting,' he told her. 'Justin will not leave Jennie with Mum indefinitely. He'll be back by the end of the month. Surely the pottery can get by without him for a few weeks? He hardly ever goes there anyhow.'

'We have to decide on the Christmas plate now, otherwise it won't be ready on time. I'm sorry, darling, but we simply took it for granted he would do the plate, and now we have been thrown into chaos.'

It was the first of a succession of visits she made over the next few months. She had been the last person to see Justin and did not have Nicholas's faith. The person who suffered most from his absence was his daughter. To desert her so soon after her mother's death was cruel. Sarah disagreed, saying he had been under a tremendous strain and needed to get away for the sake of his sanity. But as the year drew to a close, Philippa became increasingly concerned as the once pert little girl began to withdraw into herself.

By Christmas, even Sarah was worried. A present arrived for Jennie. It was a doll with a china face and real hair, which had been packed and posted by Harrods. A card came separately, bearing an Italian postmark. There was no message, no indication of when he was coming back, and no return address. Jennie never played with the doll. She kept it on a chair beside her bed, where she could see it when she went to sleep, and when she awoke.

'He'll be back,' Sarah insisted, but she sounded less sure.

Philippa was glad to see the end of 1973. It had been a miserable year. The price of oil had shot up, with resultant inflation; there were power strikes and miners strikes, and industry was crippled by a three-day working week. Moor View was strong enough to withstand the worst of the onslaught, but had this happened six years before it would have been a different matter.

Profits dropped, and the Christmas plate, one of their yearly boosters, was a disaster. She and Rodney had chosen a seasonal painting by a popular artist with a good reputation, but orders for fewer than half the plates were received. By extensive advertising and distribution to a handful of shops they got rid of them, but the additional costs bit deep into their profits. It brought home more than ever how valuable Justin had been. There were no prints of his paintings in circulation, and the people who bought his plates did so because they could not afford an original.

Philippa's optimism about the new year being better than the old was short lived. The three-day working week carried on into January, while the strikes simply carried on, with the unions holding the country to ransom, contributing to the soaring inflation, massive unemployment, and a crippling system of taxation which hit her and Nicholas particularly hard. She made another three trips to Moor View during January and, after the third, decided to confront Nicholas about something which had been on her mind for a long time.

They had been out to dinner, and she had successfully desisted from going to a nightclub afterwards. Up to a year ago Nicholas would never have given in so easily, but many of the old crowd were falling away and they met few people they knew well. Kit was long asleep when they got home, and Eileen watching television in her room.

Eileen Brown was a spinster in her mid-forties whom Philippa had employed soon after Kit was born. They already had a woman who came in six days a week to clean, and Philippa did not want a nanny. But Nicholas put his foot down, refusing to have their lives ruled by a baby. So they compromised, looking for a live-in housekeeper who would not mind babysitting. Nicholas also suggested it would be a good idea if she could cook, his wife's culinary skills never having progressed beyond the basics.

After looking in on Kit and thanking Eileen, Philippa made coffee. She took it into the living room where Nicholas was sipping brandy. He had switched on the television set, not to watch the programmes, but the advertisements. It was flickering soundlessly and she switched it off.

'It's past peak viewing time,' she said.

'There's a new coffee ad being released tonight which I want to see. It's sure to be repeated.'

'You can see it tomorrow. We need to talk, Nicholas.'

'What about?' He sounded suspicious.

'You and me and Moor View.'

'I should have known Moor View would be involved. You're been there more often than you have been here during the past three months. And please don't insult my intelligence by blaming my brother's absence. You are obsessed with it, and always have been.'

Philippa let that pass. He had been short tempered for a long time. Lang & Wakefield was not finding it easy either.

'Rodney cannot make all the decisions on his own and we're having problems getting orders out on time.'

'So is three quarters of the country.'

'I want to buy a house down there. Somewhere close to

Tavistock with a few acres attached to it. Then, when he's older, we can buy Kit a pony.'

His glass thudded on to a side table. Brandy splashed over the polished surface.

'And what is that supposed to mean? That you intend moving down there permanently?'

'Of course not. But for one reason or another we are both spending more time down there. I get embarrassed sometimes, the way we turn up on your mother's doorstep. It makes sense to have a second home where we could go during the holidays, and it would be good for Kit to spend more time in a country environment.'

'And it would also suit you down to the ground.' His eyes flashed with anger. 'The answer is no. I am not buying you another house. I bought this place because you wanted a garden, but I've never seen you do anything in it.'

'I never realised I was expected to pull weeds and cut grass. Or haven't you noticed the gardener who comes in every Saturday morning? You've been paying him for the past three years.'

His expression hardened. 'Sarcasm does not become you, darling, and it's certainly not going to persuade me to buy you a house, in Tavistock or anywhere else.'

'I have not asked you to buy me a house. I said I wanted to buy a house. I have my own money. You do not need to contribute a penny towards it.'

Nicholas leapt to his feet and grasped her right arm above the wrist.

'You're hurting me!' Unsuccessfully, she tried to pull away.

'Then stop struggling!' He pulled her closer to him, so that she felt his breath against her cheek. 'You are my wife, Philippa, and your place is here with me. I am sick to the back teeth of coming home and being told you are about to make another trip to the pottery. I have tried to be considerate, although you have shown little consideration for me or my own business. But I'll be damned if I am going to stand by and let you make a laughing stock of our marriage by spending more time there than you already are.'

'Let go of me, Nicholas!' She was as furious as he was. 'You're talking rubbish and you know it. Had I shown a little less consideration, Lang & Wakefield would not be doing as well as it is now. I have not only modelled for your clients, but have entertained them lavishly, sitting through hours of tedious conversation for your sake. You have never done anything for Moor View, other than one advertising campaign, and only because it suited your purposes at the time.'

She winced as his grip tightened. She found this dark side of his character alarming, not because she was afraid of him, but because she was no match against brute strength.

'Be careful, Philippa.' His voice was threatening. 'You are walking a fine line. Don't push me too far, because you may not find the consequences to your liking. If you persist in putting Moor View first, you can't expect me to sit here awaiting your return.'

The insinuation was clear and she reacted automatically. He caught hold of her hand before she could strike him across the face. The air between them crackled with tension, with neither about to give way to the other.

'Let go of Mummy – you're hurting her!'

The shrill voice startled them both. As Nicholas released her, Philippa saw the colour drain from his cheeks. Kit was standing in the doorway in rumpled pyjamas and no slippers. His angry expression was the image of his father's.

'Daddy wasn't hurting me,' she said, walking towards him. 'We were playing a grown-up game. It's late, darling. You should be asleep.'

'I woke up and heard you shouting.' He rubbed his eyes. 'I'm thirsty.'

Philippa glanced at Nicholas, but he avoided her gaze as he picked up his glass and finished the brandy. She reached for Kit's hand.

'Daddy and I weren't shouting at each other. I left the door open, so I expect it sounded like that when our voices drifted up the stairs. Come into the kitchen, and I'll get you a glass of milk.'

'Can I have a glass of coke with ice in it?'

'No, you can't. Your teeth will fall out, and you'll have nightmares.'

Nicholas looked sullen as he watched them. He had not expected his son to turn on him like that – neither had Philippa.

'Say goodnight to Daddy.' It was almost an after-thought.

'Goodnight.' Kit's voice was clipped and he made no attempt to run to his father and kiss him like he usually did.

Nicholas mumbled back, then transferred his gaze to Philippa. 'I am going into the study to do some work. I would rather not be disturbed.'

She did not know what time it was when Nicholas came to bed. He deliberately switched on the top lights and slammed shut cupboards and drawers. But Philippa lay with her back to him, refusing to be drawn into a fight.

'I still intend to buy a house,' she said when the lights went out and he climbed into the other side of the bed.

'Do what you want, Philippa. You usually do.'

Nicholas did not mention the house again and, for a while, an uneasy peace existed. In March a general election was won by the Labour Party and the country returned to a five-day working week. Even the striking miners agreed to go back to work, having been conceded almost every demand they made. Somebody had to pay, and the new government's policy of taxing the rich for all they were worth was the major reason for Nicholas dropping his opposition to Philippa buying a second home. He was a practical man and it was something she could legitimately do without the tax man jumping down her throat. There was also the added bonus that they were in a buyer's market. Property prices were low, especially in the country, where the spiralling cost of petrol was frightening people away from the less populated areas which had little in the way of public transport.

Because it was Sarah who heard about Dovestail Cottage Nicholas had no option but to drive his wife and son down to see it. Sarah had good taste. Dovestail was enchanting. It was inside the national park boundaries, one mile out of the nearest village, and eight miles from Moor View. It was not a cottage in the strict sense of the word. It had four bedrooms, two bathrooms, living room, study and dining room, all of which boasted natural wooden beams. There was a roomy granny flat above the double garage and a narrow stream bordering the lower end of the garden. There was also an orchard and a separate three-acre field. The kitchen was in need of modernisation and there was no central heating.

Kit loved it, and wanted a bedroom at the back which overlooked the garden and orchard. On the other hand, Nicholas pointed out the faults, including parts of the slate roof which he declared to be dodgy. A resulting survey brought to light some loose tiles which could easily be rectified. So Philippa bought it, and arranged for the builders and decorators to move in. If she furnished it during the spring, the cottage would be ready for summer.

CHAPTER TWENTY

It was midsummer, the longest day of the year. Helen was out with friends and Pauline with her fiancé.

'It's hardly worth cooking for the two of us,' Sarah told Jennie. 'I'll take you into Plymouth for a meal.'

The child's face lit up. 'Can we have hamburger and chips?'

Why was it the young always craved food which held no nutritional value, and even less appeal to someone of Sarah's generation?

'All right,' she agreed. 'But you'll have to put on a frock.'

'Oh, Grandma, it won't be any fun if I have to dress up. And it's far too hot!'

Sarah smiled. Jennie could twist her around her little finger and knew it. She was pure tomboy, climbing trees, scrambling on to the ponies, and bearing little resemblance to the quiet child who had come here ten months ago. Sarah knew her son was not entirely to blame for suffocating his daughter's natural exuberance. Those last couple of years had not been easy for him, and circumstances had dictated Jennie should be quiet when her mother was feeling unwell.

'Then you can wear your green shorts, a white shirt and clean ankle socks.'

Jennie pulled a face. 'Nobody wears ankle socks any more, except for school.'

'Cheeky monkey!' Sarah remonstrated. 'Go and get ready before I change my mind.'

Jennie sprinted up the stairs, confident she would get her own way. Her bedroom had belonged to her father and was virtually unchanged, although Sarah had hung new pastel-coloured curtains and bought a pale pink bedspread. Jennie had insisted the pictures remain on the walls and the old books in the bookcase. If she could not have her father, then she had enough to keep his memory alive. She was about to put on the green shorts when she remembered she had not washed.

The bathroom window was open and, if she stood on tiptoe, she was able to look on to the drive. She did so now, her heart sinking as she saw a strange car approaching the house. She dried her face and hands, leaving most of the dirt on the towel, then ran on to the landing.

'Grandma, there's someone coming.'

Sarah was in the kitchen shutting windows. She twisted the catch on the last one before going to the front door, followed by the yellow Labrador which had replaced her other two, the last of which had died a year ago.

The car had stopped and the driver was standing beside the open door. The dog growled at the stranger and Sarah laid her hand on his muzzle, silencing him.

'I wasn't sure of the reception I would receive, and thought it best not to telephone first.'

'You don't deserve any kind of reception. Not after all this time, with never a word, except at Christmas. Even then we knew nothing more than you were alive. You forgot her birthday. She was heartbroken.'

'I'm sorry.' He did not move and neither did she. He was bronzed by a sun stronger than theirs and was looking himself again. 'Would it be easier if she did not see me? She would not know any different if I left now.'

'And shirk your responsibilities altogether?' Sarah's voice was cutting. 'You can't run forever, Justin.'

'You know why I left, and you also know it would have been wrong to drag a child around with me. She needed the stability you could give her, and a proper education.'

His eyes focused on something behind her. Sarah turned and saw Jennie standing in the doorway. The child's hair hung in rats' tails down her back, and she was still wearing the denim shorts and a filthy T-shirt. She was staring at her father with wide, unblinking eyes.

Sarah looked at her son. She could see no visible emotion on his face, and she prayed he would not reject his daughter. Jennie had waited so long for this. One harsh word, or wrong move, and the child's world would come crashing down.

'Daddy?' Her voice was hesitant and her face pale. 'Daddy?' she repeated.

He did not reply and she broke into a run. Sarah couldn't bear to watch.

'Oh, Daddy, Daddy, I've missed you so much.'

'And I've missed you too, darling.'

Then Jennie was in his arms. He kissed her cheek and hugged her. Sarah smiled. Everything was going to be all right.

'I've got a present for you,' he said, lowering the child to the ground. She clung to his hand as though she was never going to let go. He opened the back door of the car and reached inside.

'Here,' he said. 'You'll have to look after her yourself.'

He placed a collie pup in Jennie's arms.

'She's mine?'

'Yes. What are you going to call her?'

There was a pause as the pup opened its mouth and yawned.

'Bess?' Jennie suggested. She was doing the Elizabethan period of history and Good Queen Bess had left a strong impression.

'Then Bess it is,' said Justin, placing an arm around her narrow shoulders. He looked at his mother. 'I saw a notice outside a farm when I was driving here. I hope you don't mind.'

Sarah would not have minded had he brought a litter of puppies home. They would not be going to Plymouth now. She would cook a celebratory dinner instead, with chips.

Moor View's financial year ended in April and towards the end of June Philippa received the annual balance sheets from the auditors. She went into the study with a mug of coffee and spent the morning going through them. They were worse than disappointing. They were terrible. And it was unlikely this year would be any better.

Rodney would also have copies and she needed to discuss the implications with him. They had to decide if there was room for improvement, and whether they should drop some lines so as not to over extend themselves. She picked up the telephone, then decided it would be better to see him in person. Nicholas expected her to entertain a prospective client on Wednesday evening. He had booked a table at the Savoy, and afterwards they would probably go to one of the gambling clubs. Ernest was coming too, which gave an indication of the importance of the account. They had theatre tickets for Thursday and had accepted an invitation to a cocktail party on Friday. She did not want to wait until the next week, and decided to catch an early train the following day and return that evening.

Nicholas objected, like she knew he would, saying she should go the following week when they had fewer commitments. She refused. They argued, and she went anyway.

She arrived at Moor View shortly after ten-thirty, only to discover that Rodney was out and not due back until midday. Philippa cursed. She should have let him know she was coming.

She was in her office, tackling the mail Louise had brought in, when she heard a sound from the floor above. She put it down to imagination. Justin's studio was up there, and it was out of bounds to everyone excepting herself and Rodney. This was an old building which often creaked for no apparent reason. She glanced through a verbose letter from a charity seeking financial help. They would be supporting no charities this year and she wrote the word 'regrets' at the bottom of the page.

A clatter above her head made Philippa jump. There was somebody snooping about up there and she wanted to know who it was. No one was in the studio, but the store room door was ajar. She was about to call out when something small and furry dashed towards her. She screamed, thinking it was a rat, and the creature turned tail and fled. It was not a rat, but a puppy.

'Bess, come here!'

Philippa stared as Justin came out of the store room. Stripped clean of sorrow and pain, here was the man who had swept her off her feet ten years ago. Was it really so long? It must have been, for this was the summer of 1974 and they had met in Scotland during the autumn of 1964.

He scooped the pup into his arms, then his eyes met hers and he smiled. Philippa felt something of herself go out to him and recoiled, horrified by her response. If Justin was aware of it he gave no indication.

'Where did you spring from?' He spoke as though he had seen her a week ago, not last year.

'I could ask the same of you. Do you intend to stay or are you passing through?'

He frowned. 'I shall be staying, of course.'

'What about Jennie?'

'She will live with me. Do you think I would desert her?'

'I thought you already had.' She went to an open window and leant against the casement, staring at the cloud-speckled sky. 'You were cruel to leave her for so long. Nor was it right to expect Sarah to support her indefinitely.'

'I didn't.' He was equally blunt. 'One of these days you will get your facts right. I arranged for regular payments to be made to my mother, although I doubt if she touched the money. As for Jennie, I set up a trust fund before I left, in case anything happened to me.'

Philippa flushed. 'I didn't know.'

'You should have asked Nicholas. He did.'

She could not admit Nicholas never shared family secrets with her, but she sensed Justin already knew. She had never been able to hide anything from him.

'There was a legitimate reason why I had to go away,' he said.

'You don't have to tell me.'

'I should like you to know. It's the reason I was unable to supply last year's Christmas plate, or any other work.'

'Alice was dying. You were under a lot of strain. I never expected you to keep going like an automaton.'

'I couldn't paint at all. Even when I picked up a pencil and pad nothing happened. It was something which had never happened to me before. I suppose you could compare it to writer's block. Mum knew, and I think Nick suspected.'

Her horrified eyes met his. 'And now?'

'I have some sketches I would like you to see. Tell me what you think of them.'

She followed him to a table which ran half the length of

a wall. On it was a bulging portfolio.

'I am no expert,' she said, her hand trembling as she opened it.

Justin perched on the edge of the table. 'I am not asking for the opinion of an expert.'

She did not know what to expect and was afraid of hurting him. The first sketch was of horses in a stark landscape. Wild horses? She flipped through half a dozen similar drawings before reaching a series where the horses were ridden by men dressed as cowboys. Only they were not cowboys, not conventional ones. He had lost nothing of his genius. The sketches had a magical quality, even the rough ones on which he had written detailed notes.

She glanced up. 'You were in the Camargue?'

'Yes. I arrived by accident and stayed for three months.'

'They must rank amongst the best you have ever done.' She laid some sketches on the table. A series of plates based on these would not only be an instant sell out, but would give Moor View the boost it badly needed. She dismissed the idea. He would want time to settle down and bring some normality back to his life.

'How long are you here for?' he suddenly asked.

'Nicholas expects me home this evening. Why didn't you let us know you were back?'

'I intended to. Is Moor View in trouble? I can think of no other reason for you to come on a flying visit.'

At her insistence he was still a director of the company. He had a right to know what was happening.

'It seems unfair to burden you immediately, but I received last year's figures yesterday. We scraped by with a marginal profit, and this year promises to be worse. We could even slide back into the red, which will be disastrous. I know we're in the middle of a recession and the entire country is in a bad way, but we shouldn't be hit this hard. That is what

261

I wanted to discuss with Rodney.'

'You must have some idea where the trouble lies.'

She balked.

'Philippa?'

'The Christmas plate was a disaster, and we have not dared to issue any more plates since then. As you know, they have become the mainstay of the business. Rodney and I appear to lack judgement in certain fields. I think we became too reliant on you. Your work was always in demand and you also supervised the outside artwork. Everything went wrong after you left.'

'I can give you the Camargue horses if you want them.'

He understood her better than anyone. He always had.

It was midnight when Philippa arrived home. Nicholas was waiting and made a point of looking at his watch. 'I want to talk to you,' he said.

'It's late and I'm tired. Rodney promised to telephone and tell you I was delayed.'

'Oh, he phoned, so did my brother. It's him I wish to talk about.'

Philippa shuddered as his pale eyes rested on her face. Whatever this was about, she sensed it was not going to be pleasant. She went into the living room, waited until he closed the door, then took the defensive.

'What is it?'

'You have been rather careless, darling. I found this in the study.'

He picked up a typewritten sheet of paper and waved it in front of her. For one awful moment she thought it might be part of the accounts she had been reading yesterday. But it couldn't be. She and Rodney and Justin had gone through the figures this afternoon, and none of the pages in her copy had been missing.

'Get to the point, Nicholas.' Her irritability showed.

'Why didn't you tell me Justin is a joint owner of Moor View?'

'Because it is none of your business.' She snatched the sheet from him. 'What he owns is negligible. He has earned every one of those shares and a lot more besides. Moor View belongs to me, and I can do what I want with it. Whether you approve is immaterial. Did you say anything to him?'

'I found this after we had spoken. Why? Should I have?'

'Don't be childish. He would have wondered how you found out, that's all.'

'How many other secrets do you and my brother share?'

'This is ridiculous. I'm going to bed.'

He stood in front of her. 'I asked you a question, Philippa. I expect an answer.'

'If you dare touch me, then be prepared to entertain your clients alone. And the same goes for the rest of this week's engagements.'

She meant what she said, and tomorrow was too important to jeopardise.

'Go on, run away,' he snarled. 'But remember this is not over.'

Her cold eyes met his. 'It is as far as I am concerned.'

Hope Stevenson was a woman in a man's world, a feminist of the Sixties, who had reached the high-powered position of marketing manager with a leading manufacturer of small electrical goods. She had got there by clawing her way up the executive ladder, using whoever stood in her way before callously discarding them.

Her managing director had invited her tonight because she had done the initial groundwork with Lang & Wakefield. Hope was an attractive woman of thirty-two, a natural brunette with a sexy figure which she used to its best advantage, but did not openly flaunt. She invariably made an impact, and was used to men staring at her.

She never walked into a situation without being pre-armed. She had researched Nicholas Lang and Ernest Wakefield before opening negotiations with their firm. But she had not bothered with Philippa Lang. Hope had no time for other women, and had learnt to freeze wives out of conversations by concentrating on subjects about which they had little or no knowledge.

Her nose was put out of joint from the moment the ex-model glided in on a chic cloud of elegance, drawing the eyes of every man and woman in the room. Hope retaliated by launching into the advertising campaign but, to her chagrin, Philippa not only took an active part, but knew what she was talking about. By the time they reached their third course Hope had steered the conversation towards more complicated business matters, at which point her boss took over. Then something happened which had never happened before. The ex-model joined in.

'You are well informed,' Hope remarked over coffee.

'My wife has her own business,' Nicholas told her.

Not for the first time tonight, Hope was aware of a suppressed under-current between Nicholas and Philippa Lang.

'Really,' she said, feigning interest. 'What kind of business?'

'A pottery,' said Philippa.

'How very quaint. One of those little studios where people can watch a potter at work? Or am I underestimating your abilities? Are you the potter?'

The woman was a bitch, but Philippa's smile never wavered. 'I couldn't throw a pot if I tried. But I expect Nicholas will agree that quaint is an apt description.'

★

After an important business dinner Nicholas liked to relax with a large brandy, and he expected Philippa to do likewise, although she wouldn't drink anything stronger than tea or coffee. She had resented the enforced late-night sessions at first, but now they numbered amongst the increasingly rare occasions when she and Nicholas were able to talk without their conversations deteriorating into arguments. She never changed beforehand. Nicholas preferred her not to.

'You were very impressive tonight,' he said as she kicked off her shoes and tucked her long legs beneath the full-length gown she was wearing. 'I never realised how well versed you are in company strategy.'

Philippa took the compliment as it was intended, and smiled. 'You never asked. Do you think I sit back and do nothing when I visit Moor View? It may be quaint, but we have worked hard to make it a viable business.'

The muscles in his face tightened, then he sipped his brandy and the moment passed.

'Quaint is not a word which features in my vocabulary. It was Hope who used it. I was surprised you did not slam her down.'

'And risk losing the account?' There was no malice in her voice. Realism often meant putting aside one's personal feelings. It was something Nicholas understood.

'What did you think of her?' he asked.

'On a personal or a professional level?'

'Both.'

There was no need to ponder. Philippa had weighed up Hope Stevenson in less than a minute. 'Professionally, she is quick witted, clever and knows her job. On a personal basis, I would not trust her as far as I could throw her. She has a killer instinct and will go straight for the jugular to get what she wants.' She saw his irritation. Why were men so easily taken in by attractive women who were well versed in the art of flattery? 'I'm sorry. But you did ask.'

He lit a cigarette. He smoked less frequently than he used to, but refused to give up altogether. 'Yes, I did,' he agreed. 'We have decided to bring her into the business. She'll be joining the agency in the autumn. Ernest and I will be spending more time in America, so will need someone else in the office.'

It was like receiving a slap in the face. Nicholas sensed his wife's disapproval and frowned. 'Do you dislike her because she is a woman?'

'Don't be ridiculous! Was that the point of this evening, to impress her?'

'No. We want the account, and I think we can safely say we have it.'

'She hands you the account on a plate, then walks out to join you. It's a dirty trick to play on her employer.'

'It's business.'

'Not my kind of business,' she said distastefully. 'You are making a mistake. She will do the same to you given the opportunity. A year or two with Lang & Wakefield will give her the experience she needs to walk into any top agency and demand executive status.'

'She will have executive status with us. Once she proves herself we will offer her a partnership. It has nothing to do with you, Philippa.'

He was angry but, at the same time, was trying to avoid another row. Like her, he must be growing tired of their continuous arguments. Anything, however trivial, set them off these days.

'I think we should call it a night,' she said.

'Not yet. Will you get me another brandy?'

When she took it to him he grasped her hand. 'Is there anything else I should know about Justin's involvement with Moor View?'

She thought of the document which Leonard Perkins kept in his safe.

'No,' she lied.

'Do you think we can make an excuse and wheedle out of Friday night? It's not important. You could always use Kit as an excuse.'

'Why?'

'Because I should like to go home for the weekend. It's a long time since I have seen my brother. We could leave on Friday morning and come back on Sunday night.'

'Kit has school.'

'At his age an odd day makes no difference.'

'I'll telephone Sarah tomorrow and tell her.' She paused. 'For the record, I am not jealous of Hope Stevenson.'

He smiled. 'I know. But I am not so sure she wasn't jealous of you.'

At times, his moods swung back and forth like a pendulum. She slipped her hand from his and returned to her chair.

'Please be careful,' she warned.

The unexpected closeness of that night continued into the succession of days, then weeks, which followed. Nicholas even changed his mind about her and Kit spending the summer at Dovestail. She had already bought most of the furniture, but needed time to make it into a proper home. She also wanted to find a gardener and a woman to come in part-time.

Sarah said Kit could borrow Sam, provided he looked after the pony properly. There was a local branch of the Pony Club in the village, where he could meet children of his own age.

The last day of term came. Philippa picked Kit up from school but did not treat him to lunch like she usually did.

Nicholas was taking them out this evening, and in a couple of days he would drive them to Dovestail. He would only stay for the weekend, but had promised a fortnight towards the end of August. They might, or might not, see him in between.

It was Eileen's day off and when Nicholas came home he was in a foul mood. Philippa hoped he was not going to cancel this evening, not when Kit was looking forward to it. She sent the child upstairs, telling him to change into the clothes she had laid out. She knew he would prefer jeans and a T-shirt, but Nicholas would never put up with that. His family had to look the part when he took them out.

Nicholas was in the living room drinking straight whisky, a bad sign.

'What's gone wrong?' Philippa asked.

'Everything! The Americans are getting temperamental. We produced some of our best work, which they agreed to. Now they say the campaign is too revolutionary for middle America, and if we don't tone it down they will go to another agency.' The flat of his hand slammed on to a table. 'Damn them to hell! We'll have to fly over at the weekend, and convince them the point will be lost if the campaign is altered. If they won't listen, we shall have to scrap it and start again.'

'When will you and Ernest be leaving?'

He looked at her as though she were mad. 'I shall need Ernest here. You and I will be leaving on Saturday morning. Kit can stay with my mother. You'll have to take him there tomorrow. I have no idea how long this thing will drag on, but we could be looking at a fortnight.'

'What do you need me for?'

'I should have thought that was obvious. Our American friends are impressed by you.'

'No, Nicholas. I am not about to drop everything in order

to impress your clients. And I most certainly have no intention of doing your dirty work. I have made my own plans for this summer, and they do not include dumping Kit on your mother. Anyhow, New York is hell at this time of year. If Ernest cannot go, you must go alone.'

'You bitch! This has nothing to do with Kit. It's your damn pottery! It's all you care about. All you have ever cared about.'

He moved quickly, so quickly she did not realise what he was about to do, not until it was too late, and his hand slammed into her cheek. The impact sent her reeling across the room, and she would have fallen had she not grabbed the back of an armchair.

'You leave Mummy alone! Don't you ever hit her again, or I'll . . . I'll . . .'

Her head was spinning and she could taste blood in her mouth, but suddenly Philippa was afraid for her son. He was pounding his fists against his father, who seemed unaware of the child's blows as he stared at her. What she saw in his eyes was frightening.

'Kit, go to your room.' She knew she sounded hysterical, but could not help herself. 'Now.'

He turned to her, his clenched fists hanging at his sides. 'He hurt you.' His face was pale but determined.

It was not what he said, but how he said it. The tone of his voice conveyed anger and disgust. Even Nicholas flinched at the condemnation in the young voice.

'No, he didn't,' she said. 'Daddy would never hurt me, or you either. We were having a silly quarrel.'

'Yes, he did. I saw him. And I'll never forgive him – never!'

Kit ran to her and she held him tight. Only when she heard the front door slam did she look up. Nicholas was gone.

CHAPTER TWENTY-ONE

Shepherds Fold was not large, being functional rather than decorative. It had lain empty for a decade and the dust was inches thick. Plaster and faded paper were peeling from the walls, and the ceiling on the top landing was discoloured and sagging where water had leaked in. Justin shook the banister. Even that was loose. The place was falling apart. No wonder the main farm was willing to sell it for next to nothing.

'Daddy, where are you? Come and look at the view. You'll love it.'

He glanced in the direction of Jennie's voice. She had not noticed the dirt or peeling paper as she ran from room to room with Bess yapping at her heels.

'I'm coming,' he called.

He paused to look through an open door to his left. It was the bathroom, an archaic wreck which must have dated back to pre-war days. Jennie was in the larger of the bedrooms, leaning out of an open window, with Bess in her arms.

'Be careful,' her father warned, placing steadying hands on her shoulders.

'See, Daddy,' she enthused. 'The moors go on for miles and miles without a house or road in sight.'

'You like this cottage, don't you?'

'I love it, and so does Bess. Can we live here?'

He sighed. 'It needs so much work, sweetheart, even

before we can consider moving in.'

'I can help.'

'I know. But it needs a complete overhaul. I suppose I could get someone in to have a look at it.'

'Does that mean you're going to buy it?' Jennie asked.

'We'll have to wait and see.' He tousled her hair. 'You're quite right, the view is magnificent.'

He kept a restraining arm around her as he leant against the windowsill. The wooden frame was rotting, but the walls were built of Dartmoor granite and, except for one or two places where the slates had dislodged, he was pretty sure the roof was in a reasonable condition.

'There are other considerations as well, Jennie. Like school. It's pretty isolated out here, more so than at your grandmother's.'

'The school bus goes past the end of the lane,' she said.

'We're half a mile from there, down a flint road. What happens when it snows?'

'We'll be trapped,' she cheerfully stated. 'When it snowed last winter the bus couldn't get through until the snow ploughs cleared the road. I stayed home and helped Grandma and Pauline with the ponies. It was great fun.'

Justin was beginning to realise how much he had missed her. She was nine years old and only now was he getting to know her. 'I hope you will find it as much fun when you have to help me dig a path from the front door to the car.'

'Oh, Daddy!' she squealed. She put down the squirming pup and ran to the door. 'Let's explore the garden. I bet there are all sorts of interesting things in that old shed.'

'Like spiders,' he said, watching her.

She shuddered and then, quite unexpectedly, ran back and hugged him.

'I love you, Daddy. You'll never go away again, will you?'

'No,' he promised.

Kit and Sarah were loading Sam into the double trailer when Justin came back. Jennie rushed to help, leaving her father to follow more slowly. His eyes were on Philippa. She was standing in the shadow of the barn and looked anything but pleased to see him.

'I'm going in the trailer with Sam,' Kit was saying to Jennie. 'Do you want to come?'

'Can I?' Jennie asked her father.

'If you want.' His eyes were still on Philippa's face. 'We didn't expect you until the weekend. Is Nick with you?'

'No. He has to go to New York on Saturday. I thought Kit and I might as well come down early.'

There was an edge to her voice, and he could swear she was keeping her distance from him.

Sarah came out of the trailer. 'What was the cottage like?' she asked.

'A mess, but Jennie loved it.'

'She would love anything if she was with you. You can tell me about it when I get back.'

'I can drive Sam to Dovestail. You must be tired.'

'I am a little. Thank you, dear.'

Philippa was less enthusiastic. 'I'll follow in the car,' she said as he bolted up the ramp.

After turning Sam into the orchard Kit and Jennie went to fill a water bucket at the tap by the kitchen door.

Justin took the saddle and bridle and a box of grooming tools out of the Land-Rover. 'Where do you want me to put these?' he asked.

'The shed would be an ideal place, but there could be mice in there. I suppose they'll have to go in the kitchen. Let Kit do it. He wanted the pony here, so he should take responsibility for it.'

They were standing in the narrow drive, yet she had contrived to leave a four-foot gap between them.

'What's the matter, Philippa?'

He started towards her, but she retreated a couple of steps, out of the shadows and into the bright evening sunshine.

'Nothing. This has been a long day and I could have done without the pony.'

'You are here for eight weeks. There was no urgency to fetch him today.'

'I know, but when I telephoned Sarah to say we were here she said . . . she said it would be all right.'

'She said I was out, and you wanted to avoid me.' His emotionless voice brought a flush to her cheeks. 'Why are you wearing make-up?'

The question took her by surprise. 'I always wear make-up.'

'You always wear eye make-up, not foundation and all that other stuff. What are you trying to hide?'

This was what she had been afraid of. Sarah had not noticed, but he was an artist and had been her lover.

'What could I hide from you?' she bluffed.

Now she was standing in the sun's glare he could see the lack of symmetry in her features. This time she did not move away when he approached, but her turquoise eyes blazed fire.

He desisted from lifting his hand to her face, or touching her in any way. 'What happened?' His voice was angry.

'I walked into a cupboard door which had been left open. It's easily done.'

'Do you expect me to believe that?'

'It's what happened.'

'Of course,' he said. 'I know any number of people who make a habit of walking into doors.'

Kit and Jennie came round the side of the cottage,

carrying the bucket of water between them.

'I'd prefer you not to come in. The house is a mess and I have a lot to do.'

'I had no intention of coming in.' He was abrupt. 'Hurry up, Jennie. We have to leave.'

'Do you want to come to London tomorrow and see where your mother is buried?'

Justin had come to kiss her goodnight, and Jennie sat up, her eyes sparkling. 'Can we take some flowers?' she asked. It was a year since Alice had died, and her memories of the beautiful, fair-haired woman were growing dim.

'The biggest bunch we can find,' Justin promised. 'We'll catch an early train and spend the day there. Now lie down and go to sleep.'

She kissed his cheek, then snuggled down so that he could tuck her in.

'Can we go somewhere nice for lunch?'

'For lunch and dinner too, if you can last the day. Goodnight, sweetheart.'

'Goodnight, Daddy.'

Children were so resilient, he thought. Jennie was more excited at the prospect of a day in London than seeing her mother's grave. As for him, he had a totally different reason for going there.

'There are a couple of people I have to see first,' Justin explained while they were on the train. 'This afternoon we can do whatever you want.'

They bought three bunches of freshly cut flowers at a stall outside the station, then went by taxi to Pimlico. Jennie gazed from the window. She had forgotten the bustle of the city where she had been born.

'Who lives here?' she asked.

'Steve Noble. You met him a long time ago.'

Steve had lost interest in fashion after Philippa's retirement and expanded into other areas of photography, building upon an already established reputation. Justin had taken a chance he would be home and he was.

'This is an unexpected visit,' he said. 'Come in.'

To Jennie it was like walking into a treasure trove. She was fascinated by the jumble of lights and backdrops and props, but it was the photographs covering the walls which took her breath away.

'They're all of Aunt Philippa,' she said.

As Justin followed her gaze Steve saw his eyes soften. There is still some feeling there, he thought, then suddenly realised why Justin had come.

'She was a model,' he told his daughter. 'Steve is a photographer and she used to work with him. Now be a good girl and sit over there. I shall not be long.'

'I have a better idea,' said Steve. 'Come and sit on this stool, and I'll take some pictures of you while I talk to your father.'

'We don't have time,' Justin protested.

'Of course you do. I'll do some roughs now and a proper portrait when I come down in August.'

Maggie had cajoled Steve into doing the catalogue for an exhibition of Justin's work she was planning for the autumn. He had agreed because it gave him an excuse to spend a week with Philippa at Dovestail.

Steve placed the stool in front of a plain backdrop and sat Jennie on it. She was wearing a pale pink frock with white ankle socks and white shoes. Her dark hair, which reached her waist, was held back from her face by a pink headband. He arranged some strands over her shoulder and gave her a bunch of pink and white carnations to hold. She was a picture within a picture.

'Watch your father,' he said. 'And try not to wriggle.'

It was unnatural for Jennie to sit still for any length of time, but she did her best.

Justin stood at Steve's shoulder while he adjusted the camera angle. 'How did Philippa get that bruise on her cheek?' he asked.

'What bruise?'

Had he looked up, or sounded surprised, Justin would have known he was barking up the wrong tree. But Steve did none of those things. He kept his eye on the view-finder and continued to focus the camera.

'Don't act the innocent with me, Steve. We both know she confides in you.'

'Not as much as she used to. We don't live in each other's pockets any more.'

'Did Nicholas hit her?'

He spoke softly, not wanting the child to hear. Steve also wished he had not heard.

'Is that what she told you?' His voice was casual as he reached for a filter and placed it in front of the lens.

'She said she walked into a cupboard door.'

'Then that's what she did. Why don't you stand next to Jennie? It will make an enchanting family portrait.'

'I am not interested in a family portrait. I want to get to the bottom of what happened between Nicholas and Philippa.'

Steve straightened up. 'Nicholas is your brother. I suggest you ask him.'

'I intend to. But you might as well tell me what you know, as I shall find out one way or another.'

Steve was silent for a moment. 'I told her she should leave him. If he has hit her once he will do so again. She refused to go to America with him and he lost his temper. Tread carefully, Justin. I know you are brothers, but Nicholas has a malicious streak, and you will only make matters worse for Philippa should he suspect there was ever anything between you.'

'I can deal with Nicholas.' He sounded cold and confident.

'Have you finished?' Jennie asked.

'No,' said Steve.

'Yes,' said her father.

Jennie did not see her uncle, for Justin left her sitting in the reception, where a disdainful young woman looked down her nose at the child. She was new and had tried to stop him from going through. He ignored her and marched into his brother's office. One look at Justin told Nicholas why he was there. He stood up, his face hardening.

'Why didn't you let me know you were coming? We could have arranged lunch. As it is . . .' He shrugged.

'This isn't that kind of visit.' Justin's eyes were smouldering. 'I'm giving you a warning, Nicholas. You were not dragged up in a slum, and there can be no excuse for your behaviour. Should you ever again lay a finger upon Philippa you will be answerable to me.'

'What did she tell you? That I beat her up? Come off it, Justin. We had a row. We're always having them, but they blow over in time.'

Justin felt something snap inside him. It took every bit of self control to stop himself from physically assaulting his brother, from wiping the supercilious grin from his lips.

'She didn't tell me anything. She didn't have to. I know you hit her.'

'What are you proposing to do, big brother? Play at fisticuffs? Don't be ridiculous. I am not only younger than you, but a good deal fitter.'

This time it was Justin who smiled. 'There are more

effective methods of restraining you. With a word in the right ear I could create the sort of scandal you would do anything to avoid. Think of the feast the tabloids would have if they learnt you were a wife beater, and that Philippa Russell happened to be the wife. It would not only be your reputation which suffered, but that of Lang & Wakefield.'

Nicholas paled. 'You're bluffing. You would hurt Philippa and the boy as much as me.'

'On the contrary, it would win them public sympathy. I am not bluffing.'

Nicholas knew Justin would not hesitate to carry out his threats and watched in sullen silence as his brother walked to the door.

'Goodbye, Nicholas.'

He did not reply, and they both knew nothing would ever be the same between them again.

Justin was working on a painting when Philippa burst into the studio.

'What right did you have to go and see Nicholas?' she demanded.

He put down the brush he was using and turned towards her. 'Every right considering he is my brother. Who told you?'

'He did, of course.' She stared at him, sensing it did not end there. 'Who else did you go and see while you were in London?'

'Steve.'

'Oh, Justin, how could you? I didn't ask you to meddle in my affairs, nor did I want you to. What goes on between me and Nicholas is our own business and has nothing whatsoever to do with you.' She suddenly seemed to deflate. 'I wish you hadn't. You have not improved matters, only made them worse.'

'No I haven't.' His voice was gentle. 'All I did was ensure he never laid a hand upon you again. There is no shame in asking for help, Philippa. We all need it sometimes. If you could trust Steve, why couldn't you trust me?'

She stood very still, with tears filling her eyes. 'I had no choice. It was Kit who telephoned Steve and asked him to come over. He saw what happened, you see.'

Justin did not move immediately, but when he did, it was to stride across the studio and take her in his arms. She offered no resistance. She laid her cheek against his shoulder and wept. Not only because of Nicholas, but for what might have been.

Nicholas did not come near them that summer, nor did he ask Philippa to return to London. She went back a few days before the start of the new school term. Nicholas knew she was coming, but it was fifteen minutes after midnight when he let himself into the house. He did not expect to find her waiting for him. She was wearing jeans and a check shirt. Her hair was pushed back from her face, which was highlighted by the glow of a lamp, making her look serene and very lovely. She looked up as he walked into the living room.

'I thought you would be asleep by now,' he said when she did not speak.

'And I thought you would make an effort to come home earlier than this.'

'We have a lot on at the moment. I don't have time to pander to your whims.'

That hurt. 'From what I recall you never have.'

His eyes turned to ice and his mouth hardened into an uncompromising line. He crossed the room, to stand beside the fireplace.

'Why did you have a towbar fitted to the Jag?'

The question was casual enough, but it was not what she expected.

'I am surprised you saw it in the dark. Or were you looking for dents?'

'It's your car. You can do whatever you want with it. You parked under a street light. I could hardly miss seeing the towbar.'

He was as officious as she was. The chasm between them was widening, with neither about to give way to the other.

'It meant I could borrow the trailer and ferry Sam around. Kit has spent practically the entire summer on horseback. He won some rosettes at the Pony Club Gymkhana last week and is very proud of them.'

Their son was neutral territory and safe to discuss, but Nicholas was thinking in another direction.

'I expect you took every opportunity to poison Christopher's mind against me.'

Philippa's stillness was attributable to her early training. What she wanted to do was slap his face.

'If his mind is poisoned then you only have yourself to blame. In eight weeks he has seen nothing of you. A weekend would have been better than nothing at all. It's up to you, not me, to rebuild the bridges. I have said nothing malicious about you. There was no need.' She stood up. 'Do you intend to keep coming home at this ungodly hour?'

'For the moment, yes.' He was stiffly formal.

'Then I trust you will have no objection to us having separate bedrooms – for the moment.'

'If it is what you want.'

'It is. I have made up the bed in the spare room. I'll put whatever you need tonight in there, and move over the rest of your things in the morning. Goodnight, Nicholas.'

He waited until she reached the door.

'Philippa?'

'Yes.'

'Did you enjoy the break?'

'Yes, I did.'

She did not attempt to grasp the olive branch. He had offered it too late.

When does a marriage fall apart? Was it the smaller things which gradually built up, or the larger ones which left a festering resentment? Was it taking too much and giving too little? Or was it waking up one morning and finding the love which had sustained you through the past ten years no longer existed? That you no longer cared?

Philippa asked herself all those questions, and many more besides. She found no satisfactory answer, for there was no single factor. It had happened. She occasionally wondered if Nicholas had a woman somewhere, or women. He had made no demands on her since she came back from Devon, which was just as well, for she did not want him in her bed.

She knew they were reaching the point of no return, and that she should consider leaving him, but Kit was at an age where he needed a father, and Nicholas had been making an effort to win him round. It was not his fault the child was slow to respond. Kit had not forgiven him for hitting her. Philippa sometimes despaired he ever would. He accepted without question her explanation of the separate bedrooms. She doubted Eileen was fooled, but Eileen was not a gossip.

To the outside world nothing had changed. They were still the glamorous couple society columnists wrote about. She was the charming hostess and perfect wife, he the ideal husband, good looking and industrious. In private, they had very little to say to each other.

She made a couple of one-day trips to Moor View during the autumn, seeing Justin on neither occasion. The pottery was doing well. The rest of the country might have been heading deeper into recession, but for Moor View the days of prosperity returned when Justin came back. His series of plates featuring the Camargue horses was a runaway success. The first plate had been issued in September and the last would be marketed the following February. Justin had also contributed a Christmas plate, which had been over-subscribed within a few days of its details being published. For the first time, they were going to give a proper staff Christmas party, and there would also be a special bonus. A Yuletide thank you for loyalty and hard work.

In the event, she was unable to be there.

'How would you like to spend three days in Disneyland?' Nicholas asked Kit at the beginning of December.

Philippa was startled. He had come home early, expecting dinner, which meant Eileen had to hastily rearrange the menu. He and Philippa were sitting at opposite ends of the table, with Kit between them.

'Really?' he asked. 'When?'

'For Christmas. It's the only time I can get away.'

Nicholas looked at Philippa as he spoke. Her frosty gaze met his.

'When did you decide this?'

'Last week.' He turned to the child. 'Well, Kit, would you prefer to spend Christmas at Disneyland or with your grandmother?'

Philippa knew what he would want, even without seeing the excitement on his face. What comparison was there with Dovestail in winter?

'I cannot force you to come,' Nicholas told her later, when they were alone. 'But I should like you to.'

Perhaps that said more than anything about the sorry state of their marriage.

'I shall come for his sake, not yours. I presume this trip is tied in with business. I doubt if such a generous offer would be forthcoming otherwise.'

'You are becoming shrewish, Philippa. There are a couple of people I need to wine and dine. I would prefer you to be with me, but will leave the final decision to you.'

'Are we meant to entertain these people on Christmas Day?'

'If your opinion of me is so low, it does not bode well for the future. Of course I will not be entertaining anyone then.' He paused. 'I am trying, Philippa. Couldn't you give a little in return?'

'I have grown tired of continually giving. As for the future, I cannot see beyond tomorrow. Be honest with yourself, Nicholas, we are not working.'

To give him credit he did try. At both hotels they shared a bedroom, but the beds were separate, and they somehow managed to keep themselves to themselves. Only once did Nicholas come near her. It was on Christmas night, after they had enjoyed an unexpectedly congenial day. She and Nicholas were sitting on the sofa, laughing over some ridiculous programme on the television. She did not notice him move closer, not until he put his arm around her. Give him a chance, she thought. Give yourself a chance. He kissed her, his hands gently caressing. She tried to respond, but was incapable of doing so. She felt nothing for him and, not being altogether insensitive, he drew away.

'I'm sorry, Nicholas.' She stood up. 'I'm going to bed. We have an early start in the morning and Kit is sure to be up with the dawn. Thank you for a lovely day.'

They had become strangers, no longer able to communicate on a personal basis. This could not go on for much longer, even for their son's sake.

★

Leonard Perkins always welcomed a visit from Philippa Lang, despite her irritating habit of turning up without an appointment. She was a ray of sunshine, and he welcomed her short intrusions into the humourless world of corporate law.

'Tea?' he asked, although there was not time. He had squeezed her in between appointments, which meant he would be running late for the rest of the day.

'No, thank you. I know you are busy and I only want some advice.'

He settled back into his chair, his hands crossed in their customary manner over his stomach.

'Well, my dear, how can I help you?'

'I want to know my chances of obtaining a divorce.'

He was shocked. 'I thought . . .' he began.

'So does everybody.' Her gaze met his. 'In public we both put up a front. In private, we no longer have any life worth speaking of. I do not want a protracted court case where every detail of our marriage is raked through the mud. Neither, I think, would Nicholas.'

'Have you discussed this with him?'

'No. Before doing so I wish to know my own position, and that of my son.'

'You are talking to the wrong person. Mr Simpson is our best divorce lawyer.'

'I would prefer to talk to you.'

'My knowledge in that field is limited.'

'I am sure it is sufficient for my needs.'

'Then I shall try to help, but I would urge you to discuss it with your husband before you make any decisions. An amicable agreement would be best all round.'

Would Nicholas be amicable? Would she have come here had she thought so?

'What grounds are you looking for?'

'I am not sure.'

It was an honest answer, but not an encouraging one.

'Mental cruelty is unadvisable. You are both featured too often in the popular press for it to hold up in court. Adultery perhaps? Have you reason to suspect your husband is consorting with other women?'

'No.' She paused. 'Let's say I have no knowledge of other women, but Nicholas and I have not . . . we have slept apart for the last eight months.'

Such a handsome couple, Leonard Perkins thought. They appeared perfect for each other, yet beneath the surface was a cauldron of simmering emotions.

'A detective would be able to obtain the proof we need.'

'It seems a filthy thing to do,' said Philippa, her face pale.

'I am afraid divorce is a filthy business.'

'Then I shall take your advice and talk to him first.'

CHAPTER TWENTY-TWO

———————◆———————

Hope Stevenson had gone to a lot of trouble, even buying a designer dress which showed her figure to its best advantage. It cost more than she could afford, but she looked fabulous in it. Tonight, every eye, male and female, was going to be on her, not the ex-model. She had spent the afternoon having her hair styled and nails manicured, ignoring Ernest's disapproval. They had never got along on a personal level and it was unfortunate she had to partner him tonight, when she would have preferred to take herself to the dinner they were giving for the middle-aged American.

Ernest had not wanted her to go at all.

'Do you realise the risk you are running?' he asked Nicholas. 'Philippa . . .'

'. . . knows her as someone from the office. Hope has done a lot of work on this campaign and deserves to be there. You need not worry about Philippa. Her manners are impeccable.'

Ernest looked cynical. 'I trust the same can be said for Hope.'

Nicholas realised it was folly to bring together wife and mistress, but there was no way Philippa could know about Hope. Nobody did, except Ernest, while Hope was too ambitious a woman to sacrifice everything she had worked so hard to achieve.

The dress turned out better than Hope had envisaged. Even Ernest was generous in his praise when he picked her up at seven-thirty on the dot. They were meeting at an exclusive club, the sort of place which would impress an American, impossible to get into unless you were a member, and to be a member you needed a lot more than money. It was also the sort of place where Nicholas would never take Hope, and she felt a stab of resentment as she entered the plush elegance. This was a world she wanted to be part of. She was nearly there but, somehow, she always found herself sitting on the outside, peering in.

They were the first to arrive and waited in the bar. Hope sipped a cocktail as she took in her surroundings and put names to faces. She was pleased with the minor sensation she had caused when she walked in. Let Philippa Lang top that, she thought.

Philippa was ready on time. It was Nicholas who dawdled, to the extent of slowing down at every traffic light, rather than jump them on orange as he was prone to do. Philippa sat with her eyes half closed, wondering when she should tackle him about the divorce. She could not keep up this façade for much longer.

'Did I tell you Ernest is bringing Hope Stevenson?' Nicholas asked. 'She has put a lot of work into this campaign and deserves the recognition.'

'No, you didn't,' Philippa replied. And you know you didn't, she thought.

'You and she did not hit it off the last time, but she is an employee now and will be on her best behaviour.'

'I am unconcerned either way,' said Philippa, gazing from the side window.

Ernest was talking shop with Lang & Wakefield's client,

David Sachs, who Hope felt had been appreciative of her appearance but not sufficiently over-awed. She was not interested in their conversation. She was watching for Nicholas and his wife. They were nearly twenty minutes late and when they arrived, with him lightly gripping her arm, Hope realised she might as well have worn an old rag rather than shell out on this dress. Philippa Lang wore a black gown with a high neckline and long sleeves. Her only adornment was a string of pearls and matching earrings, but she looked stunning. Hope was aware of Ernest watching her, but she schooled her features into a bland expression which gave away nothing. Nicholas and his wife appeared to know everyone there, for it took a long time for them to cross the short distance between the doors and the bar. David Sachs was enchanted, even before introductions were made.

There was a live band of four musicians who played unobtrusive melodies. For those who wished to dance there was a small floor. Hope watched as Nicholas guided his wife around it. There was no denying they were a good-looking couple who were perfectly at ease with each other. But Hope knew something of the stresses behind that perfect picture. She wished she knew more, but Nicholas refused to discuss his relationship with his wife. He had an odd sense of loyalty, or perhaps it was self preservation. For all Hope knew, he left her bed to go straight into the arms of his wife. Her resentment was beginning to fester when Nicholas led Philippa back to the table.

'Why Hope, I expected you to have David on the floor by now,' Nicholas said. His pleasant voice barely disguised the rebuke. She had been brought here for a purpose, which she was not fulfilling.

'I was waiting for you to ask me first.' The challenge was unmistakable and his eyes hardened. He could not say much with his wife here. Hope held the whip-hand and he did not like it. 'David says he is a terrible dancer and would prefer to watch.'

'I have two left feet,' David Sachs explained, aware of a sudden tension.

It was in that instant Philippa understood. She understood only too well.

'Nonsense,' she said, focusing her attention on the dumpy American, whose balding head barely reached her shoulder. 'I am sure you are a marvellous dancer. I have no sense of rhythm, so between us we are sure to do well.' She reached for his hand and, delighted, he let her lead him to the floor.

'I suggest you develop a headache.' The coldness in Nicholas's voice shocked Hope. 'I shall arrange for a taxi to be waiting for you in ten minutes. I see no reason why Ernest's evening should be ruined because of your lack of tact.'

As he walked away Ernest poured more wine into his glass.

'Did you believe he would leave her for you?' he asked. 'If you did, you made a serious miscalculation. Nor will he forgive you easily, if he forgives you at all.'

Hope was gazing at the dance floor. They should have looked ridiculous together, the tall, elegant woman and the fat man who, indeed, had two left feet. But she could see nothing to laugh at. Ernest was right. She had never stood a chance.

Philippa was in the habit of saying goodnight in the hall before going to her own room. Tonight, for the first time in months, she went into the living room and waited for Nicholas to join her.

'I want a divorce,' she told him. 'I would prefer it to be amicable, but if you are going to be awkward, I have sufficient grounds to go ahead.'

She had flung it at him, catching him unawares. 'What grounds?' he snapped.

'You and Hope Stevenson.'

'You are jumping to conclusions, Philippa. You have no proof, nor will you find any.' His composure had returned and the anger he had shown towards Hope was now directed at her. 'There will be no divorce. Not now. Not ever. Do you understand?'

'You do not own me. If you will not release me from this sham of a marriage, then I shall be left with no option but to leave you. I have my own house and my own money. Kit and I shall do very nicely.'

Nicholas did not move, but there was something threatening in his stance.

'Christopher is as much my son as he is yours. I will not tolerate you taking him from this house, or putting him in another school. Try it, darling, and I shall do everything in my power to have you declared an unfit mother.'

Philippa's laughter was brittle. 'You could never do that.'

'By taking him out of a school where he is doing well, has friends, and is happy, would be construed as a disservice. I have no objection to you taking our son wherever you wish during the holidays, but during term time he will remain here, where he belongs. And so will you.'

'You cannot get away with this, Nicholas.'

'Can't I?'

She stepped forward and slapped his cheek. He grabbed her wrist with the speed of a viper.

'Let me go!'

They stood glaring at each other. Philippa refused to give way, and she knew Nicholas would not. What she did not expect was his laughter.

'My God, you're gorgeous when angry!'

Before she could stop him, his mouth bore down upon

hers. She tried to turn her head away, but he was too strong, and the harder she struggled, the more frenzied he became. And then, for no apparent reason, he let her go.

'Run up to your sanctum.' He laughed, and was still laughing when she left the room.

Philippa could not sleep and was lying in the dark when she heard him come up the stairs. His room was further down the passage, but he stopped outside her door. She stiffened when he opened it.

'What do you want?'

'Good, you're not asleep.'

She switched on the lamp. 'What do you want?'

'To finish what we almost started.'

'Get out of here, Nicholas.'

'Not tonight.' He closed the door. 'I am growing tired of spending my nights in an empty bed.'

'Then spend it in Hope Stevenson's bed.'

'I don't want Hope Stevenson. I want you.'

As he shed his clothes she knew there was nothing she could do. To scream, or to fight him, would frighten Kit, whose room was opposite, and wake Eileen on the floor above. There was no law to prevent a man from raping his wife. For that was what Nicholas did. He violated her repeatedly before rolling over to his side of the bed and falling asleep.

Philippa did not need a doctor to tell her she was pregnant. All the signs were there, including the waves of nausea which were a warning of the morning sickness still to come. She made an appointment with her doctor because this was something she was unable to ignore. He told her she was too thin, run down and a little anaemic, then put her on a course of vitamin and iron pills. His concern made it impossible for her to tell him she did not want this baby because of the brutal way it had been conceived. She did not like to ask about a legal abortion when she was unsure about it herself, and there was always the possibility he would want to talk with her and Nicholas together. Nicholas, she knew, would never agree to it.

So she carried on as though nothing had happened. Her doctor was right, she was too thin, and it would be a long time before the baby began to show. She told nobody. Maggie had her own troubles, and not only with Noel. She had taken over Harlequin House the previous year, when her father sold the other hotels to an American chain. It meant Sarah's trekking centre was safe, and Helen's job, but now she was fighting off a trade union which was trying to muscle in. Steve, in whom Philippa might have confided, was in America, working on a series of articles for *Vogue*.

She had been throwing up for a fortnight before Nicholas noticed anything was wrong. It was a Friday and, for once, he had come home at a decent hour.

'I thought we might go out for dinner,' he said. 'It's a long time since we have done anything together.'

'And what makes you think I want us to do anything together? You have won the battle, Nicholas. I am still here and I don't expect you to go out of your way to be pleasant.'

'I am not going out of my way.' His voice was sour. 'Don't you think it's time we called a truce? Look, I'm sorry. I'm sorry for treating you like I did, and I'm sorry about Hope Stevenson. But she's gone now, and there is nobody else. Don't you think we should forgive and forget?'

Philippa stared at him. She did not know what methods he had employed but, within three days of that terrible night, Hope Stevenson had left, not only the firm but the country. She had accepted an executive position in New

York, a position which needed to be filled immediately.

'I don't think I can ever forgive you,' she told him. 'And I shall certainly not forget. Our marriage is in tatters and if it were not for ... if it were not for Kit, I would have left you a long time ago. Your threats are hollow, Nicholas. There is no court that would deprive me of my son, nor could you produce any proof to make them think otherwise.'

'I would still fight you. Think of the effect on the boy. Every detail of our married life would be splashed across the newspapers.'

'Do you think I care? No, I do not want to go out to dinner with you.'

'You are looking wan.' He spoke as though this were the first time he had seen her in a long while. 'Didn't you visit the doctor recently? What did he say?'

'That I am run down. He has given me some vitamins.' It was difficult to tell with Nicholas whether this surge of sympathy was genuine, or merely a way of getting round her.

'Then dinner will do you the world of good. As it's Friday we can take Kit. Make it a family night out.'

He was trying to get round her. 'I really don't feel up to it.' She had been eating patchily and the thought of food turned her stomach.

'For heaven's sake, Philippa! Do you always have to fight me? I am trying, and all you can do is throw my good intentions into my face.'

'How many times have you tried before? Yet we always end up where we started. For the sake of peace I shall come, but I would prefer to go somewhere quiet where we don't need to dress up.'

He smiled. 'I know the ideal place. Do you remember the pub in Henley where we used to go when you were pregnant? It's a pleasant evening. We could sit in the garden by the river. There would be nobody who knows us, and perhaps we would find it easier to talk in neutral surroundings.'

It was strange he should choose there, when she was pregnant again.

Oh, to be in England ... there were still places that had changed very little over the centuries, and this pub was one of them. It was like stepping back seven years, to a time when she and Nicholas had been happy. Or were they? There had been problems then, but they had not been insurmountable.

'You've barely touched your food,' said Nicholas.

'I am not hungry.'

'And you've lost weight.'

'Only a couple of pounds.' His solicitousness was getting on her nerves. 'I don't like Kit standing so near the edge.'

She was rising to her feet when Nicholas reached for her arm. 'We are both watching him. He can swim, and even if he does slip in, I can reach him in a couple of seconds.'

Philippa had no choice but to sit down again. Kit was enjoying himself. He had persuaded the waitress to bring him a pile of rolls, which he was breaking into small pieces and feeding to an increasing number of ducks.

'You have lost more than a couple of pounds, Philippa. You are a terrible colour and are beginning to look ill. Are you sure vitamins is all your doctor prescribed? Perhaps I should have a word with him.'

'Can't you leave me alone? I told you, I am a little run down. Is it any wonder after what you put me through?'

He was not about to be riled, which was just as well. They could both be equally stubborn when they put their minds to it.

294

'I said I am sorry. How many times do I have to repeat myself?'

'Until I am convinced you mean what you say.'

'Will you ever be?'

She shook her head. 'I don't know. We have gone through all this before and I have grown tired of it.'

She was aware of him watching her while she watched Kit. A motor launch passed by on the far side of the river, leaving a swell in its wake on which the unconcerned ducks bobbed.

'You've not visited Moor View for a long time.'

Like so many things Nicholas said, it was unexpected. Philippa glanced at him. He was a handsome man, but there was an increasing hardness about his eyes and mouth.

'I have not been needed there,' she said. It was not entirely true. Rodney was growing anxious. There were matters which could not be dealt with over the telephone. Matters which would require urgent attention if left for much longer. It was not that she no longer cared but, feeling as she did, she could not face the long journey.

'Why don't you go down next week? It never fails to invigorate you. And I expect you'd like to get the cottage ready for summer.'

'What about Kit?'

'Eileen and I are here. I can bring him down next weekend. If we come by train, we can all drive back on Sunday, like we used to.'

Kit had scattered the last of the bread rolls and was walking back, trailed by a couple of persistent ducks.

'Perhaps I will,' she said.

'Good. The country air will revitalise you more than any vitamin pills.'

Philippa intended to spend Tuesday at Moor View, but was

so exhausted by midday that she left. She did not see Justin, which was a small mercy, for she knew he could not be fobbed off with the same story she had told Nicholas.

She decided to stay home on Wednesday, but it turned out to be one of those days when the rain never stopped. Halfway through the morning she went to the pottery, where she tried to get to grips with the problems she had barely managed to dent the day before. Rodney had an appointment with a supplier and would not be back until the afternoon, so she was able to work undisturbed.

The offices emptied at lunchtime, as the staff drifted to the canteen. It had proved to be the most popular of the improvements they had made, and the year before an adjoining leisure room had been added. Philippa did not go. Her stomach was sensitive today, and weak tea was all she could face. She made it herself, in the kitchen behind the photocopy room. When she returned to her office Justin was standing by the window, watching the grey sheets of rain. He turned, a frown cutting between his eyes.

'Now I can see why you didn't let me know you were here.'

Philippa's hand shook as she put the cup on a bookcase. 'I was told you were working from home and did not want to be disturbed.'

'You may be able to fool most people, but not me. Has Nicholas been maltreating you?'

'Of course not.' The words came out in a rush. 'He was the one who suggested I come here. If anything, he has been killing me with kindness. I was glad to get away.'

His arms were folded across his chest, and the way his eyes narrowed reminded her of Nicholas. She had stopped comparing them a long time ago, but sometimes it was impossible to ignore the similarities.

'Then you must be pregnant.'

She stared at him, her eyes like saucers.

'When you walked in I saw Alice. She had the same gaunt look. Have you told Nicholas?'

Unbidden tears filled Philippa's eyes. 'I have told nobody. How could I when I don't want this baby?'

'Starving yourself will not get rid of it.'

'I am not starving myself. Most of the time I feel too ill to eat. What am I going to do?'

It was one of the few times in her life when she felt utterly helpless. Nicholas would not have understood, but Justin did. He put his arms around her and held her tight.

'Why don't you have a good cry? You'll feel better for it.'

After a while he sat her in a chair and pulled over another for himself. He held her hands as she told him everything, except the circumstances in which the child was conceived, but even then she suspected he guessed part, if not all of it. He urged her to leave Nicholas. There was nothing he could do to her, no way he could take Kit.

'I cannot leave him until after the baby is born. Not only for the child's sake but, if I go now, Nicholas will do everything in his power to discredit me.' She stood up and walked to her desk. 'I am trapped. Whichever way I turn my back is against a wall. Nicholas is quite capable of denying this baby is his and saying I had a lover. Eileen knows we have been sleeping in separate bedrooms. That we still are.'

'Philippa . . .' He was also on his feet.

'I want you to promise that none of this will go any further.'

'How can I?'

'You will if you feel anything for me. Confiding in you has lifted a weight from my shoulders, but I am not going to change my mind. I shall tell Nicholas about the baby when he comes down on Friday. Don't ruin it, Justin. Please.'

A smile tugged at his lips. 'You know I would never hurt

you, even though I think you are wrong. You have my promise.'

'Thank you. And now I am going home.'

'You should never have come in the first place.' He cupped his hand against her cheek. 'You are still upset. Let me drive you.'

'I'm all right, and it's not far.'

'I'll telephone this evening. Perhaps we can have dinner tomorrow. You don't want to stay at Dovestail by yourself.'

'I should like that.'

She did not attempt to stop him when he kissed her tenderly upon the lips.

The memory of his kiss lingered as Philippa drove through the pouring rain. She knew now that a part of her still belonged to him. It always would.

A shabby Morris loomed ahead, the first car she had met since turning on to this stretch of moorland road. She accelerated past it while she could, for less than half a mile ahead the road became a series of looping bends where it was impossible to pass anything.

She was slowing down to negotiate the first bend when a car appeared from nowhere, coming too fast out of a blind corner on the wrong side of the road. Philippa felt a momentary surge of panic. There was a steep bank to her left and all she could do was slam on the brakes and pray a collision would be avoided. The tyres screeched on the wet tarmac, and the back end of the car slewed into the bank.

Too late, the driver of the other vehicle tried to turn out of her path. In that instant Philippa saw his face. He was a boy. He did not look old enough to shave, let alone drive a car. Then there was an explosion and the Jaguar's bonnet reared up towards her. The force of the impact threw her forwards, but the seat belt locked, forcing her back into the seat, which was moving anyway. She heard shattering glass and rending steel and, as excruciating pain shot through her, she was certain she was about to die. She remembered Nicholas saying her Mini would crush like a sardine can. Before she lost consciousness it occurred to Philippa that any car would.

CHAPTER TWENTY-THREE

Nicholas continued to come home late, not intentionally, but because his life was dictated by work. On Monday Kit was still up, watching television, but the night before it was after eleven when Nicholas came in, by which time his son was long asleep. He was already beginning to regret his spur of the moment decision to send Philippa away. He was not cut out for minding a six-year-old, even though his responsibility went no further than dropping Kit at school every morning. But on Wednesday he made a special effort, coming home early so he could take his son out for a meal.

So it was Eileen who answered the telephone at seven-thirty. She was tetchy. No, Mr Lang was out. He had taken his son to dinner and she had no idea where he could be reached, or when they would be back. They were unlikely to be late, for the boy had school tomorrow.

'When he comes in tell him his wife has been in an accident. If he rings this number they will allow me to talk to him.' Justin Lang sounded agitated.

Eileen wrote down the number. 'Has she been hurt?'

'Badly enough to justify my brother coming here immediately,' he said before ringing off.

He need not have been so rude, Eileen thought. She was not to know how gruelling his day had been, or how frayed his nerves. He had telephoned Nicholas first because Philippa was his wife. Then he poured the last of his pennies into the call box and dialled his mother's number. Oh my God, he thought while waiting for an answer, he had forgotten Jennie. She would have arrived home from school hours ago, and was probably preparing supper and wondering where he was. His mother would have to collect her and take her to Flint Iron Farm. He couldn't leave here, not while Philippa was undergoing emergency surgery, with her life hanging in the balance.

Nicholas arrived home at ten minutes past ten, to be met by the agitated housekeeper. His face was colourless as he dialled the number she had written down. The woman who answered was awkward at first, insisting this was not a public telephone. Then she realised who he wanted, and sent a student nurse to fetch the haggard-looking man who was pacing the corridor outside the operating theatre.

Justin was brief and to the point. Philippa had serious internal injuries and had been in the operating theatre for three hours. There was no indication when she would be brought out.

'I'll be there as soon as I can,' Nicholas said.

He grabbed nothing other than his sleepy son. He put the protesting child in the back of the Porsche, threw a travelling rug over him, and told him to keep quiet and try to sleep. As an afterthought, he told the boy his mother had been hurt and they were going to see her. Kit was too confused and frightened to ask questions. He did as he was told, except he did not sleep. He lay with his eyes open, clutching the blanket and worrying about his mother.

Nicholas drove down because it was quicker. He would waste too much time trying to catch a plane or train at this time of night, and time was the one thing he could not afford to waste. When Justin said Philippa was fighting for her life, he meant it.

Nicholas was luckier than his wife had been earlier that day. He was lucky not to be involved in an accident himself, and luckier still not to be spotted by a police patrol. On the open road the Porsche touched speeds which were well in excess of a hundred miles an hour, and in the towns he had to pass through the speedometer was rarely below fifty.

He reached Plymouth in the early hours of the morning. Kit had fallen asleep through sheer exhaustion and cried out when his father shook him.

'Come on,' Nicholas said, taking his hand. It did not occur to him to carry the child, even when he stumbled on the hospital steps.

Nicholas was afraid as he dragged his son through the empty corridors. He had not allowed his thoughts to dwell on Philippa until now, for he had needed all his concentration to drive the powerful car. He saw his brother first. He was standing alone at the end of a corridor, looking like he had two years ago, on the night Alice died, only worse.

'Oh, Nicholas, this is not a place to bring Christopher!' Sarah came out of a waiting room, dropping to one knee as she gathered the frightened child in her arms. Kit clung to her.

'I want my Mummy.' He was close to hysteria. 'Where is she?'

'She can't see you now, darling. She is not very well. You shall have to come home with your Aunt Helen and me. Jennie is also staying the night.'

'Can I see Mummy tomorrow?'

'Perhaps.'

She gazed at her younger son. There were dark shadows beneath his bloodshot eyes and deep lines of exhaustion etched into his face. To reach here in so short a time he must have driven like the devil itself. She picked up Kit. Nicholas was a fool to take unnecessary risks when he had his son in the car.

'How is Philippa?' he asked.

Sarah did not answer immediately. She turned to her daughter, who stood in the doorway behind her. 'Could you take Kit to the beverage machine and get him whatever he wants?'

Helen understood. She took the child from his grandmother, lowered him to the floor, and grasped his hand. Helen was good with children, which made it more the pity she had none of her own. Nor was she likely to if she continued shying away from any man who showed more than a passing interest.

Sarah waited until they were out of earshot. 'She is in intensive care and will be allowed no visitors, not even you. It is touch and go, Nicholas. Justin saw her briefly when she was brought out of surgery. They let him in because he had been with her during the four hours it took to cut her out.'

Startled, Nicholas gazed at his brother, who stared back with something bordering on disdain. Had he been involved in the accident? If so, how had he come through it unscathed? He was dishevelled, but uninjured.

'Go and talk to him, Nicholas. You owe him a lot for what he has done today. Helen and I'll take Kit home. There is nothing more we can do tonight.'

They'd had their differences over the years, but this was the first time Justin looked at Nicholas and felt nothing but loathing. It had been difficult enough speaking with him over the telephone, but seeing him face to face was another matter. He wanted nothing to do with him.

When Philippa was brought out of surgery, still unconscious from the anaesthetic, she looked pathetically frail, something she had never been. The weary surgeon told Justin she had been badly crushed, and although the miscarriage had contributed to a massive haemorrhage, it had not been the main cause. Because of the risk of infection, they had removed all but the most vital organs which she needed for normal bodily function. A broken rib puncturing one lung had brought about more problems. There had also been multiple fractures, not only to her ribs, but her left arm and leg. Oddly enough, apart from heavy bruising, she had suffered relatively few external abrasions, the worst being a foot-long gash along her right thigh. Had she not been wearing a seat belt, it was doubtful she would have survived the head-on collision.

Knowing all that; knowing they had been unable to stop the haemorrhaging; and knowing her chances of pulling through were still in the balance – fifty-fifty he had been told – it was little wonder Justin had no time for his brother. When Nicholas and Sarah walked towards him, he steeled himself for a confrontation.

'Helen and I are taking Christopher home,' his mother said. 'Nicholas will telephone immediately there is any change.'

'There will be none. Not tonight.' Justin pushed himself away from the wall. 'She is in there,' he said to his brother, pointing towards a closed door with a notice reading PRIVATE on it. 'If you tell the sister in charge who you are she will arrange for a doctor to fill you in on the details.'

Nicholas was puzzled by his hostility and if Sarah had not been so emotionally drained she might have seen the warning signs.

'I think it would be easier on Nicholas if you told him first,' she said.

Too late, she saw the flash of anger in her older son's eyes.

'Why?' His voice was like a whiplash. 'So that I can tell

him how Philippa miscarried his child while she lay trapped in the wreckage of her car. You didn't know she was pregnant, did you, Nicholas?'

It was cruel, and did what he intended. It caught Nicholas off guard. Justin watched dispassionately as his brother's expression ran the gamut from shock to disbelief, then guilt.

'Justin!' his mother admonished.

His cold stare switched to her face. 'Isn't that what you wanted me to tell him? Let the doctor fill in the details. He is better qualified than me.'

He turned away, brushing past Helen. He even ignored Kit, who was trailing behind her, his eyes wide with sleeplessness and his hands sticky from the chocolate bar he was chewing.

'Justin . . .' Sarah called, but he did not stop.

'Let him go.' Nicholas took hold of her arm. 'Is it true?'

'Yes.' Her face was ashen.

'Then I had better talk to the doctor like he suggested. Go home, Mum. You are worn out.'

He took the coffee which Helen offered him. It tasted of nothing in particular. As he drank it he frowned at his son, certain Philippa would not approve of his eating a chocolate bar at this time of night. But this was not an ordinary night and, this once, Philippa might understand.

'Here, drink this.'

Justin ignored the coffee which his brother thrust under his nose. He was sitting on a hard bench in an empty reception area. A nurse had walked through earlier and then a security guard, but other than them the hospital could have been deserted.

Nicholas placed the cup on the bench beside him. He remained standing. 'Mum went home half an hour ago and

I have spoken to a doctor. They are hoping this haemorrhaging will stop of its own accord, with the help of the drugs they are giving her. If it doesn't, they will have to operate again. They refused to let me see her.' He sat down and covered his face with his hands. 'What shall I do if she dies?'

'You bring up your son and you carry on. What else can you do?' Justin picked up the coffee. 'Here, I think you need this more than me.'

Nicholas looked at him. There was no warmth in his brother's voice, but he was not ignoring him.

'You drink it,' he said. 'I'd prefer a cigarette.'

'You can't. Not in here.'

'Who is there to see? She will never be able to have another child. If she lives, that is. I suggested she come here for a week because I thought the break would do her good. Had I known she was pregnant I would not have let her drive down.'

'She was going to tell you this weekend.'

Justin leant against the wall, his eyes half closed. His face was a mask of weariness.

'When did she tell you? After the accident? They say she was conscious when she was brought here.'

'She was conscious the entire time, except for the first fifteen minutes or so. She told me about the baby earlier.'

'Was she in a great deal of pain?'

'No.'

'For heaven's sake, Justin! You could try and be more forthcoming. Philippa is my wife and I have a right to know what happened. For a start, how did you become involved?'

'Always suspicious, aren't you, Nick?' He gazed at a dirty patch on the wall opposite. He couldn't say how worried he had been after she left the office, which was why he decided to follow her. Nor could he tell his brother of the dormant emotions which had been roused, not only in him, but

306

Philippa as well. So he bent the truth, for her sake rather than his. 'She forgot to sign some documents before leaving Moor View. I was about to go home, and thought I'd drop them off on my way. I drove into the place where the crash happened shortly after the police arrived. They let me through when I convinced them we were related. And because they were reluctant to drug her without knowing the full extent of her injuries, they let me crawl through a gap in the wreckage and stay with her while the firemen cut their way through.'

He drank the coffee, then walked to a bin and dropped the cup into it. 'You should go back to the waiting room, in case you are needed.'

Nicholas blanched. 'You think . . .'

'She won't die. She has fought all her life. She is not going to give up now.'

Nicholas believed him. 'Will you stay with me?' He crushed the cigarette beneath his heel, then picked up the butt and shoved it into his pocket.

Justin would have stayed anyway. Nicholas was an irritation he had to put up with. It did not mean he had forgiven him. He would never forgive him.

They spent what was left of the night in the stark waiting room. An old woman and her middle-aged daughter shared it with them. The woman's husband was also in intensive care, having suffered a heart attack some time after midnight. He died shortly before dawn. Nicholas felt numb when a doctor took the mother and daughter into the corridor and broke the news to them. He looked at Justin, whose eyes were closed.

He was not asleep. 'She will pull through,' he said.

The cleaners came and went. The day shift took over from the night, but it was the same doctor who came into the waiting room. He looked as exhausted as the two brothers.

'She has come round,' he said. 'You may see her for a couple of minutes, Mr Lang. No longer. She is extremely weak and unable to talk, but a familiar face should set her mind at ease. I have no idea how much she remembers, but she is bound to be confused. One other thing, she is not out of danger yet. She is still haemorrhaging.'

Nicholas was pale. 'Can my brother come with me? He was with her when she was brought in.'

'I know. I was on duty.' In fact, he had thought the dark-haired man was her husband, for she had clung to his hand until the last moment, when they wheeled her into the operating theatre. 'It will probably do more good than harm.'

'Philippa . . .'

The voice came to her through a swirling mist, and it was with reluctance she opened her eyes. She knew she was in hospital, and had guessed from the tubes connecting her to drips and machines that she had been badly hurt in the crash. How long she had been here she did not know. Long enough, it would seem, for Nicholas to come down from London. He was bending over her, repeating her name over and over again.

But his was not the face she wanted to see. She tried to turn away, but the effort was too great. She heard another voice, sharply rebuking. It belonged to the doctor who had been standing over her when she awoke. She did not know what he said, but Nicholas moved back, which was when she saw Justin. He did not speak, but reached forward and brushed his fingertips across her cheek. Then he smiled, that wonderful smile which told her everything was going to be all right.

★

Three days later Philippa was moved out of intensive care into a ward. She was heavily drugged and only vaguely aware of the concerned family and friends who tramped the corridors. Because the accident had received national press coverage, cards and gifts and flowers were arriving from total strangers, and soon there was nowhere to put them. Sarah, always practical, suggested the flowers be distributed to less fortunate wards. On the other hand, Nicholas demanded his wife be transferred to a private room. He was told one was not available and, even if it was, she would receive better attention in the ward.

He was seething. 'As soon as she is strong enough I am having her transferred out of there into a private hospital. Better off in a public ward, indeed! In no time at all every Tom, Dick and Harry will be tramping through it. In fact, I shall arrange for her to be moved into London, where she will receive better treatment than this backwater could ever hope to provide.'

'It was this backwater which saved her life.' His mother was equally furious. 'And as for moving her, don't you dare contemplate such a thing. She may be out of intensive care, but she is far from being clear of the woods. They are quite right, she will be easier to monitor in a ward. And as there are only four beds I would hardly call it public.'

Her son looked suitably chastened, but once Philippa showed signs of improvement he would be itching to lock her away in a private clinic. Something must be done before it came to that. Briskly, she passed to other matters. 'Now we know the immediate danger is over, you will have to turn your attention to Christopher. You cannot keep him off school indefinitely, and you have your business to consider. I think you should take him home tomorrow, then arrange to spend Monday to Friday in London and the weekends here. You don't have to drive. The train is quick enough and you can always use my car. When school breaks up he can spend the summer holidays with me, while you arrange your life as you see fit.'

'I cannot go back to work as though nothing has happened.'

'Why on earth not? Philippa is doped to the eyeballs, and will be for some time yet. She won't even know you are gone. Helen and I can visit her every day. Justin is here, and both Maggie and Steve are going to stay for another week. Go back, Nicholas. I do not want you moping about underfoot with nothing better to do than come up with ridiculous and highly impractical ideas.'

'I suppose I should look in on the pottery,' he said. 'I don't want her to worry about it. Justin can fill me in on the details. He must have some idea of what goes on there.'

'I am sure Rodney is capable of handling any problems which arise. Take one step at a time. Get yourself organised before you take on additional responsibilities.'

She was right. At the moment he did not know whether he was standing on his head or his feet. He would take Kit home and see how much work he could hand to Ernest. He could tackle Justin about the pottery next weekend, and also the increasing hostility he had felt since that long night in the hospital.

Kit did not want to leave. He was frightened he would never see his mother again. He had been allowed to visit her the day before. She was pale and drawn, with plastic pipes running into her arm and beneath the bed covers. Her eyes were out of focus as she whispered his name and tried to lift her hand to his anxious face.

'She needs to rest,' his father explained as he drove back to London at a more sensible speed than he had left it. 'Her body will mend while she sleeps.'

His unsatisfactory explanation did little to alleviate Kit's anxiety, but he was afraid to ask questions in case his father got angry.

There was a registered letter waiting for Nicholas when he arrived home. Eileen had left it on the top of a pile of post, most of which consisted of sympathy letters from acquaintances, business and otherwise. Nicholas opened it at breakfast the next morning, and his face flushed with anger. He took Kit to school, then drove to the offices of Perkins, Crisp & Perkins, where he demanded to see Leonard Perkins. The intimidated receptionist called for reinforcements, and a buxom, middle-aged woman appeared. Mr Perkins was due in court. An appointment would have to be made. Nicholas shouted her down, and the entire office would have been in an uproar had the elder Perkins not come to investigate the cause of the commotion.

He eyed his favourite client's husband with something bordering on contempt. 'Please come into my office, Mr Lang.'

'I want to know the meaning of this.' Nicholas waved the letter at him.

'In my office, Mr Lang. Please. It's this way.'

He left Nicholas with no option but to follow.

'I was extremely distressed to hear about Mrs Lang,' said Leonard Perkins as he settled behind his desk. 'Thank God she is going to be all right. And now, Mr Lang, what may I do for you? Please feel free to sit down. Ah, it's the letter which has upset you. It was necessary under the circumstances. What don't you understand?'

'What right you have to send me this.'

Nicholas did not sit. He stood glowering on the far side of the old-fashioned wooden desk. An intemperate young man, Leonard Perkins thought.

'I have every right. I understand your wife will be incapacitated for a considerable length of time, and I am therefore invoking the clauses of a Power of Attorney which I hold. Both Mr Slater and Mr Justin Lang, your brother I believe, are aware of the terms of the document. The letter is perfectly clear. Please do not interfere with Moor View Pottery in any way whatsoever. If you do, I shall obtain an injunction to prevent you from entering it. Should you not believe me, I have no objection to your own lawyers scrutinising the document. I can assure you they will find no loophole. I drew it up myself.' He glanced at his watch. He would have to leave within the next five minutes if he was going to get to court on time. 'I am extremely sorry you had to find out like this, after what must have been a harrowing week.'

Nicholas was white with fury. 'I shall certainly have my lawyers contact you,' he muttered through clenched teeth. He strode to the door, where he stopped. 'As a matter of interest, when did my wife have this document drawn up, or do ethical reasons prevent you from telling me?'

'No, of course not. I remember it clearly. Your son was born shortly after it was signed and sealed.'

The document was binding. It was perfectly valid for the other two directors, who were also shareholders, to run Moor View jointly and take whatever policy-making decisions they deemed necessary. Nicholas was like a volcano at the point of eruption. It was both ludicrous and insulting that Philippa should entrust his brother, who had never been a businessman, with a share of the pottery, while effectively blocking any attempt he might make to look after her interests in this time of crisis.

He drove down early on Friday, collecting his son from school at three-thirty.

'We're meant to play cricket until five o'clock,' Kit said, throwing his satchel on the back seat.

'These are extenuating circumstances. I have explained to the headmaster and you will not get into trouble. Sit in the back, Christopher.'

'But I always sit in front when Mummy's not here.'

'Not any more.'

'But . . .'

Nicholas clipped the boy on the arm. 'Do as you are told. And use the seat belt. I had it fitted today.'

This new rule, together with the rear seat belt, were Ernest's suggestions. 'Considering the speeds you drive at it makes sense,' he had said. 'Be careful of that boy, Nicholas. It would kill Philippa if anything happened to him now.'

It was a sombre warning and, because of it, Nicholas kept a watchful eye on the speedometer during the long drive from London to Devon. He drove directly to the hospital, ignoring Kit's complaints that he was hungry.

'Next week you can stay home with Eileen,' he said after reaching Plymouth and hitting three sets of red lights in a row. 'You will be able to play cricket to your heart's content and eat yourself sick. I thought you wanted to see your mother.'

'I do,' said Kit, fighting back a flood of tears. 'And I hate cricket.'

'Don't go out,' Sarah told Nicholas the next morning. 'We're having a family meeting. Justin will be here shortly, and I have arranged for Pauline to take the children on the first ride. It will be better if they are out of the way.'

Nicholas stared at his mother. 'What on earth for?'

'I should have thought that was obvious. Philippa is part of this family, and we need to discuss her future.'

'She is my wife and I shall do whatever is best for her. I

313

am grateful for everything you are doing, but this is not a family matter. I have no intention of discussing my wife's future with my brother.'

Sarah was annoyed. 'Stop talking like a pompous ass! I am not concerned with what you think is best, but with what is best for Philippa. And where has this animosity towards Justin sprung from?'

'Ask him.'

'I shall. The kitchen at ten, Nicholas. If you care for Philippa as much as you profess, you will be there.'

He was. It was a rare occurrence for Sarah to intervene in the lives of her sons. Neither of them were obliged to take any notice of her, but it was gratifying to know they had enough respect to defer to her wishes, if grudgingly.

Justin had not come into the house yet. She had spoken to him in the barn, where she found him helping Kit and Jennie saddle their ponies. Out of earshot of the children she had asked what was wrong between him and Nicholas. His reply had been short and sharp and not altogether satisfactory, but she gathered it was to do with Moor View. She also sensed there was something else, something more deep rooted, which he had no intention of telling her.

Helen was making tea and Nicholas standing beside the Aga.

'If this is meant to be a family meeting, then Jennie and Kit should be here,' Helen said.

'Kit is too young,' Sarah told her. 'And hearing us talk about his mother would serve no useful purpose, other than to distress him further.' She was looking at Nicholas as she spoke. He ignored her.

'Jennie is ten,' Helen mused. 'I was only nine when the decision was made to come back here. You included me then.'

'Because it directly affected you,' said Justin from the back

314

door. 'This really has nothing to do with Jennie, and it would be unfair to include her while excluding Kit.'

He came into the kitchen, Bess at his heels. Sarah saw his eyes flicker in his brother's direction. She could feel the coldness in the air, and wished she knew what had happened, for without that knowledge she was helpless to defuse the situation.

Justin sat at the head of the table. Bess lay beside him, her chin on his foot.

'Sit down, Nicholas,' Sarah said.

'I'll be damned if I sit at the same table as him. I am only here because you requested it, but I warn you now, any decisions to be made concerning my wife are mine, and mine alone. They certainly have nothing to do with him.'

Helen blanched, while Sarah was stunned by his malevolence.

Justin had expected it, and his voice was steely. 'You always were selfish. You talk about Philippa as though she were your personal property, a possession to be jealously guarded. Your wife, as you repeatedly tell us. I sometimes wonder if you remember she has a name. Not once since the accident have I heard you say how much you love her, or display as much affection as I do to Bess here. As for Kit, he is a confused little boy whose feelings you have callously tossed aside. You are his father, and he is terrified of you.'

'My God, you've got a bloody cheek trying to lecture me on how to be a husband and a father. You treated Alice like dirt until you knew she was dying. I didn't have to marry Philippa because she was pregnant, and I have never run away from my responsibilities. It was you, not me, who deserted the child you now profess to love so much. And you would leave her again if it suited your purposes!'

'Stop it!' Sarah shouted. 'Both of you. You are bickering like children. I wanted you here to discuss a young woman of whom I happen to be very fond. If you must squabble, then do so elsewhere.'

Nicholas transferred his gaze to her face. 'There is nothing to discuss. As soon as she is well enough, I intend to take Philippa home. If necessary, I can employ a nurse to care for her.'

'Why not lock her in a cell and throw away the key?' his brother said. 'She might as well have died in that car rather than be stifled by you.'

The situation was getting out of hand, and Sarah took the only action she could think of. She picked up the nearest object and flung it on to the tiled floor. It was a wooden bread board and the clatter was deafening as it bounced, then split in half. A cat leapt off the windowsill into the garden, and Bess whimpered. But Sarah had the attention of her sons.

'Sit down, Nicholas. Now. No arguments. And, Justin, I don't want to hear another word from you, not unless you have something worthwhile to contribute.' Her eyes flashed with rarely seen anger as they rested on her younger son. 'And the same applies to you. I don't care how old you are, but this is my house and while you are in it you will both show me some respect. Do I make myself clear?'

'Nothing you say will make me change my mind.'

'Sit down, Nicholas.'

He was a man of thirty-four and she thought he was going to refuse. But he did as she asked.

'And you too, Helen. I'll pour the tea.' She felt drained as she filled the cups and handed one to each of her three children. Then she sat down, deliberately placing herself between Justin and Nicholas. She could have cut the atmosphere with a knife.

'I want Philippa to stay with me until she is completely recovered,' she said. 'After she is discharged from hospital she will need continuing treatment and all the moral support we can give her.'

'She can have both in London.' Nicholas was obdurate.

'The treatment, certainly, but the moral support?' Sarah could also be stubborn. 'Do you realise the enormity of what has happened to her? Being a man, you obviously do not. She has not only lost a baby, but has yet to learn that she will never be able to have another. She is thirty-one years old, and that is the greatest tragedy to come out of this accident. Her injuries will heal in time, but what about the scars you can't see? Will you be there to help her cope with those?'

'He will be working all day and half the night.' Justin's voice was flat and unemotional. 'Even if he says he won't, it is the nature of advertising. And then there is the American market he is trying to cultivate. Are you willing to sacrifice that for Philippa's sake?'

Nicholas bristled. 'Ernest will be doing any travelling. If necessary, I can arrange to work from home.'

'You won't bend, will you? Your damn pride will not let you. You are determined to be right, whatever it takes.'

'Oh, for heaven's sake! Surely the sensible thing would be to ask Philippa what she wants.' Three pairs of surprised eyes turned to the usually reticent Helen. Her cheeks flushed. 'None of you has the right to decide what she must do. Not even you, Nicholas. As for Kit, he should be allowed to stay here until Philippa is out of hospital.'

'He has school,' said her brother.

'There are fewer than three weeks of this term left. It is not going to set his education back if he misses them. He was crying last night. You didn't know, did you? I got up to let the cat out and heard him. He was breaking his heart and, from what I could gather, he has cried every night since you took him back to London. He can't cope with what is

317

happening. If he was here he could visit his mother every day. It would help him, and her too.' The colour spread through her face. 'I'm sorry. I spoke out of turn.'

'No, you didn't, sweetheart.' It was Justin who spoke. 'What you did was put us to shame.' He looked at his brother. 'Well, Nicholas, are we going to argue over this for the rest of the morning, or are you going to see sense?'

'Helen is right,' Sarah stated. 'We all know it. You have a business to run, Nicholas. Nobody is expecting you to give it up. And I am sure Philippa will be grateful if you keep an eye on the pottery.'

Immediately, she felt the antagonism and anger emanating from him and remembered, too late, that Moor View had something to do with Justin and Nicholas going hammer and tongs at each other.

Nicholas sprang to his feet. 'Didn't he tell you? He is not only a director but a shareholder. Both he and Rodney Slater have been made custodians of Moor View, with the power to kick me out should I go within a mile of the place.'

Sarah shuddered as he slammed out of the kitchen. Her stark eyes turned to Justin.

'Is that true?'

'Yes,' he dismally replied. 'It was Philippa's idea, not mine. I never realised it would come about like this. I don't think she did either.' He stood up, leant across the table, and squeezed his sister's hand. 'I think he will consider what you said. You took him by surprise. You took us all by surprise. I need some fresh air. Can I take one of the cobs?'

'Of course,' said Sarah. She remembered a more amicable family meeting, when they decided to move back here. It was a move she never regretted. Justin rode on that day too. Some things never changed.

★

The cob was sweating when Justin brought it back. As he led the horse into the barn, Nicholas stepped out of the shadows.

'How many times do you have to be told not to smoke in here? There is a notice above your head!'

His brother walked outside and ground the cigarette into the dirt. 'I am not a child.'

'Then stop behaving like one.' Justin undid the girth and lifted the saddle from the cob's back. 'What do you want?'

'To warn you to stay away from my . . . from Philippa. I don't know how you wheedled a chunk of Moor View out of her, but I am not going to stand by and let you turn her against me.'

'You don't need me for that. You are making a pretty good job of it yourself. At least some good came out of the accident. It rid her of a child she never wanted.'

He thought Nicholas would hit him. His fists clenched and his eyes blazed with uncontrolled fury.

'She told you that?'

'She told me enough. I was able to guess the rest. Why didn't she want it, Nicholas? Was it because of your mistress? Don't look so surprised. I still know people in London. There have been rumours circulating for a long time about you and a woman who suddenly landed a top job in America. Your doing, no doubt.'

Nicholas started forward.

'Daddy . . . Daddy . . . where are you?' Jennie ran into the barn.

'What is it?' His eyes remained on his brother's face.

'Kelly bucked and I fell off. Look, I scratched my arm and there's a bruise coming up.'

She lifted her left arm for him to see. There was a sticking plaster below the elbow and a little discoloration which would not amount to much.

319

'Next time you'll remember to use your legs to stop him from getting his head down. Be a good girl and fetch me a headcollar.'

Nicholas watched with hard eyes as she skipped away.

'I warn you, Justin, stop meddling in my life. And if you know what's good for you, stay away from Philippa.'

'If she wants me to visit her then I shall continue to do so. And another thing, don't go upsetting her over Moor View ... or any of this. She doesn't have the strength to stand up to the traumas.'

'What do you think I am?'

'What you have always been. Selfish and insensitive.'

Nicholas turned on his heel and strode back to the house.

'Here you are,' said Jennie, holding up the headcollar. 'Grandma is making shepherd's pie for lunch.'

'We won't be having lunch here. We're going home.'

CHAPTER TWENTY-FOUR

Philippa became more aware of what was going on around her as she was weaned off the heavier drugs, but there was still a lot of pain and the punctured lung obstinately refused to mend. It was July before she asked about the full extent of her injuries. Her pale skin was even paler afterwards, but the hospital staff agreed she took the news well. That night she cried silent tears into her pillow, not for the baby who had never known life, but because there would never be another. She did not speak of it again, nor did anybody else, even Nicholas, who had never been so caring. It was impossible to dislike somebody who pandered to her every whim, but a leopard could not change its spots, and neither could he.

'They hope to kick you out in a couple of weeks,' he told her during one of his regular weekend visits. 'In time for Kit's birthday. Have you any idea what we should get him?'

'A pony. He's been wanting one for a long time.'

Nicholas frowned. 'You know a pony would be impractical. What happens when we go home?'

She did not want to think about home, or the continuing unhappiness it represented. She turned her head away.

'Are you in pain? Shall I call a nurse?'

'No. I'm a little tired. Get him whatever you think best.'

Before returning to London he asked his mother if she

could look out for a suitable animal, adding that she would be stuck with it for nine months of the year. She found Bertrand, or Bertie as he was affectionately called. He was a twelve-year-old Dartmoor pony and had been ridden regularly at Pony Club rallies and in local shows. He was being sold because his present owner had outgrown him. Nicholas arranged for him to be delivered on the morning of Kit's seventh birthday.

'You'll be able to see his expression when the pony arrives,' he told Philippa.

Her lung collapsed two days later. It meant more drugs and an indeterminate stay in hospital. She was too ill to see Kit on his birthday, let alone see how thrilled he was.

It was nearly September. Ernest did not have the right touch with their American clients and a crisis was looming. If Nicholas wanted to save the accounts he had worked so hard to get, then he would have to go to New York himself. With Philippa still in hospital and Kit due back at school, he was being pulled in two directions. At one time he would have sought advice from his brother, but their ill feeling was running too deep. So he shared his problems with his mother, expecting no sympathy, and surprised to get it.

'Kit will have to stay here. There should be no trouble getting him into school. The bus can pick him up by the gate, and he'll have Jennie to keep an eye on him. Perhaps now you can understand my concern about your grandiose ideas of moving Philippa back to London. It would have been disastrous.'

Philippa left the hospital on a cold November morning. Nicholas came down from London for the occasion. He was driving a new Jaguar.

'It's yours, darling,' he said, placing a rug over her knees.

'To use when you feel up to it.'

She shuddered. She didn't think she would ever feel up to it again. Sarah, who was sitting beside her, squeezed her hand.

'He means well, even if he is a bit premature,' she whispered, when her son slid into the driver's seat. 'Thirty miles an hour maximum, Nicholas. We are not on a race-track.'

After five months Philippa found the outside world a noisy and intimidating place. When they reached the moors, she felt an uncontrollable fear. Again, she saw that out-of-control car careering towards her, and the terrified face of the boy behind the wheel. He had not survived the crash. She had known as she lay trapped in her own car, when nobody would tell her about him, not even Justin. By the time they reached Flint Iron Farm she had broken out in a cold sweat and Nicholas insisted on carrying her to the room which would be hers. It was Justin's old bedroom. She recognised the beams and the bay window with the box seat. Otherwise it was nothing like the room Helen had shown her all those years ago. There were new flower-patterned curtains, and where the desk had been was a kidney-shaped dressing table. The rugs had been replaced by a carpet and on the freshly painted walls were prints of local scenes.

'Nicholas is next door,' said Sarah. 'And Kit is further along the passage, next to Helen. He wanted to stay off school, but we made him go. You don't want everyone confronting you at once. You ought to rest for a while, my dear. You look exhausted. How about a cup of tea?'

'That would be nice,' Philippa said. She turned to Nicholas. 'I'd like to see Bertie before Kit comes home.'

'Mum's right, you need to rest first.'

A small flame of rebellion sparked inside her. She had lost five months of her life, lying in the same bed in the same ward, doing what she was told and never complaining.

'I want to see him. I have rested all morning and I can rest all afternoon. You can bring him under the window.'

'Of course he can,' said Sarah. 'Go and fetch him, Nicholas, while I help Philippa to the window.'

'I can help myself, thank you. I may be weak, but I am not helpless.'

Sarah and Nicholas exchanged glances.

'I'll make the tea,' said Sarah. She pushed her son out of the door.

Philippa crossed the room slowly. She stopped in front of the dressing table mirror. This was the first time she had seen herself properly. She lifted a hand to her cheek. She was so pale and thin. There were purple shadows beneath her eyes, and her hair was limp and lustreless. Steve would not want to photograph her now.

She moved away from her reflection. She did not know it yet, but the rock-hard determination which had carried her through the worst times was beginning to reassert itself.

Nicholas stayed for a week, during which time she never saw Justin. But when Nicholas had gone his brother re-entered her life. She knew there had been an argument, and wondered if it involved her. There was nothing else for them to fight about.

She was determined to gain weight and whereas breakfast was a meal she had always avoided, Philippa now forced herself to eat a slice of toast and the thick, milky porridge Sarah made for her. While Nicholas was there he had brought it to her room on a tray and sat with her while she ate, but on Monday she went downstairs to find Justin sitting at the kitchen table with the rest of the family.

He smiled. 'Good morning, Philippa. You are looking remarkably well.'

'What are you doing here so early?'

'I am going to drop the children at school, then spend the rest of the day at Moor View. The place has gone mad and Rodney is insisting I put in some proper hours.'

That was an exaggeration. Rodney had told her how Justin had been putting in a lot more than proper hours since her accident.

He came every morning for breakfast, and Philippa made a point of being in the kitchen when he arrived. They were rarely alone, except on the few occasions when he dropped by during the day, putting his mother's mind at ease by walking with her. He did not fuss like the others did, nor did he make concessions, other than to slow his pace to match hers.

'What happened between you and Nicholas?' she asked him on the morning they got as far as the main gate. It was further than she had gone before, but no distance at all when looked at in perspective. It was going to take a long time before she was halfway fit again. 'Did you quarrel because of me?'

She was leaning against the gate and the cold wind had whipped some colour into her cheeks.

'We quarrelled over a number of things. You are not to blame for what Nick is. He always did put himself first.'

'But the reason you are not speaking is because of me. Sarah has been upset by it.'

'As have we all. Come along, we'd better get back.'

'I feel fine.'

'I know. But I have an appointment in an hour.'

'To do with Moor View?'

'Yes.'

'I appreciate everything you and Rodney are doing.'

She fell into step with him, resisting an urge to grip his arm.

'Isn't it what you wanted? That's something else Nicholas resented. It was the straw which broke the camel's back.'

She stopped. 'I don't understand.'

'Your Mr Perkins is not an idle man. Within hours of hearing about the accident he invoked the clauses of the Power of Attorney he was holding.'

'How would that affect Nicholas?'

'Everyone involved was sent a letter. Rodney, me, the bank, our accountants. And Nicholas.'

'Nicholas?'

'His letter told him to stay away from Moor View. I understand he went to see Leonard Perkins and they had a stinking row. Needless to say, my brother came off the worst. You should have told him years ago.'

'He would have understood no more then than he has now. I don't regret what I did. My only regret is you had to suffer because of it.'

She started to walk, not seeing the mixture of emotions which pulled at Justin's features. Her strength was returning and it was time he withdrew, before she became too dependent upon him.

That year Philippa was determined to be at Moor View's Christmas party. Nicholas was not there to stop her, Sarah could not, and Justin refused to get involved. But he did promise his mother he would take her there and ensure she did not get too exhausted.

Everyone was pleased to see her. She was given a bouquet of fresh flowers and there was a cake for her to cut. Sarah's fears were not unfounded, for Philippa did find it tiring. After an hour Justin suggested they leave.

'I'm glad I went,' she said as he drove through the wrought-iron gates.

'I thought you would be.'

They lapsed into silence. He was a careful driver who kept within the speed limits and she relaxed, not noticing the road he took. She was not sure what brought on the panic. It could have been that she recognised a farm they passed, the one with rusting milk churns standing outside the gate. A runnel of fear passed through her.

'Where are we?'

He pulled over to the side of the road and switched off the engine.

'I think you know,' he said.

She did. It was here she had passed the Morris, and not far ahead were those looping bends. Her fear turned into anger. 'You have no right to bring me here. Take me back to your mother's.'

'I am. I thought you would like to see Dovestail on the way.'

'You can reach Dovestail without using this road.'

'Only by making an eight-mile detour. Is that what you are going to do for the rest of your life?'

Philippa was silent. He turned the ignition key, then drove straight on.

'Please, Justin, I can't. Not yet. It's too soon.'

There was no traffic and he stopped the car in the road. Her face was colourless and she was verging on self-induced hysteria.

'This place does not hold pleasant memories for me either. You have to meet your fears head on if you are going to conquer them.'

'I can't . . . I really can't. I'd rather get out and walk.'

'Then you had better start walking. I remember when you had guts. Now you are proving that you possess the same cowardly streak as the rest of your family.'

Her expression hardened. 'Take me home. I don't want to see Dovestail, nor do I care which road you take.'

She did. She relived the horror of that day as they approached the first bend.

'The probability of it happening again in the same place is a million to one chance. Look, there is nothing here, not even a mark.'

'A boy died.'

'Not because of anything you did. You were trying to avoid a collision.'

She knew he was right. Lightning rarely struck in the same place twice. But his harsh treatment was not something she could easily forgive.

'I won't come in,' he said when they reached Flint Iron Farm. 'Nor will I be seeing you again for a while. Noel and Maggie have invited us to spend Christmas with them at Lochdunnan. Nicholas will be here and it will be less awkward.' He handed her the flowers. 'I am not going to apologise, Philippa.'

'I never expected you to.'

She walked away without saying goodbye.

Nicholas was furious when he learnt Philippa had gone to Moor View, and even angrier when she came down with a cold on Christmas Eve. She said it was nothing, but he insisted the doctor be called. Antibiotics were prescribed and he was told she must rest and not get over-excited.

The cold lingered, and after New Year Philippa returned to hospital for X-rays. There was fluid in her lungs, but not enough to justify her being re-admitted. She was given more medicine, and throughout a long and dismal January was confined to the house and, more often than not, to bed. She had caught colds before, and the odd bout of flu, but this was the first time her health had let her down. She was irritated by the weakness of her body and bored to tears. Kit was back at school and Nicholas in London, with little hope of coming down until the end of the month.

She wrote to Justin, thanking him for the Christmas present he had left for her and Nicholas. It was a painting of Kit riding Bertie, which she was going to hang over the fireplace at Dovestail. She kept her letter short and breezy, playing down the illness which continued to plague her. She thought he would come and see her on his return from Scotland, but it was now halfway through January and he had not been near the farm. Rodney, who had, was forbidden to involve her in Moor View.

January slipped into February. She had seen Nicholas once since Christmas. He was in New York at the moment with no idea of how long he would be away. He promised to drop everything and spend a week with her when he came back. Philippa did not miss him, but his being there would have broken the tedium. She came to a decision. She was going back to work.

Sarah was horrified. 'You can't,' she said.

'Why not? I appreciate everything you are doing for me, but it's about time I stood on my own feet.'

Sarah wondered if she should appeal to Justin. He could stop her. He had telephoned regularly to ask how she was, but had not come round. She did not ask why. She presumed he was trying to smooth things over with Nicholas. She was always the last to know what was happening.

'If you must go, I shall drive you there,' she said.

Philippa refused the offer. Justin had been right. She needed to take her life back into her own hands.

There was so much to catch up with. While Rodney got her up to date, she drank weak tea and wondered if Justin would join them. He was there, for his car was in the yard. After a while she realised he was not coming, but pride prevented her from asking Rodney the reason.

He waited until three o'clock before walking into her office. Philippa looked up as he closed the door, guessing from his expression why he had come.

'Have you had enough yet? You look awful.'

'Why should you care?'

He did not answer immediately. He was thinking she was not much different from the fifteen-year-old girl who had challenged his right to stand on her doorstep.

'I care, Philippa. I would not be here otherwise. One of us had to walk away.'

'We were doing nothing wrong. I was ill.'

There was something gloriously naive about the way she said that.

'You are not ill now, only weak and run down. But you will be ill if you continue to be obstinate. Let me take you home.'

'And give everyone the satisfaction of saying they told me so?'

'My mother may seem over-protective, but only because she thinks of you as a second daughter. Will you take my advice and leave now? You have had little experience of winter in this part of the country. Look out of the window. Fog is drifting in and once it settles driving across the moors will be difficult. In your case it would be foolish.'

He gave her no chance to reply, but left as quietly as he had come.

She went to Moor View for a few hours each day, but rarely saw Justin, who came in less regularly now she was back. He had employed a resident artist specialising in design work and had also built up a network of independent artists, people they could commission individually. In short, he had ensured Moor View would survive without him. So could

Philippa, but that did not stop her from missing him.

She quarrelled with Nicholas when he turned up. He said if she was well enough to spend time at Moor View, she was well enough to come home. She told him she had no intention of hauling Kit out of school as his life had been disrupted enough during the past year. Nicholas retorted there was nothing to stop her coming back after Easter, when Kit could start the summer term at his old school. Then he made the mistake of suggesting he share her bed, if only for the sake of appearance.

'What was that about?' Sarah asked when he came into the kitchen. 'The two of you were shouting loud enough to raise the dead. I wish you wouldn't upset her, Nicholas.'

'I want her to come home, but she refuses.'

'You have to be patient, darling. She is beginning to find her feet, but needs more time. She will come back when she's ready. Shall I talk to her?'

'I can handle my own wife.' He gazed from the window. 'Where is Christopher?'

'It is not Philippa who is at fault. You have come home in a foul mood.'

He sat down. 'I only got in from New York this morning. I spent a couple of hours at the office, then drove here. My internal clock is in another time zone.'

'Then you should have gone to bed and come here in the morning. Behaving like a bear with a sore head will not endear you to anyone. It's as well Kit is out.'

'Out? Out where? It's seven o'clock.'

'Justin has taken him and Jennie to the cinema. I think *Bambi* is doing the rounds again. He often takes them out after school on a Friday.'

Nicholas rubbed his tired eyes. 'I am fed up with the influence he is exerting over my family. He made a mess of his own life, and now he's trying to ruin mine.'

'If you bothered to come here a little more often, you could exert your own influence over your family. Don't blame Justin for what is happening to your marriage. He rarely comes here either, other than to drop off or pick up the children.' Sarah slammed a mug of coffee on to the table. 'Drink this. It will clear your head and put you in a better frame of mind.'

'I don't want coffee.' He pushed it away. 'I could do with a double brandy.'

Had he been a child she would have slapped him. He was behaving like a child, spoilt and petulant because he could not have what he wanted, and was not prepared to work for it. Sarah threw the coffee down the sink.

'I finished the brandy last week, on a trifle. If you don't want coffee, you can go without.'

'Then I'll go to the Pack Horse. I shall be welcome there.'

Frustrated and angry, he slammed out of the house, and equally frustrated and angry he returned to London on Sunday evening. He did not say when he would be back. The agency was busy, and he wanted to open an office in New York by autumn.

He was in America over Easter and was not missed. Pony Club activities were in full swing and Philippa ferried Kit and Bertie to the various rallies. There was always somebody who was willing to unhitch the trailer, and she would leave it at the grounds while she went shopping or to Doves-tail.

Steve came for a short visit in May. He had last seen Philippa at Christmas, and was delighted by how well she looked.

'I was in New York last month and saw Nicholas in a restaurant,' he told her one lunchtime, when they were sitting in the garden behind the Pack Horse. 'He didn't see me.'

'He's opening an office there.'

'He was not alone, Philippa.'

She placed her hand over his. 'I didn't think he would go all this time without another woman. I don't care, Steve. I am happy here, and so is Kit. I am never coming back to London.'

'What about Nicholas?'

'I intend to divorce him.' Her calm eyes met his. 'What else are you trying to tell me?'

'That the woman was Hope Stevenson.'

They were going to have a hot summer. There had been little rain and the grass was withering. Justin saw the signs as he walked from the main farm, carrying a can of fresh milk. Bess ran ahead, yapping shrilly. As he came round the side of the hedge he saw his mother's Land-Rover. The gate was open and the dog had disappeared.

He was partway along the path when something made him pause. He was not sure what – a rustle, the snap of a twig, or a scent which was alien to these surroundings. He turned slowly, knowing who it was before he saw Philippa standing beside the boarded-up well. Sunlight filtered through the branches of a tree, its rays caressing her face and flecking her hair with gold. The skimpy top and denim shorts would have looked provocative on anyone else, but she wore them with the same unconscious elegance she would have afforded a designer gown.

'I know I've broken all the rules by coming here, but I have missed you, Justin. I've missed you so very much.'

She spoke quietly, and with such serenity that his breath caught in his throat. She had made her decision. She was not going to walk away. As she came to him, he saw the scar which ran down the inside of her right thigh, its whiteness accentuated by her tan. It was a permanent reminder of her accident.

She stopped an arm's length from him, her eyes searching his. He put down the milk.

'This is wrong,' he said.

'I don't care. I am going to divorce Nicholas, and shall tell him so the next time he bothers to come down.'

He took her hands in his. Where her wedding ring should have been there was no mark. It was a long time since she had worn it.

'Are you sure this is what you want? You can still turn back, Philippa.'

'I don't want to turn back.' She leant forward, brushing her lips against his.

At that, he gripped her shoulders, his mouth closing over hers with the intensity of a man who has found an oasis in the middle of a desert.

CHAPTER TWENTY-FIVE

The freak temperatures continued into July. No rain fell. Reservoirs shrank and streams became trickles, or disappeared altogether. There was serious talk of water rationing, and the government drew up a Drought Bill.

Everyone was affected. Sarah changed her routines. Her regular pupils and the handful of holidaymakers who turned up every summer rode before ten, while the treks went out after five, when it was cooler.

Industry was warned of impending water shortages and instructed to cut back on its usage. Initially, the South West was the worst-hit area, with Moor View finding itself an early victim of the abnormal weather conditions. Rodney got around the worst of the problem by dividing the work force into day and night shifts, like he had done during the power strikes a few years earlier. Water supplies tended to be erratic during the day, with demand fast outstripping supply, whereas late at night the demand dropped away. Rationing was a necessity, but the pottery kept going, completing its orders with the minimum of disruption.

'If I'd known what was going to happen we could have sunk our own borehole years ago,' said Philippa.

Justin laughed. 'There's not been a heatwave like this in two centuries, and it will probably be as long before we have another.'

But he unboarded the well at Shepherds Fold, and fitted a pump to bring up the water. Sarah did the same at Flint Iron Farm, except her brackish water could only be drunk by the ponies. Philippa would have followed suit had she been living at Dovestail, but she was not. Common-sense won when Justin reminded her of what had happened the last time she told Nicholas she wanted a divorce. He would have to be more restrained in his mother's house.

She was growing impatient. His irregular telephone calls told her nothing, other than he was flitting back and forth between London and New York – between the office and Hope Stevenson, she sourly thought. On the other hand, Philippa did not regret her one indiscretion. Justin had made her feel like a woman again. But further liaisons were out of the question. In this small community somebody would find out, and too many people could get hurt. Yet it was during this strange, in-between period, when her life was floating in limbo, that the flames of love and hope and happiness burnt at their strongest.

School broke up for the summer, and Kit was chosen as a team member for the Pony Club competitions which were held at the end of August. It was a summer like no other as hot day followed hot day, with the sun beating down from cloudless skies. Wild ponies drifted towards the villages and farms in search of water. Grass fires became a common occurrence, and the parched earth cracked, taking on an ugly, desert-like appearance. Moor View ran into difficulties as water shortages bit deeper. It was the same all over the country. Standpipes appeared in town and village alike, with people queuing for something they had always taken for granted.

Still Nicholas did not come.

He turned up a week late for his son's eighth birthday. It was after midnight and Philippa was in her room, going through the monthly figures, when she heard the unmistakable roar of his Porsche. She was relieved he was here, for now she could put her plans into motion, but she did not want to face him tonight. Her dilemma was solved when she heard Sarah's door open and her footsteps on the landing. She put away the papers, then sat in the dark beside the open windows. Nicholas came up half an hour later, but went past her door and into his own room.

He slept soundly, not waking until late the following morning. The sun was beating down with a fierce intensity and the house had an empty feel to it. But when he went into the kitchen Philippa was sitting at the table, reading a newspaper and sipping orange juice.

She looked up. She was wearing a pale blue, sleeveless top and faded jeans. Her hair was pushed back from her face and only her eyes bore traces of make-up – enough to flatter and enlarge, but not intrude upon a natural loveliness which never failed to take him by surprise.

'Hello, Nicholas,' she said.

He leant forward to kiss her, but his lips met her cheek. He frowned, but refrained from remarking upon the deliberate slight.

'Where is everyone?' he asked.

'Your mother is in the stables, Helen is having her hair done, and Kit has gone riding with Jennie.'

'Alone?'

'No.' She folded the newspaper. 'Your brother is with them. Would you like coffee?'

'I can make it.'

'I don't mind. It's only instant.'

'You were asleep when I got back last night. Mum told me not to disturb you.'

'I know. She told me this morning.'

He watched her spoon granules into a mug, pour in the boiling water, then add milk. When she brought it to him, he took an elaborate jewel case from his pocket and laid it on the table. It was from Tiffany's in New York.

'An apology for staying away for so long,' he said.

This was difficult enough and he was making it no easier. She lifted the lid. Inside the case was a gold necklace, linked, and undoubtedly valuable. Nicholas had never gone in for cheap gifts. She ran her fingers over the shining gold, but did not pick it up.

'Thank you. It is beautiful.'

'You can wear it tonight, when I take you to dinner. We need to get to know each other again.' He reached for her hand, but she snatched it away.

'Nicholas . . .' she began.

'Sit down, Philippa. Hear me out first.' He was angry, but knew she would retaliate in kind if he lost his temper, then they would get nowhere. 'I have been away for a long time, but it has been for a purpose and you were in good hands. I have set up the American company and it will be in full swing when we go there in September.'

'We?'

'Let me finish. I have rented a flat with marvellous views over Central Park, and found a proper English school for Christopher. Prominent businessmen and diplomats send their children there, so you don't have to worry about him picking up Americanisms. It will only be for six months or so. By next summer I should have trained someone to take over.' She was staring at him, her eyes wide and unblinking. 'Look, it's my work. Ernest is hopeless with people, and is not keen on us having a New York office in the first place. He thinks we are over-extending ourselves.'

'Are you?'

'No. That's where the work is. Over here there are too

338

many agencies struggling for survival, and too few big accounts to go round. I will accept no more excuses, Philippa. I want you and Christopher with me.'

She took her empty glass to the sink. Outside, a cat was playing with a dead mouse.

'No, Nicholas. I am not coming to New York, nor to London. Kit and I are staying here. All I want from you is a divorce. You can keep the London house and every penny of your money. You will probably need it. I hear Hope Stevenson has expensive tastes. Did you buy her a gold necklace, or a less obvious trifle?'

Neither her expression nor voice conveyed emotion, but he saw the knuckles of her clenched hands whiten. He saw something else as well.

'Where is your ring?'

His anger was not unexpected. The reason for it was. She lifted her left hand, studying her slender fingers and short, unvarnished nails.

'Upstairs. You can have that too. I mean it, Nicholas, I am not coming back.'

'You know I will not give you a divorce.'

'It is out of your hands. I have the grounds.'

'And what are those?' His voice was ugly.

'Hope Stevenson. It's a small world. Steve saw you with her in New York.'

'He may have seen us, but he cannot prove anything.'

'Leonard Perkins can. He has the evidence he needs. If you won't agree to amicable grounds, I shall have no qualms about naming her. I've had a lot of time to think about the future. The one lesson I learnt in hospital is you need to live for today, because there may not be a tomorrow. To put it in a nutshell, I don't want to share my life with you any more.'

His eyes were blazing. 'There is something else behind

this – or someone else. Are you whiter than white, darling? Or do you have a lover? My brother is always hanging around.'

Philippa's face was the colour of marble. 'That is the kind of underhand remark I have learnt to expect from you. I do not consider it worthy of a reply.'

She turned away from him and left by the back door. Nicholas slammed the lid on the necklace. Let her sue for a divorce. He would fight her every inch of the way.

He was still sitting there when his mother came in.

'Good morning, dear,' she said. 'We didn't wake you as it seemed best to let you sleep. Did you miss Philippa? I saw her walking through the upper paddocks. If you hurry, you can catch her up. She's probably gone to meet Kit. Justin took him and Jennie riding. They should be back soon.'

'Does he come here often?'

Sarah switched on the kettle. 'Who?'

'My brother, of course.' He could not bring himself to say Justin's name.

'I hardly ever see him. He takes the children riding occasionally, but Jennie usually cycles over. I believe he is working on some paintings, and you know how involved he gets.'

'Then he spends his days at the pottery?'

'He works from home while Jennie is on holiday. Can I get you anything?'

'No.' He had not touched the coffee. 'Perhaps I'll catch up with Philippa after all.'

She was by the gate which led on to the moors, standing beside a tall horse upon which his brother was mounted. Kit and Jennie were riding ahead and he moved into the shadow of the barn, not wanting to be seen. There was no reason why his wife and brother should not be talking. They were in the open. The children were in full sight. Yet Nicholas felt a mindless rage as he watched them.

The ponies leapt into headlong flight and Kit gave a whoop as Bertie cleared a two-foot jump at a flat-out gallop. Nicholas heard his brother shout, but the children ignored him as they raced across the paddock. He went into the barn. It was cool there, and filled with the familiar smells of hay and straw, dung and warm horseflesh.

He listened to the children chattering ten to the dozen as they unsaddled their ponies and sponged them down.

'Hello, Kit . . . Jennie,' he said when they came into the barn.

Their flushed faces turned to him. 'Hello . . .' they replied in unison.

'Mummy said to let you sleep this morning,' Kit told him. He did not look overjoyed to see his father and Nicholas felt another surge of anger as he wondered what lies the boy had been fed.

'Did you have a nice ride?'

'Yes, thank you.'

'I want to take you and Mummy out this afternoon. We could go down to the sea. It will be cooler there and you can swim.'

'Can't,' said Kit ungraciously. 'It's the Pony Club Gymkhana tomorrow. We're both riding in it, and this afternoon we have to clean tack and wash the ponies.'

Nicholas took a deep breath. 'I suppose your father is taking you,' he said to Jennie.

The child grinned. She was going to be a stunner when she was older. She had inherited the best from both parents. 'No, Aunt Philippa is. Daddy has to work.'

'Come on,' Kit said, sounding annoyed. 'We have an awful lot to do.'

Nicholas scowled as they walked away, leading the ponies

to the far end of the barn and putting them in adjacent boxes.

'I think I shall wait for your mother,' he told Kit when they came back.

'She was going for a walk.' He was polite, but displayed no affection.

'I know. I'll see you later.'

Kit nodded, and Nicholas saw relief on the boy's face before he and Jennie hurried outside.

Someone else spoke. It was Justin.

'If I see either of you do anything like that again I shall knock your heads together. Do you understand?'

'Yes, Daddy,' said Jennie.

'Did you see Bertie sail over that jump?' Kit asked.

'You were lucky not to fall off.'

Kit laughed, and Nicholas found himself resenting the easy banter his son could have with his brother, but not with him.

Justin had no idea his brother was in the barn. When he came in, leading the big-boned hack, Nicholas stepped from the shadows and lashed out at him. The blow to the side of his jaw sent Justin reeling into the horse, which plunged forward, ripping the reins from his hand. He lost his balance and fell. Shod hooves flashed past his head, one striking him on the shoulder.

He pushed himself into a sitting position, wincing at the pain which shot down his arm.

'What was that about?'

'As if you didn't know!' Nicholas lashed out again, this time with his foot. There was a grunt of pain, and he smiled as Justin doubled over. 'I warned you once before, big brother. Perhaps you'll listen this time. Stay away from my wife and son.'

He forced himself to back off before he was tempted to lunge out for a third time.

Justin struggled to his feet. 'You have already lost her, Nick.'

'I wouldn't take any bets on it. I haven't begun to fight back.'

He walked out of the barn. Philippa was nowhere to be seen, so he went back to the house. She would not stay out long in this heat.

CHAPTER TWENTY-SIX

The horse had done more damage than Nicholas. There was a dull ache in Justin's right shoulder, and his arm was stiff. He had not realised the extent of his brother's resentment and was glad Philippa had agreed to remain here rather than return to Dovestail. He was also glad Jennie would be staying for the day, as it meant he could slip away before she saw him. But he had to see to the horse first. It was at the far end of the barn, flirting with Copper.

His arm was unwieldy and he struggled to remove the saddle and bridle before fetching a bucket of water to sponge down the sweating animal. When he came back the horse was circling its box and refused to stand still. By now Justin's patience was wearing thin and he reached for the rope halter which hung from a hook outside the door. As he slipped it over the horse's head he noticed how agitated the ponies in the adjoining boxes were, while those nearest the entrance had laid-back ears and flaring nostrils.

He looked round, unable to see anything out of the ordinary. There was a herd of wild ponies on the moors beyond the paddocks. The close proximity of a stallion was probably exciting the mares which, in turn, were upsetting the others. He was about to tie up the horse when he heard a gushing roar. At the front of the barn, close to the doors, a bolt of flame shot upwards. It ignited a wooden partition which enclosed the area where the tack and grooming tools and winter rugs were kept.

Because of the flies and heat, Sarah was keeping the ponies in during the day and there were close to thirty animals in here, each one in a separate box. The barn was wooden and bales of hay and straw were stored in the loft above his head. This was the worst nightmare of all. There was one way in and one way out and, should that become impassable, the animals would be trapped, dying most horribly in a fiery inferno.

Justin forgot the pain of his shoulder as he led the horse into the wide passage. He was about to throw open the doors of the adjacent boxes when it struck him that the ponies were liable to run away from the fire, to the back of the barn, not the front.

He broke into a run, the horse reluctantly following. The flames were spreading at an alarming speed. The partition was ablaze, and tendrils of fire were creeping across the floor towards one of the main support poles. The horse shied away from the flames, but Justin dragged it to the entrance, slipped off the halter, and slapped its rump. The horse disappeared at a gallop. One saved, he thought. But what should he do now? The house was too far away and nobody would hear him yell. Yet to go for help would condemn many of the ponies to death. He went back into the barn, praying somebody would see what was happening before it was too late.

He grabbed one of the two fire extinguishers which were kept in brackets on either side of the doors. But he was trying to tackle something which was already beyond control. The foam stopped the fire from shooting up a wall, but there simply was not enough to douse the pinpricks of red heat which ran in rivulets over the straw-strewn floor. No sooner had he killed one pocket of flame than another

345

sprang up somewhere else. A cardboard box filled with brushes was smouldering. Fire licked at a row of saddles which were piled on a wooden horse.

The extinguisher was empty. He didn't bother with the other one. It was a waste of time. He had to rescue the ponies which were nearest the flames. The terrified animal in the first box was wearing a headcollar, which made it easier to grab hold of. But even so, it almost wrenched his arm from the socket when it jerked back. One by one, he led out the plunging ponies, but it was a slow task. He not only had the fire to contend with, but an increasing amount of smoke which was forming a thick band near the doors. He was never going to get them all out, not by himself. He would have to throw open the boxes and hope they had the sense to save themselves.

Justin had led eight to safety when he saw a flicker in the rafters. Why had nobody seen what was happening? Surely the smoke was visible, and the loose ponies? A shudder of fear overtook him, but he had to keep going. Somebody must come soon.

Philippa did not walk far. She followed the boundary fence towards the house, watched by a herd of wild ponies. There was little grass here, but they came for the water Sarah put out each evening. She climbed over the rails into what had once been the vegetable garden, but was now a barren wasteland. A thunder of hooves startled her, but when Philippa looked round the wild ponies were staring at the paddocks. She followed their gaze and saw two of the riding school ponies gallop on to the road. Then she saw the smoke and realised the barn was on fire.

She shouted, hoping somebody in the house would hear. But a dog started to bark, drowning out her voice.

★

'Shut up, Bess!' Jennie yelled.

The dog ignored her.

'Let her out,' Sarah said.

'If I do that, Daddy will take her home with him.'

Nicholas put his hands over his ears. 'I'm going to look for Philippa,' he told his mother.

'She'll be back in a couple of minutes. Jennie, please let Bess out.'

'But . . .'

'Oh, for heaven's sake, I'll do it!' Nicholas flung open the door.

'Bess!' Jennie sprinted after the dog.

Kit was taking a bridle to pieces. He threw it on to the kitchen table and started to follow her.

'Not so fast, young man.' Nicholas blocked his way. 'You are not going to run off and leave that mess there.'

'Grandma . . . Grandma . . . come quick . . . some of the ponies are loose.'

As Sarah leapt to her feet, Philippa ran in from the hall.

'The barn is on fire! Somebody is trying to get the ponies out.'

Nicholas needed to be quick witted in his line of work, and did not hesitate now. 'I left Justin in there no more than five minutes ago. There was nothing wrong then. You'd better call the fire brigade,' he told his mother, and to Philippa, 'Don't let the children out of your sight.'

Jennie was still standing in the doorway. He thrust her into the kitchen, then ran out, slamming the door behind him.

'Bertie . . .' Kit whimpered.

'Daddy . . .'

Philippa flung herself across the room, grabbing hold of the child before she could follow.

*

347

The fire was spreading randomly, devouring whatever lay in its path. As there was no wind, Justin hoped it would remain confined to the area where it had flared up. He was wrong. Smouldering flecks of straw floated on the smoke-laden air, starting innumerable new fires across the front of the barn. The main passage leading to the doorway was comparatively clear, but the ponies did not want to go through the smoke or past the crackling flames.

What Justin feared most was what he could not easily see – the fire which was spreading through the rafters. He knew the beams were solid and would burn slowly, but should the floor above them collapse, neither he nor the animals trapped with him would survive.

He had resorted to leading them out two at a time. It was not easy. The two he had now suddenly realised the doorway was only feet away. He let them go as they plunged forward, managing to slip the halter from one, but not the other. He would have liked to follow, to fill his lungs with something other than smoke. Instead, he turned back.

In their rush to get out, the ponies narrowly missed colliding into Nicholas. He leapt aside. What on earth did Justin think he was doing? Some of them were already on the road. It would only take one speeding car to cause a serious accident. He went into the barn and was gripped by horror when he saw the hell which had broken loose in there. A dull roar drew his eyes upwards. Through the smoke he saw orange flames flickering in the overhead beams. They were also creeping along the wall towards the doorway, and had engulfed the area where the tack was kept.

He could not see the ponies, but he could hear them crashing around their boxes. He took a deep breath and went in search of his brother. The pall of smoke which lay across the front of the barn thinned suddenly, making breathing easier, and allowing Nicholas a clear view of the real state of the fire. It was confined to the front of the barn, but spreading fast. The electricity must have blown, for the only light was provided by the flickering flames.

He saw his brother trying to force the larger of the two cobs out of its box. When the horse reared up Justin was barely able to hold it.

'You're done in. Give him to me.'

Nicholas took the lead rope, using brute strength to bring the horse down. Submissive, the cob stood shivering. Nicholas gripped the headcollar and, momentarily, blue eyes met grey, not with hatred, but with respect and understanding.

'There has to be a quicker way than this,' he said, alarmed by the number of animals still in there.

'There is, but I couldn't risk it on my own. If we let them loose, we can get behind and drive them out.'

'You do that while I get rid of this one.'

The cob refused to walk into the wall of smoke. Justin hit it on the rump with the rope halter he was holding. Still it baulked. He hit it again, this time finding an unexpected ally. Bess must have followed his brother in here, and when she leapt forward, snapping at the cob's heels, the horse plunged into the smoke, dragging Nicholas with it.

Justin threw open the doors of a line of boxes, but none of the ponies would come out. They were too frightened. Nicholas came back and the two brothers worked together, leading the terrified animals into the passage, where they stood in a tight bunch, watched by Bess. The bitch had never been trained to herd. What she did came from inbred instinct.

Neither Justin nor Nicholas spoke. The smoke might have been less of a problem there, but it stung their eyes and affected their breathing. And then, when they least expected it, one of the main support pillars exploded from a deadly combination of fire and heat.

Flaming debris was showered into the air as part of the loft collapsed into the empty stables at the front of the barn. A shaft of burning wood hit Nicholas in the back, knocking him to the ground, while another glanced off his brother's already inflamed shoulder. A pony screamed as flecks of burning straw showered upon its back. Justin, who was closer, ran to it, brushing off the smouldering straw. He dragged the animal into the passage, where he suddenly leant against a partition, his face grey and his body racked by a paroxysm of coughing.

'We have to get out of here now,' Nicholas was yelling. 'Those rafters are not going to last much longer, and when they go the loft is going to cave in.'

Justin straightened up, his eyes on the animals still shut in their boxes. He couldn't bear to leave them, but common-sense told him they had to save what they could, rather than lose them all.

It would be over by the time the fire brigade arrived. Sarah looked her age as she trained a hose-pipe on the left side of the doorway. Philippa was doing the same on the opposite side, using water pumped up from the well. The pressure was low, even from the mains supply, but between them they were keeping the doorway clear of flames. They would have gone inside to help, but Nicholas stopped them when he brought out the panic-stricken cob. It would be folly for them to go into that smoke, especially Philippa with her weakened lung. They were of more use out here, damping down the doorway and catching the loose ponies. The latter was a task delegated to the children. It kept them away from the burning barn, and was one less worry for the two women.

Jennie and Kit were rescuing a pony from the side of the

road when Helen drove up. She had seen the smoke from Povey Ashton, but had thought it another of the grass fires which were ravaging the moors. She stopped the car and went to help them. As she did so, she heard a terrifying crack. Within seconds a section of the roof was on fire and black smoke was billowing into the sky. She saw the horror on Jennie's face.

'Daddy is in there,' the child gasped.

Kit was holding the pony, but his eyes widened as the enormity of what was happening dawned on him. Up until now, this had been a game.

Helen could see Philippa and her mother, but neither of her brothers. 'He won't be in there now,' she said with an assurance she did not feel.

Jennie was not listening. She started to run. Kit thrust the pony's lead rope at Helen and followed her.

Without warning, the mains water slowed to a trickle, then stopped altogether. There was no break in the hose. The supply had simply run dry. Simultaneously, the floor collapsed and a cloud of smoke sent both women staggering backwards. When it cleared they saw the doorway was still intact, but not what had happened beyond it. For all they knew, Justin and Nicholas could be trapped, or injured or, worse still, dead.

Philippa started forward. Sarah stopped her.

'Don't be a fool. There is nothing you can do.'

'We can't leave them in there.'

'And we can't get them out.'

Unbelievably, a pony emerged from the smoke. Behind it were another twelve, all scarred with varying degrees of burns. Bess was with them, her coat filthy and her tongue lolling. Then Nicholas stumbled out. His hair and clothes were singed and he was coughing. Philippa took hold of his

351

arm and led him away from the smoke, to where the air was clearer.

'Sit down. Don't try to talk.'

He couldn't, even if he wanted to. His lungs were bursting. He put his head between his knees and gasped for breath.

Philippa straightened up, her stricken eyes searching for his brother. Sarah also turned. The terrified ponies were too shocked to run any further, and neither of the women noticed Jennie push her way through, with Kit and Helen following.

'Where's Daddy?' The frightened voice said everything.

Nicholas looked up. Justin had been behind him. 'The fool must have gone back.' He lurched to his feet.

'Where's Bertie?' Kit wailed. 'You left Bertie in there to die!'

'No he didn't.' Helen grabbed hold of the child. 'He did the best he could. You have to be brave, Kit, like Bertie is being. He won't feel a thing. I promise.' It was a lie, but the truth was too shocking to contemplate.

If Bertie was trapped, so was Jennie's father. 'Daddy!' she screamed, running towards the blazing barn.

Nicholas tried to stop her, but his leaden limbs responded too slowly. It was Philippa who caught her by the shoulders. The child's screams became hysterical, and she shook her hard. Sobbing, Jennie crumpled into her arms.

Only Sarah saw the determination on her son's face as he walked towards the raging inferno.

'Nicholas, you can't!'

'I must. I can't leave Justin in there. From out here it looks much worse than it is.'

Philippa had one arm around Jennie. She lifted her free hand to his cheek. 'Be careful, Nicholas. Don't take unnecessary risks.'

She meant what she said. They had shared too much for her not to care.

Justin could not desert Copper. Of the six animals left, only the elderly horse stood quietly as she waited to be rescued. So he turned back when he knew the others were safely out, and his brother with them.

The smoke was everywhere now, and only the rear of the barn was free from fire. In the rush to get out those from the front, he had forgotten that the animals left behind were more personal to the family. Sam and Bertie were here, and Kelly, the ugly bay pony which Jennie rode. There was also Cloud, his mother's riding horse, and Garland, who belonged to Pauline.

Justin led them into the passage, closing the doors behind them. They bunched together, staring at the fire with bulging eyes. Last of all, he brought out Copper. The mare nuzzled his hand as she followed him. The others were not so trusting, and he could not drive them out single-handedly. He tried, but they went no more than a few steps before swinging round and charging to the rear of the barn. It seemed nothing was going to persuade them to go through those flames, and time was running desperately short. Another section of loft crashed down. Justin could not see where it fell. He could see nothing through the dense smoke.

Only Copper stayed with him. True, he was leading her, but had she pulled hard enough it was doubtful he could hold her. The others were clustered behind him, terrified, but resigned to their fate. There was another way. The chances of it working were slender but, at the very worst, he might be able to save himself and the mare.

He did not have the strength to vault on to her tall back and had to mount from a rail. She shuddered once, but responded to his commands. From her back he was better able to herd the others. He got behind them, using the rope halter as a whip to drive them forward. He could not shout. His throat was raw and breathing was becoming more difficult. His idea was working. The bunched animals were moving away from the back of the barn. But then Sam dodged behind him, and when Justin tried to head off the pony, the others scattered.

He would try once more. If they would not come he would have to leave them here. Somewhere above him a beam splintered. A lump of blazing wood crashed down beside Copper and the mare leapt sideways, almost unseating him. She shied again when something low to the ground shot past her. Justin saw a flash of black and white, and heard a snarl.

Confidence returned as the wild-eyed animals moved forward. The dog snapped at their heels and the chestnut mare with her aggressive rider barred any retreat. They plunged into the smoke, shying away from burning wood and straw, always trying to turn back, but prevented from doing so. Copper was trembling, but continued to obey her rider.

Justin felt raw heat pass close to his face, and something else as well – the merest suggestion of fresh air. He knew he was almost there and the doorway must still be clear. It was at that moment he heard the crack as the beams above him gave way. Fire rained down and the terrified animals broke into a mindless gallop. Justin thought he heard someone call his name before a beam hurtled past, missing his head by inches. As it rammed into what remained of a line of stables, Copper reared up. Justin would have stayed on her under normal circumstances, but he was too exhausted and fell heavily.

Sarah knew the front of the barn was about to collapse when flames burst through the walls. She tried to stop Nicholas, but if he heard her frantic call, he chose to ignore it.

'Get back!' she shouted as the wall shuddered and began

to collapse from the top, falling inwards upon itself.

Helen dragged Kit to a safe distance, but Philippa did not move. She shielded Jennie's eyes from the horror, while watching it herself. Tears poured down her cheeks as she tried to comprehend the full depth of this tragedy. Nothing could possibly survive in there.

But against all the odds, something did. Even as the wall toppled there was a thunder of hooves and the six horses burst through the flames. Behind them was Bess, burnt and limping badly. As the animals wheeled towards the dejected group still clustered in the driveway, the dog collapsed into a puddle of water forming around the hosepipe Philippa had abandoned.

The wall fell with a deafening crash which sent bursts of orange flame shooting skywards. The entire barn was an inferno. Philippa closed her eyes, the pain more than she could bear.

'Where's Daddy?' Jennie whimpered.

Philippa forced herself to move. 'We have to go to the house now.' She could not bring herself to answer the child's question.

It was like being trapped inside a nightmare and, for the first time in his life, Nicholas knew the meaning of real fear. Moments before the front of the barn collapsed he pulled his semi-conscious brother into the shelter of a box which was not yet destroyed. It probably saved their lives, but for what purpose? If the fire did not kill them, the smoke would.

The partition which sheltered them sparked, then ignited. The straw on which they lay caught fire. Nicholas grabbed a half-full water bucket and doused the flames. Oddly enough, there was relatively little smoke at this level. Justin eased himself into a sitting position. His arm was useless and his head pounding.

'Why did you come back?' His voice was barely audible.

'Because I'm a fool, and despite what happened you are still my brother. Do you realise we are both going to die in here?'

'It seems highly likely. Did the horses get out?'

'Sod the horses! If you hadn't been so sentimental we wouldn't be in this position. They may have. I don't know.'

Another beam fell, scattering burning debris and engulfing them in choking clouds of smoke.

'For what good it will do, we've got to try and get further back,' Nicholas said. 'Can you walk?'

'I'll manage.'

Nicholas helped him to his feet, and together they stumbled into the passage. It was difficult to see, and even more difficult to breathe. They had to skirt burning chunks of wood, while trying to avoid the consuming flames which clawed at them. They reached Copper's box. The bedding was alight and fire was creeping along the rear wall, but there was nowhere else for them to go. Behind the box was a fixed ladder leading into the loft. It was from there that hay and straw was lowered by hook and tackle to this end of the building.

Nicholas sank to the floor, his shoulders against one of the few partitions which was still intact and his hands resting on his updrawn knees. He closed his eyes and tried to ignore the pain of his burns.

'There will be no cavalry charging to our rescue,' he said. 'This is it.'

Justin was coughing again. He was finding it difficult to stop. He must have hit his head when he came off Copper. Waves of dizziness were affecting his sense of balance, and it was a struggle to concentrate on what was happening around them. He was fast reaching a stage where he no longer cared. But deep down inside him something rebelled. He was not about to give up without a fight. The ladder leading into the loft niggled him, but he could not think why.

'It was my fault,' Nicholas was saying. 'I was smoking before you came in. I thought the cigarette was out. It couldn't have been.'

'You never learn, do you?' Justin watched as a solitary flame flickered around the base of the ladder. 'The window, Nick. You nearly fell through it when you were three years old. Mum had it boarded up.'

Nicholas had forgotten. The window was in the loft, close to the ladder. The boards had been nailed across it over thirty years ago. They must be rotten by now and loose enough to pull away. He struggled to his feet. It was not much of a chance, but the only one they had.

A stream of cars was coming from the village. They parked alongside the road, and while some people set about catching the loose ponies, others ran down the drive.

Jennie was no longer screaming. Her face was buried in the dog's charred coat and her body was shaken by heart-rending sobs. Kit clung, white-faced, to his mother's arm as both Philippa and Helen tried to coax Jennie to leave. Sarah stared helplessly at the blazing barn, her life lying in ashes at her feet.

'Bess is hurt. Don't you think we should take her to the house?' said Philippa gently. She had to lay her own grief to one side, otherwise it would overcome her.

'She needs a vet,' Jennie sobbed.

'We'll get one. Come along, darling.' She glanced at Helen.

'I'll bring Bess,' said her sister-in-law.

Jennie clung tightly to Philippa's right hand, Kit to her left. Slowly, they walked away.

The loft was an inferno from one end to the other, and most of the roof had already collapsed. Even so, it was impossible to see the sky through the smoke, only glimpses of a bright ball which was the sun.

Choking, burnt by the intensity of the heat around and above them, the two brothers struggled to push aside the bales of straw which blocked their way. When they finally uncovered the window, Justin collapsed, his breathing ragged and painful. He had not left the barn since the fire began, and it was a miracle he had got this far.

'Save yourself, Nick.' He closed his eyes, not wanting to see the blazing beams above them.

'What sort of sadist do you think I am?' Despite his own exhaustion and fear, Nicholas was able to instil humour into his voice. 'We go together or not at all.'

It took every ounce of his remaining strength to pull away the boards. The window might have been dangerous for a three-year-old, but was barely large enough to take the width of a grown man. He swore on discovering the frame had been nailed closed. The beams cracked. It was a sound he had come to recognise. In desperation he kicked out the glass and a gust of air hit him in the face.

'Come on, big brother. You go first. It's a long way down, but there is grass underneath.'

'You go. I'll follow.'

'Don't be ridiculous. You can hardly move. Don't worry, I shall be right behind you.'

The ideal way would have been to climb out, hang by the arms, then drop, but there was no time for such manoeuvres. Even if there had been, Justin was in no condition to try them out. Anyhow, the window was still ringed by jagged pieces of razor-sharp glass. As Nicholas bundled him through the tiny space he heard the beams give way.

'Jump!' he yelled. Then he was falling, plunging helplessly downwards.

Nicholas did not follow. The first beam struck him across the head, knocking him unconscious. The second killed him.

CHAPTER TWENTY-SEVEN

'I'll look after you, Mummy,' said Kit.

His heartfelt promise and the small hand which clutched hers got Philippa through the service and afterwards, when the coffin was lowered into the ground and she knew Nicholas was gone forever. Who could have foreseen such a tragic end to her marriage? Rather than this, she would have chosen to stay with him, even if it meant condemning herself to a life of misery.

Only family and a few close friends had attended the burial, although the small church had been filled to capacity. Sarah bore up staunchly, but could not hold back her tears at the end. Helen supported her mother throughout, and led her away when she could decently do so.

'I want you to go back with the others,' Philippa told Kit. 'I should like to be alone for a while, to say goodbye to Daddy.'

He hugged her and then left. She was aware of hushed voices fading into the distance, the slam of car doors and engines being revved. Finally, everyone was gone and all she could hear were the sounds of the countryside – a thrush calling, sheep bleating on the moors, and the clop of hooves as a rider passed through the village. This was a pretty spot. It overlooked the moors and was shaded by a tall sycamore tree. Not far away, at the bottom of the churchyard, was a narrow brook overhung by weeping willows. The brook was dry now, but when the weather broke it would soon fill from the natural gullies that ran into it. Philippa was comforted by the knowledge that it would never be silent here. Nicholas would not have been happy if it was. He had enjoyed life too much.

She threw a red rose on to the coffin before she turned away, crossing to the flagged path along which she had walked as a bride. She hesitated when she saw a solitary figure seated on a bench, his head bowed as he waited for her.

'I thought you had gone,' she said when she came closer.

Justin looked up, his dark eyes unreadable. 'I didn't think you should be alone at a time like this, nor did I wish to intrude.'

'You could never intrude. No, don't stand up. I am in no hurry to get back. I need to be in the right frame of mind for tea and sympathy.'

'Close friends aside, the majority of people think they are helping you cope with your grief. I remember what it was like after my father's death, and how glad we were when everyone left.'

Philippa sat down, not beside him, but further along the bench. Justin should not be here. He was gaunt and grey, with angry red burns marking his face. His right arm was strapped up to relieve the pressure of a cracked collarbone, while his hands and forearms were swathed in bandages. She suspected he was in constant pain, though he would not admit it. He had discharged himself from hospital at the weekend, returning to Shepherds Fold with Noel's collusion. It was the latter who had driven him back, then come to the farm to collect Jennie. And it was Noel who was staying with them until Justin could use his hands again.

'You look ill,' Philippa said. 'You should have stayed in

hospital. Nobody would have condemned you for not being here.'

'He was my brother, Philippa, and he lost his life saving mine. A little discomfort could not keep me away. Anyhow, there was nothing more they could do, except give me painkillers and change the bandages. I can take the pills at home, and Noel takes me to Out Patients every day. It shouldn't be for much longer. In another week or so our local GP will be able to take over.'

'How bad are your hands?'

His shrug was non-committal. 'They could be worse.'

'Will you still be able to paint?'

'I expect so.'

He was avoiding her gaze and she instinctively knew the damage must be extensive. Tears stung her eyes and she turned her head away, watching a blackbird peck at the hard ground. Lost in their own thoughts, neither of them spoke, and yet each drew comfort from the closeness of the other. It was Philippa who broke the silence, voicing a subject which was no less emotive, but one which had been preying on her mind.

'Nobody knows what started the fire. The best the experts can come up with is spontaneous combustion. I suspect it was caused by something else, and you know what it was.'

'Why should I know more than them?'

'When I met you in the paddock that morning I omitted to say Nicholas had accused me of having a lover. He suggested you. I denied it, of course, but I shall never know whether it was conjecture or if he knew something.'

Justin looked at her with the understanding she had come to expect from him. 'He was angry, and clutching at straws. Any straws. Nobody else knew, so why should he?'

Philippa felt no less guilty, for it was she who had gone to him. Now they were both paying for what they had done. She met his gaze.

'I know Nicholas was waiting in the barn when you got back, which means the fire must have started during the short time it took me to walk around the perimeter fence. I saw the smoke from the back of the house. What happened in there? Did Nicholas start it deliberately?'

Justin laughed. It was a dry, humourless sound.

'My brother had a temper, but he was not a psychopath who went about setting fires for the sheer hell of it.'

'I am not saying he was. But something happened in the space of five or six minutes. Perhaps he wanted to teach you a lesson, and the whole thing got out of hand?'

'No, Philippa, it was nothing like that. Now you are the one who is clutching at straws.'

She was certain now that he knew what had happened. 'Please don't try and protect me, you'll only make matters worse, not better. Because of me, Nicholas is dead and your career as an artist hangs in the balance.'

She saw in his eyes the anguish he must be seeing in hers. 'It takes so little to tip the balance and create a tragedy. Nicholas and I quarrelled, but he threw no direct accusations at me. He simply told me to stay away from you and Kit, then stormed back to the house. He had many faults, but so do we all. The one thing I never doubted was his deep sense of family loyalty. He would never have tried to kill me, either deliberately or otherwise.'

'Then how did the fire start?' she persisted.

'I am not sure. He admitted to smoking a cigarette before I came in, but thought it was out. Perhaps it was. Who can say for certain? He has smoked in there before and nothing came of it. Perhaps it was spontaneous combustion. In this heat anything is possible. I know I am asking a lot of you, Philippa, but it would be better if you repeated none of this, not even to my mother. My father died with a slur on his name and I do not want the same to happen with Nicholas. The truth will make little difference now. If it is the truth.'

Philippa reached out and touched his bandaged hand. 'What you have said will go no further. I only wanted to know for my own peace of mind. In return, I would like you to say nothing to Sarah about the state of our marriage, or that I intended leaving him.'

'Did you think I would?'

'No,' she said. He looked exhausted and the strain was beginning to show. 'Do you think this is God's way of punishing us?' She had never been a church-goer, but Sunday morning services at school had been compulsory. From what she remembered the sermons contained a good deal of fire and brimstone.

A smile tugged at Justin's lips. 'You don't believe that kind of rubbish any more than I do. It was an accident. Like your car crash last year was an accident. You were not to blame then, nor are you to blame now. Neither of us is.'

'But because of what has happened nothing will ever be the same again.'

'How can it be? Have you decided what you will do now?'

'Kit and I shall move to Dovestail, but first I must go to London and sort out our ... my affairs. I intend to sell the house, and will have to ask Ernest if he wants to buy me out. I prevented Nicholas from becoming involved in Moor View, and he left me everything, including his share of the agency. It appears he and Ernest did not have an agreement to safeguard their respective interests, which I find rather strange.'

'There is probably a reason for it. Nicholas did nothing without a reason.'

A middle-aged man walked around the side of the church. He was carrying a shovel.

'I think we ought to leave now,' said Justin. 'There are a lot of people at the house who have come a long way to pay their respects.'

They walked slowly along the narrow path, neither of them looking back.

'Will you go to London immediately?' he asked.

'No. I shall wait until Kit is back at school. There's a lot to be done, and I may have to stay there for a while.'

'I wish I could do more to help you, but circumstances being what they are . . .'

'You need to rest,' she said. 'And it would be better for me if I kept busy. It's not so much the loss of Nicholas which I find devastating, but the way he was lost.'

'Time is a great healer. One day you will be able to look back without sadness. Until then, remember you and Kit are as much family to my mother as the rest of us.'

There was something in his voice that alarmed Philippa. 'Why are you telling me this now?'

'Because it is important you should know.'

The drought broke the next day, condemning that long, hot summer to memory. Soon after Kit returned to school Philippa went to London. There was not only the house and business which required her attention, but countless other trivial matters which she was unable to ignore. She asked Leonard Perkins to liaise with Nicholas's solicitors and sort out whatever he could. There were outstanding taxes to be paid, and a minefield of legalities which had to be dealt with. In the middle of it all, Leonard Perkins dropped a bombshell.

'I have decided to step down, Mrs Lang, and I'll be retiring in the spring. My son will take over your portfolio.

You will find him extremely capable.'

She would miss him. He had always been there when she needed him, never refusing to see her when she turned up without an appointment.

Thomas Perkins was a younger edition of his father, fortyish, with the same intent expression and the beginnings of a paunch. There was one marked difference between them. He insisted on being called by his first name.

Philippa decided to sell the house furnished, except for a few pieces which she sent to Dovestail. The worst part was having to sort out Nicholas's personal belongings. Both Maggie and Eileen offered to help, but it was something she had to do herself. She gave his clothes to charity, but kept a few items, such as the three advertising awards he had won. She would give them to Kit when he was older.

She had automatically presumed Eileen would want to stay on, despite the difficulties of integrating her with Celia Paine, who was less formal but unable to live in. But Eileen wanted to remain in London, so Philippa said she could stay in the house until it was sold. In addition, she promised to keep the housekeeper on full salary until she found another position. Eileen had been good to her and Nicholas.

She did not see Ernest until she had been in London for a fortnight.

'Why did Nicholas leave his share of the business to me without any stipulations concerning what I should do with it?' she asked. 'You should have been given first option to buy his half. When you started this agency you both invested what capital you had.'

'I knew what Nicholas was doing and agreed to it. We both trusted you not to do the dirty and sell to an outsider.'

She watched as he poured tea into delicate china cups. They came from Moor View, and Philippa would have given them to Nicholas had he asked. But he hadn't. He must have purchased them from the pottery's Knightsbridge stockist, which told her how far apart their lives really had been.

'That was a foolish assumption,' she said. 'Why did he do it?'

'Because I am no businessman. Nor do I have his knack of dealing with people. He knew you had those qualifications, and more besides. He always admired the way you ran your pottery, building it up from nothing.'

Had he told her so when he was alive they might have avoided some of the strife.

'What do you want, Ernest?'

'For you to retain his shares and become a director. The continuing connection with your name will keep the business flowing in and, quite honestly, there will be times when I shall need somebody to bail me out of awkward situations. You are respected in the advertising world, both as Nicholas's wife and one of the country's top models.'

'That was a long time ago. And I know nothing about advertising. What possible assistance could I be?'

'Quite a lot. There is also Christopher to consider. He may decide to follow in his father's footsteps.'

Philippa was unprepared for this. She sipped the tea, stalling for time as she ran the implications through her mind.

'Try it for six months,' he urged.

'Surely you would be better off with an experienced partner?'

'Nicholas and I were successful because we worked well together. It would not be easy to find somebody of his calibre.'

'I cannot see how my being here will help.'

'Six months, Philippa. Please. I know you have your own life to rebuild, but I shall demand very little from you. Those six months will give me breathing space. This is not the best time for an upheaval. There is no cash to spare. As you know, Nicholas was determined to break into the American market and we have over-extended ourselves by opening offices there. In fact, as things stand at the moment, it could turn into a catastrophe. I flew over last week and found everything in a shambles. We're having to prepare all the major work from here.'

Philippa did not need this on top of everything else, but how could she leave Ernest in the lurch? Nicholas had always said he was brilliant when it came to artistic interpretation, but lousy at making vital, policy-making decisions. She owed him too, for in the beginning Ernest had done as much, if not more than Nicholas, to boost her career.

'All right,' she said. 'I'll give you six months, subject to one condition.'

'Which is?'

'You cut your losses and close down the New York office. We cannot stay in this recession forever. Once we start climbing out of it you need to be in a strong position to attract potential clients.' She smiled. 'You are right, I could help there. Nicholas had a solid core of contacts, all of whom I have entertained over the years.'

She saw the relief in his face. He looked a lot older than forty and, for the first time, she noticed how grey he was.

Philippa telephoned Kit regularly but remained in London for a month, until everything was sorted out to her satisfaction. She resisted the temptation to return home for weekends, for coming back would be harder than staying. On her last day in London she did a little shopping, lunched with Leonard Perkins, and said goodbye to Ernest. Last of all, she visited the house for a final time. It was empty now. Eileen had left a couple of days ago when a domestic agency placed her with a diplomatic family in Belgravia. She wandered through the rooms and then she also left.

She was staying with Maggie, who must have been watching for her. She was at the front door before Philippa could lift her hand to the bell.

'Someone is waiting to see you,' she said. 'I put him in the study.'

Philippa shrugged off her coat. 'I am not expecting anybody. Who is it?'

'An old friend of yours, I believe.'

She paused outside the study door, certain Maggie knew who it was. But the tubby little man with a bald patch and grey hair was nobody she knew. He wore wire-rimmed spectacles and a badly fitting suit which had seen better days.

'I know ten years is a long time,' he said. 'Have I changed that much? You haven't.'

She recognised the voice and, on looking closer, she recognised the man.

'Mike?'

'The very same. I am sorry about what happened.'

'I am learning to cope. And I have my son. How did you know I was here?'

'Justin Lang contacted me. Gideon Slater and I always exchange cards at Christmas and he traced me through him. He asked me to come here. He said you needed me. I obviously mistook him, for I was under the impression it was you who was looking for me.'

Perhaps she should have been. The years had not been kind to the smart chauffeur she had known. 'I believe I do need you, Mike. Are you working at the moment?'

'No. But I did not come here looking for charity.'

'I would not insult you by offering it. I don't need a chauffeur, but could do with someone I can trust to look after Kit. I am not talking about anything so mundane as babysitting, although it would be handy to have someone living in. What it would entail is taking him to an endless stream of Pony Club rallies and horse shows. I simply haven't the time any more. There is an empty flat above the garage which you could have and, quite honestly, I think such an arrangement would solve both our problems. Look, I'll have some tea brought in and we can talk it over.' She paused. 'I should also like to know what has happened since I last saw you.'

That had been on her wedding day, when he had given her a sprig of white heather for luck.

Philippa arrived at Flint Iron Farm much later than planned. The rain was bucketing down as though it would never stop, and a bitter wind was whipping across the moors. Helen was working night-shift and Kit was in bed with flu.

'You should have let me know,' she told Sarah. 'I would have returned immediately.'

'He only came down with it yesterday, and I didn't want you to worry. He'll be right as rain in a couple of days. The doctor has been and left some medicine. Children are always catching something or other. You can't spend your life running around them. Go and see him while I get you something to eat.'

Kit was sleepy, but pleased she was back. She kissed him goodnight and promised he would get a present in the morning, after she had unpacked.

'You look tired,' Sarah said when she went down to the kitchen. 'Go into the living room. I'll bring you some tea, or would you prefer coffee?'

'Tea will be lovely.' Sarah made lousy coffee.

There was a log fire burning in the grate and Philippa stretched her hands towards it. Sarah brought in a tray and placed it on a side table.

'There is something you should know. Justin has gone.'

Philippa stared at her. 'What do you mean? Gone where?'

'I don't know. He wouldn't tell me. He wanted to leave Jennie here, but she found out and threatened to run away. So he took her with him. Her and the dog.'

Waves of shock reverberated through her and when Philippa spoke her voice was unsteady. 'Why?' she asked.

'He refused to tell me, but I suspect his decision is tied in with what happened to Nicholas. He also seemed to think it would be easier on you if he left. I told him he was being ridiculous, but once he makes up his mind nothing will sway him. I hope I am wrong, but this time I don't think he will come back.'

'What about Jennie? He can't disappear, not with a child in tow.'

'Children soon forget, and she is devoted to her father.' Sarah wiped a tear from her cheek. 'He left you a letter. It's on the mantelpiece.'

Philippa looked at the envelope but did not pick it up. She was too numb. He had known on the day of the funeral. It was the reason he had sent Mike to her.

Sarah opened the door. 'Drink your tea before it gets cold.'

Alone with her thoughts, Philippa gazed into the fire. She remembered the afternoon they had spent together. How gentle Justin had been, sweeping away the horrors of a night which had left her pregnant. And later, when she was bereft because she could never bear his child, he had held her in his arms, saying nothing, but giving her strength when she most needed it.

Her hand trembled as she reached for the envelope and ripped it open. Inside was a single sheet of paper. The writing was scrawled and she sensed the effort which had gone into these few lines.

'There is nothing more I can do for Moor View and so

370

I have handed Rodney my resignation. He will not rip it up as you once did. You and I never stood a chance, and I believe we never shall. Fate will always intervene to keep us apart. I am not running away. I would not tell you the truth before, but you deserve to know it now. I may never be able to paint again and want nobody's pity, least of all yours. It is better this way. You can survive without me. You always could.'

He had written his name at the end and nothing else. Where was he now? What would he do? He could have stayed on at Moor View without anybody pitying him. But it was more than that which had driven him away. Art was his life. Where would he be without it?

A log split and Philippa suddenly realised that the pungent aroma filling her senses was burning pine. It brought back memories of Lochdunnan. Of the wide-eyed innocence of first love. Times remembered which were best forgotten.

She buried her face in her hands and wept.

PART FOUR

1982 to 1984

CHAPTER TWENTY-EIGHT

Philippa had kept a low profile over the past few years. Because she shunned publicity the gossip columnists soon lost interest in her, although they occasionally mentioned her name if she made an appearance at an official function. One such function was the New Year Charity Ball. She did not want to go, but the invitation had been sent by one of the principal organisers, who was also a client of Lang & Wakefield.

She had stayed with the agency, despite the initial difficulties of going into a business about which she knew virtually nothing. She and Ernest had hit some rough patches, but perseverance paid off and they were now planning to bring in a junior executive.

The constant trips into London had meant she needed permanent accommodation. She could not expect Maggie to put her up all the time, and Philippa disliked hotels, so she purchased a two-bedroomed flat in a luxury Knightsbridge block. The choice had been practical, for she was only there a few days each month and the flat was serviced, with doormen on a twenty-four-hour rota, a sophisticated security system and basement parking. It was also within walking distance of the agency.

It was from there that Steve fetched her on New Year's Eve. He was always a willing escort when she needed one and, being a close friend, she felt comfortable with him. There had been no men in her life since Nicholas had died, not from lack of opportunity, but because she did not want a serious involvement.

The ball was everything she disliked, bright and noisy and brimming with celebrities. Ernest had already procured a table in an unobtrusive corner, where they were joined by a handful of mutual friends. The evening was turning out to be more congenial than Philippa had anticipated when she became conscious of somebody watching her. She looked up, her eyes meeting those of a tall, broad-shouldered man who was vaguely familiar. He walked towards her, his smile both intimate and sensuous. Her companions were laughing at a private joke and did not appear to notice, even when he stopped a foot away from her.

'Sitting at tables is far better than waiting on them.' His voice bore the faint trace of an American accent. 'Speaking for myself, I never want to wash another dish for as long as I live. I often wondered if we would meet again. This is certainly classier than Lady Jayne's ever was.'

Philippa's eyes widened. 'Vincent?'

'I wasn't sure you would remember. I've been watching you for an hour, trying to pluck up enough courage to come over. Would you like to dance?'

'Very much.'

She leant forward and whispered in Steve's ear. Startled, he glanced round. Philippa rarely danced with anyone, even him.

The orchestra was playing a slow waltz and Vincent held her close as they moved around the edge of the crowded floor. He had the self assurance of a man used to money and power.

'I read about the death of your husband,' he said. 'You were widowed tragically young.'

'The tragedy was his. He died, while I am still here. What about you, Vincent? Did you stick with acting, or turn to a more lucrative career? I am afraid my knowledge of the theatre is limited, and I rarely go to the cinema.'

'I did a little repertory work, but was never a success. After a while I accepted I was a lousy actor and started looking in other directions. I am still in the theatre, but now I produce shows, both here and on Broadway. At the moment I am negotiating to open a new musical in the West End.'

The orchestra paused before launching into another number.

'I ought to go back,' said Philippa.

'When we have spoken barely a dozen words to each other? Your partner does not appear to be unduly worried.'

'What about yours?'

'I came alone,' he said, whirling her into the middle of the floor. 'And before you ask, there is no wife sitting at home, either here or in the States. We were divorced a few years ago.'

Further conversation was impossible, and Philippa relaxed. It was a long time since she had been in the arms of an attractive man. But when the number ended she insisted on returning to her table.

'I'd like to see you again,' Vincent said. 'How about dinner tomorrow night?'

'I am going home tomorrow. My son is expecting me.'

'I can fetch you from there.'

She laughed. 'I live in Devon. You would find three hundred miles a long way to come.'

'I shall if I must. I always liked you, that's why I used to walk you home.'

She looked at him. 'I never knew that. You gave no indication of how you felt. You wouldn't even come in for a cup of coffee.'

'I didn't have two pennies to rub together in those days.'

'Neither did I.'

'And I was in awe of you. I thought you would refuse if I asked you out.'

'And now you presume I will accept?'

He grinned. 'Nowadays, I don't give up so easily.'

Philippa handed Steve a brandy, then settled opposite him, her legs folded beneath her. 'It was an enjoyable evening,' she said, remembering how she and Nicholas used to sit like this.

Steve smiled. 'I thought so too. It's about time you shed your widow's weeds and had some fun.'

'When did I ever wear widow's weeds?'

'Figuratively speaking, for the past five years. Vincent Grant is the only man who has got past first base. When are you seeing him again?'

'He is taking me out tomorrow night – or is it tonight?'

'What do you know about him?'

'Not a lot. Do you remember when you and I first met?'

'How could I forget? What has Vincent Grant got to do with it?'

'We worked at the same restaurant. He washed dishes and walked me home at night. I haven't seen him since I left there.'

'He has a reputation as a womaniser.'

'He told me he is divorced.'

'Twice, and up to six months ago he was living with an actress in New York.'

Philippa sipped coffee from a mug. 'You didn't waste much time finding out about him.'

'He doesn't live the life of a recluse. I am fond of you, darling. I saw you get hurt once and don't want it to happen again.'

'I appreciate your concern, Steve, but I was a gullible young girl then.'

For the past two years Kit had captained his Pony Club team through to the national championships, winning them on both occasions. He rode Bertie in the mounted games and his second pony, Delight, in the jumping events. Christopher Lang was fast becoming one of the country's up-and-coming young riders, and those in the upper echelons of the horse world had their eyes on him.

Kit had long ago decided on the course his life should take, but it was not until the spring of 1983 that he took his first step in that direction.

'I need a horse,' he said.

They were having tea in the living room and Philippa put down the cup she was holding. 'You have Bertie and Delight. Why do you need another horse?'

'They are ponies, and ideal for Pony Club, but I need a cross country horse to bring on for when I graduate into adult classes.'

'You are still only fourteen and a long way from being an adult. As a matter of interest, where do you propose to keep this horse?'

'You could have an extension built on to the stables.'

She sighed. 'I am not made of money, Kit. You have chosen an expensive hobby which I indulge because I am away such a lot and know how much it means to you. That motorised horsebox cost a fortune and every year the price of fodder and clothing, vets, petrol and entrance fees escalates.'

'The horsebox is a better way of transporting the ponies

379

over long distances. And it saves money because Mike and I live in it when we're away.'

'Finances aside, how do you propose to look after and exercise three horses? I will not tolerate your school work suffering any more than it does now.'

The determined look which reminded her so much of Nicholas came into his face. He tossed a biscuit to Tag, the labrador Sarah had given him for his twelfth birthday. 'You're putting obstacles in the way. When I am old enough, I want to be chosen for the Olympic Equestrian Team. I won't unless I have the right horse.'

Philippa gazed at her son. He was tall and slender, with the powerful legs and shoulders of an athlete. In his eyes she saw a reflection of herself, not Nicholas, for he did not have his father's calculating streak.

'I suppose you already have one in mind?' she asked.

He suppressed a smile. 'Not exactly, but there might be one coming on the market soon. He was bred by his owner and has been ridden in novice classes. She is getting married, and the rumour is she will be giving up eventing. He's a great horse, and I think he has the potential to get me to the top.'

'I'll think about it,' she said. 'Have you any idea how much this great horse will cost?'

He shrugged. 'It depends who else is after him, but we could pick up a bargain.'

A month later Philippa wondered at her son's grasp of mathematics when the horse came on to the market at an asking price of twelve thousand pounds. She took him to view the animal, otherwise she would get no peace.

Silver Mist was a mountain of rippling muscle which dwarfed them both. He was a six-year-old gelding and silvery white, as his name suggested.

'He is one of the gentlest horses I have ever known,' the young woman who owned him said. 'He also has the potential to go a long way with the right person.'

Kit looked small and vulnerable when astride that tall back, but he rode the horse competently, trying out its paces in a large paddock.

'Your son is a talented rider,' the woman said.

'He is obsessed.' Philippa watched, her heart in her mouth, as he put the horse over a line of brush jumps.

'But you are not sure about Mist?'

'He is a big, strong horse and I think Kit should wait a couple of years before taking on something of this magnitude.'

'In a couple of years he and Mist could be a viable partnership. I want him to go to the right home. I bred, reared and trained him myself, and the only reason I am selling him is because my fiancé travels, and when I marry I won't have the time to bring him on to his full potential.'

'If a good home is your first priority, why are you asking so much?'

'It is a fair price. I have already turned down an offer of sixteen thousand because I did not like the man who wanted him. Mist is an exceptional horse, Mrs Lang. He could be worth a great deal more in a few years' time. If your son likes him, I am willing to let you have him on approval for as long as you want. He is also open to whatever veterinary inspections you require.'

Kit trotted the horse over to them. 'He is super, Mum. Really fantastic.'

Philippa knew she had lost. Silver Mist came on approval in July, at the start of the summer holidays, but there was never any question of him going back.

'There go your birthday and Christmas presents for the next ten years,' Philippa dryly informed her son as they stood together, watching Mist explore the new box which had been added to the existing block. 'And if I see so much as a scratch on him I shall throttle you. That animal represents a major investment.'

Kit laughed and put an arm around her waist. He was nearly as tall as she was now. 'Mist and I are going to make you proud of us.'

'You don't have to prove yourself to me, darling. I shall always be proud of you. But there is one little thing you could do in return.'

'Anything.'

'I'd like to ask Vincent down for a weekend. It's about time you met him. Will you be polite, even if you don't like him?'

'Is there any reason why I shouldn't?'

She kissed his cheek. 'Not that I can think of. But I don't want your nose pushed out of joint if I bring another man into the house.'

'Will he be staying with us?'

'No, darling. I'll book him into Harlequin House.'

'That's all right then. Do you know if Grandma is coming over to see Mist?'

'She and Aunt Helen are coming for supper. I knew you'd want to show him off.'

CHAPTER TWENTY-NINE

———◆———

The Gertrude Mullins School for Girls had been established by Millicent Turner's grandmother in 1894, as a private academy for the daughters of well-to-do northern families. It was situated on the outskirts of Durham, in a gloomy building which had once been a monastery, and accepted girls from the ages of eleven to eighteen. The majority of them boarded, but a handful were accepted as day pupils. The girls were expected to work through their A Levels but, despite a respectable pass rate, few bothered to go on to university or worthwhile careers. When they left school, it was to be sucked into a social whirlpool which invariably led to comfortable marriages with the right young men.

It was the second week of the summer term, and Millicent was reading through the long list of improvements that needed to be done if the school was to remain open. The official letter had arrived this morning, out of the blue. She would have to convene a meeting of the board of governors to discuss its contents, although she knew there was no possibility of completing even a fraction of the requirements within the stipulated time. They did not have sufficient capital, and she could see no way of raising the vast sum which would be required.

There was a knock at the door. Millicent frowned. She was a severe-looking woman of fifty-five with narrow, unsmiling lips and grey hair which was permed into an unattractive frizz. Her life was this school. She had married young, divorced, and brought up a son who was a house-master at Eton. She wanted him to take over when she retired. Now everything had changed. There might not be a school after the end of the Christmas term.

She slipped the letter inside a folder.

'Come in,' she called.

'If it is not inconvenient, I should like a word.'

'No, it is not convenient, but sit down, Mr Lang.'

Six years ago Justin had answered an advertisement for an art teacher and Millicent Turner had employed him because she was desperate, the last teacher having walked out without giving notice. The Gertrude Mullins School pre-ferred women teachers in this all-female environment, the only other men being a Latin teacher and the gardener-cum-caretaker, both of whom were over fifty and balding. A good-looking widower under the age of forty was not Millicent Turner's ideal choice. She knew what fantasies teenage girls indulged in, and the fact he had a daughter would make no difference. Half of them would be mooning over him, while the other half used every wile to play him up.

He admitted to not having taught for a long time, and never senior students, although he had the qualifications to do so. She took him on until the end of term, haggling down the salary when he asked for his daughter to be accepted as a day pupil. Jennie Lang had been Millicent's charity case. She was given a free education and lunch, her father being expected to provide the regulation uniform and books. He did so without any apparent difficulty. He rented a small house not far from the school and he drove a decent car, but nobody knew anything of their past. It was a subject which neither would discuss.

Millicent's worst fears came true during those first few weeks. The girls were eager to attend his classes, and in no time at all the school was in the grip of a collective crush. She deliberately intruded upon his classes, walking in at odd times without warning, then staying for a while, watching and listening. Not once had she found a class rowdy or undisciplined, and if he were conscious of the effect he had upon the girls, he gave no indication of it. She finally conceded he was a good teacher who knew how to get his pupils' attention and how to keep it. Consequently, she made his position permanent.

He kept himself to himself, rarely mixing with the other members of staff, and never joining them during the break periods or for lunch. On the negative side, he was always pestering her for new and better equipment, while his teaching methods were unconventional to say the least – unconventional but effective. They crossed swords regularly, especially when he made spur-of-the-moment decisions to take his classes on unauthorised field trips.

It was the dog which had caused most dissent. She wandered into his class when he had been there for less than a week and had seen it lying on a blanket in a corner of the room. They had argued time and time again about that dog, and even when she threatened to terminate his employment he continued to defy her. In the end, rather than lose someone who was good at what he did, she turned a blind eye and, within reason, let him go his own way.

Guessing what he wanted now, she spoke first. 'Before you ask, the answer is no. You are not getting so much as a new paint-brush this term. You shall have to make do with the equipment you have. Your department has received more funds than all the others put together, and you are still not satisfied.'

Justin smiled. 'I am here for another reason. I wish to

leave at the end of the term and wanted to tell you before I put it in writing.'

It was the last thing she expected from him. 'Why? You are given everything you want.'

'It has nothing to do with my position here. The Royal College of Art have agreed to accept Jennie in September, providing she obtains her grades.'

His daughter was a bright girl who could get into any university. Instead, she had chosen to follow in her father's footsteps.

'There are other colleges which have excellent reputations. There is no need for you to go to London. Or are you getting out while the going is good?' Millicent's mind was still on the letter. She forgot he had no way of knowing about it.

The vehemence in her voice startled him. 'I went there, and would like my daughter to do the same. Is the school in trouble?'

He was an astute man and she had said too much. 'No. Thank you for telling me of your intentions. I shall advise the governors accordingly.'

'The school appears to be in trouble,' he insisted. 'Is it financial?'

'That is none of your business, Mr Lang. Is there anything else you require?'

He stood up. 'When you interview for my replacement I suggest you allow me to spend some time with the applicants. I can ensure you find the right person, who will continue what I have started.'

'I shall consider it.' Her cold eyes rested on his face. 'I am curious as to why I have never seen you paint. You must have the talent. The teachers I had prior to you were more interested in their own work than that of their pupils.'

He turned over the palms of his hands, revealing a crisscross of faded scars. 'Your other teachers did not have these.'

She knew there had been a fire for the scars had been vivid when he came here. He had mentioned it, but she did not want to pry into something which was obviously painful to him.

'Is that how your wife died?' she now asked.

'She died of leukaemia in nineteen seventy-three. It was how my brother died. Thank you for your time, Mrs Turner.'

'You are right, the school is in financial trouble.' For some reason she felt she owed him an explanation. 'I should appreciate your keeping this information to yourself, but we may have to close at the end of the year.'

Jennie knew her father did not have a class until the next period and walked in without bothering to knock. He was stretching a canvas across a frame and had his back to her.

'I thought you were studying,' he said without turning round.

She closed the door and stood with her back against it. She had grown into a tall, willowy girl, with her father's colouring and the same depth of compassion in her grey eyes.

'How did you know it was me?'

'Bess.'

The collie was lying in a patch of sun, her tail swishing back and forth. Jennie walked further into the room, her shoes creaking at every step. The brown uniform was bad enough, but she hated the shoes. They would be the first thing to go when she left here.

She saw her father had prepared two canvasses, and was now on his third.

'Who are they for? Me?'

He looked round. 'If you want a canvas, you can prepare

387

it yourself. What are you doing here?'

'Lucy has invited me to study at her house. Is it all right if I go? Her mother will bring me home. It's her bridge night, so she has to go out.'

He frowned. Afternoon lessons had been suspended for the senior girls, the time being allocated to study. The boarders had no choice, but many of the day students went home at lunchtime. 'You start your exams in two weeks. Are you really going to study, or is this an excuse to gossip, then slip out and meet some boys?'

'Honestly, Dad, what a rotten thing to say! Because Lucy is boy-mad doesn't mean I am. It'll be better at her place. And her mother will be there.'

'All right, sweetheart. Telephone if you are going to be late.'

Jennie ran her fingers over one of the canvasses. 'This doesn't belong to the school. The quality is too good. Old Turnip Face . . .'

'Jennie!'

'Mrs Turner,' she corrected, pulling a face at him. He knew every teacher's nickname, including his own, which had made him laugh the first time she told him. 'Mrs Turner would have a fit if she knew you were buying this.' Her eyes widened as they met his. 'They are for *you*. You are going to start painting again.'

He kissed her forehead. 'I am going to try. Whether or not I succeed is another matter. Now run along. I want to get this done before my next class. And, Jennie, I know I don't have to tell you, but keep this to yourself.'

'Nobody knows anything about us. They never have.'

It was part of the bargain he had struck when he brought her with him, and she had kept her promise, difficult though it often was.

'Do you still write to your grandmother?' he asked.

A flush of colour stained her cheeks. 'I haven't done so for a couple of months. How long have you known?'

'Since we came here.'

'Why didn't you say anything?'

'Because I trust you, and I can't stop you from keeping in touch with your family.'

'She is also your mother. I always regretted not being able to tell her where we are. I haven't even said you are teaching. It was best not to.' She glanced at her watch. 'I'm late. Cheerio, Dad. Don't bother to keep me any dinner. I can eat at Lucy's.'

He watched her go. She was growing up. Not very long ago she had sat in a corner of this room, doing her homework while he took his last class, or tidied up ready for the next day. He went back to stretching the canvas on to its frame. Three canvasses for the three chances he was giving himself.

The last day of term came and went. The girls who had finished school said their goodbyes, many of them tearful in the heat of the moment. The new art teacher would start next term. She was a competent woman in her mid-thirties, who had been singled out by Justin as having the right qualifications. She would live in staff quarters and be more involved with the school. It was unfortunate she might not have a job after Christmas. Nobody knew how bad the situation was. If there was a way out of this predicament, which Millicent Turner doubted, then she did not want to frighten away the new crop of pupils starting in September.

This was the first day of the summer holidays. Most of the staff had already left, and there was an eerie silence about the place. There is nothing more melancholy than an empty school, Millicent thought as she filed some timetables. A knock at the door startled her. Nobody knew she was here.

'Come in.' Her response was automatic.

'I have left everything tidy and inventoried,' said Justin. 'I came to say goodbye.'

'I thought you had already gone.'

'Not quite.' He smiled. 'We leave in the morning.'

No wonder the girls fell for him. They were going to miss him, and so would she. There would be nobody to argue with. Nobody to stand up to her and not give a damn.

'Italy isn't it?'

'Yes. For a couple of weeks.'

'What will you do with the dog?'

She would miss that too. It was odd how easily one adjusted to another person's eccentricities. He took his daughter abroad every summer, but she had never wondered about the dog before.

'She goes into kennels. I can see you are busy, so I won't detain you. I only wanted to thank you for everything.'

'It is I who should be thanking you. I know we have had our differences, but I shall not hesitate in recommending you for another position.' She took his outstretched hand. 'I wish you well, Mr Lang. Both you and Jennie. I look forward to the day when I hear she has become an accredited artist.'

'Thank you. Goodbye, Mrs Turner.' As he withdrew his hand he pressed a card into her palm. 'There is something by the door which I want you to have. You may keep it if you wish, but you will benefit by taking it to the person whose name is on the card. Insist on seeing her personally. She will give you a fair price. I hope it will help keep the school open.'

Millicent Turner stared at the printed card. On it was the name of an art gallery in London.

'I am afraid I don't understand . . .'

'You will, Mrs Turner. Goodbye.'

The following week she went to London, taking the oil painting with her. The picture of a horse standing beneath a tree, with a row of hills forming the background, was attractive, but she doubted it was of any value. In fact, she'd almost not come today, but local enquiries had established the Huntington Gallery to be highly reputable, and she was curious to learn what connection it had with her art teacher.

The canvas was awkward to carry and it was raining, so Millicent took a taxi to Bond Street. There was an elegance about the gallery which was hard to define. The young man who greeted her was polite and well spoken. She could see his eyes resting on the shabbily wrapped picture.

'Do you require a valuation, madam?' he asked.

'Yes. I have been told to ask for this person.' She handed him the card. 'Does she work here?'

'She owns the gallery, madam. I am afraid she is not here at present.'

Why didn't she think to telephone first, get her facts right and make an appointment? Why had she allowed herself to be taken in? The painting was sure to be worthless.

'Would you like to speak with her assistant? I am sure she can help.'

'Thank you,' she said in a voice which would have had her girls snapping to attention.

The woman who appeared from an inner office looked more like a fashion model than someone who was interested in art. She took Millicent into a well-lit room, offered her tea or coffee, then asked if she could see the painting. Millicent refused any refreshments. The sooner she got out of there the better. She handed over the picture. The woman cut the string and removed the paper. She lifted it to the light, then placed it on a table and studied it.

'This is freshly painted,' she said. 'May I enquire how it came into your possession?'

Millicent felt a cold shiver run down her back. 'It was given to me. Is something wrong?'

'I think you ought to see Lady Margaret.'

Millicent felt even more uncomfortable. There was nothing on the card to indicate that Margaret Buchanan was titled. 'I was told she was not here.'

'She isn't. She is at home. Can you wait for half an hour?'

The damn thing was a forgery. Millicent knew nothing about art, but she knew when she had been taken in.

'I can see I am wasting my time. Someone has gone to a great deal of trouble to play an elaborate hoax. Please could you re-wrap it?'

The young woman looked startled. 'I don't think this is a hoax. I think it is genuine. If so, what you have here is worth a great deal of money.'

Maggie smiled as she traced her fingers over the signature. This was no forgery. She was too familiar with his style. There was less detail than in his earlier paintings, but she knew from Noel how severe the injuries to his hands had been.

'This is the first Justin Lang to surface in seven years,' she said. 'I would have heard had any new paintings come on to the market. Did he give it to you himself?'

'He has been teaching at my school for most of that time. I had no idea who he was. To the best of my knowledge, this is the only painting he has done.'

'Is he still with you?' Maggie asked. 'He is a dear friend of many years. His first exhibition was held in this gallery. He is godfather to my son, and I also know his family well. His brother was killed in a fire. I think he may have blamed himself, although it was not his fault. And ... well, there were other things. He disappeared you see. Both he and his daughter.'

'He left at the end of last term, which was when he gave me the painting and said to bring it here. Jennie starts at the Royal College of Art in September, so they will be living in London now. Are you interested in purchasing the painting?'

'I sell on commission, but could have a buyer by the end of the week. Are you sure you want to sell it?'

'He gave it to me for that purpose. The money is for the school building fund.' Millicent wondered what it was worth. A thousand pounds perhaps, or was she aiming too high? Whatever it was, the money would be a drop in the ocean. As the bank would only extend a loan for half the amount it was inevitable the school would soon close its doors for the last time.

'I have half a dozen clients who are avid collectors of his work,' Maggie was saying. 'The old paintings are changing hands for between fifteen and eighteen thousand. This one should fetch twenty.'

'I beg your pardon?'

'Twenty thousand pounds, Mrs Turner. Will that be satisfactory? I shall also waive my commission. I rather think Justin would want it that way.'

Millicent clutched her handbag. Twenty thousand pounds for such an ordinary-looking painting?

'It would be more than satisfactory.' A smile parted her thin lips. The school would not be closing after all.

Maggie was waiting in the main gallery when Noel arrived.

'What's happened?' he asked.

'Nothing terrible,' she assured him. 'Thank you for coming so quickly. I wasn't sure when you were returning to the States, and I needed to see you.'

'I intended to leave tonight, but can delay my departure if necessary.'

'Everything is all right, Noel. I am sorry if I sounded hysterical on the telephone. This has been a morning of surprises. Come into the office. I have something to show you.'

She had placed the canvas on an easel, in a position where the light from the windows shone upon it. Noel stopped inside the doorway, staring at the painting. Maggie closed the door and stood at his shoulder.

'Well?' she asked.

'Did he bring it himself?'

'No. I only wish he had.'

Noel had recognised the artist immediately. After Millicent Turner left, Maggie found herself doubting the authenticity of the painting. But Noel had swept aside those doubts. Fondly, she linked her arm through his. Since their divorce they had become friends. He spent most of his time in America, living with a girl half his age. But he never brought her with him on his frequent visits to see the children. It was better this way, for now they were free to lead their own lives without recriminations.

'I believe it could be the first painting he has done since the fire,' Maggie said as he studied the canvas more closely. 'You know him better than I do. There is a distinct variance in style, and I would like your honest appraisal.'

'I prefer this to his earlier work. I always thought him too precise. If this is his first attempt in seven years, then he has lost none of his talent.'

'Do you think he will continue now he has started?'

'It's in his blood and he won't find it easy to stop. Where did it come from?'

Over coffee she told him about Millicent Turner and what little information she had gleaned about the Gertrude Mullins School for Girls.

'Did this Turner woman know where he was going?' he asked when she was finished.

'No, only that Jennie is starting at the Royal College in September, and they will be living here. It should be easy to trace them.'

Noel frowned. 'Leave him, Maggie. Hounding him could drive him away again.'

'I have no intention of hounding him. But I think Sarah should know, and Philippa too.'

'I suspect Sarah already knows a lot more than she is letting on. As for Philippa, do you think it wise?'

'What happened between them was a long time ago, when she was a girl,' Maggie said. 'They are close, Noel, in the same way she and Steve are close.'

'Philippa and Steve are friends, but I have never been sure about her and Justin. I often used to wonder if they simply buried their feelings away. Don't interfere. You may regret it.'

Maggie was silent for a moment. 'Philippa has someone else in her life now, but perhaps you are right.'

'There is no perhaps about it. I am right.'

CHAPTER THIRTY

Justin had not wanted to move back into his old stamping grounds, but he knew Chelsea, and it was one of the few districts which had changed little since he first moved there in the Fifties. He rented a flat in a narrow side street close to the Thames, then got a job as an illustrator of children's books. He had walked into one of the larger publishers with an impressive portfolio and a false name, been commissioned for one book, and kept steadily working thereafter. He was better suited to it than teaching, and the money was good. The years at Gertrude Mullins had eaten into his capital, and although the sale of a couple of paintings would set him and Jennie on their feet, he had lost faith in himself as an artist. The canvas he gave Millicent Turner fell far short of his exacting standards, but he knew it would fetch a good price, on curiosity value alone.

For Christmas, Justin had given his daughter a second-hand car, giving her the freedom to come and go as she chose. But she rarely went out, despite having made plenty of friends at college. He tackled her about it on a warm evening in June. He had a deadline to meet and was putting the finishing touches to a water-colour.

Jennie came into the room and peered over his shoulder. 'That's enchanting.'

'It's the cover for *Benny the Badger*.'

'You are far too good for this sort of thing.'

'It's undemanding and I enjoy doing it.' He reached up and squeezed her hand. 'Are you going out this evening?'

'No. I'm taking Bess for a walk. Will you come with me?'

'I have to finish this for tomorrow.'

'You can do it in the morning. There's some stale bread in the bin. We can feed the ducks in Battersea Park, then go for a drink. Some fresh air will do you good. I don't suppose you've been out today.'

He hadn't. His eyes were sore and his hand growing numb. It would eventually force him to stop, whether he wanted to or not.

'Give me another fifteen minutes,' he said.

It was pleasant outside. He sat on a bench watching Jennie feed the ducks. They squawked around her feet and, when the bread was finished, the bolder ones followed her to the bench.

'You should be enjoying this evening with someone of your own age, sweetheart, not trailing around the park with your old father.'

'Forty-six isn't old.'

He placed his fingers beneath her chin. 'It is too old for you. Why aren't you out with one of those bright young men you see every day? I can't believe none of them ever asks you.'

'Oh, they ask me.' Her voice was flat. 'They ask me out for a cheap meal, then expect me to hop into the sack.'

'Not all of them can be like that.'

She laughed. 'Of course not, but sooner or later they want the same thing. Blame yourself for bringing me up with a strong sense of morality. Look, Dad, don't worry. I am in no hurry to tie myself down.'

'The last thing I want is for you to be tied down, but you

should be out enjoying yourself.'

'I enjoy being here with you. Come on, Bess is looking bored.'

She clipped a leash on to the dog's collar before she and her father walked arm in arm across the Albert Bridge.

'You've not arranged anything for this summer, have you?'

He shook his head. 'You know I haven't. I can't tell you what to do any more.'

'I have already decided what I want to do.'

'What's that?'

'Go home.'

He stopped. 'Home?'

'To Shepherds Fold. I know you never sold it. You still have the key to the back door. I also want to see Grandma and Aunt Helen again.'

He gazed beyond her, at a barge chugging down river. He had been dreading this.

'You can go back whenever you want, Jennie. You always could.'

'You know I won't go without you. It wouldn't be the same. What are you frightened of? Uncle Nicholas has been dead for a long time.'

'Nicholas is only part of it. I cannot go back. Nor do I have any desire to do so.'

'You always taught me not to run away, but to face my fears. I think it's about time you confronted yours.'

'You don't understand. There are too many painful memories.'

'I am not a little girl any more. I can help if you will let me. You are throwing away a wonderful gift. You shouldn't be teaching unappreciative children, or illustrating trite books. There are others who can do those things. I am beginning to think you are never going to paint properly again, not until you resolve whatever is troubling you.'

'You should have gone into psychiatry.'

'Now you are changing the subject. I love you, Dad. I want you to be happy.'

He was touched. 'I am happy, darling.'

'No, you're not, and you never will be until you go back.'

She hugged him, and he kissed her forehead. It was marvellous to be young and naive and still believe in fairy tales.

Pauline kept her horse stabled here but, being married with a family of her own, was rarely able to help out any more. Sarah had employed another girl who lived locally, but she was off today and Pauline volunteered to take out the afternoon ride, leaving Sarah free to sort out the monthly accounts. She was about to start when Helen telephoned to say she was going to the cinema with a friend and would sleep at Harlequin House tonight. Sarah saw more of Pauline than she did her daughter. When Maggie had promoted Helen to assistant manager a year ago, it had meant she had to live in when she was on duty. But she always came home at other times, until this mysterious friend, about whom she never spoke, entered her life. Sarah often wondered whether it was a man, a married man, otherwise Helen would have said something.

She returned to the accounts, entering figures in a cash book as she wrote out each cheque. She was startled when her labrador growled and, looking up, she saw a strange dog standing in the doorway. She stared at the collie, wondering where it had come from. The dog wagged its tail and walked towards her. It was Bess.

Justin parked behind the new brick stables. Most of the boxes were empty and a few ponies were grazing in the paddocks, Copper amongst them. She must be thirty, he thought, shuddering when he saw the ugly burn mark which ran across her back and into her flanks.

When he had left here, the burnt-out shell of the barn was still standing. There was nothing there now, except grass and a solitary sycamore, too large to be called a sapling and too small for a tree. Justin knew every inch of this ground. The tree had been planted approximately where Nicholas died.

'Grandma did the right thing,' Jennie said. She was clutching his arm. 'She took away all the memories. Have you seen Bess? She's disappeared.'

'She knows her way around.' He gazed at the house. That had not changed. It was how it had been during the war years, when he was a child, and when they came back to it after his father's death in 1959. How it was when Nicholas and Philippa were married, and when Alice died and he went away, leaving Jennie here. How it was when Nicholas died and he left again, this time taking his daughter with him and never intending to come back.

'Grandma must be out.' Jennie sounded disappointed. 'Most of the ponies are.'

'Not necessarily. Let's go and see.'

'Don't you want to take the car?'

He smiled. 'To walk a few hundred yards? You're getting soft, sweetheart.'

'Oh, Dad!' she giggled.

He walked slowly, which she found irritating, then stopped a short distance from the house. She was about to say something reassuring, but changed her mind. This was something he had to do on his own.

'Justin . . .'

Jennie saw the colour drain from her father's face as he turned towards the voice. She turned too, staring at the dumpy woman with grey hair and her father's warm smile.

Sarah had not expected a child, but neither was she prepared for such a lovely young woman.

'Grandma . . .'

The girl ran to her, and tears filled Sarah's eyes as she hugged Jennie tightly. There was so much she had missed. All those important years where childhood ended and adolescence began. She looked at her son, who was watching them.

A smile pulled at his mouth. 'I may have made a mess of the rest of my life, but I don't think I did too badly with her.'

'No,' his mother agreed. 'You didn't do badly at all.'

Jennie wanted to visit Moor View, and expected her father to go with her. Sarah said Philippa was in London until the end of the week, so Justin suggested his daughter wait for her aunt's return if she was too timid to go on her own. But Jennie had another motive for wanting him there. She was convinced he would rediscover the desire to paint once he set foot inside his studio. So she nagged until he gave in and took her there on the Friday morning.

The pottery was not the massive place Jennie remembered from her childhood, but there was an air of prosperity about it. The sign by the front gates was freshly painted, and a couple of delivery vans were being loaded at the far end of the building. The car park had been resurfaced and there were special bays for management. Her father parked in a space reserved for visitors.

'I resigned before we left here,' he told Jennie when she asked why.

The main entrance had been altered. Double glass doors had replaced the wooden one, leading into an attractive reception area, rather than a maze of passages. But the rest was much the same. The offices had expanded and many of the faces were new. Louise was office manager now, and Rodney had put on weight.

'Nobody has been allowed in the studio since you left, except for a cleaner.' Rodney smiled as he handed over the key. 'We still get enquiries about when you will be doing another plate.'

'I came to look, Rodney, not to stay. I wouldn't be here at all if it were not for Jennie's persistence. I have no idea what's up there, but perhaps she will find something she can make use of.'

It was not what his daughter wanted to hear. 'I think you should go in by yourself,' she said as he slotted the key into the lock. 'I'd like to look round. I won't be long.'

'The reason I came was because of you.'

'I know, Dad. I also know you did some of your best work here, and I want to see you painting again, not illustrations for children's books, but the bold canvasses with which you made your name. You may be slower than you were, but you are still capable of doing them. I found out how much the painting you gave Mrs Turner fetched. You could live comfortably off one painting a year, luxuriously off two.'

'You are walking a fine line, Jennie. I will take only so much, even from you. Go ahead if you want to look over the pottery. I shall wait in the car.'

He was angry and went to pull the key from the lock but, as sometimes happened when he was in a hurry, it slipped through his fingers and dropped to the floor. Jennie snatched it up. Then, before he could stop her, she opened the door and pushed past him into the large room.

Oil paints, water-colours, pastels and brushes lay where he must have left them. There were canvasses stacked everywhere, and pinned on the walls were some of the original sketches upon which he had based many of his paintings. Jennie stared at them, wondering at her audacity in thinking she could be her father's equal. She would be lucky to stand in his shadow. She had been too young to appreciate his work before they left. Now she saw the touch of genius which still made people ask when he would be issuing a new plate.

She propped a couple of canvasses on a table. One was part of his original series of Camargue horses, and the other a detailed oil of Shire horses pulling a plough.

'Now do you understand?' Justin asked. 'My hands have lost their flexibility and will not always do what I ask of them. I can never hope to paint like that again, however hard I try.'

She turned to him. 'Then you will have to change your style to accommodate the stiffness of your fingers. It will not make you any worse an artist. It could make you better. Come to think of it, I rather like the simplicity of Benny the Badger.'

He walked to a window, where he stood with his back to her. 'Hurry up and take whatever you want. I am going to tell Rodney to throw everything away, then put this room to better use.'

Tears of disappointment stung Jennie's eyes. 'For as long as I can remember I wanted to be like you. I believed you could take on the world and win. But you are not trying to fight back.'

'There are too many things you don't understand.'

He did not elaborate. It was the first time she had stood up to him like this, and he was unprepared for a verbal attack. Jennie mistook his silence for complacency, which infuriated her even more.

'What is there to understand? You have an impediment. So do thousands of people. They learn to live with their disabilities.'

He turned slowly, his eyes seeking hers. 'I am not the artist I was and am too old to start again.'

'Rubbish! You are too stubborn to start again. I don't want anything from here. If you want to burn it, do so. I couldn't care less!'

She snatched up a blank canvas and hurled it across the room. It crashed into a row of glass jars which contained hardened paint-brushes. They toppled like a row of skittles, crashing to the floor and shattering. Her father said nothing, but his face was grey.

Even when she slammed out of the studio Justin did not move. He was overcome by a sense of helplessness, coupled with a deeply imbedded hurt. She was right. He had opted for the easy way out. There had already been too much pain in his life, so who could blame him for wanting to avoid more?

It seemed Jennie could.

A buzz of excitement preceded Jennie as she wandered through the pottery. She might be the initial cause of it, but the real reason was because her father had come back.

'Excuse me, but this area is not open to the public. What are you doing here?'

Jennie's eyes smouldered, like her father's did when he was angry. There was something familiar about the dark-haired young man who was standing in front of her. He was tall and lean with strong features, and she would have found him attractive were he not scowling so disagreeably.

'I am not the public.' Her tone matched his. 'If I were, I would be unimpressed by your rudeness.'

He did not expect her to retaliate and took a backward step, which was when she saw he was using a walking stick. She felt guilty for tearing into him like that, then remembered it was he who had been rude to her, so he should be the one to apologise. Whether he would was a matter of speculation. At the moment, he was staring at her as though he had seen a ghost.

In a way he had. She was the most beautiful girl he had ever set eyes upon. There was a captivating sparkle in her grey eyes, and he admired her forthright manner. From what he remembered, she had been fearless as a child.

'Jennie . . . Jennie Lang. It *is* you. Don't you remember me?'

A distant memory stirred. 'Peter? Peter Slater?' She sounded uncertain.

'Yes. You have grown, and very nicely if you don't mind me saying so.'

Her laughter was unaffected. 'What are you doing here? I thought your ambition was to join the army.'

'It was, and I did.' If anything, his expression darkened.

'What happened?'

'My leg. Surely you noticed?'

'You have a stick but, for all I know, you could have fallen down a flight of stairs.'

'I was shot last year, while I was in the Falklands. The limp is permanent and the army no longer wanted me.'

He spoke with such bitterness that Jennie did not dwell on the subject.

'And now you are working here?' she asked.

'Sort of. I am meant to be familiarising myself with the place until my father decides what to do with me. I expect he will give me an obscure desk job where I will be in nobody's way.'

'You don't have much faith in yourself. Surely you have some training?'

'Only in combat, which won't do me any good here. Are you looking for anywhere in particular?'

'No, but I'd like to see the art department.' She paused. 'I presume you have one?'

'Of course. Your father laid its foundations. I'll take you there.'

'Thank you. My father is obviously well thought of.'

'He was one of the major forces who helped to make Moor View what it is today. He also ran it with my father after Philippa's accident.'

They fell into step, Jennie moderating her pace to his more faltering one. Take away the outsize chip on his shoulder and he would be a likeable young man.

'What are you doing now?' he asked.

'Studying art.'

'To become an artist like your father?'

'To become an artist,' she corrected. 'I could never be like my father. He is unique.'

Peter could think of no suitable answer and remained silent, needing all his concentration as they climbed the stairs to the second floor. He cursed the gammy leg which had not only robbed him of his career, but his youth. How could anyone as vital as Jennie Lang notice him? All she must feel was pity.

He was unable to tear his eyes from her face as she flicked through the pattern books and when she stood up so did he. 'My father must be wondering where I am. How do I reach his studio from here?'

'By following me.' He reached for his stick. 'Would you have dinner with me?' His impulsiveness startled even himself.

'When?'

'Tomorrow night?'

'Only if I can impose one condition.'

He stiffened. 'What condition?'

'That you try to smile occasionally. You look so much more approachable when you do.'

Justin could not leave the broken glass scattered over the floor. He started to pick up the razor-sharp slivers, cursing when one cut into the palm of his hand, slicing across the

406

existing scars. He was wrapping a handkerchief around it when the door behind him opened.

'Is that you, Jennie?'

'No, it's me. Rodney said you were here.'

He straightened up. She had been thirty-two when he last saw her. Now she was forty and, unlike so many women, Philippa had improved with age. Physically, she was no different. Her figure was as slender and her long legs as shapely. Her tawny hair still floated about her shoulders, although it was styled with a more deliberate carelessness. The changes were in her face. Again, there was nothing dramatic, but the quick-fire succession of her own near-fatal accident, followed so closely by Nicholas's death, had left their marks.

'My mother did not expect you back until this evening,' he said.

'My business was finished, so I was able to return earlier. You have been gone eight years, Justin, and now you walk back as though it were yesterday. I still don't understand your reasons for leaving.'

'I left you a letter.'

'Which was a cruel and cowardly way of saying goodbye. You know I would have stood by you, that I needed you.'

'It would never have worked, Philippa. Everything has conspired against us since the day we met. Anyway, you do not need me now.'

There was no warmth in his voice. She could feel him distancing himself from her, like he had before he left. When Rodney told her Justin was back, Philippa had experienced a surge of emotions which had sent her rushing up here. Now she was confused and resentful.

'No, I don't need you any more,' she said. 'There is someone else who I am fond of. Why did you come back?'

'Because Jennie wanted to. We will be leaving at the end of summer.'

407

Philippa saw the canvas lying on the floor and the broken jars. 'Are you painting again?'

'I sketch a little.' So Maggie had not told her about the painting. 'Jennie is the artist now. I brought her here to see if there is anything she could make use of. I will not be needing this studio again.'

'If you don't want it, Jennie might.'

'I cut my ties with Moor View when I left here. It is yours. Do with it what you will. I no longer care.'

She recoiled at his sharpness. 'You always did have the capacity of hurting those who were closest to you. And you did not cut your ties, not entirely.'

His eyes bored into her. 'What do you mean?'

'Rodney and I were unable to accept your resignation.'

'Why?'

'Because we decided it would be in our best interests to bend the rules. We had no idea where you were, so could not advise you. Officially, you are still a director.'

'You had no right, Philippa!' He was furious. 'If nothing else, what you did was illegal.'

'We had a two-thirds majority. I would also add that our motives were purely selfish. You left at a time when we were fighting our way through the recession, and it benefited us to have your name linked with the company.'

'My life is my own and I will not put up with you or anyone else meddling in it.'

'You can interfere with my life, yet I must remain on the perimeter of yours. If you are still determined to sever your links with Moor View see Rodney before you go. He will make the necessary arrangements. And leave that broken glass. I'll send somebody to clear it away.'

She left, slamming the door behind her. He should never have let Jennie persuade him to come back. It had been a mistake from the beginning.

CHAPTER THIRTY-ONE

When Justin heard a car draw up outside the house he thought Jennie and Peter had come back for something his daughter had forgotten. He was wrong, it was Helen.

'I don't have long.' She kissed his cheek. 'We have a special function tonight and I must be back by eight-thirty. I wanted a word with you before the family get together tomorrow.'

'Do you want a drink?' he asked as she picked up a sketch-pad and flicked through the pages.

'Sherry, if you have it.'

'Only semi-sweet. I bought it for Jennie.'

'That's fine. Is this her work?'

'Yes.'

'She is good, but you were better at her age. You always will be better, Justin.' She put down the pad and took the glass from him. 'Why won't you paint any more? I know you can. Maggie told me about the canvas which found its way to her gallery last year. I never saw it, but Noel did. He is the one person whose opinion you always valued, and he preferred it to your earlier work. He thought it less cluttered with trivialities.'

Helen had been a plain child and now, at thirty-four, she was a plain, dumpy spinster. She wore a dark suit and her mousy hair was swept upwards into a timeless style which would have been better suited to someone twice her age. But during the years he had been away she had blossomed into a woman who was no longer afraid of her own shadow. The responsibility of Harlequin House must have helped, but he sensed another, stronger influence.

'You should have come when Jennie was here to back you up.' His eyes sought hers. 'Why is it so important that I paint again?'

'Because you are an artist, and a good one. Do you think Nicholas would have let you forget it if he were here now? You and he did not always see eye to eye, but he was your staunchest defender. Jennie is growing up and has her own life. What will you do when she leaves? Without your art, you will have nothing.'

'I'll survive. You have changed, Helen.'

'I had to learn to stand on my own feet. We all relied on you to get us through the bad times. When you left ... well, nothing was easy. Mum was devastated, and if Mike Taylor had not turned up when he did, I hate to think what might have happened to Philippa.' She sipped her sherry. 'Now she has Vincent Grant. Do you know about him?'

'I know of him. Will he be joining us for lunch tomorrow?'

'No. He lives in London. He has only been here a couple of times. He is rich, charming and good for her. Don't ruin tomorrow, Justin. Mum is looking forward to having the family together.'

'Why should I ruin it?'

'You will if you upset Philippa like you did yesterday. When you first met her she might have been a flippant young girl with more money than sense, but she is now a capable businesswoman, who not only runs Moor View, but is the driving force behind Lang & Wakefield. She plays

410

down her part in the latter, but I doubt if the agency could have survived without her.'

His dark eyes rested on her face. 'Why do you think Nick married her? He saw her potential and used it mercilessly. For someone who spends her life closeted in a country hotel, you are remarkably well informed. Who do you share secrets with? Mike Taylor?'

The blush which spread through her cheeks was the old Helen. 'I see him occasionally.'

'Occasionally?'

'Quite a lot, actually. I like him and he likes me and, before you ask, yes we are lovers. I trust you to keep that information to yourself.'

'Why the secrecy?'

He could see the whiteness of her knuckles as she gripped the glass.

'He is much older than me.'

'Old enough to be your father,' he agreed. 'Even were he ninety and on crutches there is nothing any of us could do to stop you.'

She smiled. 'How do you propose we circumvent the other awkwardnesses? Philippa is my sister-in-law, Kit my nephew, and Mike their handyman.'

'Those are your awkwardnesses. Philippa has never treated Mike as an employee. What happens at Christmas and birthdays, and on other special occasions?'

'I don't understand.'

Justin refilled her glass. 'When the family get together for Christmas, which I presume you still do, what happens to Mike? Is he left alone at Dovestail, or expected to clear off – out of sight and out of mind?'

'Don't be ridiculous! He joins us, of course.'

'So where is the problem?'

'You make it sound so uncomplicated. I only wish it was.

411

What do I tell Mum? *How* do I tell her?'

'You are not a child. Nobody can dictate what you must do. Personally, I think Mum would be delighted. And Philippa too.' She looked less than enthusiastic, so he did not press the point. 'And now you can tell me what has happened since I have been away.'

'Why?'

'Because none of you will forgive me if I put my foot in it tomorrow.'

Helen frowned. 'From what Mike has told me, you knew Philippa a long time before she became involved with Nicholas.'

'We met a couple of times. Nothing ever came of it.'

The sharpness of his voice told her a lot more than he intended.

Sarah went out to make sure the afternoon ride got off safely, while Jennie borrowed her father's car and drove to Dovestail with Kit, who wanted to show her Silver Mist and the ponies. During lunch the two young people did not experience the awkward lapses of silence into which their parents frequently fell. Sarah and Helen struggled to keep the conversation alive, but when the opportunity arose Philippa slipped outside. Justin was talking to his sister, and it was unlikely she would be missed.

She was leaning against a gate, gazing towards Flint Iron Tor, when he came looking for her. She did not see him, and he was in no hurry to make his presence known. She wore slacks and an open-necked shirt, with her mother's pearls about her neck. He had rarely seen her in any jewellery other than those pearls. At one time they were all she possessed, but he knew Nicholas had bought her some valuable pieces. He wondered if she wore them as a good luck charm, or because they were the only link with

412

a mother she had never known.

His expression softened as he watched her. It was a long time since he had come into contact with the combination of elegance and sophistication which were as natural to Philippa as breathing. They were nothing to do with money. The parents who sent their daughters to the Gertrude Mullins School were wealthy, but the mothers he had met were dowdy by comparison.

Emotions he had thought long dead stirred inside him. But it was too late to revive them. He had made his choice when he left here, and now they must remain buried forever. He was about to turn away when Philippa sensed his presence.

'I wanted some fresh air,' he said. It was a lame excuse.

'I don't think there is any. It's too muggy. Sarah says we'll have a storm later on.'

Her voice conveyed all the tension he was feeling, and she would not meet his gaze.

'I want to get in touch with Noel. Do you know where he is?'

'He lives in Florida, but should be back next week. He usually spends part of the summer here, and at Christmas he takes Maggie and the children to Lochdunnan. They are far happier divorced than they ever were married.' She paused. 'You always valued his opinion, and Maggie's too. Will you take their advice now?'

'Even if I start painting again, Moor View will not benefit.'

Their eyes met, but she could read nothing in his. 'I am not thinking about Moor View. I am thinking about you. The past is over and done with but I still care, Justin. Is that so wrong?'

He watched the line of ponies plod through the paddock to the gate his mother was holding open. 'I have lost the passion I once had. I can live without painting now.'

'Nicholas's death affected all our lives in one way or another. You were wrong to cut yourself off. Sarah and Helen and I picked up the threads of our lives. Did you even try?'

'You have seen my hands.'

'They are unsightly, but you are not crippled. Jennie says you illustrate children's books. If you are capable of that then you are capable of painting. How will you know what you can do unless you try?'

'I have tried. It is not easy, and I can only work for short periods of time. Whose idea was it to plant that tree?'

'Sarah's. I wish she hadn't, for whenever I come here it reminds me of what happened. I suffered from dreadful nightmares afterwards.'

'I still do,' he said. 'Every so often something triggers one off.' It had happened on the first night he returned to Shepherds Fold. He had woken up in a cold sweat, and spent what remained of the night with the lights switched on, terrified of sleep because of the horrors it brought.

Philippa watched him, sharing his pain, like he had always shared hers. She reached towards him, but suddenly withdrew her hand. It was over. She could not revive something which was long dead, nor did she want to. When Justin looked at her again, Philippa's expression was as unemotional as his.

Philippa should have been elated, but the two encounters with Justin had left her depressed. She turned to Vincent for consolation, but he had troubles of his own and the night they spent together ended in an argument. Philippa returned to Devon and when Vincent telephoned to apologise she snapped at him, rejecting his suggestion that he come down for a couple of days.

She immersed herself in the pottery, where she saw a lot of Jennie, who was interested in their methods of design. Justin occasionally dropped her off during the morning, but he never came in, and more often than not she left with Peter. One of the few times they did come face to face was when Rodney insisted on an informal meeting between the three of them. Philippa took little part in the discussions, despite their relevance to Moor View's future. She sat apart, listening, but passing no comment unless asked to do so. The result was that Justin agreed to remain with the company until the following March, which tied in with the end of their financial year. He wanted no payment, and offered nothing, other than a remark which made Philippa bristle.

'You are allowing an element of the modern to creep into your designs,' he said, his eyes resting on her face. 'You could be creating future problems.'

'It happens to be the future which we are considering,' she retaliated.

She expected him to argue like he had always done in the past, but he shrugged, then let the subject drop.

Philippa was arranging a bouquet of flowers which Vincent had sent her when Peter unexpectedly turned up. He was no longer the embittered young man who had returned from the Falklands, hating everyone and everything. Jennie had changed him, bringing sunshine and laughter into his life. She would be returning to London shortly and Philippa wondered if Peter would sink back into that mindless despair which was so distressing, not only to his family, but everyone who came into contact with him.

'I wanted to see you away from the office,' he said as she made them coffee.

'What about?'

'It's rather awkward.'

She glanced through the window. Kit was schooling Mist in the paddock.

'Come into the living room. We won't be disturbed there.'

She did not rush him, but let him bring up the subject in his own time.

'I should like to know what sort of future I can look forward to at Moor View.'

'Your father could tell you that.'

'My father is biased. You know how he opposed my joining the army. To tell the truth, I don't think he knows what to do with me. What plans do you have?'

'None,' Philippa said. 'Because you have no idea what you want to do, we have allowed you to drift. Perhaps we were wrong, but your father and I could see no point in pressurising you into something you would grow to resent. If you want a worthwhile position at Moor View, you must earn it. The pottery's future will eventually lie in the hands of the younger generation, and it is up to you to decide what you will contribute. Your father would like you to take his place, as I would like Kit to take mine.' She paused. 'But the final decisions must come from you and him. And Jennie too, for she is also a part of it.'

'You know, of course, that Moor View is hopelessly outdated?'

'We are a traditional pottery, Peter. It is what our reputation is based upon.'

He smiled. 'There is a difference between outdated and traditional but, if properly handled, the old and new can live side by side. I know how it runs, and what improvements I would like to make, but lack the knowledge and skill. I was thinking of doing a business management course, and I'd also like to learn something about computing. Willing or not, Moor View needs to be dragged into the twentieth century. Will you still want me under those circumstances? In time, it could mean radical changes.'

Apathy had turned into ambition. It bode well for the future if channelled in the right direction.

'Your father and I have never shied away from making radical changes. We have even discussed the need of installing a computer system, but got no further than that because we know nothing about them. From what you say, I presume you want to take a full-time course. How will you support yourself?'

'I have my disability pension, and a little money put by. I am also prepared to work in the evenings and at weekends.'

Rodney would finance him, but Philippa sensed pride had its place here.

'If your studies are for the benefit of Moor View, then I see no reason for not giving you a company grant. After all, large organisations offer training facilities. Where will you study?'

'London. That's where Jennie will be. There is still time to enrol if I leave immediately. Otherwise, I might have to wait until next year.'

Philippa stared at him. He spoke with an intensity which suggested a lot more than a summer romance, and she wondered how Justin felt about losing his daughter to this good-looking young man who obviously adored her.

Dawn was breaking when Jennie crept into the house. Bess ran from the living room to greet her, and the girl glanced at the partly open door before looking in.

The curtains were undrawn, and the first rays of sunshine were reflecting on the windows. Her father must have been here all night. At first, she thought he was asleep, but then she saw him watching her.

'I should have telephoned,' she said.

'You are not answerable to me, Jennie, any more than I have a right to censor you.' His voice was gentle. 'Did you spend the night with Peter?'

The blood rushed to her face. 'Yes.'

'There is no need to be ashamed. I was young once. I thought you might want to talk. It must be hard sometimes, not having a mother in whom you can confide.' There was a look of Alice about her as she stared at him. 'Of course, if you would prefer not to.'

She kissed his cheek. 'I don't think any mother could be more understanding than you. I'm glad you stayed up.' She sat on the floor beside him, with her legs tucked beneath her. The sun was rising above the moors in a magnificent golden ball and, as tendrils of light and warmth reached towards her, Jennie thought she would burst with happiness. 'I love him, Daddy.'

'I know, sweetheart.'

She leant against him and, gently, he stroked her hair. How could he not know? She was his daughter, and the glow which radiated from her was one of love and of being loved. She had spent most of this summer with Peter, and it had only been a matter of time before they consummated their love physically. When she had not come home that night Justin felt what all fathers must feel when they know a beloved daughter is lying in the arms of another man. But his anger had been short lived and, seeing her now, he was able to share her happiness.

'I am glad I took your advice and waited for the right person.' She spoke quietly, without embarrassment.

His hand became still. 'Did you take precautions?'

'Peter did. He said he wasn't going to take any chances until I was on the pill.' She twisted round, her eyes searching his face. 'Is that why you married my mother – because you had to? I found your marriage certificate in one of the boxes I was unpacking after we moved to London. My maths may be poor, but she must have been pregnant when you married her.'

She had taken him by surprise and he was unable to reply immediately.

'You were very young when she died, and it seemed unimportant later on.'

'Did you love her, or were you doing the correct thing?'

Again he hesitated. As the sunshine spread through the room she saw his face more clearly, saw the lines of weariness and regret. She reached for his hand. When he spoke, he did so haltingly.

'What you ask is not as straightforward as it may seem. I was captivated by your mother from the moment I met her. I thought I loved her but, on reflection, what I felt was a compulsion to protect her. We waited a long time before deciding to live together. I am not sure when we started to go wrong. We had very little money and there were other pressures, but in the end it was her helplessness which wore me down.'

'Helplessness?'

'It is something you will never understand, sweetheart. Your mother became more and more dependent upon me, until I felt stifled and told her I wanted to end our relationship.' He paused, and Jennie was aware of a sudden tension. 'I fell in love with somebody else and, had Alice not become pregnant, I think we would have married. Instead, I married your mother. Looking back, I have no regrets. You made it worthwhile and, towards the end, we rediscovered a fondness for each other.'

Jennie was silent. In the garden a chorus of birds broke into song. Further away, she heard the shrill whinny of a wild pony. Something stirred in her memory.

'Who was the other woman?' she asked. 'The one you fell in love with?'

The light disappeared from his eyes. It was as though a curtain had been drawn across them.

'It is irrelevant now.'

Was it? Jennie was not so sure, but knew better than to press him. She stood up. 'It's morning. I'll make some tea.'

While she was in the kitchen he opened the windows. It was going to be a beautiful day. He was still beside them when Jennie came back. China rattled as she put down the tray.

'I made some toast,' she said. 'Do you have any idea what perfume Philippa uses? It always seems to be the same one.'

He turned away from the window. She was chewing a slice of buttered toast as she poured the tea.

'Chanel. She has never used anything else. When she couldn't afford it she wore nothing rather than a cheap scent. If you want some, I suggest you persuade Peter to buy it for you.'

She put down the toast. 'Was it her you fell in love with?'

Emotions which she could not interpret pulled at his features. 'What brought you to that conclusion?'

'Little things which I was too young to notice before. For a start, you act differently with her than you do with anyone else. She is different with you too. This summer you have both gone out of your way to antagonise each other, but I don't think you mean it.'

He was standing so still he could have been carved from stone.

'Philippa and I have been friends for many years. We reserve the right to antagonise each other.'

'What about the perfume?'

'You've lost me. What has perfume got to do with anything?'

'Quite a lot. I'd forgotten until now. You must remember how hot it was when we were last here. Inside the house was airless, even with all the doors and windows open.' It was at that point she saw he had guessed what she was about to say. 'One day when I came home from school that perfume was wafting through the house. At the time I thought nothing of it, even though the smell was strongest upstairs, in your bedroom.' She stopped, her eyes downcast. 'I am sorry if I have hurt you.'

'It's my fault for letting you open that particular bag of worms. What Philippa and I did was wrong. She intended to divorce my brother, but at the time she was still married to him.'

He sat down. His face was grey and he looked his age.

'Is she the reason you never wanted to come back?'

'Part of it, but not all. Jennie, I want your promise you will keep this to yourself. Not even Peter is to know. Too many people could get hurt.'

'It's not too late to start again.'

'For us it is.'

'But . . .'

'That's enough, Jennie. The subject is closed. I want your promise now.'

She had seen him angry before, had been at the receiving end of his anger. But she had never seen him quite like this.

'I promise,' she said.

CHAPTER THIRTY-TWO

October was cold and dank and when Ernest asked Philippa if she could spend a few days in London to help with a potential client, she was glad of an excuse to get away for a few days. She arranged to go up by train. Vincent said he would meet her, while Mike could take her to the station after dropping Kit at school.

Of course it had to be the morning when Celia was late and Kit dawdling.

'When do you think the exercise ring will be ready?' he asked as he poured himself a second cup of tea. 'The evenings are starting to draw in pretty fast, and it won't be long before the clocks go back.'

'Soon. They promised to have the floodlights up by the weekend.'

At the moment, he was riding Mist at dawn and the ponies after school. The floodlit, all-weather arena would enable him to exercise the three of them during the dark winter evenings. He wanted it to be under cover, but Philippa had to draw the line somewhere, and told him he must graciously accept what he was getting, or have nothing at all.

She glanced at the kitchen clock. 'Do hurry up, Kit. I'm going to miss my train.'

'Vincent won't mind waiting. Are you going to marry him?'

The colour drained from Philippa's cheeks. 'You're a little premature. He has not asked me.'

'Everyone expects him to. What will you say if he does?'

'I'm not sure. I didn't know it had become a matter of public speculation.' Vincent had never discussed marriage, but he had dropped hints, leaving her in no doubt he would ask when the time was right. 'How would you feel about having him as a stepfather?'

Kit gulped down his tea. 'I haven't given it much thought. I don't suppose I would mind, unless he started interfering. Would he live here?'

'Some of the time. But I wouldn't marry without your approval. Now hurry up and fetch your things. We'll talk some more when I get back from London.'

She started to clear the table, stacking the dirty dishes on the draining board. Would she want to marry Vincent if he asked her? It would mean more than him coming here occasionally. It would mean she would have to uproot, as he would want her with him in London and New York. And she would see less of Kit, for his life was here with his horses. Nor could she remain so involved with either of the businesses. It was a major decision and one she had to face sooner or later.

The door opened. 'I've put your luggage in the car,' Mike said. 'Where's Kit? If we don't leave in five minutes you'll miss the train.'

'He's upstairs.'

Mike closed the door and stood with his back against it, looking embarrassed. 'Do you have a moment?'

'Of course. What is it?'

'I was wondering how much you've heard about Helen and me.'

She smiled. 'Disjointed rumours. I have also seen you together, and am not blind.'

'We want to get married in spring. Would you object?'

'Why should I?'

'Helen is your sister-in-law. The situation could be awkward.'

It was an odd coincidence that he should be talking of marriage when she was contemplating the same thing. She kissed his cheek.

'There is something wonderfully old fashioned about you, Mike. I might have been snobbish a long time ago, but now I shall be delighted to have you as my brother-in-law.'

Philippa was in no hurry to leave London. Vincent was not the only incentive. She had an urge to see bright lights and bustling shops, to gossip with Maggie, and laugh with Steve.

Her first couple of days were devoted to the agency. The prospective new account was a large perfume manufacturer which was represented by an aggressive young executive and an older man whose name Philippa recognised. He had been working for a different company in the Sixties, and had chosen her as the model for a series of perfume ads. She did not envisage any difficulties, even when Ernest said the younger man had the final say. She had learnt how to handle aggressive young executives. After all, she had been married to one.

Their first appointment was early on Thursday morning and Philippa was on her way to Ernest's office when she was waylaid by his secretary, who said she was needed in reception. She backtracked, hoping that whatever it was would not delay her for long. Ernest could handle the initial presentation, but was liable to flounder if left alone for any length of time.

As she walked into the reception area Jennie leapt to her

feet. The girl was wearing a tatty anorak over a navy pullover, faded jeans and trainers. Her hair fell to her waist in a shining curtain and, for an instant, Philippa saw a strong resemblance to Alice. Then Jennie smiled, and was purely her father.

'Have I caught you at a bad time?' she asked.

'It's not the best, but never mind.' Philippa hugged her. 'What are you doing here?'

'I want to beg a favour from you.' She pulled a face. 'Two actually.'

'Then you had better come through to my office.'

'I don't have much time as I'm late already. My first class starts in fifteen minutes.'

Philippa glanced at the receptionist, but she was busy with the switchboard. She sat down.

'What are these favours?'

Jennie took a deep breath. 'Peter and I have decided to live together, and I don't think it's fair to expect Dad to keep on supporting me – not entirely. I was wondering if I could come to you for a holiday job. I am willing to do anything, and wouldn't expect to be paid much. I know it's a cheek, and if you say no I'll understand.'

'Of course it's not a cheek,' Philippa assured her. 'You are family, Jennie. When you were a little girl, before your father became famous, Nicholas was always pushing work his way. I doubt if he would have survived without it. Whenever you want a job, for however long, there will always be one for you in the art department. Not only here, but at Moor View too. What is your second favour?'

This time she was more hesitant. 'Dad is starting to paint again. Noel persuaded him he was a fool not to, and . . . well, there are one or two other things which I am pushing him into. It is not easy. He can be terribly stubborn some-times.'

Philippa smiled. 'It runs in the family. What has all this got to do with me?'

'He is going to give up the flat and move back to Shepherds Fold. I am worried he will shut himself away, and want you to get him involved with Moor View.'

'He has already said he will not come back.'

'He will if you, and not Rodney, asks him. I know he doesn't show it, but he is still fond of you.' She glanced at her watch. 'Oh golly, I must go, otherwise I shall be in trouble!' She kissed her aunt on the cheek, then sprang to her feet and rushed off.

Philippa did not move. How much did Jennie know? She suspected it was a lot more than the girl was saying.

'Can you stay for the weekend?' Vincent asked. 'I'd like to arrange something special for Saturday evening.'

Philippa had an inkling as to what part of that something special would be. Vincent was not an impulsive man. He would not propose to her like Nicholas had done, on a Sunday morning while looking through the newspapers. And Nicholas would not have left her at the top of the basement steps night after night, as Vincent had done when they were working at Lady Jayne's.

'Of course I can stay,' she told him.

On Saturday morning Philippa had her hair styled and her nails manicured, then popped into Harrods for some last-minute shopping. It was a little after one when she returned to the flat. The telephone was ringing, but stopped before she could unlock the door. Almost immediately it started again.

'Thank goodness you're back!' Helen said. 'I've been trying this number for the past hour, and in between have rung everybody you know.'

Helen had never telephoned her here before. The urgency of her voice filled Philippa with foreboding and she felt fear run through her veins like ice.

'What's happened?' she asked.

'Kit is in hospital. Mike is not sure how badly hurt he is. The last time we spoke he was still unconscious. He was taking part in a cross country event and the horse fell at a jump.'

'Where is he?' Philippa's voice was trembling.

'In Taunton.'

She rang Vincent as an afterthought, while waiting for a taxi to take her to the station. He wanted to drive her to Taunton, but she would not let him. It would be quicker by train and she preferred to go alone. He did not press her and Philippa was too distraught to sense how dismayed he was at being excluded when she was most in need of support.

It was the worst journey she could ever remember. There was no direct train and she had to change, wasting more time than she could afford. She sat beside a window, worrying about Kit as she watched the sky become blacker and the rain heavier. She had telephoned the hospital before leaving the flat, but they would not tell her the full extent of his injuries, only that he was comfortable.

Taunton was a town she did not know, and she had to ask the ticket collector where the taxis were. She started to run, but someone grabbed her arm.

'It's me, Philippa. I almost missed you.'

Their eyes met. Justin's were filled with all the compassion and understanding she remembered from the past and, without hesitation, she flung herself into his arms. He held her tight, shielding her from the people who were rushing past.

'He is all right,' he said, taking her to one side. 'He came round before I left the hospital, and I was able to talk to him.

He was groggy, mostly because he has a bad concussion. They want to keep him in overnight, but you should be able to take him home tomorrow.'

'Thank God. I was imagining all sorts of things during that awful journey.'

Justin looked cold, as though he had been waiting for a long time, but his smile was reassuring. 'You have to expect the occasional accident. He must have fallen off before.'

'Umpteen times. But the worst injuries have been to his pride.' She hesitated. 'There is more, isn't there? Otherwise you would not be here.'

'That is not entirely true. But you are right. The concussion is only part of it.' He took both her hands in his. 'He was lucky, considering the horse rolled down a bank and over him. His right arm is broken, a couple of ribs are cracked, and he has some nasty bruises. He should have known better than to try out a young and inexperienced animal when the ground is a quagmire.'

Philippa's heart missed a beat. 'He wasn't riding Delight?'

'No. Silver Mist. I thought you knew.'

'If I had, I would have stopped him. He promised not to jump Mist in competition until next summer. What on earth was Mike thinking of?'

'It was a practice event rather than a competition. No prizes were being offered. And you cannot expect Mike to pass judgement on the condition of the ground. He has to rely on Kit for that.'

'Which does not condone what he did. On top of everything else, Mist cost a fortune.' She stammered to a halt. 'Is he dead?' How would she tell Kit his horse had been destroyed?

'Of course not. A broken leg was suspected at first, but the course vet confirmed a bad sprain. On the negative side,

428

there could be a fracture. I told Mike to get your own vet to X-ray it immediately.'

'Then there is a possibility he may never jump again?'

'It is something which has to be considered.'

'Kit's ambition is for him and Mist to get into the Olympic team. I know it is nothing more than a pipe-dream. But we all have our dreams. I had mine. You had yours.' This had become too much and Philippa was unable to stop the tears which spilled down her cheeks.

'Come on,' Justin said. 'I'll take you to him.'

There was a gentleness in his voice which she had not heard since the time before he went away. He put his arm around her, holding her close, and when she fumbled for a tissue, he thrust a handkerchief into her hand.

'How did you know about Kit?' she asked when they were sitting in his car. 'And get here so quickly?'

'I was at Shepherds Fold. Helen couldn't leave the hotel as half the staff are off with flu. Mum came down with it yesterday, so she didn't want to get her involved. Mike didn't know what to do. Whether to leave Mist and go to the hospital with Kit, or leave Kit and take Mist home. So Helen asked me to come. Do you mind my being here?'

Philippa shook her head. 'I've missed having you around when things go wrong.'

Kit's face was as white as the cast on his arm. He was wearing a tie-up surgical gown, but if he was here for one night Philippa did not suppose it mattered. Only when she came close to him did she see that one eye was swollen and half closed. A row of neat stitches ran along his upper lid and into his eyebrow.

'Were you kicked as well?' she asked.

'I can't remember. One moment we were flying over some rails and the next through the air. Are you mad?'

'I was.' She sat on the edge of the bed and kissed his cheek. 'The trouble is you are growing too big for me to scold. No doubt you have learnt your lesson the hard way. However, Mike has a couple of things to answer for.'

'It wasn't his fault. I persuaded him to let me bring Mist. None of the fences were over two foot three, and I took Delight round first. She popped over them without any trouble, so we agreed it would be all right to give Mist a try. I've jumped him higher at home.'

'You obviously did not take into account that Mist is a headstrong, young horse, whereas Delight is a wily old bird who has learnt something about self preservation.'

'Will he be all right?'

'Justin is phoning Mike to find out. If he is ruined there is nobody to blame but yourself.'

His hand reached for hers and she gripped it tightly. 'I'm sorry, Mum.'

'I know, darling. But it's no good worrying until we hear what the vet has to say. How about you? How do you feel?'

'A bit light-headed. A nurse gave me an injection before you arrived. She said it would help me sleep. I wish I didn't have to stay here tonight.'

'It's only a precaution. You can come home in the morning if there are no after-effects.'

'You are fortunate it is only one night. According to Mike, one side of your hat is split from top to bottom.'

Philippa jumped as Justin came up behind her, but did not turn round, which was why she saw the sudden alarm in her son's eyes.

Anxiously, she leant forward. 'What's the matter?'

'Nothing. I thought it was Dad standing behind you. I must be having hallucinations.' His gaze shifted to Justin's face. 'I never realised how like my father you are. How is Mist?'

'He'll be out of action for a few weeks. When you start

riding him again he will need to be brought on slowly. Jump him too soon and you could find he has lost his nerve and will try running out.'

Kit was silent. Philippa saw his relief, but he was also looking dazed. She suspected the medicine was taking effect.

'Can you exercise him for me when he is sound?' he asked Justin. 'It's going to be at least six weeks before the cast comes off, and by then he will be jumping out of his skin.'

'Kit, how can you ask such a thing? Justin doesn't even live here any more.'

'He will be by then. Jennie told me when she telephoned last night.'

Philippa looked at Justin. She could read nothing in his expression, but sensed something was unravelling which she was incapable of grasping right now.

'It is too much of an imposition,' she said.

'Who else is there? Uncle Justin is the only person I can trust with Mist. Grandma is getting old and would find him too much of a handful. I can arrange for friends to hack the other two at weekends, and I can always lunge Delight in the arena.'

'You will do no such thing!'

'Oh, Mum, I can manage her with my left hand. As it is, I'll miss out on the Pony Club games at Wembley this year.'

Philippa felt her self control slip away. 'You could have been seriously injured today, perhaps killed. Can't you think of anything but those horses?'

Justin placed a hand on her shoulder. 'Take it easy,' he said, and to Kit, 'I'm a bit rusty, but don't mind exercising him, providing your mother agrees.'

'Do I have any choice?' She saw Kit's expression and realised how haggish she must sound. 'I'm sorry, darling, but this has not been the best of days. I know you hate it when

I am sentimental, but you really do mean so much to me. And don't get your hopes up too high. You may have been told the cast will come off in six weeks, but that does not mean you can leap straight on to a horse and carry on as though nothing has happened.'

'I don't expect to.' His eyes were blinking. 'Will you definitely be taking me home tomorrow?'

'Definitely,' she confirmed. 'I'll bring some decent clothes with me. You don't want to be seen dressed like that.'

'Undressed you mean.' He grinned. 'I'm sorry, but I can't keep my eyes open. When you leave here, why don't you and Uncle Justin go somewhere for dinner? You look good together, and he isn't really like Dad.'

Philippa was grateful Justin could not see her face at that moment.

'He is Nicholas all over again,' she said as they left the hospital.

'What makes you think that? Nicholas was ambitious and determined to have his own way in everything. What Kit has inherited is your stubbornness.'

Philippa glanced at him. 'I am not stubborn.'

'Neither is a mule.' He smiled. 'Would you like to take up his suggestion about dinner? You can't have eaten, and we still have a two-hour drive ahead of us, longer if there's fog.'

'I'd like that.' She remembered the special dinner she was meant to be having with Vincent that night, then put the thought to the back of her mind.

Justin took her to one of those intimate restaurants he was so good at finding. As they sat down Philippa had her first misgivings. What if they found conversation awkward or stilted? She should have foregone dinner and asked him to take her home. But without conscious effort the eight-year gap was bridged, and she found herself feeling like she always had in his company, perfectly at ease. They did not hurry. There was no need, for neither of them had anybody waiting.

They lingered over coffee. Because he was driving Justin had drunk very little wine, and Philippa left her glass half full.

'They'll probably finish this in the kitchen later on,' she said, running her fingers down the bottle.

'Is that what you used to do?'

'Sometimes. They were pretty awful wines that I remember, or maybe my tastes were more refined in those days. Lady Jayne's seems a lifetime away. Vincent tells me there is an Indian Tandoori there now. Clive died and nobody knows what happened to Malcolm.' She lifted her eyes. 'What are we going to do, Justin? If you are coming back to Shepherds Fold we can't continue avoiding each other like we did in the summer.'

He reached across the table, laying a hand over hers. She felt the rough callouses of his burns, but neither of them were free of scars, physical or mental.

'We have learnt from the lessons of the past and there is no reason why we cannot be friends. Will you marry Vincent?'

'I think he intended to ask me tonight.' She looked at their hands, his fingers loosely entwined with hers. She did not want to discuss Vincent with him. 'Jennie tells me you are painting again.'

Justin was aware of her reticence, even if his expression did not show it. 'Yes, I am. Has she also told you the Royal Academy wants to set up an exhibition of my work next summer, preferably to include some recent canvasses? I have a feeling she has her finger in that pie as well.' His eyes sought hers. 'She knows about us, Philippa. She guessed most of it, and I told her the rest.'

'She came to see me a couple of days ago, and I suspected as much then. Nor would I like to swear that Kit is totally ignorant.'

'She never mentioned calling on you.'

'Probably because she was cadging a holiday job. She wants to be independent. Well, partially independent. Do you mind her living with Peter?'

'She is not a child and it's a situation which I have to accept.' He sipped his coffee. 'She knows I will always finance her. I had to work my way through art school and, as things turned out, Nick did the same at university. There is no need for her to do the same.'

'Personally, I think she is making a token gesture. She also said you would come back to Moor View if I asked. Will you?'

'What could I do there? The art department has become self sufficient in my absence.'

'Perhaps too self sufficient, and lacking a guiding hand. If you are uneasy about the mixture of modern and traditional, why don't you do something about it?'

He let go of her hand. 'Finish your coffee,' he said. 'It's getting late.'

She did as he asked, for she knew he would come back.

And come back he did, a fortnight later. Philippa arrived late at the pottery, to find he had swept through the art department like an avenging angel, leaving nobody in doubt about who was in charge.

'Don't interfere,' Rodney told her. 'There are only two people up there who have worked with him before. To gain the respect of the others he must establish authority in his own way. He won't do anything drastic without consulting us first.'

Philippa heeded his advice and, consequently, the few times she and Justin met were in busy corridors, where a few words had to suffice before they went their separate ways. He gave her no encouragement, yet she was always conscious of his presence, instinctively knowing when he was in the pottery and when he was not.

Alarmed by the effect he was beginning to have on her, Philippa turned to Vincent, whom she had neglected during the turmoil of the past three weeks. She had spoken to him once, when he telephoned to ask about Kit. Now she felt a desperate need to see him, but he told her he was flying to New York for an important consultation with some backers and would be away for a fortnight.

Her personal crisis was not helped when Justin came to Dovestail the following Sunday morning. Kit had asked him to try out Silver Mist, who was sound again. Philippa took her son to one side and tartly told him he should have informed her beforehand. And then, knowing she was being unreasonable, she stood with him, watching Justin ride Mist in the exercise ring. He finished by jumping the horse over a two-foot pole. He has lost none of his skill, she thought, wondering if he had put in some practice on one of his mother's horses.

He came over to them, but it was to Kit he spoke. 'If you are serious about training Mist to international level, I suggest you devote a year to schooling. He has the scope, but lacks discipline in confined spaces. It is no good jumping brilliantly in the cross-country section if you are going to lose out on the dressage and show-jumping phases.'

'Thank you,' Philippa said later. 'Kit thinks you are wonderful, and I won't have to worry about his risking his neck for another year.'

'He still has to jump Mist, but he should be a little more cautious. Will you have lunch with me next Saturday?'

She stared at him. 'Why lunch?'

'Why not?' he asked.

On Thursday evening, shortly after six, Ernest telephoned.

'You have to come up tomorrow,' he said. 'We have a crisis on our hands. There has been a mix-up at our end, and now one of our top accounts is threatening to walk out and go to another agency. I have tried to smooth things over, but they won't listen. You'll have to talk with them. I've set up an appointment for eleven. If you catch an early train you should be here in time for me to fill you in on the details.'

'Which client, Ernest? And what happened?'

'Sorry, darling, I have a call from the States waiting on the other line. I'll see you tomorrow.'

'Ernest . . .'

He hung up and try though she might, Philippa could not raise him again, either at the office or his home, where an answer-phone had been switched on. She wondered if she should cancel lunch on Saturday, in case she had to stay over, but decided she could telephone Justin from London if the situation was anything as desperate as it sounded.

She drove to Exeter, caught a train to Paddington and then a taxi to Kensington. She walked into Ernest's office at ten on the dot. His sheepish grin told her she had wasted her time.

'The panic is over,' he said. 'I am afraid it was a storm in a teacup. I telephoned Dovestail, but you had already left. Never mind, there are one or two other things I'd like to discuss while you are here.'

CHAPTER THIRTY-THREE

Mike had gone to see Helen, Kit was visiting a friend and Philippa had had to hang around for half an hour because Justin was late. Yesterday had been a fiasco and this luncheon date had the makings of a disaster. She should have cancelled it.

'Do you mind if I pop into Moor View?' Justin asked as he turned on to the Tavistock Road. 'I want to drop off a couple of designs.'

'Of course not.' Philippa gazed at his profile. The lines were deeper and his hair was flecked with grey, but he was still a good-looking man who had lost none of the sense of purpose which she had always found so admirable in him. 'Why are you taking them in today?'

'Because they are needed today.'

'We are well within our schedules. There's no need for anyone to work overtime.'

He glanced at her. 'Relax, Philippa. Rodney okayed it. You cannot expect to keep your finger on every pulse. The business has grown too large, and you were away yesterday.'

'I should still have been told.'

'You've become quite the despot, haven't you?'

She knew he was laughing at her and, angrily, she turned her head away. They did not speak again and Philippa was glad when they reached the pottery, for it was a diversion of sorts.

'Are you coming in?' he asked.

'I'd prefer to wait here.'

He got out of the car, then came round and opened her door. His fingers closed around her arm.

'I might be a while, and I don't want to find you in a blind fury when I get back.'

'You won't.'

'Won't I? I know you, Philippa.'

'I have no intention . . .'

'Can you never do anything you are told?'

She glared at him. 'I want to go home when you have finished here. To go on for lunch is pointless.'

He shrugged. 'Suit yourself. I have never pandered to your whims, and don't intend to start now.'

She had to go with him because he left her no choice, and had she not been so furious, Philippa would have been suspicious when he headed towards the main doors. Outside of normal office hours those doors were kept locked.

'Smile, sweetheart,' Justin said moments before reaching them.

Then the doors swung open and she was grateful for his solid presence as they walked into a sea of familiar faces. One face, more familiar than the rest, loomed directly in front of her.

'You'll never know how hard we worked to keep this secret,' Kit said. 'Congratulations, Mum, for your twenty-one years at Moor View.' He grinned. 'Actually, double congratulations are in order, as you also turned forty this year. Although I don't suppose you want everyone to know that.'

'It's too late now,' she said, hugging him.

This was something she had never expected. All the staff

were there, and mingled with them were the people who had taken a hand in shaping her life – Leonard and Thomas Perkins with their wives; Gideon, now eighty-seven and robust as ever; Noel had flown over from America; Maggie and Steve and Ernest were here; Rodney and Daphne with the twins, and Peter and Jennie; Mike and Helen were holding hands, and Sarah was standing with them. And perhaps the greatest surprise was Vincent, who stepped forward and kissed her cheek.

Harlequin House had provided a sumptuous buffet which was laid out in the canteen. Champagne flowed freely and, after Philippa had blown out the candles on a two-tiered cake, Rodney made a presentation.

'It was the simple idea of a limited edition of collector's plates which was the turning point for Moor View,' he said. 'So it is appropriate that we give you a plate which is more limited than any of the others. It is the only one in existence, hand-painted by the artist who worked on the original series. I promised not to mention his name, but we all know who he is.'

Everyone clapped and tears stung Philippa's eyes. The plate which Rodney handed her lay in an open box, on a bed of pale satin. The painting was of Moor View, but not the functional Moor View she knew. A lyrical quality had been introduced by setting it beneath a sky of gold which reflected against the randomly growing daffodils in the foreground.

She looked up, her eyes searching for Justin, who she had not seen since Vincent took his place at her side. He was standing with Jennie at the back of the room. He did not avoid her gaze, but met it with a directness which set her pulse racing. It was as though they were the only two people in the room and, in that instant, Philippa knew there had never been anyone but Justin. There never would be.

Someone asked the same question three times before she realised it was directed at her. The spell broke and she found herself caught up in a welter of congratulations from which she was unable to escape. When she did extricate herself, Justin was nowhere to be seen. Jennie was standing with Peter and Kit. She started towards them.

'Alone at last,' said Vincent, blocking her way. 'Come over here, darling. There is something I want to ask you.'

'Can't it wait?' she asked impatiently.

'It has waited long enough already. This is an ideal time to announce our engagement. We could make it a triple celebration.'

Had he asked five minutes earlier Philippa would have said yes, a decision she would have regretted for the rest of her life.

'I'm sorry, Vincent, but I can't marry you.'

It took a moment for the shock to register. 'What do you mean? Why not?'

'Because I am in love with somebody else. Please forgive me.'

'Philippa!'

She was gone.

'Noel, do you know where Justin is?'

'He slipped away after Rodney gave you the plate. I suppose you know he would never have done it for anyone else but you? That fine brush-work is difficult for him now.'

'Where is he?'

'What's wrong with Vincent? He looks shattered.'

'*Please*, Noel!'

The urgency in her voice got to him. 'Try his studio. He went in that direction.'

'Thank you. If anyone asks . . .'

'. . . I have no idea where you are. Or him either.'

He was standing beside a window, staring into the yard. He did not look round when she came into the room.

'I am sorry about this morning,' he said. 'I never meant to upset you. There was no other way of keeping this a secret.'

'I never suspected a thing, right up to the last moment, when the doors opened. I am touched so many people bothered to come.'

'They came because they like you, and admire what you have achieved.' He turned slowly. His expression was grim and his body taut as a coiled spring. 'You have come a long way from the haughty young madam who ordered me to use the tradesmen's entrance. That was twenty-five years ago.'

A quarter of a century, yet it could have been yesterday. 'I was fifteen and fell head-over-heels in love with you. Mike told me I had a schoolgirl crush, but what happened later proved otherwise.' She hesitated. 'The irony is I still love you. I always shall.'

He smiled. That wonderful smile which enveloped her in its warmth and chased the cold shadows from his face. She barely dared breathe as he walked towards her. And then she was in his arms, tasting the sweetness of his mouth pressing down upon hers. Her doubts fled. He wanted her as much as she wanted him.

It was Justin who broke away, holding her at arm's length, his grey eyes tender upon her face.

'Will you come back to the beginning with me? To Lochdunnan? It is virtually unchanged since we were last there, and ours for as long as we want it.'

Philippa's nerves felt as though they had been stripped bare. 'A dirty weekend?' she asked, treating his suggestion with humour because she was unsure how else to respond.

'If I had wanted a dirty weekend I would have suggested Torquay. It's nearer.'

This was no joke. As she studied the strong contours of his face she saw he was deadly serious.

'An affair then?'

His sudden laughter sounded brittle. His nerves were also on edge, making Philippa feel less vulnerable.

'With Jennie and Kit breathing down our necks? It is hardly practicable, and would create more problems than it solved. I want to take you to Lochdunnan as my wife, not my lover.'

He lifted his hand to her cheek and mirrored in his eyes she saw all the love she felt for him. There was no need for words. He held her close, and she laid her head against his shoulder.

To love was to trust, and this was for always.

Warner now offers an exciting range of quality titles by both established and new authors. All of the books in this series are available from:
Little, Brown and Company (UK),
P.O. Box 11,
Falmouth,
Cornwall TR10 9EN.

Alternatively you may fax your order to the above address. Fax No. 0326 376423.

Payments can be made as follows: Cheque, postal order (payable to Little, Brown and Company) or by credit cards, Visa/Access. Do not send cash or currency. UK customers: and B.F.P.O.: please send a cheque or postal order (no currency) and allow £1.00 for postage and packing for the first book, plus 50p for the second book, plus 30p for each additional book up to a maximum charge of £3.00 (7 books plus).

Overseas customers including Ireland, please allow £2.00 for postage and packing for the first book, plus £1.00 for the second book, plus 50p for each additional book.

NAME (Block Letters) ....

ADDRESS...

....

☐ I enclose my remittance for _____

☐ I wish to pay by Access/Visa Card

Number ☐☐☐☐☐☐☐☐☐☐☐☐☐☐☐☐

Card Expiry Date ☐☐☐☐